REVENGE

REVENGE

S. LEIGH MEDEIROS

THE PAPER HOUSE
PUBLISHING

For Michael, today, tomorrow, and always.

ONE

Hyacinth couldn't take anymore; she channeled the inner strength from within her soul and knew that if she faltered now, it would bring death to the Gnetgnu and their whole civilization. She was the Prophet Warrior taken from the human realm to stop the Quarternewt demons. Only with the elixir from its heart would she ever bring forth the antidote of the Frezton Flower plague destroying the various inhabitants of the planet. The most impacted natives were the Gnetgnu, her new people, and she fought for them unconditionally with all the love and devotion as if she were of their blood. She drew her sondya higher. Forged from the native Flutotious of the planet's center, it was custom-made to fit around her elbow, bringing its blades past her hand.

She charged the Quarternewt with all her might, screaming, "I will not fail!" As she felt the sondya plunge through the razor-like flesh of its chest, the indigo-colored blood sprayed onto her face, saturating her skin and hair. She squeezed her eyes shut, being forewarned that the substance was toxic to humans. Her sondya ripping the creature in twain sounded like the cracking of rocks in the quarries she remembered from her home planet. She wished she could cover her ears. She slightly hummed to drown out the sound, fearful of opening her mouth and getting Quaternewt blood within her system. The creature gurgled in distress as its massive body fell to the heated ground of its nest. Hyacinth landed with a thud to the bottom. She quickly wiped her mouth with the back of her hand, disgusted by the viscous substance that seemed to be drying at an alarming rate.

"Your kind will never injure the Gnetgnu again!". She removed her sondya from the beast. Her new people needed each blade saturated in the indigo substance from its hearts. Hyacinth removed the sacred vials from her satchel. She vividly remembered the directions by the wise Jom and filled them in the specified order. She placed them in her satchel, then ran the back of her hand over her forehead, vividly reminding her that she was still covered in the substance. The indigo blood continued to dry quickly like a mud mask from a spa on her Earth planet. As she was taught, once it was thoroughly dried, it was only a matter of time before it would burn her flesh. She ran to the nearest puddle and tried to decipher if it was Septtronium, Decttronium, or Marttronium. She placed her index finger over the top, and the rings formed were dark blue. She knew instantly it was Septtronium. She quickly washed her face and hair, running her fingers through each strand, she breathed in deeply. This whole year of training and planning, for hours upon hours daily, barely sleeping, perfecting each technique to its finest. Now, she was fully accomplished, and it was over far too quickly. She was unfulfilled.

This was supposed to be her moment, righting all of the wrongs of her new people, engaging in the battle of a lifetime, the crucial closing to decades of terror and fear. She sneered for a moment and felt somewhat slighted. Perhaps full-blown climax on other planets was different than on Earth. She regained her focus and lowered her gaze to her core piece. She stored it in Gnetgnu discarded threads she weaved for safe keeping. She ran her fingers over the hard orange stone, but its decahedron shape had not softened. "What did I miss?" she shook her head.

Something was unsettling in how easy it was to defeat the Quarternewt, not just any Quarternewt, an alpha. They were twice the size of a typical Quarternewt with skin twice as razor-sharp, making it harder to pierce. Her journey to its nest was far more dangerous than the battle itself. Even in video games, the final boss is the most epic, not the side quests that take too long or the level boss where you have to jump on a generic character three times to claim victory. The whole playback didn't make sense to her, and it didn't even attack her when she entered the nest. It didn't become aggressive until she unveiled her sondya, the only weapon known on the planet that could drain a Quarternewt. She was trying to understand *why* that victory made her so uneasy. She stared at the lifeless beast. She tried to equate its characteristics to something Earthly to understand its make. It was as if a salamander and gecko merged with a dragon and then transformed its skin into multi-colored razor blades with out-of-proportion oval eyes that appeared fully dilated at all times.

She crouched down and examined the beast's snout; it didn't look evil or menacing as she had been taught. She slowly stroked its snout and was surprised it was soft. She looked at its chest and slowly touched it with her finger, and she retracted immediately. It was razor sharp. If it were at a different angle, it would have sliced her finger open like the business side of a pair of scissors. The contrast in textures made her believe their species meant certain death for the Gnetgnu, even if by accident. Hyacinth still couldn't shake the uneasy feeling that this was just too simple and shook her head at how she could take it down with her sondya with one blow. The act took seconds once she pierced the skin. She continued to stare at the lifeless creature, only now realizing that she had taken the life force away from this being.

It wasn't like buying processed meat at the grocery store, was personal. Part of her would permanently be bonded to this moment, remembering she was the one who drained it. She turned her head to the side. If she looked at its features differently, it was actually cute. She felt as though she slayed a harmless rabbit instead of a supposed razor-wielding demon. She slowly leaned over and pushed it out of its nest as it gently glided to the ground below and disappeared into the heated mist of the ground. She finally processed what she had done. She never wanted to die in her bed, and she felt as though she violated some trust the animal once felt in the sanctity of his nest. For reasons she didn't understand, she dipped her finger in the Septtronium puddle and made the Gnetgnu symbol for sorry on the nest.

She had been guided to her destiny underneath Gretgen, the absolute trainer of the Gnetgnu. She sighed, "Well, that's that...I guess," everything felt out of place. Why was this so easy? It didn't make sense; all her teachings painted these creatures as monstrous beasts, and while they resembled the artwork depicted in the ancient texts, their fighting technique did not match. Was this particular Quarternewt simply unprepared for their battle? Was it chilling in its nest after a hard day with a beer, and she merely stabbed it to death? She shook her head. That was impossible; the prophecy pages she had read showed the exact color patterns of its flesh. The picture looked like her. Only her face was blurred, but her demeanor and her sondya were depicted identically.

Was this beast simply undertrained for this moment? She shook her head, there were so many unanswered questions. She knew as soon as she made it back to the Gnetgnu, she would speak with Gretgen and Jom. Then her mind started to wonder, did she actually look like the figure in the picture, or did she blindly believe and her brain told her that she looked like them? Now she was uneasy, as though she had been lied to. She felt gullible which infuriated her.

Once she ensured she was cleansed with Septtronium, she took a large jar from her satchel and filled it to the brim. She didn't know how many puddles of the substance she would come across on her journey back. She wanted some on hand just in case there were any lingering effects from the Quarternewt's blood. While the Gnetgnu needed this for their cure, she was warned human flesh could not withstand the indigo juices without being horrifically burned and scarred. She wondered if that sensation was anything compared to the sting of the Mrshti flower. The Mrshti flower felt worse than fire ants on her skin. She looked at her finger where the flower had clung. It took six months, but the flesh returned to its normal color. She could feel the hard shell of scar tissue. She wondered if that experience made her immune to the Quarternewt's life juices, because she didn't feel even the slightest stinging sensation from the indigo substance. Or maybe, once again, she was lied to. She felt stupid and somewhat vulnerable, which was a feeling she loathed more than anything else.

She sighed as she knew her journey back to the Gnetgnu village would be long and arduous. Her trusty Hunterna succumbed to the heat as they entered the realm of the Quarternewt's nests. Its form could take on any shape. When the heat became too high, it melted, appearing like wax and then emanating into a gas as it danced across the sky. She started her journey back on foot. "Well, this kind of sucks." The only human on an alien planet in an alternate galaxy, she found herself talking to herself more and more to try and keep her sanity. She longed for someone to say something sarcastic to her, something funny. This whole planet seemed devoid of all comedy and emotion.

She tried to fill her mind with the joy that would overcome the Gnetgnu when she finally arrived. As she was taught, when the Prophet Warrior defeated and protected the Gnetgnu, there would be feasting and celebrating throughout the village. Her victory meant so many could be cured from the fury of the Frezdon Flower illness created by the Quarternewt to destroy the Gnetgnu. Perhaps she would finally have a night of rest to heal from this ordeal. Until her core piece softened, she would take her place next to the all-mighty Jom as the sworn protector of the people. She wanted desperately to fulfill the prophecy so she could be returned to Earth.

Until her core piece softened, she needed to compile righteous acts at the direction of Jom to show she was worthy and that the Gnetgnu, her adopted people, were safe. Only then would her part of the prophecy be fulfilled. She had completed several journeys and slaughtered many more. Her first kill was a small Quarternewt that had fallen from its nest. She disliked taking its life, but after training for six months and learning why it was needed for the Gnetgnu to restore order to the planet, she did as she was told. She didn't stop to analyze the situation as closely as she had done with the alpha.

That time felt more like the first item on a checklist. She justified all of her actions as necessary to soften her core piece. Only then would she be granted access to the rainbow portal. She knew it wasn't her choice to stay or leave, and while she loved her role here, she wanted to return home, to Earth.

On her fifth moon shift of walking, her feet ached, and her muscles grew weary. When she thought her body could not endure another step, she thought of Caleb. Her destiny tore her away from her fiancé. What must he be going through with her gone for so long? She wondered how his reaction to her disappearance unfolded. She knew he more than likely cried. He was the crier in their relationship, with his heart perpetually on his sleeve. She wished the decahedron turned soft so she could travel the portal and be back with her love.

She and Caleb were celebrating another Valentine's Day together when she was struck by a wave of pure light that pulled her through the portal by the back of her neck. She wrinkled her nose at the thought as it was like someone grabbing a kitten by the scruff to be selected from the litter. It was the first time she saw this as overly rude and obnoxious, instead of a privileged selection to fulfill a need for multiple parties.

She shook her head and refocused her thoughts on Caleb. They were to be married that June, and she mourned how she missed her wedding to fulfill this new destiny she never knew existed. The thought of his kiss, the memories of all their nights together cuddling in their bed, how she would forge the life she always wanted with the man who loved her endlessly. This comforted her soul, motivating her to carry on. She needed to return to him as he must have been in agony without her. She was far too busy training to process her agony without him. In her mind, he was her actual future. This was a detour, one she intended to end. She was slightly annoyed she didn't have more answers as to why she was not granted access to the portal sooner. She knew she had to carry on; the Gnetgnu needed the vials, and the leader of the people, Jom, needed to explain why she would be delayed in returning to her Earthly world. But the more pressing question, *why was this so easy*, was still on her mind, as the anger built with each passing footstep.

The village was in full view as she reached the final land mass of the Strythocket Hills. She smiled at what she had called home for the past year on the horizon. "I'm back." She put her satchel down only momentarily and bowed her head to recite the prophecy speech she was taught to chant when she returned from a victory. "I have found answers and brought them home once more, another life will live, and another life no more. I will save my people, the ones who need me most, and I have returned to Jom, my master and host." She picked up her satchel, and she thought it made a noise; she shook it, and two vials made a clanking sound. She would have inspected it further, but the thought of a hot cup of Strezma syrup made her dismiss the sound.

She ran to the edge of the village, but the gates didn't open. She did the secret knock as she was taught when entering from the outside, but still, there was nothing. *What the fuck?* She thought. She rolled her eyes and knocked again, three hard, three soft, two rigid, one soft. The gatekeeper looked from his perch. She waved, "I have the vials!" She smiled brightly, but the Gnetgnu guard did not react. The Gnetgnu were odd creatures. They did not have faces per se, they had eyes and mouths but no noses as they did not require oxygen, and they didn't breathe at all. Their planet had oxygen, but it was not for them. It was for the Quarternewts and the Mustleknapps.

Their bodies were frail, like that of paper. If they ran directly into a blade, they tore apart. They could morph their bodies, either flat like a sheet of parchment or rolled like a scroll. In times of emergency, they'd fold like gliders on the wind to travel faster. Their eyes could move anywhere on their flat rectangular body at any time. They could have one in the front and one in the back, close together or far apart.

Their mouths were always in the top left corner. Their appendages presented as strings with leaf-shaped extensions on the end. She did the knock for the third time, a little bit harder. It made the gatekeeper quiver in fear.

The doors slowly opened, but her eyes were disappointed to see everyone working as per routine. There was no celebration of her return, no feasting, no gratitude, no change whatsoever.

She snarled to herself she was definitely lied to on some level, but the severity was still unknown. She trudged down the center path, giving a dirty look to all she passed. Then she saw Gretgen, and she ran to him, and finally her scowl softened, "Gretgen!"

He adjusted his eyes to see her come toward him, and his left appendage struck out quickly to stop her from approaching him. It was as fragile as a maple leaf attached to a piece of yarn as it wavered in its execution. She found it pathetic.

"Gretgen, what's going on?" her heart broke in half. He was her trainer. He taught her the way of the warrior; he had been her everything since arriving on this planet. Why would he keep her away from him? She looked at his mouth, but his speaker stone had been removed, "Who took your speaker stone?"

Gretgen's eyes moved from the front of his parchment to the back, and he walked away from her. "Stop! Look at me, if nothing else, look at me!" She called desperately.

He didn't understand her words. All he could feel was the nervousness in her tone. She did not speak their language, and they did not speak hers, but with the speaker stone attached to the edge of their lip, and one attached to her jaw, their words translated automatically, and they knew what they were saying to one another. For all he knew, her words could be threatening or hurtful.

The Gnetgnu knew nothing of empathy, sympathy, love, or hatred and appeared to have no emotions. Gretgen was the only Gnetgnu to understand their feelings since he met her. He taught her the warrior's skills, and she taught him about the different emotions. His eyes returned to the other side of his body, and she reached her finger out to him…she saw what looked like a tear go down his eye. The Gnetgnu did not have guilt or regret, when they spoke, they were condescending but logical. It appeared as if he wished to speak to her, but he could not without his stone. Until it was returned, he was silenced by anything or anyone who was not Gnetgnu. His eyes sparkled in the light of the seven moons, and then he touched her finger.

She could still feel their bond to one another in their secret way of touching, Gnetgnu were so fragile that touching them anywhere else, even embracing one, could damage their core and render them broken beyond repair. She could tell he wanted to tell her something, but he ran away before jumping into the air, morphing his form to glide into the wind to be as far away from her as possible. She felt as though she was stabbed through the heart. Why would he run from her? Night after night, staring at the horizon, observing the moons, learning of his people, hours upon hours of training to make her the most dangerous weapon on the planet.

Something was off, something she didn't know about, and she needed to find out.

She ran to the Great Hall, "What the fuck is going on around here?" she asked herself as she pushed the doors open. None of the servants were there. Usually, there were ten guards to protect Jom from the threats of the Quarternewt assassins. She walked down the hall and studied the portraits of the grand prophets before her. She stared at a couple longer than she typically did, some portraits indicated attire from the 20s, and others almost modern, like from the millennium. She saw the picture of one in particular, and she smiled at him, he seemed to be looking after her through the whole journey. She never gave much thought into life outside of Earth, and she viewed him as someone that was more her guardian than anything else. If she wasn't with Caleb, she imagined what her life would be like with him. She shook her head to regain her focus. She went to open the door to Jom's altar room, when a Gnetgnu guard flitted in front of her and blocked her.

"I demand audience with his eminence our Jom, I have retrieved vials needed for the Frezdon Flower antidote." She shoved her hand into her satchel instead of opening it properly and held the vial in his viewpoint, hoping that would be enough to convince him to let her pass.

The guard was hesitant, he too was missing his speaker stone. His eyes moved throughout his body confused. She rolled her eyes and flicked his right corner, and it ripped. The Gnetgnu quickly retreated, attempting to mend the piece she tore.

She gasped, "My apologies, I'm frustrated, I didn't mean…" she shook her head, why lie? He couldn't understand her anyway, "I did mean it, I'm not sorry, I need answers." She walked in and saw Jom at the altar without even adjusting his gaze when she walked through. "For fuck's sake what the fuck is happening?" she was annoyed, exhausted. She looked over his face, he was slightly wider than a typical Gnetgnu, and he was the only one of their kind who wore the sacred robes.

"Did you retrieve the vials?" he was monotone in his speech, but she was relieved his speaker stone was still in place.

She reached into her satchel and placed them on the altar. "As instructed."

"Thank you." He took the vials and went to walk away.

"Thank you?" she asked, confused. He continued to walk away, unaffected by her tone or facial expressions, "Hang on a second, I single-handedly took down an alpha Quarternewt and traveled the journey here without my Hunterna, and I have been without food or drink for two days, and all you have to say is, *thank you?*"

"What did you expect?" he did not turn to her or stop what he was doing.

"You told me this was going to be the final righteous act! And yet, my core piece is nowhere near softened!"

He appeared to sigh, uncharacteristically of the Gnetgnu, then turned and stared at her, "Again, what did you expect?" While she was taught Gnetgnu demonstrated no emotion, it appeared as though

Jom was finally understanding the concept of annoyance, given this human's attitude.

"I thought this was the finale, you said this was." She couldn't cover the anger in her tone. "I say a lot," he lost his patience.

"I want to go home!"

"Then go, I'm done with you," and before she could say another word, he blew some white dust on her, and she felt her body pull backward, once again like the scruff on the selected kitten. She was in the rainbow portal.

"What the hell!" She screamed as she staggered backward, the force faster than the speed of light.

This was not what she was promised. She saw the rainbow crystals surrounding her. The speed sent her flipping and spinning, forcing her body forward. Even the weight of her satchel was powerless to slow her momentum within the portal. Before too long, she heard what sounded like the shattering of glass. She turned, and there was a Gnetgnu guard behind her, following her.

He had a modified sondya. He manipulated it in such a way he implied the intent on removing her core piece; he tried to stab her heart but failed, and she subdued her attacker. Then he used the sondya to cut off her core piece. She grabbed the guard, ripping and ripped him in half with her full strength. She tried to reach for her piece, but it was nowhere to be found. She tried to stay within the portal's boundaries but bounced about from being off balance.

One of the crystals sliced the back of her neck, she watched as the droplets of blood morphed the color of the portal to a crimson red as opposed to clear rainbow light. She finally centered herself and realized she moved with more incredible speed. She ripped her sleeve and tied it around her neck, "They tried to kill me…" she said in disbelief as her thoughts raced while she pulled herself tighter into a ball.

Her mind flooded with many questions: Why did they send me back this way? What were the vials really for? Why did they try to kill me within the portal? Why is my satchel so heavy? Is gravity different in the portal? What happened to my core piece? Did it disappear?

What the fuck just happened? He was done with me? What did that even mean? Before too long, she felt her body hit solid ground. She rolled on impact to minimize any damage to her body. It took her a little while to recover and examine what she was on. The ground was hard, what was this? Then she shook her head and realized it was linoleum. She slowly peered at the body in the hospital bed.

"What the fuck?" she said aloud to herself.

TWO

Hyacinth opened her eyes slowly. She could hear her heart monitor, she felt the oxygen tube across her nose. She blinked, but everything was blurry. She blinked again, went to rub her eyes, and became fully aware of the IV on the back of her left hand. It hurt. Whoever put it in must have done a rushed job because she could feel it tugging in places she knew it shouldn't pull. What happened? The last thing she remembered was being with Caleb for their Valentine's Day tradition. She would make him croque monsieur as she had for the first episode of her YouTube channel where he was featured. They would share a glass of wine, eat the sandwiches, and then she'd make him vanilla bean Crème Brulee. Her body longed to be with him, and her heart ached for him to hold her. She never knew what it felt like to be loved until she met Caleb.

He was going to give her the life she had always wanted. She knew she was in a hospital, which meant he wasn't out of reach, but she was slightly startled he wasn't at her bedside. She tried to sit up, but her body was far too frail. She heard in the distance a familiar voice, and it said sarcastically, *fucking weakling*. She was confused. Who would say something like that to a person lying in a hospital bed? She tried to move again, but she couldn't bring her eyes to open or her back to sit up. She heard the voice again. *Are you fucking kidding me?* She grew frustrated and stubbornly made up her mind to sit up in the bed. She slowly brought her hands to her face and realized her eyes were dry, she forcibly blinked using her fingers. She kept doing this until she could see the ceiling. Once her vision was intact, she lowered her gaze, staring at her from across the room was herself.

"Hello, replacement me. I'm so glad you finally got up."

"Who are you?" she stared at herself. It looked like her, but it was a different version of her. This version was muscular and gruff. She could see bruises on her knuckles and a small line of blue beneath her eye, as if she was punched in a fight. There was dried blood on the back of her neck, which snaked its way down the front decorating her collarbone. She wore an odd-looking outfit, as if she wrapped her whole body in a tan tapestry and secured it with some crudely tied purple ribbon.

"I am you." She laughed looking at what her former self looked like. Soft, sweet, innocent; that being was padded, and her fingers never knew what it was like to harvest her food from the growing vegetation around her. She never spent days without food, water, or a bed to sleep, forced into the elements of an unknown planet coping with weather conditions she never knew existed. She never entered the battle and took the lives of creatures she didn't know for reasons she didn't understand, putting her safety and well-being in jeopardy. For a split second, she pitied the being on the hospital bed; her world only knew one way, and the actual world was far from one perspective. She shook her head sadly. Her former self was weak, and that would never be her again.

"No, I am me." She questioned herself, she knew who she was. Hyacinth had her own YouTube channel, she was going to marry Caleb, she had a beautiful apartment, and she had a whole plan for how her life would unfold. She had no active memory as to why she was in this hospital room staring at a parallel version of herself. In a split second, nothing made sense anymore. Being in a hospital meant something medically went wrong, but staring at a parallel version of yourself who looked like she was about to slaughter you made no sense to her. Was she losing her mind?

"That's where you're wrong, simpleton." She sighed at the true sinister nature of what she thought were her gentle abductors. The Gnetgnu were so deceitful they sent a body double so there would be no suspicion of her abduction. Whoever concocted this double paid specific attention to detail. Even the scar on the back of her neck from childhood was there. "Do you have a belly button ring?"

"Yes," she answered timidly.

"No, I meant touch where it exists. Is it there?" The being reached down, "No…"

"Couldn't copy what you couldn't see, Jom?" She rolled her eyes, they depicted a snapshot of her and nothing more.

"Why don't I have a belly button?" the being asked panicked.

"Because you're not real." Hyacinth widened her eyes, annoyed that this creature couldn't put two and two together quickly enough.

"Who are you?" she was frightened.

"You know who I am."

"No, I don't…" She shook her head, afraid, delicately naïve as to what was happening, desperately wanting Caleb to come into the room and chase away this imposter.

"You're the next level of identity theft."

"You don't make any sense."

"Stop being so fucking gullible, you know your own self."

"You are not me."

She laughed, "I am Hyacinth."

"No, I am Hyacinth."

"No, you're a clone made by the Gnetgnu."

"What's a gnetgnu?"

"Doesn't matter. In about 5 seconds, you're going to disappear anyway."

"What are you talking about? You sound insane." She hit the call button to summon the nurse.

"Their pathetic attempt to destroy me altered my approach back to Earth. You were never meant to wake up and see me. They thought they killed me in the portal; they sent a guard on a suicide mission, but they were wrong about me. They underestimated me based on your frail figure, they never thought I'd rise above and be greater than they ever knew."

"Where am I?"

"The hospital."

"Why?"

"You don't need to know."

Hyacinth in the hospital bed looked at Hyacinth in her warrior clothing standing in the room. The warrior approached her and gently pulled around her former self's throat. She took a step back, the Hyacinth in the bed looked at her hand as it started to break into chunks resembling kinetic sand.

"What's happening to me?" She didn't feel pain. She felt her whole body go cold and then numb. "You were never meant to know."

The whole-body double in the bed turned into a sand-like substance. Hyacinth quickly took a jar from her satchel, gathered as much as she could and sealed it shut, "I'm sorry they did that to you." She purposefully pushed a single tear down her face with no emotion or the intention to grieve. She touched it with her index finger and then used it to draw the Gnetgnu symbol for sorry on the lid. She equated it to be similar to an ampersand, but instead of ending in the small tail on the right, it spiraled to the center, went up through the entire symbol, and ended with half an arrow at the top. She found this experience paralleled her final battle with the Quarternewt. She was glad she pushed it out of its nest, like she removed the sand from the bed. She did not create the being in the hospital bed, but she was sorry she disintegrated. The body double must have activated when her real being landed back in this world, or that's what she assumed, slowly realizing it was because the Gnetgnu never anticipated her return. She was shocked it all happened as quickly as it did, not realizing she touched the deactivation system within the throat of the double.

She looked around the hospital room, "Was this your curse for a year?" she asked the jar. She heard rustling behind her. She slipped the jar back in her satchel and readied herself to fight as she had been trained to do so. She adjusted herself to be in the first position Gretgen taught her. She lunged back on her left leg with her arms spread before her face, her elbows pointed out, and her satchel guarded behind her back.

The nurse stared at her, frightened, she was wearing a face mask, some face shield that made her look more like a dental hygienist than a nurse, guarded with a whole-body plastic gown and gloves tucked into the sleeves. She also had on some weird-looking goggles that were underneath the shield. "Ma'am, you cannot be in here."

"This is my hospital room. I am Hyacinth. I demand to be released immediately." She stated clearly as if she were negotiating a treaty for her freedom from prison.

"Where did you get those clothes?"

"That's not your concern. I demand to be released immediately." She spoke assertively, putting the nurse on edge.

The nurse was not convinced this wasn't some hoax. She glanced at the empty hospital bed and then relaxed, realizing the only logical conclusion was the coma patient wasn't in a coma anymore, "When did you wake?"

"Moments ago."

"You need to put a mask on right now."

"Why?"

The nurse took a face mask, placed it on a tray, and put it on the stand beside the bed.

Hyacinth walked toward it, "Six FEET!" screamed the nurse.

"What?"

"You have to maintain social distance!"

"What are you talking about?" she rolled her eyes. The term seemed made up.

"You need to wear that mask and stay six feet away from others."

"What are you a germaphobe?"

"Slow the spread of the pandemic!"

"What pandemic? Unless I am in the heart of the outbreak, I demand to be released at once!" She was more insistent than before; her voice grew deeper and she cracked her knuckles.

The nurse went to her chart, "My poor dear, you've awakened at the worst possible time in all of human history."

"That seems slightly exaggerated. Is the inquisition back?"

"Excuse me?"

Simpleton, she thought, "The Spanish inquisition killed so many…never mind. I'll be blunt. I want out. If I slept this whole time, I'm awake now and want to go home."

"Is there someone I can call for you?"

"Caleb, my fiancé." She shook her head. Caleb would never leave her side; he'd be next to her, holding her hand, singing to her softly, waiting for her eyes to look at him. He would NEVER abandon her in such a way.

"I can bring you our iPad after it has been sanitized so you can FaceTime him."

"Why can't he just come here?"

"No one is allowed in."

"What?" the thought sounded too science fiction for her to comprehend.

"Where did you get those clothes? Did they come from your personal bag?"

"Umm…" She quickly assessed her situation drawing from her personal memory bank of hospital experiences. She quickly sifted through her mind each time and came up with the most reasonable explanation she could, "I couldn't take another moment in that hospital gown." She picked up the gown from the bed with slight traces of sand on the fabric. She held it up and half smiled, waving it in the air.

"How did you remove your IV?"

"Not rocket science," Hyacinth held her hand up. There were enough bruises on her hands from her battle with the Quarternewt that no one would be able to tell she never had the needle in her arm.

"I need to put it back."

"That won't be necessary. Consider this my refusal of treatment. I am Hyacinth, I want to go home. I will sign whatever I need to. You will not be personally liable."

"Excuse me?" The nurse was confused.

"I want out." She articulated each syllable to illustrate her frustration fully. She was the Prophet Warrior. She returned to Earth prematurely; she would not cower like an animal in a cage.

"I'll speak to the doctor." The nurse turned to leave, shaking her head, confused. Hyacinth assessed the room for an escape route. The window indicated she was on the top floor and could not risk breaking it open to climb down. She looked to a vent on the ceiling. Even if she stood on the bed, she would never be able to remove the screen, nor did she know where it went. She wanted out of this room, she wanted Caleb. She had to tell him what happened to her. If anyone on this Earth would believe her, it would be him. "Pandemic, my ass. The sting from the Mrshti flower, that is more of a plague than whatever the fuck this is."

She cracked her neck and then paced in the room. She couldn't escape the feeling that something was wrong, something was off, and the tension in her muscles was screaming at her to seek the truth. She couldn't uncover the truth as quickly as she liked because this planet didn't hold the needed answers. She needed to find her core piece, go back through the portal, and confront Jom. She started her first set of strength training for the day. She didn't know how long her journey through the portal took, and she needed to be at her full strength at any moment.

A doctor passed by and stared at her for a moment. When she was done, she looked up, "Can I help you with something? Or do you want to knock off the obnoxious staring and move the fuck on?"

She was particularly nasty as her anger overtook her better syntax skills as the unanswered questions festered in her mind.

"You need to put your mask on."

"Putting a mask on, depriving my body of oxygen while I'm engaged in strength training is a bad idea, doctor." She rolled her eyes.

"You need to put your mask on."

"Do you have the plague, or do I?"

"This is for overall safety. Place your mask on," he said forcefully. "Will you go away if I do?"

"Yes."

She took the paper mask, put it on, and raised her eyebrows. *Fucking happy tool bag?* She thought to herself. She took it off as soon as he walked away, "You did a great job two-handed. Now let's see you do it with one hand."

A different nurse appeared after an hour. She stared at Hyacinth, entirely balanced on her right hand with her left at a perfect 90-degree angle, with her left foot straight in the air and her right at the other 90-degrees. Hyacinth breathed in through her nose and out through her mouth as she concentrated on the position. She meditated, keeping her body perfectly balanced, thinking of Gretgen's teachings. She was the Prophet Warrior, and while they double-crossed her and sent her back without a reason, she knew she found solace in her mind that she would find the answers she needed in time. While she was balanced, she used this time to tighten her core and then slowly shifted so she was balanced in the same fashion on her left hand, methodically shifting each of her appendages to a perfect 90-degree angle.

"Miss," the nurse said timidly. The original nurse asked her to go to the room, saying she would not believe what she saw.

Hyacinth pushed with one hand and flipped backward into the air. She landed into a kneeling position and slowly stood straight again, a slight amount of sweat dripped from her brow, given the severity of the workout and the room temperature. She slowly brought her gaze to meet that of the nurse. The look behind her eyes conveyed the message that one wrong move could result in Hyacinth attacking her like a wild animal.

"You need to put your mask on."

Hyacinth placed the pathetic paper mask on her head like a birthday party hat.

The nurse said, "The proper way to wear a mask is to cover your mouth and nose." She sounded like a flight attendant explaining how to put oxygen over your face in an emergency.

"What makes you think I fit the definition of proper?" She snapped the elastic band, indicating she was not moving the mask.

"You need to put your mask on over your mouth and nose so you can use this," she held up the iPad, hoping this would be a good enough incentive to gain her compliance.

"Technically, my mask is over my mouth and nose…" she laughed.

"Look, Miss, either put it on the right way, or you can't use this to call whoever you need to call." Hyacinth retreated to the corner where she emerged from the portal, as the nurse placed an iPad that was wrapped in plastic on the stand next to the bed. She had no desire to put that stupid paper mask over her face.

"I'm more than six feet away."

"That doesn't matter; you must put the mask on."

"What frightens you more?"

"What?"

"The look on my face or the plague?"

"Please, put your mask on."

"So which is it?"

"What do you mean?"

"The mask or the distance? Surely you do not need both."

"Please, Miss, I need you to put your mask on over your mouth and nose."

"What exactly is going on?"

"Put your mask on." The nurse was losing her patience.

"Why?"

"Put your mask on."

"Not until you tell me why!"

"Slow the spread; the virus will kill you if you catch it. This is for your protection and mine. You need to put your mask on, or you'll catch the virus."

"You are aware that makes little to no sense to the coma patient."

"Put it on, or I'll call security!"

"So, exercising a simple civil liberty makes me a criminal?"

"It is the new state mandate, which must be done!"

"Or what?" Hyacinth folded her arms like a stubborn child.

"I already told you I will call security to make you wear your mask."

"So, they'll come up here and yell at me from six feet away, telling me to put on a mask?"

"Don't be non-compliant, or they will force the mask onto you!"

"But if they can't come within six feet of me, what are they going to use? The poles animal control uses?" Hyacinth laughed. Let them try and get her, she'd take every one of them down like they were daisies.

"Listen," she changed her approach and spoke bluntly, "I'm on the last hour of a 12-hour shift. This is the policy everywhere. Please put the mask on and call your next of kin. Given you have been here as long as you have, I don't think you need to quarantine before your release."

"What happened? Did a monkey spread an outbreak again?"

"A bat."

"What?"

"Mask, call, get out while you still can."

Hyacinth put the stupid mask on correctly. As soon as the nurse left the room, she removed the mask. She took the iPad and called Caleb. It was hard to activate the touch screen with the plastic. "Why the fuck would you wrap an iPad in a fucking condom?"

He didn't pick up on her first call. She shook her head. If he didn't know the number, he would never pick it up. She texted him, "It's Hyacinth! Pick up the call!" she tried again, "Caleb?" she asked, confused when she saw his face.

He was wearing a scary-looking mask. It was black and shiny, it wasn't some paper ridiculous thing, this looked like something out of a horror movie. His beautiful almond-shaped eyes were bloodshot as if he hadn't slept in a week, "Hy?"

"Yeah, it's me, honey!" she wished she could see more of him she wanted to verify that this was actually Caleb.

"You're awake?"

"Yes." She looked around her, *obviously*, she thought.

"You're not dead?"

"No," she shook her head. He was acting so oddly, stating the obvious. She smirked, thinking how emotional he could get; he was relieved, and she needed to be understanding.

"I missed you."

"Why are you wearing a mask?"

"There's a virus going around, and so many people are dying."

She rolled her eyes, "After what I've been through, been there, done that."

"What are you talking about?"

"I have so much to tell you!"

"Do you need to quarantine?"

"What does that even mean?"

"Two weeks in isolation before seeing someone again after being exposed."

"Exposed? I believe my body was in a coma for some time, I saw me wake up."

"What are you talking about?"

"Caleb, you're not going to believe me when I tell you what I've been through. When can you come get me?"

"I can't come pick you up."

Her heart deflated, "Why not?"

"I can't leave the apartment."

"What are you talking about?"

"The whole state, the whole country, the whole world is on lockdown."

"What?"

"It's called quarantine."

"Okay, so come get me, and I will quarantine with you."

"I can't risk getting the virus; I have asthma."

"Caleb, think about this: your fiancée woke up from a coma and wants to come home…"

"We'll figure something out."

"Do you expect me to walk?"

"I'll call an Uber if they're still running. I don't know if they are, but if they are, I'll send one for you."

"Wait, you won't leave the apartment because of some virus, but you want me to get into a stranger's car and come home?"

"I'll quarantine in our room for the next 14 days until you're safe to see."

"You don't want to see me now? I've missed you!"

"I can't risk the virus, 14 days isn't that long. We've already proven we can handle a little longer."

"Wait, what do you mean? How long have I been gone?"

"About two months."

"A year." She shook her head in disbelief.

"No, it's been a little over two months,"

"No, I counted the days, the moons, all of it."

"You were dreaming in your coma."

"What day is today?"

"April 24th 2020."

"So, I've only been away from you for a couple of months?"

"A pretty long couple of months."

"It's been longer for me."

"What are you talking about?"

"I have so much to tell you! I can't wait to hold you, I miss our bed, I missed our Valentine's Day, I want us back!"

"Hy, you can't come near me until you've quarantined."

"What does that mean?" she was beyond frustrated.

"You cannot be in the same room with me until I know you're not carrying the virus."

"Excuse me?"

"We have to be separate until we know you don't have the virus. You could be carrying it and give it to someone without even knowing if you have it."

"Same thing happens with chicken pox. Are you insane?"

"Hy, you cannot come in this room with me, or the germ you could have could kill me."

"Do you have any idea how asinine that sounds?"

"It'll only be 14 days if you keep your social distance and stay in the apartment."

"Are you trying to tell me that you want me to sleep in the other bedroom and use the other bathroom because you won't leave the apartment to come get me, and you won't even hug me when I get there?"

"If I get the virus, I could die."

"If you got any virus, you could die."

"Hy, now is not the time for your sarcasm."

"What the hell happened while I was gone?"

"The world ended." Caleb started crying.

"Are you crying?" She had no patience when he did this. She felt as though he cried more often than she did. She took a deep breath. Caleb was Caleb, and he cried when he was sad…or overly happy… or when something didn't go the way he wanted. Now that she had 20/20 vision in her life, she found him overly sensitive.

"You have no idea how hard this has been."

"You're right," she was annoyed but tried to be caring. "So who has all my stuff, my phone, my clothes?"

"I have it all. I'll set the spare bedroom up for you nicely, and we can talk through the door."

"You're serious?"

"Yes."

"We haven't been together for over two months, and you don't want to hold me?"

"Hy, you don't understand."

"Oh, wait, that's right, the big bad virus is going to kill everyone." She rolled her eyes.

"Why are you being so stubborn?"

"That's how natural selection fucking works, a disease comes along, and if you can't cut it, you die."

"Why are you so cold?" He started sobbing again.

"Seriously?"

"Hy, I forgot how cruel you can be, but you were never this cruel to me…"

"Did they send me back to the right world?"

"What are you talking about?"

"Nothing," she didn't think she could trust Caleb, which hurt more than she was ready to handle. She seriously wanted to punch him, he was being unbearably sensitive and it bothered her. She questioned herself for ever loving him and felt guilty for doing so.

"I will send someone for you."

"Good, because I wanna come home!" She hung up on him, "Fucking jerk." She was annoyed he was crying and angry that he wouldn't get her. She didn't care if there was a plague on the Earth. She would move everything in her path to get to him if he needed her. Why wouldn't he do the same for her? She shook her head, she was the Prophet Warrior. Perhaps her year of training changed her in more ways than she acknowledged. *No*, she thought, *if you love me, you'd find me, get to me, do whatever it took, and never leave me.* She thought about when she had her wisdom teeth taken out, she had difficulty recovering from the anesthesia, and Caleb stayed by her side while she recovered. Then he carried her out of the dentist's office, took her back to their apartment, and cared for her. He cradled her in their bed, iced her jaw, and made her Jell-O. She wanted that again, she wanted to be cared about. Why was he being so distant?

The doctor arrived and stayed six feet away from her. "Put on the mask." She put it on, her will to fight decreased since her conversation with Caleb. "Where did you get those clothes and that bag?"

"I was admitted with them and changed when I woke up."

"There's more than just that."

"Enlighten me, Dr. Obvious."

He raised an eyebrow. "Your face has changed."

"How can you tell? All you can see are my eyebrows behind this mask…"

"According to your chart, you were admitted at 155 pounds."

"Your point?"

"You cannot be more than 115."

"Ouch, bedside manner doctor, you shouldn't talk about a girl's weight like that. You could be the catalyst for a fatal eating disorder."

"You can't have more than 5% body fat."

"So ask yourself, is the nutritional feeding tube sufficient, or is it possible your staff made an error?", she had been training for a year on the planet of the Gnetgnu. She was the slayer of the Quarternewt, survivor of the Grshniz plague, and withstood the Mrshti Flower's burn. She was the strongest, fastest, and most skilled Prophet Warrior that planet had ever seen. Her body was in peak condition, acting as her own weapon no matter what creature she faced.

"We just need to run a few tests to ensure you are ready to go home, and since you have been in this one room, we can consider you quarantined."

"But as soon as you run a test, I have to re-quarantine, which makes no sense because if I'm wearing a mask and you are six feet away, then I'm safe…exactly who measured?"

"What?"

"Well, first off, was it a guy or a girl who measured?"

"Explain yourself."

"Well, if a girl measured six feet, it's probably accurate, but if a guy measured length and said six feet, it's probably closer to four or three." She laughed.

"Miss, that is highly…"

"Accurate." She smiled.

"Look…" the doctor couldn't help but shake his head, feeling uncomfortable.

"The faster I can go home, the faster you'll be rid of me, I want nothing more than to leave." She did a back flip, smiled to herself, then winked at the doctor before she did another.

"What are you doing?"

"Ensuring I don't lose my training."

"Were you a gymnast?"

"Something like that." She did another backflip; her strength remained untainted by the journey, and she would maintain her skill, being deadly on the planet she once inhabited.

"I'm going to ask you some basic questions."

"Expect an acidic answers," she said sarcastically as she did another backflip.

"I need you to stop doing that and answer my questions."

"Can I take my mask off so I can do my regimen again?"

"I don't recommend that."

"Don't worry, I'll tell them you told me no, and I did it anyway." She plopped the mask on the floor, dropped down, and started doing push-ups.

"Were you always this dedicated to strength training?"

"For the past year, yes."

"What are you doing?"

"Ten straight push-ups, ten to the right, ten to the left, ten diamonds, and clap outs."

"You just did 50 push-ups,"

"Yes, I did. I will do that same regimen at least ten more times today, sometimes with one hand, others with two."

"You have been in an unresponsive coma for two months."

"And as soon as I woke up, I needed to feel powerful again."

He left the room abruptly and returned quickly with a picture of her from her admittance. "This was you two months ago."

"And this is me now." She held her arms out, "Eat clean, bro."

"What did you do with the woman in that bed?"

"I AM the woman from that bed."

"I am calling security."

"Good, go right ahead. You can't scare me."

"Why?"

"Because I am Hyacinth. Do you want a fingerprint motherfucker?"

"Actually, I would,"

"Fine," she held her middle finger up. "But you may have to come closer than six feet to get it."

After signing several sheets of paperwork indicating she was denying any further treatment, she was discharged from the hospital. She signed herself out of every test they insisted they run, and when she went to turn a page, she'd lick her middle finger to piss off the nurse. They were originally thinking of a medical phenomenon, then perhaps switched identities, but her less than tactful attitude was a strong motivator to release her. She knew exactly what had happened to her. Jom had betrayed her, and she was going to find her way back through that portal and demand to know why. She was waiting for someone to pick her up and sat on the curb. One of the nurses went to the smoking area with her mask on; she'd take the mask down, take a drag, and then put it back on. Hyacinth laughed at how the smoke would bellow out the sides of the mask, "Did the world turn stupid?" she asked herself as she sat on the curb.

After the next twenty minutes, she observed several people acting out of typical human behavior. Perhaps she was gone for so long that she forgot how typical humans behaved. She watched a man on his cell phone take his mask down when he talked then left it on when he drove away in his car.

She shook her head at each one of these happenings. There were two people in a car, one wearing a mask, the other was not. They parked the car, and the person with the mask on took it off.

The person who had the mask off in the car put one on. She

massaged her temples. *What is taking you so long?* Surely, Caleb would come to his senses after he finished his crying fit. Maybe it took him an ample amount of time to realize how he needed to get her home no matter what was going on in the world. Surely some part of his brain realized they could be together again. A car pulled up, "Hi, Hy!"

"Hi, Mr.Kim, how are you?" she swallowed her anger. She liked her downstairs neighbor just fine, but sending him to get her as though she was a delivery made her temper flare.

"Good. Caleb sent me."

She rolled her eyes. Was he serious? "Thank you for coming to get me."

"No problem, put your mask on. I put mine on, too."

She did as she was told, got into the front seat, and buckled up, "What happened?"

"Pandemic hit. Restaurant closed right now."

"I'm sorry to hear that."

"Me too."

She smiled, not that he could see the gesture behind the mask, "Is everyone on lockdown in the apartments?"

"Exit at your own risk."

"What did I wake up to?"

"Pandemic."

"Apparently…how's Mrs. Kim?"

"Scared, she stays put. I run around for her."

"Seems like that's going to be me pretty soon."

"Caleb never leaves."

"How is that possible?"

"Everything delivery now."

"Are you going to open the restaurant again?"

"Can't…only take out."

"Yikes."

…

She knocked on the apartment door, and it felt unnatural to

knock on the door to her own home. She scowled at the thought. She wanted her life back, she wanted to pull that stupid mask off Caleb's face as soon as she saw him. After she shook some sense into him, she had to tell him everything that happened on that foreign planet. The adventures she had, her transformation into the Prophet Warrior, and her confusing return to Earth. She was so anxious she felt like her skeleton would jump out of her skin. She held her ear to the door, but there was no sound. Her anxiety switched quickly to anger, and she smacked the door with her fist. She stared, shocked at the sound it made. There was a slight indentation from her force. She was stronger than a typical human on the other planet. She didn't realize that this would carry over onto Earth. She traced the indentation with her fingertip, and then she smirked to the side. Part of her laughed to herself that if he didn't open the door in the next 15 seconds, she'd kick it down.

Caleb didn't undo the chain or unlock the top lock, he called to her, "Hy, I'm going to unlock the door, but I want you to wait until the count of 10 so I can get back in our room before you come in."

She smacked the door with her clenched fist. This time, the noise didn't bother her. Instead, she reveled in her ability, "Are you serious right now? Unlock the door, remember this is my apartment too! I want to talk to you face-to-face!"

"Absolutely not! You were in a hospital and then Mr. Kim's car… two weeks minimum separation."

"Open the fucking door!" She heard it unlock and then what sounded like Caleb running away. She opened the door, and he left the chain on. "Are you fucking serious right now with this shit?" she kicked the door and broke the chain. Her adrenaline was pumping as she walked into their apartment. She smiled immediately, and a wave of comfort instantly softened her hard, angry shell. She dropped her satchel on the end-table as she often had done when coming home from the store in her former life. She was finally home; this wasn't some thrown-together shelter she had to meander in the heat of the moment.

She loved their apartment; it was perfect for the two of them and their friends when they'd visit. Two bedrooms, two baths, 1800 square feet, top floor with no neighbors above to make noise and bother her while taping her channel. She looked at her kitchen and smiled. The wooden cabinets, fully tiled counter tops, and nostalgic walls gave it an eighties vibe, which she needed for her channel. She ran her fingers over the cold, smooth tile. She compared it to the feeling of the Strythocket tree branches; so similar to one another. She stared at her spacious countertops. She filmed her YouTube channel in this space. Her equipment had been untouched these past couple of months.

She never realized how lucky she was to have this perfect kitchen with her plethora of gadgets. She remembered the Gnetgnu planet and how all food was eaten raw; none of the species had a cooking method, and they failed to sit down for a meal. That wasn't done there, you were lucky to find something edible among them at all. Their kind rarely ate, their strands didn't require caloric intake. Over this strenuous time, she missed cooking in the kitchen for Caleb and his colleagues when they would come over to play D&D.

She slowly walked into the living room and looked at their bookshelf. There were framed pictures of her and Caleb on the shelves in front of all his history books. Again, she ran her fingertips over the edges of the shelves and took a deep breath. She closed her eyes and reflected on her surroundings, feelings, smells, touches; everything from her former life. It was pristinely kept in its place, simply waiting for her to return to it. She stared at their engagement photo, the genuine happiness behind both their eyes. She took it off the shelf, traced his face, and looked at her former self. Her reflection in the glass of her current form forced her to shake her head. She was different. Could she ever make her new self adjust to her former role? She had to wrap her arms around him to know the answer to that question, and she gently called out, "Caleb!"

"14 days minimum and you have to be symptom-free." He called from behind the bedroom door.

"You have GOT to be kidding me. This is ridiculous!"

"The original two weeks have become indefinite. Stop the spread!"

She went to open their bedroom door and literally smack some sense into him when she realized he had locked it, "You don't trust me?"

"You just tried to come in!"

"Yeah, because this is my room too!" She slammed her back against the door, this was worse than the time he locked the door after losing to her in chess and sulked for the entire night.

"Hy, you don't understand."

She slid down against the door, "Caleb, you don't think this is a little extreme?" She smirked, thinking about kicking it down to prove her point.

"You don't have the whole story!"

"I'm sure over the next two weeks I will."

"Two weeks only if you're symptom-free."

"We are in the same apartment! You are not sealed inside of there, we're sharing the same air! You're not a fucking Tupperware!" She took this time to look at her fingernails, which were dirty and uneven. It never bothered her on the Gnetgnu planet, so long as they didn't break and bleed, whatever they looked like was fine. But being back home, she did have to worry about their integrity, and if she was going to cook anything for her channel, they needed to look stellar.

"You don't have all the information!"

"Does the information include door knobs being part of the cure?" she smacked it playfully and listened to the sound.

"You need to stay out there, and when the time comes, we can be together!"

"None of this makes any sense!"

"Because you're not listening."

"There is a space between the door and the floor where I am sitting. I can literally blow through the bottom of your door."

"Can you at least try to be understanding!"

"Okay, let me see if I have this correct. There is a virus, and it spreads?"

"Yes!"

"That's true of all viruses." She sat forward and placed her palm on the wall, *home at last.*

"You have no idea if you have it or not until you have symptoms!"

"Like measles?"

"NO!"

"Viruses are just that, viruses, they morph and spread, and that's just what they do." The world seemed to have forgotten common sense while she was gone.

"You cannot come near me until you have been two weeks symptom-free!"

She bowed her head, defeated. Part of her contemplated getting a paperclip and picking the lock. She smirked; she was strong enough where she could kick it down. She took a deep breath. Spending a whole year on the planet of the emotion-free and logical Gnetgnu did harden her. Perhaps she needed to soften around the edges, "What are the symptoms?" she tried to sound sweet, but it came out sarcastic.

"Fever, chills, cough, difficulty breathing, fatigue, muscle aches, headache, loss of taste and smell, sore throat, runny nose, nausea, vomiting, diarrhea."

"You sound like the end of every pharmaceutical commercial," she laughed. She imitated the sound, "Please contact your doctor if your eyes start bleeding, you can't maintain an erection, you've lost hearing in your right ear, or if you wake up dead."

"I forgot how insensitive you can be."

"Excuse me?"

"The death toll is high, people are dying…if you have asthma, you're in a higher risk category for getting sick."

"Aren't you already in that high-risk category for everything?" She rubbed her temples. Had Caleb gone completely insane?

"Hyacinth!"

"It's true."

"This virus can spread through your eyes!"

"All viruses can spread through your eyes." She rolled her eyes, "It's a mucus membrane, it can go

through eyes, ears, nose, mouth..."

"You haven't even asked me how I feel or what I've been through!"

"According to you, I've been in a coma for two months, you wouldn't even pick me up from the hospital, you're talking to me through a door because I may or may not have some *virus*, I can't go into my own room and cuddle with the man I love, and you're upset I haven't asked how YOU feel?"

"It would be nice to know you care." He choked up on the other end of the door. "Caleb, please tell me how you are feeling," she said as though she read from a script. "I'm scared, isolated, and you don't know how hard this has been!"

"That's fair, you're right, talk to me."

"My grandmother died!"

"Oh no, I'm so sorry. I know she meant the world to you."

"It was heart-wrenching!"

"Did her cancer spread?" She leaned forward and started doing her push-up regimen again.

"No!"

"Then what happened? Her heart again?"

"She caught the virus!"

"But she had congestive heart failure and lung cancer?" She stopped and held her arms up to indicate that it seemed odd.

"She did, but once the virus got her, she couldn't breathe, and we couldn't be with her. She died alone and scared in a room without any of us near her."

"I'm sorry, Caleb, that must've been awful." She tried to sound sweet, but it was sarcastic. She decided to just be her normal tone and stop trying to be caring. She quickly went back to her push-ups.

"We couldn't even have a funeral!"

"I know you're hurting, I know what she meant to you."

"And you were not there for me! When I needed you the most!"

"In my defense, I was not on this planet." She spoke sincerely, although he took her to be metaphorical. "But I still needed you, and I couldn't get to you once March hit. I visited you everyday up until they wouldn't let me. You didn't look alive, you looked dead."

"That must have been awful."

"How would you feel if you had to visit my corpse in the hospital?"

"I don't want to imagine that because it must hurt so deeply."

"It did, and then my grandmother died, and I've been virtually teaching, and I can't leave this room or this apartment. You have no idea."

"No idea? I've been away for far too long."

"And yet you don't want to respect my life? You want to just come in here after being in the outside world where the virus could kill me?"

"Has every person who's had the virus died?"

"No…"

"Then, maybe you stand a chance."

"Stop it!"

"Take a chance. Why don't you open the door, and we can cuddle our way through this pandemic together? We're better together, you always say that!"

"Two weeks."

"You're being ridiculous." She stood and yelled at the door as if she was yelling into his face.

"Do you want me to die?"

"No, I don't want you to die, but I want to see you."

"Then be a little more empathetic to my situation. If I catch the virus, then I'm going to die."

"How do you know your immune system won't just make antibodies and you'll survive?"

"Hy, if you're not even going to try, I will stop talking."

She rolled her eyes, "They definitely, *definitely* put me on the wrong planet."

"What are you talking about?"

"Caleb, I wasn't in a coma."

"What are you talking about?"

"I was abducted to another planet." The thought hurt her heart. She was talking about it in such a way that it brought out so many conflicting feelings. She longed to be there but wanted to be here; she wanted answers, and they lied to her. She felt vulnerable, her least favorite feeling.

"You know I don't always understand your metaphors."

"Caleb, I'm serious, I was abducted into another galaxy with a different time line, a different everything, and when they returned me, it's hard to explain."

"Hyacinth, do you have any idea how crazy you sound?"

"Do you have any idea how crazy you and everybody else sound?"

"Is this how you are coping with the accident?"

"What are you talking about?"

"Do you know why you were in a coma?"

"I wasn't in a coma! My body double was in a coma."

"No, it was your Valentine's show, I had to go pick up the costumes for my history lesson, and I left you alone here, and you left the gas on the stove. I found you unresponsive in the kitchen."

"I would never do something like that."

"That's what I always thought until that moment. I feared you were trying to kill yourself."

"Why would I do that?" she was hurt on several levels. She would never do something like that, and the fact he even contemplated she would want to do something like that cut deep.

"Because you don't want to marry me..."

"Caleb," she could feel his soul shattering on the other end of the door, "Have you been holding on to that thought this whole time?" She could hear him sniffling on the other side of the door.

"Yes," he full out sobbed.

"Caleb, I've done nothing but fight every battle, hoping that with each victory, I was closer to coming home to you. For you, it has been two months. It's been over a year for me, and the thought of marrying you is the only thing that got me through so much pain."

"I thought you wanted to escape from me."

"Never!"

"I love you, Hyacinth."

She smiled, "I love you too, honey."

"Everything is shut down. What if it doesn't open in time for the wedding?"

"Then we go to city hall, we get married because we love each other, and when the world reopens, we'll have our wedding reception."

"You still wanna marry me?"

"Of course I do! Caleb, you have no idea what I have been through! And when we get married, we're going to show everyone, all our friends, colleagues, students, and Mr. and Mrs. Kim!"

"I've missed you so much."

"I can't wait for you to see me."

"I charged your phone, and we can FaceTime, not right now but later."

"Why not now?"

"I have a lot of work I need to complete tomorrow."

"You can't spare 10 minutes to FaceTime?"

"I have spared you time right now, but I will FaceTime you when I'm free."

"Are you going to take your mask off?"

"No, why…did you take yours off?" the anger swirled with panic in his tone.

"As soon as I walked through the door," she said innocently.

"Hy, that's irresponsible."

"After what I've been through, I'm not wearing a mask in my own apartment."

"You're a contributing factor to the spread." His tone shifted from a man in love to a man in shock.

"I've been awake less than a day, and the pandemic is my fault?" she asked sarcastically.

"Your attitude could bring whole cities down!" He spit the words at her as if she was the world's problem.

"Fuck, you've gone psycho."

"Will you at least read about what has been going on? Educate yourself."

"I will…now, is there anything to eat in this place?" She changed the subject. She didn't want to hear any more of his rants, about the virus, or how her nonchalant approach was making matters worse. With one breath, he told her he loved her and, in the next, angry at her attitude.

"I'm ordering take out in a bit."

That statement hit a genuine nerve, "You want me to wear a mask in the apartment, but you'll order take out?"

"Hy, I do not need your sarcasm right now."

"I think I'd rather face another Quarternewt." She shook her head as she made her way into the kitchen. The cabinets appeared empty, as if Caleb had eaten everything possible. She opened the fridge, and there were a couple of leftover containers. She picked up one and smelled it, then shook her head. She went days without food and water on the other planet and could easily wait for something decent from a takeout place. With her head held low, she trudged into the spare bedroom.

She looked around, this was their office/guest room, and even though she resented being sequestered there, it still brought a smile to her face. Her desk was in the corner where she edited her videos for her YouTube channel. She looked at the little cabinet where Caleb kept his collectibles. She smiled at the action figures; they didn't bother her as much as they used to. They were so important to him, and she stared at one from *Mortal Kombat* and noticed how the muscles were overly exaggerated. She looked down at her stomach and pulled the rags to the side, now she was just as muscular. She laughed to herself that perhaps she was training for the tournament and then shook her head, feeling the sting of betrayal when Gretgen flew away from her.

She went over to the desk where he had placed her clothes in a pile. She unraveled the hand-woven cloth she had made from discarded Gnetgnu threads to patch together her t-shirt from her abduction. This outfit was the only item wrapped around her body for the past few months. It had an odd smell, a mixture of body odor and cinnamon. She stood naked in the room and slowly ran her finger tips over each muscle. Her body was transformed into a weapon. She wanted a shower as she hadn't had one in so long. She knew she wanted to feel the warm water down her skin.

She walked into the spare bathroom. She liked this one more than the bathroom in the master bedroom, which was a small stall shower as opposed to this one which was a full bathtub with a detachable shower head. She ran the water and let out a long sigh of relief. As she stepped into the center of the stream she couldn't help but compare this sensation to sex. This was far better. She took the body wash that was in the corner of the tub and started rubbing her body down. She could see the suds mix with dirt and debris from her time on the planet and swirl down the drain. She ran her fingers over her scalp, enjoying the sensation of her hair finally being cleansed with natural soap and not Septtronium.

Even though she finished cleansing her body she stayed beneath the magnificent stream. She enjoyed the privilege of showering, not only showering but also showering with warm water and delicious smelling soaps. She finally decided she had been in long enough and laughed at how her finger tips had pruned from being immersed in the water for so long. She turned off the water and took one of the towels from the corner shelf. She hadn't felt cotton in over a year, and even this was shocking yet comforting.

"Don't know what you have until you don't have it anymore." She reminded herself. She always kept a little basket of amenities below the sink for guests staying over, and now she laughed at how she was the guest in her apartment because of what was happening. She put on face moisturizer, and every moment she rubbed the substance on her skin, she smiled and moaned in satisfaction. She used deodorant; the smell of baby powder made her giggle. She brushed her hair, rubbed the detangler through, and then thoroughly combed her hair. She reveled in the softness. She would typically tie her hair behind her to keep it out of her way in battle. Who was she going to battle on this planet other than Caleb? She smiled at herself with her cheekbones prominent, her double chin completely gone from her year of training. She would need her wedding gown taken in several sizes.

She made her way back into the spare bedroom. She pulled on an old t-shirt. It was so prominent on her that it felt like she was wearing Caleb's clothing. She pulled on her pants and rolled her eyes as she pulled the drawstring as tight as it would go. "How did you ever fit in these?" Then she laughed, "Oh right, you used to eat food, and you couldn't do more than two push-ups," she laughed to herself.

She took her phone and FaceTimed Caleb, but he didn't pick up. She was saddened by his rejection. He texted her, "You may not be aware of this, but I have to work virtually, so that means recording lessons, grading papers, and many other responsibilities. Not everyone gets to sing and cook on the internet to make money."

She shook her head; a text was mere words, but she interpreted him as angry, slightly upset in her mind. He loved her YouTube channel. Not only did he watch every episode, but he let his colleagues know when a new episode was posted. He was never the harsh one. That was always her roll, "Fuck you!" was all she texted, and then her blood boiled thinking over and over again what was said, "Get a grip you over sensitive dick."

"Just like you."

"What? What is just like me?"

"Not seeing someone else's problems, only looking at your own."

"Your fiancée was in a coma for two months, and you won't even open the door to see her! You tell me you love me, and you've been in fear this whole time I wanted to die, but you snap at me for trying to FaceTime you?"

"Hyacinth, you have to read the media coverage about the virus, and you need to be aware that the world is a bigger place than you."

"Trust me, I know!"

"Please research and read about this. This is REAL!"

"So, who am I blindly following this week, CNN, TikTok, Fox, or the history channel?"

"I am very busy preparing for tomorrow. I'm ordering takeout in a little while. What would you like?"

"Excuse me?"

"I have not left the apartment! I have food delivered."

"So, the delivery guy gets your attention, but I don't?"

"You are so self-centered sometimes that I can't take it."

"WTF!"

"Do you want something to eat or not?"

"Cheeseburger, please."

"Since when have you voluntarily eaten cheeseburgers from anywhere in Paramus?"

"Since now, with fries, extra coleslaw, and pickles,"

"You hate all those things."

"I hate that you're a paranoid dick, but we all have to face that shit now, don't we?"

"You only eat cheeseburgers from White Manna! You're not making any sense!"

"Neither are you, hence my order!"

"Hy, knock it off! Let me know if you want something to eat, but I'm not ordering you that because I know you don't want that."

She smiled to herself. Her out of character order was on purpose; she wanted to check if he was actually Caleb. He only ordered take out from three places, and they each had the worst cheeseburgers she had ever tasted. She took a deep breath, and texted, "I love you."

"Are you okay?"

"I am now."

"What do you want to eat?"

She smiled to herself. Caleb joked that he was the only man in the world who could ask his girlfriend what she wanted to eat, and she always had an answer, "Honey mustard salmon with asparagus on the side."

"It'll be here in twenty. There's money in the jar."

"I love you."

"You are confusing."

"So are you."

"I love you too."

She reminded herself that Caleb was sensitive and that she was the hard-hearted one. She was sarcastic, and he was sincere. The symbol he always said represented their relationship was the taro blossoms. Caleb grew up in Nanakuli, raised by his grandmother and grandfather. She remembered when he took her there to meet his family. They were not exactly excited about their engagement, but they loved Caleb and were supportive. She and Caleb had been together for four years in total but lived together for two. They were engaged for one year. He had asked her last Valentine's Day as a surprise on her YouTube show, and she got an extensive number of views for that episode.

Part of her was relieved she didn't miss their wedding after being abducted to the planet of the Gnetgnu. She would still find the answers she sought, but the unsettling feeling of not knowing why rose within her, taking precedence over anything else. She let it go for now and tried to place her engagement ring on, but it was too big for her finger.

She texted Caleb, "My engagement ring doesn't fit. It's too big."

He didn't text her back right away. She wrinkled her mouth, shook her head, and talked herself down, "He has things to do. It's not about you. He's going through a lot right now; this planet has feelings, and Caleb has always been the sensitive one."

The door knocked, and she paid for the takeout and brought it in.

"Caleb, your food is here." He texted her, "Leave it at my door, and go in the spare room."

She went to text back, "Leave your room, you fucking pussy," and she stopped herself. She cleared the content and typed, "OK."

When she went to place his food on the ground, she noticed he had left his silver chain beneath the door. She smiled. She took his necklace, placed her engagement ring on it, and clasped it around her neck. She texted him, "Thank you, I love you."

"Love you too."

THREE

She paced in their spare bedroom restless. It had been nearly a week since her return. With each passing day, her mind slipped further from Earth and closer to the planet of the Gnetgnu. Her sanity was also slipping, she'd speak the prayer in her sleep. She'd wake at the drop of a hat and spring into attack mode. She was convinced she had heard something; she swore someone was following her. Every night she charged her phone, and every morning, it was dead. The paranoia that grew within her mind frightened Caleb further away from her.

She had already taken down the coat rack in the middle of the night, having a flashback to the infant Quarternewt she fought. She was finally in a dead slumber from a week without REM sleep. A squeaking noise coming from a vent in the kitchen forced her from her sleep. She leapt from her bed knocking the bedroom door off its hinges, and flipped her way to the top of the counters. If Caleb dared leave his room, he would see her screaming and pulling her hair. As the world around her was growing more paranoid of the virus, she grew more paranoid that she was on the wrong planet. She tried to confide in Caleb multiple times, but he thought her ramblings were only due to the pandemic. Their relationship was an overextended rubber band that was about to snap. It was as if their years together meant nothing to him anymore as her sanity descended into madness.

Every time she tried to FaceTime him, he had an excuse. Either he was prepping for his virtual classroom, he had a 1:1 with one of his students, he was stuck in virtual professional development, he was watching the latest updates regarding the regulations and statistics of the virus, or, his lamest excuse in her opinion, he was having a panic attack and needed to focus on himself for a moment. He always told her she was insensitive, why wouldn't Caleb even look at her? She was so lonely; she spent a year away from him on another planet, and yet only one room away, she felt he was further from her than ever. She kept questioning if she was truly on the right planet. She would ask him odd questions about history to see if his answers matched her common knowledge.

She stared at her phone and had an internal debate with herself, and then she decided if she did nothing, it would always be nothing, but if she tried something, then at least that was different. She truly questioned if this was the right planet and reminded herself there was a sure way to find out. She reflected on her family, then made the hard choice and called her sister.

"Hyacinth?" the voice was bitter.

"Why is everyone so fucking shocked?" she regretted her decision immediately.

"You've been in a coma for two months…not that that makes a huge difference in your presence in my life, but Caleb thought I should know just in case I wanted to say goodbye, and for the record, I didn't, I told him never to contact me again…blocked his number, should've blocked yours again."

"Chrys, please."

"So what happened now, a sudden surge of urgency to speak to your only conscious relative?"

"No, just trying to understand the world." Her sister's tone confirmed it, she was definitely on the right planet. There was no way Jom could have known her connection to her sister, so it couldn't have been replicated in an alternative state. She was disappointed and relieved at the same time. She didn't like either feeling.

"There's a pandemic."

"I know, and the world turned upside down because of it."

"Let me guess, you just don't give a shit because it's not impacting you and your little bubble of a world."

"No, I just…I wanted…I can't…" she stumbled and stuttered, her typical confidence compromised hearing her sister's voice again. There was a saying she remembered her mother used to say that things staying the same was comforting, but this was far from it. It was awkward and painful.

"Awww, how cute! She doesn't know what to say."

"Chrys, please."

"I have no desire to talk to you, you're worse than Dad, you're worse than…" her sister choked on her

words.

"I am different, you know that." She couldn't help but choke up. "You're no different, you're just as selfish and just as bad."

"Because I wanted to live?"

"No, because you didn't care."

"I cared! I cared a great deal, but what was the point?"

"Fuck you."

"Chrys, please."

"Why?"

"I'm still your sister."

"No, you lost that right when you left."

"I couldn't take it,"

"So you put all the burden on me?"

"You could've come with me!"

"And abandon her? The way Dad did? The way you did? The way Rowan did!"

"Can you please try,"

"Awww, emotion from the baby. How are you feeling, my selfish little monster?"

"Conflicted, I wanted to reach out to you and ask how Mom is doing."

"The same," Chrysanthemum said sadly. "What year is she stuck in today?"

"I'm not sure, but it was when Dad was still around. Why do you give a shit all of a sudden?"

"Does she know about quarantine?"

"She's been in quarantine longer than the global pandemic, twat."

"Did she know I was in a coma?"

"No."

"You didn't tell her, or she didn't remember."

"I didn't tell her."

"Why?"

"Because she doesn't remember you anymore, and that's how I like it, she hasn't uttered your name in over a year, and I wasn't about to stir that fucked up pot again."

"When did your sanity snap?"

"More with every passing day, you selfish piece of shit."

"Chrys, I know we've had our differences." She started to pace in her kitchen.

"Our differences?" She started to pace, although her kitchen was a quarter of the size, she looked closer to a caged animal with a rotten scowl across her face.

"Please, this is not..."

"Oh no, you really, really wanna go there now because you wake up from your coma and it's like the last seven years just didn't happen?"

"I called you, remember?"

"So?"

"The phone works both ways."

"What are you going to do, help? You're in fucking Jersey and we're in Arizona. Did you want to FaceTime the dementia patient?"

"Look."

"No, I get you woke up from a coma, and you're all, oh no, my life, whatever, I don't give a shit whatever realization you've had."

"Please..."

"I had you listed as a missing person because I couldn't believe you would do this to us!"

"I told you every day I wanted to leave."

"Want is for the selfish, the loyal endure."

"You don't have to sacrifice your life for her!"

"That's what a daughter does, not that you know what that means."

"Look, this is just..."

"No, now I would hang up on you, but that's your go-to move, so I'll say goodbye and hang up."

"But..."

"No, fuck you, Hyacinth, don't call here again, I'm blocking this number. Goodbye," she said. She hung up the phone.

Hyacinth sighed loudly; she didn't understand why she called her sister in the first place. Then she glanced at the overabundance of takeout containers in the garbage and remembered she wanted to verify she was on the right planet. She went to her bedroom and then stopped herself when she realized she couldn't go in. She rolled her eyes and went into the spare bedroom. She didn't miss her sister or mother. There was no lingering guilt for seeking her chance to live her only life. Part of her realized she should've been there after her mother's fall, and she wasn't. She left her older sister to handle the aftermath, and Chrysanthemum refused to leave their mother in the hospital setting.

While on the Gnetgnu planet, she was the Prophet Warrior. Back here on Earth, she felt no honor or pride, but she was more relieved that she got herself out. The Gnetgnu abandoned and tried to eliminate her. She found a profound parallel between that and her abandoning her own mother and sister, worse than her brother. She hadn't thought about Rowan in so long, so she did her best to suppress the memory of him, but when she was honest with herself she thought about him daily. She curled into a ball on the bed. The sheets smelled like the fresh linen fabric softener Caleb had always bought. It made her feel comforted, and it seemed as though the only thing in her life that made sense right now was that scent.

She closed her eyes tight, trying to keep the tears from running down her cheeks. She remembered when her father walked out, his duffle bag behind him, her mother begging him to stay. Her mind could feel the sensations, the shrieks of her mother, and then the final sound of the door as it slammed shut. She couldn't remember how old she was when that happened, she couldn't have been older than five. She remembered Rowan running after him and her mother holding him back as he flailed his arms out, eventually hitting their mother across the face and running into his room.

She could hear muffled accusations from her brother blaming their mother for him leaving and how he wished he could go with him. She remembered her sister crying and her mother holding Chrysanthemum in her arms, rocking and comforting her. With a blank expression on her face, Hyacinth merely walked into her brother's room and started playing with his hand-held arcade game, which she wasn't allowed to touch, but he was so distracted she sat and played for a solid hour before he took it from her. She remembered Rowan staring into her eyes and telling her they were a team. They needed to stick together, and the two of them were against the rest of the world.

Hyacinth didn't cry when her father left. She didn't react; she remembered him leaving, and when her heart should have winced from his abandonment, she didn't feel anything. She never knew what happened to him, and at this point, she no longer cared or pondered where he was or if he was alive. She remembered Rowan dragging her to the library so he could use the computer and try and find him. She usually played games on another computer, waiting for him to take her home. She reflected on that experience and questioned if that was the catalyst for her being cold?

Or was she like that beforehand, incapable of feeling the sting of abandonment like her siblings did? Perhaps she was too young to realize that once he walked out that door, he wasn't coming back. Their mother suffered from a mental illness; none of them knew what it exactly was, but it was enough to drive their father away. When she reflected on the days her mother spent in bed, not moving, she equated it to some form of depression. She couldn't remember the exact order of events. Did her mother stay in bed all day before or after he left? Was Hyacinth closed off to emotion before or after he left? She never felt close to her father or her mother, for that matter. They were just players on a stage, in her opinion.

She never really cared for her sister the way her brother had. The only one in her family she felt connected to was Rowan. Since she was an infant, her mother would tell stories that if she was fussy, she needed to place her in his arms, and she would calm immediately. If there was a storm, she'd run into his room for comfort. He'd run his fingers through her hair and tell her stories until she fell asleep. If she tripped and fell, she went to him for a Band-Aid. Rowan always ensured she had a snack in her backpack when she went to school, and he checked her planner when she came home. He helped her with her homework, and then they cooked dinner for everyone. He was the one who read to her at night, and she couldn't sleep until he brought her a glass of water and kissed her forehead goodnight.

She remembered her mother's stroke and how they all had to sacrifice to keep her home. She dropped out of high school, and Rowan left college. Chrysanthemum was the oldest, and she took on managing the house, the bills, and all of those horrific details associated with caring for a loved one in the home setting. Rowan worked day in, day out. Chrysanthemum and Hyacinth took shifts to care for their mother, who never regained the use of her left side. They couldn't understand a word she said, and trying to get her to comply during her rehabilitation was arduous. It was almost as if their mother had given up on life itself.

Hyacinth hated every moment, as if the three of them had to sacrifice their future to keep this one heart beating. To her, it never seemed fair. If their mother lost the will to live, why were they keeping her here? She stopped smiling after that, she stopped singing with Rowan in the living room at night, and she went through the motions of the day and nothing more. The light behind her eyes died, and it wasn't until it was too late that she realized the same could be said for Rowan.

After almost a year of living in this fashion, her brother started acting strange. She didn't know what type of drugs he started taking, but she could see a change behind his eyes, and she had to start shaking him awake in the morning to get to his first job. She could still hear the sound of the gentle rain from that night Rowan came into her room. He handed her a playing card, the Joker. He gave the Queen of Hearts to Chrysanthemum the night before, but Hyacinth did not know this until later. She could still hear his voice, *Hy, remember this always, you are a wild card, you deserve more than this, and you will have it. I love you. No matter what, be strong.* She could remember lying in her bed, Chrysanthemum asleep next to her, snoring as usual. She remembered trying to focus on the sound of the gentle rain.

Rowan brought her a glass of water and kissed her forehead. He tucked her in, warm and safe, as he ran his fingers through her hair until she fell asleep. While she was in a perfect dream, Rowan silently closed the front door to execute his endgame. He spray-painted the words "All in all," in the center of a brick wall, then turned off his airbag, unclipped his seat belt, and crashed at 85 miles per hour into the wall.

His body was ejected through the windshield, and glass went through his trachea. His face was so deformed they had to use dental records to identify him. Hyacinth and Chrysanthemum tried, but even they were skeptical if that was his body. He didn't have tattoos or birthmarks to assist in identification. Hyacinth made an extraordinary request and walked over to the body. She placed her hand within his, and she nodded. She knew instantly that this dead body was her brother. Her hand fit the way it always had in his. Her thin fingers fit perfectly between each of his knuckles, as it had since she was a child.

His wake was closed casket, Hyacinth remembered wheeling her mother into the funeral home; her mother tried to reach for him and fell out of the chair. It took both her daughters and the funeral home director to get her back in as she refused to accept help. She shook her head over and over again, crying and desperately trying to tell the girls how upset she was, but her words were so mumbled that no one understood. While the girls were asleep that night, their mother entered the kitchen, turned on the gas, and put her head in the oven. When Hyacinth woke in the night to get a drink of water, she found her mother's body unresponsive. Part of her always wished she left her there, but she alerted Chrysanthemum immediately. The EMTs revived her mother, but her brain would never recover completely from the lack of oxygen.

Hyacinth and Chrysanthemum were on their own, 17 and 23, to care for this broken human. Hyacinth started working, taking over Rowan's role as the breadwinner. Chrysanthemum took care of their mother during the day and night. Both girls were perpetually exhausted. Hyacinth worked two jobs, cleaning houses and stocking a warehouse overnight, but she made enough money to support them.

After a year, she understood why Rowan committed suicide. She started feeling the same way, the monotony of each day showing no light at the end of the tunnel, surrounded by sadness and darkness with the growing desire to escape. She thought about taking something to relax but used her better judgment; she did not want to walk in Rowan's footsteps. Part of her believed it was the drugs he was relying on that led him to take his life, not his true inner desire. She tried talking to her sister, but that didn't help. Chrysanthemum always made her feel guilty, that she was selfish for wanting to put their mother in a facility and have their own lives. Her mother's mind was gone; she would wake up and ask what day it was but then forget the next moment and mumble. She had no recollection, and bathing and feeding her became more and more challenging as she had no concept the left side of her body did not work. While her mother was hospitalized after another fall, no one remembered it was Hyacinth's birthday. She took that as a sign that she didn't exist to them. She was finally 18, packed a bag, and just like her father, she opened the door and left.

Hyacinth started dry crying and refused to shed a tear for her mother. Whenever she remembered these feelings, Caleb always held her. She never told him why she felt that way, and he never asked. He just knew she was upset, and he would hold her. Now, he was galaxies away in the room next door. Hyacinth had never known love until Caleb. She had known a man's touch, and what dating was, but being in a relationship, Caleb was her first. She never understood what he saw in her, but she could see happiness within him. He often bought her sentimental gifts that she didn't understand, and she often used his facial expressions and joy to comprehend how to react.

She had no background knowledge of emotional gestures other than her brother kissing her goodnight before bed. Again, she assumed that was a routine, like waking up and turning off the alarm. The first morning, she woke up to Caleb holding her, she was confused. He ran his fingers through her hair and kissed the tip of her nose. She just smiled revelling in his happiness, which in turn made her happy.

She felt a slight pain in her jaw from withholding herself from crying. She touched the side and felt the small hole carved to place her speaker stone in so she could communicate with the Gnetgnu. The all-knowing, all-powerful, and understanding Jom was the one who initiated the contact. She was frightened at first. When she arrived on the planet, she was horrifically confused. The first thing she remembered was the bright light and the rainbow colors surrounding her as she was transferred through the portal to the planet. She landed in a weird tuft of what seemed like fur. It was white, iridescent white, reflecting the spectrum of light around it. She landed on her face, and when she sat up, regaining consciousness, she saw seven full moons spaced in the sky.

The sky was a deep purple, but the stars were orange. She felt calm when she saw the orange hue brighten the purple sky, but she couldn't identify a single constellation. There was no big or little dipper. She couldn't remember if she heard a sound or not. She fixated on locating the North Star but couldn't find it, and she couldn't find Orion's belt. Those were the only constellations she knew from being in school. Combining these observations, she realized she wasn't on Earth. She doubted she was even in the Milky Way.

She thought she heard a rustle behind her, but in reality, she felt the vibrations of something approaching her, and her mind interpreted this as noise. That was the first time she saw Gretgen. He appeared before her, and before she could scream, he held his appendage over her mouth. They stared at one another. His eyes came to the front of his body. She noticed that his eyes were similar to hers, and she was calm. That was when Jom, in his ceremonial robes, grabbed her arm, pulling her backwards in a way she was instantly paralyzed, and he forced the stone inside her jaw.

The pain was excruciating that she screamed and attempted to kick her attacker, but the powers of the Jom kept her subdued. Once her stone was inserted, she could hear him soothe her, cooing over and over again that he was sorry and that the pain would go away and how relieved he was that he found her. She shook her head and kicked and screamed if anyone came within a foot of her. She was extremely distrusting to begin with, and now being here, with these strange-looking beings on a planet she didn't know, she grew colder and colder.

She lost consciousness at some point, and her body was taken into some grand hall and locked in a strange room. When she awoke, she touched the walls but didn't understand the material it was made of. They were solid, but it moved like a deflated balloon when she pressed her hand against it. She was given something that resembled a lunchroom tray but didn't recognize the offering, and she feared it was poison. She spent her first week crouched in the corner of the room she did not know, scared out of her mind. The pain in her jaw was as if someone took a screwdriver to break her jaw, and she cried and cried.

She never cried, but this experience finally brought emotion out of her. She wanted to return to Caleb, to Earth. Fearful her mind was broken, she longed for something to make sense. The pain would not ease, and she couldn't understand what she was going through. Each moment it seemed as if she was losing her mind. She thought her sanity had snapped, and perhaps this is what her mother saw the world to be. She feared she had lost her sanity, and the thought of being on another planet was a delusion to protect her mind from understanding her decent into her own mental illness.

It wasn't until Gretgen entered the room did she accept the realization that she was abducted. The first day, he stayed for an hour, sitting. He didn't force anything in her direction or say anything. The second day, he came again, and the only words he uttered were *the tray is food.* On the third day, he noticed she nibbled some of the purple puff and sipped the red liquid. He left briefly and brought her more. On the fourth day, he sat beside her, but did not attempt to touch her. Finally, by the fifth day, he approached her, held one appendage out, and whispered, "I can help." She remembered staring at him; it took a very long time before she finally unfurled from her fetal position, came toward him, and placed her finger against his paper-thin appendage. She never understood true desperation until that moment.

The memory stirred emotion within her, and the sting of betrayal morphed into the bloodlust of revenge. She rarely felt emotion as strongly as this; centered on pain and hurt, projected outward, as opposed to coping within herself to handle the hurt of abandonment. She sniffled, remembering the assassin creeping after her in the portal, attempting to take her core piece. She wished she still had it. How did it vanish into thin air? Then she started to question why she needed it. Jom sent her reeling through the portal without it being softened. Was it a placebo? Did she blindly believe what she was told about the stone? Could Jom send her back that whole time? Or did they need to retrieve the core piece for another purpose? She wished she understood, the tears could no longer be held back and streamed down her face, and the arms she longed to comfort her were nowhere to be found. She didn't want Caleb; she wanted Rowan.

The pain hit her hard again, and she touched the spot again, and her eyes widened. There was a pattern to the hole. She could feel it, it was there. She started to hyperventilate. There was a pattern! She knew it. She touched it over and over again, studied it, memorized it. She ran into the kitchen, grabbed a Rubbermaid and a container of salt, and made it quickly back into the spare bedroom. She sat on the ground in the lotus position, then poured the salt into the Rubbermaid. She traced her jaw with her right hand and traced the same image into the salt with her left. Then she switched and touched her jaw with the left and the salt with the right. She repeated this exercise for close to an hour.

She finally looked down at the impression of the salt. She grabbed a pencil from her desk and sketched it on the wall. She erased, modified, and kept going back to the salt. She was like a crazed animal, shaking her head, erasing and redrawing. It was similar to an infinity symbol. The center burst into a clover-like formation but transitioned smoothly to a tear drop before re-entering the infinity symbol. She worked for hours, drawing, redrawing, all the while touching her jaw. Finally, the sun rose in the sky, she finally had it.

She laughed and laughed and then traced her drawing. An outside party would think her mad. From a vent up in the corner of the room, two eyes stared at the symbol and smiled.

"You sent me back with the intention of me being dead…but I made it! There has to be at least one other person on this Earth who knows what this symbol means! And I will find them, I will not rest, I will not falter. And once I have my allies assembled, I'm coming for you, Jom. I'll take you all down unless you tell me the truth!"

She texted Caleb, "I know how to prove this to you!"

"Not now."

"Please…"

"NOT NOW."

"When?"

"7:30. I'm taking a break, and we can talk then."

"I'm not crazy!"

"In your opinion."

"No, I can show you proof. I found it!"

"Stop texting me."

"Why?"

"Because you have lost your mind."

"No! I found the answer."

"Stop texting me."

"Seriously?"

"Stop texting me."

"Is that all you're going to say to me?"

"Stop texting me."

She shook her head and spoke to herself, "I'm not losing my mind, I can prove it, and you're a fucking tool bag."

...

She waited, and at 7:30, the takeout arrived. She paid the delivery person, placed his box outside his door, and entered the spare bedroom. She heard him open his door and bring the box inside his room.

She slowly exited and sat against his door, "You know it's been a week, and I have no symptoms. Can you at least open the door or FaceTime me?"

"Hyacinth, there is a lot on my mind right now, and I am not in a place where I can exude the patience I need to hear you ramble about your metaphorical world to which you retreat to cope with the pandemic."

"It's not coping I WAS on another planet, and now I can prove it. I have a symbol that..."

He interrupted her quickly, "Tonight at 8:00, we have a Tele-health session with a couple's therapist."

"What? Why?"

"We are going to do a zoom meeting with each other."

"Caleb, I figured out the symbol. I can't be the only one, there must be more people like me out there..."

"You sound like a conspiracy theorist, and I fear your brain is damaged beyond what you can accept."

"No, I'm not, I was abducted to another planet, and they forged a body double with no bellybutton who left the gas on, and it looked like me, but it wasn't me, and their timeline works differently than ours. It could be from the seven moons and how they shift. I'm not entirely sure how the whole thing works. But the portal is a rainbow, and there are crystals. It wasn't very comforting at first, but now I know I was there. I was there for over a year, and I trained, and I'm amazing. You have to see me! I can flip. I have muscles, and I can move in ways I never knew I could, and now that I have the symbol."

"STOP IT!"

She disliked how he yelled at her, "Caleb, listen, I have the substance they made the body double out of. It looks like sand, but it's more powerful than that and..."

He interrupted her again, "I can't take this anymore! It's like talking to a deranged stranger!"

"Caleb, you love me. You know me."

"Do I?"

"You do!"

"It's been a week with you here, and I don't feel like you're here at all." She heard him move in his room, "What are you doing?"

"I have things to do! It's much harder to be a teacher than a YouTuber."

"Caleb, something happened to me on that planet. I was trained to be a warrior, and they hurt me and betrayed me, and you don't believe me."

"You are sick, and you need help. I think the gas from the stove scrambled your brain, and you didn't allow them to test you before you left the hospital, I think you have something wrong with your brain."

"My brain is working just fine, thank you very much!" she was offended, "I have a bigger problem."

"And what is that?"

"The only man that I've ever trusted doubts me."

"8:00, we have Telehealth. Hopefully, a professional can get us through this."

"Through what?"

"Your delusion!"

"It's not a delusion! This actually happened to me! I was abducted and trained, and now here I am, and the only person in the world I trust thinks I'm insane."

"Because you are!"

"What?"

"There are no other planets like ours, you need to stop this now. I can't *even* with you right now!"

"Stop talking like this. I am NOT insane."

"I don't believe you."

"So then, why bother telehealthing? Whatever the fuck that means."

"I need another rational person to confirm this is you and not me."

"And if they can't?" She asked, panicked.

"I need to think of myself and what I need."

"What about us?"

"If you are not you, then there is no us."

She felt a tear go down her face, and she gasped in pain. She smacked herself across the face for feeling that way. "You really want me to cry over you, don't you?"

"Hy, you are delusional, and I don't know where that will lead us."

"I'm not delusional, and if you would just take a few moments to realize what I am telling you, then you'll see. Then you'll be there for me."

"Eat your food. At 8:00, we have Telehealth."

She went back into her room without another word. She traced and retraced the symbol on her wall. The eyes from the vent were worried about her. She traced and retraced the symbol and then punched the wall, and her hand went through the dry wall. She coughed from the dust and powder that surrounded her, and then she couldn't help but laugh. She shook her head and then looked at her takeout. She was so sick of honey mustard salmon…she wanted her own food and cooking. She had had enough of this stupid quarantine and made up her mind that she was going to the store the next day. She didn't care anymore about being symptom-free or holding Caleb at this point. She knew that she was NOT crazy and that he just wasn't listening. She wanted her revenge on Jom, and she would get it. She had waited a week, and she was done biding her time.

FOUR

Hyacinth worked diligently over the next week. She etched the symbol in her cabinets so that they would be visible from her next show. She transferred her drawing onto the computer and printed the symbol onto iron-ons that she had placed on the t-shirts that she would wear during her show. She started an alternate YouTube channel featuring the symbol accompanied by zen-like meditation music she played on her keyboard, hoping it would draw out someone. She knew she couldn't be the only one who knew what this meant. She joined an online forum for memes and participated in the 2020 sucks meme phenomenon, ensuring she put the symbol in the background. Unfortunately, no one commented about the symbol. They usually just laughed about the irony of her posts. Her favorite was a picture of her face covered in Amazon tape with the caption, *more effective than the mask.*

She was setting up the kitchen to make a video for her channel when Caleb came out of his room with his mask on. "Caleb!" She ran over to him, and he backed away quickly.

"It hasn't been two weeks yet!"

"It's been 13 days!" she yelled. "Put your mask on!"

"No!"

"Then I can't stay here with you." He sounded hurt and threw his arms up in the air.

"What are you talking about?"

"You have to put your mask on!"

"No, I don't." She dismissed his concern and reminded herself to distance herself from him emotionally.

"You went outside and bought food!" he stared at the counters.

"Captain Obvious comes back to join the episode!"

"Stop it!"

"I have a cooking channel, if I don't cook food, people don't watch, and if people don't watch, sponsors get upset." She laced in her high level of sarcasm. Once again, she was annoyed at stating the obvious to him.

"Do you want me to die?"

"Stop!" she rolled her eyes and pulled on her hair.

"Every time you leave here, you risk picking up the virus and bringing it home! I am at high risk!"

"You're at high risk for everything! What the fuck makes this different? You're at high risk for an asthma attack so you can't go running, you're at high risk for an emotional breakdown if your stress level is too high, you're at high risk of erectile dysfunction if you drink too much, you're at high risk for fucking everything, so take it all and blow it out your ass!"

"You are being so unreasonable that it is breaking my connection to you!"

"I had a staph infection after I had my appendix out. Do you remember?"

"Hy, this is different!"

"I had a staph infection, not just any staph infection, I had MRSA! I was in the hospital, and you sat next to me, refused to leave, slept next to me, you exposed yourself to more germs then! All with no precious mask or distancing to save you, and yet now, you won't even FaceTime me fearful the virus can somehow leak through fucking wifi!"

"You don't understand!"

"Because I have independent thought…" she rolled her eyes.

"You went into a store with other people!"

"Yes, and they were all masked, all 6 feet away."

"You still could've picked it up!"

"Then what's the point of the masks and the distance?"

"Now we have to start over again."

"Maybe you do, but I don't."

"You are being unreasonable."

"You are being paranoid! What's the difference between the food I cook here and your deliveries?"

"If you're not even going to try…"

She interrupted him, "Because you can't answer that, there is no difference. You just don't want to see it. The same way you're refusing to see this!" She pointed to the symbol. "Touch my jaw; you'll feel it!"

"Don't touch me."

He turned around without another word and slammed the door to his room. She was so angry she turned and kicked the refrigerator and dented it easily. She looked shocked and then laughed. To Hell with Caleb. She needed more attention on her channel anyway. She was about to record her intro when her phone indicated she had a text.

"Are you HyHy22?"

"Who wants to know?" she quickly texted.

"I'm a fan of your meditation channel, I'm SwitchRat3."

"How'd you get this number?"

"Not hard…a few key strokes."

"Before I block you, what do you want?"

"I know that symbol."

"How?"

"Still going to block me?"

"Depends on how you know that symbol?"

"It's on my jaw."

Hyacinth froze, "Where do you live?"

"I'm not telling you."

"Then how will we meet if I don't know where you live?"

"Good point, North Jersey."

"Do you know where Trader Joe's in Paramus is?"

"The one off 17?"

"Yes."

"Yeah."

"Meet me there in 20 minutes."

"You know?"

"Depends on what your jaw reveals."

"Just wait…"

"Seriously, how do you know?"

"I'm not saying anything until I see you."

"What do you look like?"

"I have blue hair. What do you look like?"

"I'll have on a t-shirt with the symbol."

"See you in 20, masked and gloved."

Hyacinth rolled her eyes yet again and spoke to herself, "Masked and gloved, what the fuck? Do you make your beau where a condom if you're on birth control?" She went to his door, "Caleb, I'm not crazy, and I still want you to see that…do you love me?"

"I'm questioning that every day."

"I was about to record my show, but I need to go to Trader Joe's…do you want anything?"

"No."

"Are you sure?" She asked, knowing he couldn't resist their dark chocolate-covered pretzels.

"No."

"I kinda love you…" she said the phrase he used to say before he told her that he was in love with her, and kissed her hand and touched the door. Caleb did not respond, and she sighed and left the apartment without her mask.

"Hyacinth!" she heard from behind her.

"Fuck off, I'm not even facing you." She kept moving as she went to the stairs. She went down quickly and Mr. Kim was at the bottom with his mask on.

"Hy, please."

"Why?"

"Because I am asking you," he said with sincerity as he held out a paper mask to her.

"I am doing this for you because you asked me without being judgmental or nasty." She took the mask and put it on.

"Thank you." He walked back into his apartment.

As soon as she felt the sun touch her skin, she ripped it off, "If I found at least one, then your days are numbered, Jom." She smiled to herself as she got into her car.

. . .

Hyacinth was nervous as she entered the Trader Joe's parking lot. It was packed, people lined up six feet apart with their carts. Everyone's eye communication indicated they were annoyed, scared, and ready to enter fight, flight or freeze mode at the drop of a hat. She parked at the end of the parking lot as if there was a spot close up anyway. She looked at everyone suspiciously, but then again, everyone who looked at her matched the expression. She was wearing the paper mask, and her gloves were old winter gloves she had found in one of the drawers of the spare bedroom. She returned to her people-watching as she had done outside the hospital. She noticed everyone staring at one another as if they were in a room about to be murdered. Tensions were high, and her tension was higher.

She tried to distract herself by looking over the highway, so few cars, it seemed like a fake version of Earth. She wondered if they had sent her back to an alternate dimension again, but she shook her head, remembering the conversation with her sister. This was Earth, this was happening, and everyone simply lost their minds. She carefully touched her right mandible, then slowly bit down, and could feel the mark. That symbol was the key to finding others, she'd create an army, and return for Jom. She knew that experience was real; they needed that specific shape for her speaker stone so she could understand the language of the Gnetgnu. Caleb could dismiss her, their new therapist could dismiss her, but she knew she had the proof and yet no one would even entertain the idea that what happened to her was even possible.

A small girl, maybe 5'1", approached her with beautiful tan skin and blazing blue eyes. Her hair was dyed dark blue. She looked like a human sapphire. Hyacinth enjoyed the hand-made mask with water Pokémon scattered about. Her outfit was more provocative than Hyacinth was used to. She wore a pink fur vest covering a white short-sleeved t-shirt with skin-tight pink leggings and knee-high white leather open-toed boots. She looked at Hyacinth and quietly asked, "Are you HyHy22?"

"Are you SwitchRat3?"

"That'd be me."

"How do you know the symbol?" Hyacinth asked quickly, not wanting to chit-chat with someone who may be a fraud.

"How do YOU know the symbol?" she challenged, folding her arms.

"I asked you first." Hyacinth was not intimidated, she may only be a few inches taller than her, but she was ten times stronger.

"How do I know you're not messing with me?"

"You mean other than the fact that I'm in the parking lot of a grocery store in the middle of a pandemic with no intention of searching inside for toilet paper and hand sanitizer?"

"How do I know you're not just some sicko messing with my mental illness trying to expose me to the virus?"

"Mental illness?"

"I have anxiety."

"Don't we all?"

"People who say that have no understanding of what it's like to deal with it."

"Easy, not trying to be offensive, just commentary on the situation."

"Well, normalizing anxiety to be something you feel once in a while makes people like me who *actually* endure a life of terror at the very motion of breathing feel really small."

"Again, didn't mean to offend. I'm sarcastic and nonchalant about the seriousness of most things."

"Personal tragedy?" she tilted her head and raised an eyebrow.

"Obviously."

"Explains the attitude."

"I could say the same."

"Why did you agree to see me? Did you whip that symbol up to trap me?" The girl looked around her anticipating agents to subdue her.

"Wow, you're that level of conspiracy theory?" Hyacinth could easily see how her breathing started to increase, and the vein in her neck thickened in panic.

"Well, let's see, I was abducted to another planet only to be returned to this one, where everyone thought I was dead, and it took over a year for everyone to realize I was alive, and now a viral pandemic is plaguing the world, and some weird YouTube channel materializes with a melody that matches the rhythm from the prayer I was conditioned to recite from said planet and displays the symbol that's carved into my jaw, and everyone around me is convinced I'm crazy! No one believes me!" The girl started to hyperventilate.

"Calm down." Hyacinth's eyes widened seeing this girl fall apart in front of her. "Calm down? Really?"

"I don't know, what do you want me to say?" Hyacinth shrugged.

"Something more effective than calm down!"

"That's all I got."

"Well, you need to do better because every breathing technique I've learned is not taking away this overly anxious feeling I have right now."

"Take ten deep breaths and count to ten?"

"Genius." The girl rolled her eyes.

"I don't know. I'm not a therapist,"

"But you're human!"

"I don't know. Can you think of something funny?"

"Nothing is funny right now!"

"Umm…find relief in realizing that this is a good thing?" the inflection in her voice was not comforting. "How is this a good thing?"

"I know the symbol."

"I know the symbol."

"So then *we* know the symbol." She gestured her hand back and forth between them.

"Everyone told me I was crazy," she said sadly. "Everyone thinks I'm crazy." Hyacinth shrugged. "We're not crazy." She smiled.

"I know that."

"What I need to know is why *you* know that symbol."

"Look, I need to verify your jaw, and you can verify mine, and then we both know, we know, what we know."

"I know what I know, but I need to know what you know!"

"I'm not telling you what I know until I know for sure you know what I know."

"Wait, what?" The girl raised an eyebrow, trying to keep up with the banter.

"I'm going to touch your jaw."

"You can't…" The girl shook her head back and forth and then took a couple of steps backwards.

"Why?"

"First of all, I'm not coming within six feet of you."

"You don't find these guidelines slightly suspicious?"

"How so?"

"So how does a virus know how to measure six feet?"

"The virus doesn't, but the scientists know more than I do! I believe the 6 ft is needed."

"What makes six feet significant?"

"What is your problem?"

"Sorry, I was in a coma when this all started, so having not been there on day one, I'm having a lot of trouble believing all of this."

"Well, I believe it, and you can't come within six feet of me!"

"I need to touch your jaw."

"Do you have gloves?"

Hyacinth held up her hands. "Yeah, just like we agreed."

"How are we going to do this?"

"Hold your breath?" Hyacinth suggested.

"What'll that do?"

"You think me breathing within six feet of you is going to give you a deadly virus that no one can cure?"

"Yes."

"Wow, okay, so hold your breath, remove your mask, and I'm going to touch your jaw, and then we'll go back to social distancing,"

"This is crazy."

"You have a shred of hope for finding someone who knows what you know, and you're going to let it slip through your fingers because you're afraid of a virus?"

"This virus kills!"

"All viruses kill. That's not new. What made this one the fucking exception to normal acceptance of something deadly?"

"Your relaxed attitude to the virus that has taken both my grandparents and my uncle is very disturbing."

"I'm sorry for your loss."

"Ever since this virus hit, everything sucks, and then out of the blue, I see your channel, and now I just want answers. Nothing makes sense anymore. Nothing made sense once I came back, and now, with this, I feel so isolated, I can't take this, I'm suffocating!"

"Could be from the mask…"

"I didn't mean literally. Are you always like this?"

"Kind of…"

"Tone it down a little, please. You're triggering my anxiety."

"I'm triggering your anxiety? How about the massive amount of morons behind us buying soap like they never knew it cleaned hands to begin with?"

"You must wash your hands when you return home!"

"You should be doing that anyway!"

"I'm going to lose my sanity."

"I've got bad news for you. You already have."

That statement would have normally sent her into a mental spiral, but for whatever reason, she laughed, "Why are you so sarcastic?"

"I see the world differently, I guess."

"I saw the symbol…and I just…" she winced her eyes as though she would cry.

A typical person would feel sympathy or empathy toward the girl about to cry, but Hyacinth felt annoyance. She wanted to remain logical, "Hold your breath, I'll keep my mask on, pull yours down, I'll touch your jaw and then when you bite down, and I feel the mark, I'll move away, and you can use hand sanitizer on your face, and then I'll let you do the same to me." She rolled her eyes, as everyone was practically bathing in hand sanitizer, to her, that made no sense anti-bacteria treatments for a virus were futile, she felt as if she was the only human on Earth who felt this way.

"Okay…on three."

"One, two,"

"Wait!"

"What?" Hyacinth was growing impatient.

"The people on the grocery line are staring at us…"

They both glanced over and saw all the people looking at them, there was no way they could have heard them, but they saw the intensity between them.

"Why is this any of their business?" Hyacinth scoffed.

"While a person can be intelligent, people can be surprisingly ignorant and act irrationally."

"Once again, that was already true. Now it just seems heightened."

"I'm used to people staring, but not like this." She looked down sad. "Let's go over there, and they won't be able to see us."

"Okay."

"Alright, are you ready?"

"One, two…wait, I don't know if I can do this…"

"Seriously?"

"This is scary and weird, and how do I know I can trust you?"

"What are you a Quarternewt?"

"One, two, three."

Hyacinth walked over to the girl then touched her jaw. She bit down and felt the same mark. Her eyes shot wide open, and she took several steps back. Hyacinth laughed in pure joy and couldn't wipe the huge smile from her face.

"You felt it!"

"I felt it!"

"My turn."

Hyacinth pulled her mask down, and the girl approached her and touched her jaw. As Hyacinth bit down, the girl was elated, feeling the same indentation in her mandible. She squealed louder as her heart grew larger than she knew possible as she wrapped her arms around her.

"You're closer than six feet, you know that?" Hyacinth teased.

"I don't care about the virus!"

"I thought this was a pandemic?"

"I don't care, YOU KNOW!" And the two continued to hug and squeal in delight in the back of the parking lot.

"What's your name?" Hyacinth asked, smiling without her mask on. "Skyler," she removed her mask, and smiled, "You?"

"Hyacinth."

"Where are you from?"

"Originally Arizona, but now I live here in Paramus."

"I live in Franklin Lakes…do you think that's why they picked us?"

"Because we live in Bergen County?"

"Maybe…"

"Skyler, I am so relieved. No one will believe me! My fiancé doesn't, and our new therapist thinks I have paranoia." She grabbed both her hands and gently squeezed them.

"Been there, done that. My parents think I made it up during a bad acid trip." Skyler jumped up and held her tight, and Hyacinth smiled, easily holding the girl up. She felt like a little bunny, small and delicate. Hyacinth stroked her blue hair and then put her down. They continued to stare at one another.

"How old are you?"

"24, you?"

"25, who do you live with?"

"My parents," Skyler said.

"Do you want to come to my apartment, and we'll talk?"

"Sure."

They each walked to their cars, they exchanged phone numbers, and Hyacinth texted Skyler her address.

"Put your mask on!" Screamed someone on the shopping line. "Fuck off. I'm six feet away!" Hyacinth shouted, annoyed.

The woman on the line started running toward Hyacinth and she started aggressively spraying Lysol on her. Hyacinth used her training as she spun her body in the air, rotating ten times, then kicked the person to the ground. They did not get back up.

"What did you do?" Skyler looked shocked and frightened.

"What do you mean?" Hyacinth asked plainly. "You just attacked her."

"She just sprayed me with Lysol! She got what she deserved."

Hyacinth took a moment to check herself and looked at the patrons. Before she knew it, a riot ensued in the Trader Joe's parking lot. People were knocking over carts, taking items as fast as they could, others were punching one another. Skyler looked frightened, "What did you do?"

"I didn't cause this!" Hyacinth looked confused, "They're freaking out."

"We better get outta here."

Hyacinth quickly ran to her car and locked the door once inside. She was shocked, "What is wrong with everyone?" she screamed into her steering wheel.

She looked in the distance, and there was a whole group of people around Skyler's car. Hyacinth took a deep breath. She parked her car on the edge of the parking lot, far from the insanity, but poor Skyler was stuck in the middle. She looked like a poor baby gazelle surrounded by a pack of lionesses. She grabbed her keys, "You can do this. You took down the Quarternewt, you walked through the heat of the nest and survived the plague of the Grshniz, you were able to withstand the Mrshti flower burn, and you survived the assassination attempt in the portal, you can take on a riot with idiotic humans."

She ran to Skyler's car. A panicked Skyler was inside with her mask on, putting Purell on her hands as her smart car rocked back and forth while she screamed, tears running down her cheeks.

Without hesitation, Hyacinth activated her training and dispatched the group attacking the car. She grabbed the first around the neck and used the momentum from their body to climb over the top of the car, and then she propelled their body downward, knocking over the three people on the other side. She slid down the back of the car and kicked two people using alternating roundhouse kicks from both sides. She side-kicked a third that still did not pick up on the danger.

She effortlessly performed a back handspring from the ground and landed crouching on Skyler's car roof. She smacked the roof three times, indicating to go, and Skyler started driving. Hyacinth balanced on the roof of the car as another group of individuals chased them. As Skyler passed Hyacinth's Honda Civic, she jumped into the air and somehow crashed onto the curb next to her car. She quickly got inside and sped away.

"What the fuck happened while I was away?" Hyacinth screamed as she drove out of the parking lot.

...

They walked into her apartment building, and Hyacinth removed her mask while she was in the hallway. Mr. Kim popped his head out of his door, "Hy, you know better!"

Hyacinth quickly put her mask back on, "But how will you know I'm smiling?"

"I know!" he quickly closed his door as the two made their way up the stairs to her apartment.

"You need to follow the guidelines."

"I need everyone around me to wake the fuck up." She rolled her eyes. "People are dying."

"People die every day."

"Would you feel that way if you had the virus?"

"Yeah, you've been away from the Gnetgnu for too long."

"If I could go back, I would. I miss the moons merging on the horizon of the Strythocket hills."

"I miss the orange stars illuminating the darkened sky."

"I miss the blue circles of a Septtronium puddle." She ran her fingers through her hair.

"Is that why your hair is that color?"

"Yeah, it makes me remember."

Hyacinth smiled wide, "How long were you there?"

"A little less than two months."

"I was there for a little over a year."

"That's intense,"

"I spent most of my time training underneath Gretgen. Did you know him?"

"How do you know he was a he?"

"He told me he was a he when we spoke with the speaker stone."

"Oh…"

"Yeah, that's what he used, so I used it. I don't know if the Gnetgnu have traditional gender."

"How do you identify?" Skyler asked as Hyacinth unlocked the door.

"She/her, you?"

"She/her."

"Okay, so we got that settled."

She walked down the hall and knocked, "Caleb, are you still teaching?"

There was no response, and then a muffled, "On a 15-minute break."

"There's someone here I'd like you to meet." She smiled from ear to ear. "What? There's someone here?"

"Caleb, you need to come meet this person. They know what I know. I'm not crazy!"

"Hy, now I have to start the two weeks over again! I am not leaving this room if another person is in the apartment!"

"She has on a mask, and to be honest, she's going to be around a lot. We're like quarantine cousins."

"Absolutely not! Do you have a death wish?"

"Caleb, seriously, come out and meet her. Her name is Skyler, and she knows what I know!"

"I have work to do!"

"Caleb..." there was no response. She turned to Skyler, "Sorry, he drank the Kool-Aid."

"You need to start taking this more seriously."

"And everyone around me needs to wake the fuck up."

"Seriously, you're being insensitive. How many have you lost from the virus?"

"How many did we lose on the planet of the Gnetgnu?"

"That was different!"

"No, it was similar. The Frezton Flower petrified hundreds,"

"But those were different circumstances."

"How so?"

"We had apothecary intervention, the elixirs we made, the life juices of the Quarternewt. We don't even have a vaccine here!"

"It's a virus! You're never going to have a vaccine on this planet."

"What are you talking about?"

"Viruses morph and change. How many times has the flu evolved?"

"You just haven't experienced someone leaving this Earth alone, frightened, unable to breathe!"

"Were you ever choked by the Quarternewt?"

"A Quarternewt choked you? How did you survive?"

"I used my strength training and got out of there."

Skyler lowered her mask, "I don't know how I feel about all of this."

"Do you go anywhere other than your house?"

"Grocery store when my house manager fucks up an order,"

"So then you're running a risk every time if you're listening to what they say."

"Why are you skeptical?"

"I'm not skeptical. I think it is perfectly reasonable that there is a virus with the capacity to kill, but this reaction isn't going to do shit. I have the virus, or I don't; either you have the virus, or you don't. They have you convinced that if you go out without your mask, you're going to die, but doordash is totally legit and virus-free?"

"You should have a little more compassion."

"We were abducted and had to fight in a war that was not our own, and then we were cast aside for reasons unknown, convinced by our own loved ones that we're crazy. I no longer know the word compassion."

"You're bitter."

"Totally."

"So, how is this going to work?"

"We need to find more of us. I know they're out there."

"But what if they're just crazy virus-spreading freaks?"

"We live in a world of chaos surrounded by freaks daily. We know the failsafe; only those granted a speaker stone have the mark on their jaw. That's how we identify who's legit and who's not."

"So, how do we spread the word?"

"How did you know?"

"The meditation channel you put up with the symbol."

"I also have a cooking channel. I decorated the backdrop with the symbol, and we'll see if we get anymore hits." She pointed to the etched symbol in her cabinets.

"I can add it to my podcast."

"How?"

"I'll describe it."

"Or, you could make that the icon."

"That's a better idea."

"Come on, we have a lot of work to do."

"Do you feel it?"

"What?"

"For the first time in years, I'm not alone." Skyler looked at her adoringly. "You're not alone, but I warn you I am sarcastic and cruel."

"I'm eccentric and tend to be dramatic."

"It doesn't matter. We know what we know. That's a stronger bond than idiosyncrasies, I guess."

"True, we're forever connected."

"There have to be more of us."

"I'm convinced there are,"

"Then let's find us."

From the vent in her kitchen, the two yellow eyes looked intrigued. They did not recognize this other human, but then again, there were only a handful of humans it had seen in its lifetime before coming to the apartment building.

FIVE

Hyacinth couldn't sleep, she was ecstatic she'd met Skyler and confirmed she wasn't crazy about her time on the Gnetgnu planet. She thought about Gretgen and her Hunturnah. She loved the Hunturnah, and losing it to the heat of the Quarternewt nest still stung and mimicked the pain she felt as she held Rowan's hand the final time. She missed lying on her Hunturnah's back, feeling him breathe, holding her in the night when they went on missions together. The feel of the Hunturnah was softer than velvet, the sound of its voice more soothing than any music box she had ever heard on Earth, and the gentle rhythm of its breathing always relaxed every muscle in her body. She opened her eyes and could hear Caleb sobbing in the room next to her. She opened her door, went down the hallway, and leaned against his door.

"Caleb, honey, are you okay?" There was no response, "I know you're awake."

"Leave me alone."

"Why are you acting so strange?"

"I could say the same about you!"

"How so?"

"You're pretending there is no danger because you were on a different planet."

"I WAS on a different planet."

"You brought a stranger to the apartment!"

"She's not a stranger. She was also abducted. If you would feel it, there's a symbol imprinted in my jaw, and she has the identical marker."

"You sound insane."

"You weren't there, but you will understand eventually."

"I'm calling off the wedding."

"What?"

"I'm calling off the wedding."

"Why?"

"Because you are not you…"

"And you are not you."

"You need to understand we are in a pandemic, and life is sacred. You dismiss it so quickly because of your mother, and it's only a matter of time until you go down the same path and leave me to grieve."

"How dare you say something like that to me!" She felt as if she couldn't breathe, as if she was being choked by a Quarternewt all over again.

"Because it's true! Mental illness and suicide attempts are in your blood!"

"Either you open this door right now, or I will kick it down."

"You're not strong enough to handle what is happening around you, so you have made this whole thing up, and it's scaring me."

"I didn't make it up!"

"Then I dare you. It has a deadbolt; you're going to hurt yourself in your delusion."

"Are you challenging me?"

"Stop lying to yourself."

Her anger bubbled over her like a boiled pasta pot, she leaned and kicked the door in, "Doubt me now!"

"Hy!" he looked terrified.

"Don't throw my mother in my face, you fucking pussy! I should've never told you in the first place! Yes, I run from the hurt of my past, but that doesn't mean that what happened to me didn't happen!"

"You look so different!"

"Yes, I do because I have been training!" She did a backflip.

"What did those doctors do to you? Did they give you steroids?"

"No, I have been on another planet fighting and training!"

"Hy, stop with the nonsense!" And at that point, Caleb fainted to the ground.

"Are you kidding me?" She leaned over and slung him over her shoulder. She placed him gently in their bed and sat next to him.

He fluttered his eyes, looked over at her, and then shot his body up, terrified, "What happened?"

"Seriously?"

"How did you get in here?"

"Oh no, no, no, please…not fair."

"What are you talking about? What happened?"

"I knocked the door down and broke the logic in your mind that I'm insane, so your brain shut down and didn't hit save, fuck."

She stood and turned away from him. He shook his head, afraid, "You don't make any sense!"

"I'm the only one on this planet that makes sense right now."

"You're doing it again with this nonsense!"

"This isn't nonsense! It's the truth take off your mask and hold me! Let me back in our room!"

"Get out!"

"NO!"

"Why?"

"This is my room, too! Both our names are on the lease, so you can't just get rid of me!"

"I don't love you anymore!"

"What?"

"You are so insensitive and such a jerk about this whole situation, and I can't take it! Your attitude about the pandemic has only revealed to me how self-absorbed you really are and how you don't care about anyone but yourself!"

She walked toward him, and he was terrified, "Caleb, think of what you are saying!"

"I don't know you anymore!" he crawled into a fetal position on his bed.

"I don't know you either." She wanted to break down, "We live here together, and my new friend Skyler is going to come over, and I'm going to see her at her place. We are quarantine cousins, so deal with it. If you want me gone, then each day, take another piece of me out of the room and leave it outside your door. When the lease is up, I will leave. But know this: on that day, once that door closes, I'm NEVER coming back," she turned and slammed his door back into place.

He texted her, "You broke my heart."

"How so?"

"You know."

"I don't know, hence the question."

"You agreed to a separation, and didn't even try to fight for us."

"What exactly am I fighting for?"

"US!"

"If you need to test me, your faith in me is compromised."

"I don't recognize you anymore."

"I don't recognize you either, so as such, fine, wedding off, the future I fought to get back to is gone, and now I have to accept that."

"Why can't you keep your mask on and stay in the apartment?"

"Because I have free will and a mind of my own."

"This is real!"

"I never said it wasn't!"

"Then why take the chance?"

"To live."

"What are you talking about?"

"Fear does not stop death, it stops liberation!"

"You need to be less political and more logical."

"You have no clue what logical means!"

"Educate yourself!"

"I have!"

"What evidence do you have that this is exaggerated?"

"What evidence do you have to suggest this is as bad as everyone says it is?"

"I have a college degree; what do you have drop out?"

"You're rubbing that in my face?"

"I'm pointing out reality, you're too ignorant to see what's really happening."

"Your texting tenaciousness needs to take a back seat before you say something you can't take back."

"Our future is over."

"Do you mean OUR future, as in me and you, or the future of mankind?"

"Both."

"HS…your brain is broken…I hope you come to your senses sooner than later. When the lease is up, I'm out, I hate you."

"Why do you hate ME? You're the one who is being stubborn."

"I was abducted, and you don't believe me. You act like this virus is going to wipe out the whole human race, and you refuse to try…"

"Try what?"

"Try and understand…you threw my past in my face. I told you those things because I trusted you, and now I have lost all trust in you."

"I tested your loyalty to our relationship, and you failed!"

"There should never be a test!"

"I disagree!"

"Fine, disagree, you tried to make me grovel for you, and I will not. You are a fucking asshole!"

"Stop cursing at me."

"Stop texting me!"

"Fine."

Then there was silence. She lost herself in this moment and started to destroy the room. She took her computer and its equipment into the kitchen. Then she took a screwdriver and a hammer and destroyed the desk unit. She cried and screamed the whole time. She was stuck in the spare bedroom on a futon, then fine, but that ugly wooden desk he put in there would be nothing but splinters by the time she was done. She hated the desk, she hated him, and she hated that she was the only one who could see the fake reality of the pandemic. She hit it harder and harder. Once again, the pair of eyes watched from the vent. But instead of a smile, this time panic ascended its furry brow. The eyes were hurt seeing her unravel. She screamed over and over again as she broke each piece of wood.

Then she started grabbing any object she could find to break. There was a cute little statue of cherubs that Caleb had given her one year for Christmas. He was far too into knick-knacks for her interest, but that's what he liked, so she went with it. She grabbed it and slammed it into the wall. When only one head of the two chubby angels broke, she picked it up again and slammed it harder against the wall.

Everything in the room was destroyed. She ripped apart each of his action figures, removed the glass from the cabinet, took the hammer, and smacked each shelf repeatedly. The only thing unscathed was the futon. She breathed erratically and pulled her hair. The tears attempted to leak from her eyes, and she held her head backward until she could safely proceed without tears. She entered their kitchen, grabbed the box of black garbage bags, and started putting all the pieces in.

She walked outside to the garbage bins, holding three bags in each hand, and threw them inside. She kicked the bin, and it made a loud noise, and without her intentionally doing so, she left a large dent in the side. She went back and forth with all the bags from all the items in the room five times. Then she vacuumed the floor. She made the futon, and realized that the room was far larger without the desk and all the statues and plaques. She tried to give herself a reality check; she just destroyed his shelves and smashed every one of his action figures that he cared about dearly, but she felt no feeling of dread or regret. *Good,* she thought to herself. She went into the bathroom and threw away anything she didn't want into another garbage bag. As she made her way into the hallway, her neighbor gave her a dirty look because she wasn't masked. Hyacinth snapped, "If you don't like it, go back to your apartment, you brainwashed sheep!" She made her way to the dumpster. When she returned to her door, a note was attached stating, "Wear your mask or pay the price!"

She shook her head, went inside, and grabbed a pen, she wrote on the bottom, "How much?"

She went back inside and opened her liquor cabinet. She grabbed a bottle of tequila and went into the fridge. She was relieved she had made truffles for her show the day before. She locked the door to her newly redesigned room and refused to allow herself to weep over the loss of her relationship with Caleb. She drank multiple shots of tequila and chased them with chocolate as she painted the symbol on her wall. She started painting the skyline of the Strythocket Hills with the indigo-colored sky, seven moons, and orange stars. "I am not crazy, this was real!"

SIX

Skyler arrived at the apartment early. She knocked, and an exhausted Hyacinth opened the door, "What the hell happened to you? You look like fuck!"

"So, to put it bluntly, Caleb called off the wedding, broke my heart, and I feel girly weird feelings of anguish that I need to suppress to stay cold-hearted. I don't think the tequila or the chocolate fixed that. I destroyed my spare bedroom last night and was threatened by a mask-wearing sheep, and I only finished drinking 4 hours ago..."

"What happened?" She rolled her eyes as she went inside, half dragging a-still-buzzed Hyacinth into the living room.

"He called me insensitive."

"You kind of are..."

"He told me I needed to take this pandemic seriously,"

"You really do..."

"He rubbed some emotional traumas from my past in my face."

Her face morphed, "Fuck that prick!"

"That's the part that really hurts,"

"Well, I mean, you are insensitive." Skyler walked over to the fridge and searched for that juice Hyacinth had made the other day.

She enjoyed having her around, almost as if she were her personal chef.

"I don't attempt to hide that." She locked the apartment door and followed her.

"This really is something serious." Skyler knew where the glasses were, she poured them each a glass.

"In one opinion."

"But he shouldn't have rubbed your past in your face," Skyler reached into her purse, took out a Xanax, and handed it to Hyacinth.

"I know." She took it without question.

"That's a low blow, I don't care, that crosses a friggin line!"

"Hence my reaction."

"So what happens now?"

"I'm here until the lease is up, both our names are on it, we both pay rent and utilities, he can't get rid of me until September. I'm hoping he wakes the fuck up before then."

"Maybe he will."

"I told him to remove a piece of me from our room each day if he wanted this to end. This morning he put out the freaky little porcelain doll he gave me for my birthday one year."

"Those things are so creepy. Where is it?" She looked panicked.

"Are you afraid of porcelain dolls?" she giggled.

"Only if they're babies,"

"Why?"

"They look like dead infants, and it freaks me out." She kept looking around the living room, fearful the doll was going to jump out at her.

"It was a sleeping baby."

"Even worse." Her anxiety was triggered, and she started to breathe faster.

"I shattered it between my thighs and threw it away, it can't jump out and say boo."

"Why would you do that?"

"It was a gift from him, and if he doesn't want me to have it, then I don't want it, so I destroyed it."

"Why did he give you a sleeping baby porcelain doll?"

She rolled her eyes and then collapsed on Caleb's gaming chair in front of the television. "He got it for me because I told him I wanted to have his baby, and I wanted us to be a family."

"That doesn't seem like you at all..." They were instantly bonded to one another in the short time they were together. Skyler was an only child, so having Hyacinth around was a new, enjoyable experience, and for Hyacinth, she was happier with Skyler than she ever felt with Chrysanthemum. They knew each other's moves, thoughts, as if they grew up together as best friends.

"I was drunk..."

"There it is." She felt this was the newly adopted pet phrase of their friendship.

"Wanna hear something disturbing?"

"Possibly," she raised an eyebrow. "He named it."

"Named what, the doll?"

"Yeah..."

"Creepy..."

"Told you it was disturbing."

"What did he name it?" her curiosity increased.

"Kaleki."

"Different...what's the significance?"

"It means Grace, that was his mother's name."

"I would say that's really sweet and cute, but I'm sorry those things freak me out."

"Me too, but it meant something to him, so it meant something to me. But it's over, so it really means nothing, so I transformed it into nothing..." She looked off to the side.

Skyler laid over Hyacinth's lap, then gently wrapped her arms around her, "Then why are you staying here?"

"I shoot my YouTube channel in my kitchen, I need to keep some consistency for my viewers. It's what's getting them through this pandemic in a lot of ways."

"So you do acknowledge there is a crisis," she said sarcastically. "There's a crisis, but not the same one everyone else is fighting."

"What do you mean?"

"Viruses and plagues, dying is part of life. Remember them from the Gnetgnu?" She squeezed Skyler tight and then returned to the fridge, took out two bottles of water, and tossed one to Skyler.

"Yes,"

"They were put on the planet for a reason. It's not going to stop because you put a piece of cloth around your face, or you don't sit in the movies with someone, and no one is getting that."

"But people are dying."

"People die every day." Her heart winced thinking of Rowan. Why did she always let his memory permeate her thoughts after his selfish betrayal?

"But if you can stop the spread."

"Didn't the original message say two weeks?"

"Yes."

"And how long has it been?"

"Far longer."

"So they're just going to keep this riding until they've snuffed out the weak, destroyed the struggling, and bent everyone over as hard as possible." She took a long sip of water and swallowed it hard, making a loud sound.

"You need to…" Skyler tried to sound convincing but didn't know what to say, and in her moment of pause Hyacinth interrupted.

"If they announced tomorrow that crab walking through the streets was the most effective way of travel to avoid the virus, would you do it?"

"Probably."

"I wouldn't! Think of how crazy this all sounds! Why is everyone so quick to just listen like this? People die every day, and this is not new. Everyone just needs to wake the fuck up." Hyacinth yawned loudly, walked over to the pantry, and downed a handful of chocolate-covered espresso beans.

"Come on, let's get out of here."

"Where are we going to go?"

"I have spare bedrooms in my place."

"I thought you lived with your parents?"

"I live in the pool house."

"How big is the pool house?"

Skyler smirked, "Bigger than your apartment, for sure."

"Seriously?"

"Um…I live in Franklin Lakes." She bobbed her head, implying Hyacinth should have figured out her lifestyle from day one.

"Good point."

"So yeah, grab some gear, and you can pick a room."

"I need to keep checking in on him."

"Hey, do you, but you no longer need to live with the non-believer." Skyler took her by her hand and went into the spare room to help her pack a bag, "These are your clothes?"

"Yeah, kind of underwent a body transformation during my time with the Gnetgnu."

"Our styles may differ, but I have one room dedicated just to clothing."

"Seriously?"

"I told you I'm eccentric." She put her nose in the air and didn't hide her privilege as she reveled in every moment of it.

"What do you do for a living?"

"When the pandemic hit, my parents told me my mental health was my only job."

"Wow."

"Yeah, so, for the good of my mental health, we're redefining your wardrobe today."

"Fine by me."

Hyacinth grabbed her satchel and then went to Caleb's door.

"Caleb, I'm going to stay with Skyler for a little bit. There's food in the fridge, enough for two days. I'll be back to check on you."

"Why bother?" said the broken voice from the other end.

"Because your brain is scrambled, and I'll just have to wait until you come back to your senses to tell you I told you so."

She jumped into Skyler's smart car, and the two made their way for a fun girl's day-in.

. . .

Hyacinth got a strange text from a number she didn't recognize, "Is this Hyacinth?"

Normally, she would ignore a text from a random number, but these were unprecedented times, so she decided to entertain herself, "I don't know, are you?"

"What?"

"If you're having an identity crisis, that's fine, but that's a question you must ask yourself, not someone else…Are you Hyacinth?"

"No, is this number Hyacinth."

"Your number, I don't know? Do you identify it as binary code?"

"No, is this number Hyacinth?"

"Again, your number, your call."

"Are you trying to confuse me?"

"You're the one who is confused. Are you Hyacinth, or are you 201-434-6654?"

"No, I want to know if you are Hyacinth?"

"Why didn't you ask?"

"I did! Is this Hyacinth?"

"I don't know who you are… are you Hyacinth?"

"No, I'm not."

"Okay, I'm going to call you Cliff."

"Why, Cliff?"

"From this conversation, you just seem like a Cliff to me."

"Did you just assume my gender?"

"No, you did."

"Cliff is a male name."

"If you identify it that way, it can be."

"Are you trying to confuse me?"

"Oh, Cliff, my dear, you seem so confused without my help. You don't know if you are Hyacinth, a number, or male. I hope your personal journey reveals itself to you in time."

"Wait…what?"

"What a Cliff thing to say."

"My name is Chad."

"You will always be Cliff to me."

"Is this Hyacinth?"

"I thought you were Chad? Dammit, Cliff, keep it together."

"OMG!"

"LOL!"

"Seriously, I am trying to find Hyacinth, who also goes by HyHy22?"

"Who are you?"

"My name is Chad."

"What do you want, Chad?"

"I want to know if this is Hyacinth!"

She face-palmed, "What do you want with Hyacinth?"

"I want to touch her jaw."

"Do you know where Trader Joe's is?"

"Which one?"

"The one off Route 17?"

"Yes,"

"I'll meet you in the parking lot in 20 minutes at the cart return."

"So you are Hyacinth?"

"That's a risk you have to take Cliff."

"My name is Chad."

"Is it Cliff?"

"Stop doing that!"

"Why? It's fun and easy?"

"Is this Hyacinth?"

"In 20 minutes, your question will be answered."

"So you are Hyacinth?"

"I said 20 minutes, Cliff! Like I said, keep it together."

She walked into the kitchen and texted Skyler, "There's another."

"Trader Joe's?" She heard from the second floor of the pool house. "20 minutes." She called up

"On my way down."

The two girls loved being together in the pool house. Hyacinth still checked on Caleb, she cleaned the apartment while she was there and did his laundry so he'd have clean clothes. Still, as promised, she destroyed the items he would leave outside his door. She was slightly relieved he ate the food she had left after she filmed her shows. She originally saw that as a small step in the right direction, but after a few weeks, she decided she didn't want him back. If this was how he acted in the face of crisis, how would he react to bumps down the road? She decided she didn't care. He was weak, she was strong, and she didn't need him.

. . .

Hyacinth and Skyler pulled up to Trader Joe's, and it looked more chaotic than typical, "The masses are anxious to get their organic smoked salmon this morning."

Skyler playfully backhanded her, "Hy, you really need to be more empathetic. People are scared."

"What scares you more, this virus or the heat from a Quarternewt nest?"

"I have no alchemy here."

"We have it here, it just looks different. We haven't figured it out yet."

"I just can't believe there is another one of us."

"I bet there are dozens, but some don't have the social media to see the symbol."

"Who are we meeting?"

"His name is Chad."

Skyler laughed, "So we're going to meet a blond alpha gym rat with too much gel in his hair?"

"Oh please, no, I think my sarcasm will hit overload."

"Where are we meeting him?"

"I said by the cart return."

"Which one?"

Hyacinth did her devilish smirk, "I didn't specify. I wanted to see just how Chad this Chad is."

"You're awful,"

"Sometimes." She smiled. She loved Skyler's acceptance of her sarcasm. Hyacinth enjoyed how eccentric Skylar could be. They stitched together flawlessly, and she especially enjoyed it . When Skyler would put together another outfit for her to wear, she felt like a privileged live-doll. She definitely couldn't fill out the chest cups the way Skyler could, but her fashion gift made it easy to alter the chest portion. Part of Hyacinth wanted to ask if they were real, but she knew they were real after seeing Skyler get changed one day. The two were instantly comfortable around one another. Though Hyacinth didn't divulge her past, she didn't want to relive it. They focused on their present, and she quickly learned how to comfort her through panic attacks.

They drove past each of the cart returns, and they saw a man over 6 feet tall. He was wearing an Under Armor hoodie, so it was hard to assess the muscle situation, but they could see broad shoulders. His hood was up, he wore his sunglasses and mask, and he was swiping on his phone. "I can't tell if that's him."

"I'm thinking it's him. What kind of jeans are those?"

"They look like Dolce and Gabbana…"

"Oh dear Lord, we have a genuine Chad."

Hyacinth parked the car, and she and Skyler slowly approached the man leaning on the cart return, still occupied with his phone. As they approached him, he stood straight, "Six feet."

"Seriously? Underestimating your height? Not a typical male reaction," Hyacinth stared at him. "Social distancing."

"Is for fuckwads." She interrupted and smiled at him intensely, and she tilted her head ever so slightly to be cute with her crude comment.

"Please," he matched the head tilt, "I know it's a shame to cover up something so beautiful, but please put your mask on." He stared at her, matching the intensity, and smiled beneath his mask.

"Or what?"

"I can't stand here and stare at you."

"Well, I'm not putting it on." She made a pouty face to be obnoxious, but he found her seductive.

"That's a shame," he started to walk away, "See you later, beautiful…"

"Cliff?" she called out to him.

He turned around, stunned. "Hyacinth?" He removed his sunglasses and mask, pulled down the hoodie and revealed what they had easily concluded, a perfect hair-gelled Chad. But more for Hyacinth, she recognized him immediately. This was her guardian from the portrait in the great hall.

"I don't know, are you?" she smiled, feeling relieved, having blind trust instantly.

He walked toward her, "It's you."

"Oh, so now the lack of a mask is okay?" She smirked as he approached her.

He stood before her, and with no hesitation, he placed one hand on her waist and the other on her jaw, leaving no time for her to protest. She bit down, and he felt the symbol. He smiled and started to hyperventilate in joy. He took her hand and placed it on his jaw, and he bit down. She didn't need to verify; she knew his face and his smile, but he didn't need to know that. She smiled and turned to Skyler, "He's legit." She took Skyler's hand and had her touch the symbol. All three were ecstatic together.

Chad reached out and touched Skyler's jaw.

"How long were you there?" Skyler asked. Skyler wrapped her arms around Chad and placed her head on his chest.

"Almost a year," Chad answered and cradled her to him.

"Did you face the Quarternewt?" Hyacinth did the same, though she was taller than Skyler, and landed closer to the crux of his shoulder.

"I took down 8 in my time there." He wrapped his arm around her as well, but slightly tighter, wanting her as close to him as he could.

"8?" Hyacinth looked up at him impressed.

"Yes," the comfort they found within their touch flowed through them with every breath. With his arms wrapped around each girl, they all breathed in sync. To an outsider, it would not look very clear. Still, to them, it was as if they were falling into a warm hug of acceptance and understanding that no other group of individuals could experience. They stayed in this fashion for several minutes, and there was no awkward tension to break the silence, just the sheer satisfaction that they had found one another. Every so often, they would touch each other's jaws and giggle.

"How long ago were you taken?" Skyler's curiosity got the better of her.

"I was 23 at the time," he looked off in the distance, remembering the white light and the rainbow crystals.

"How old are you now?" Hyacinth asked, staring into his spell bounding eyes.

"33."

"So it's been ten years, and you still remember the symbol?" Skyler was shocked.

"It's the only piece lingering. I wrote of my journey in my journal, but those memories can fade. This is tangible, I can touch it, I can feel it. If I get a cold, it hurts."

"It's the only piece of the puzzle that's permanent, I guess."

"Do you remember how you got there?"

"I remember a white light, a pull, and rainbows all around me."

"Us too."

"I remember everything about being there thought I was alone. When I returned, everyone thought I was crazy."

"Us too," Skyler said. "My parents made me move in with them because they thought I'd lost my mind."

"Everyone told me I was crazy and that I made it up because of what happened to me beforehand."

Chad looked down sad.

"What happened to you?"

"I woke up in my coffin, my body double had died."

"Holy Shit!" Hyacinth was shocked.

He looked into her eyes, "Yeah, it was intense." He had never seen anyone as beautiful before, and he was immediately infatuated with her.

"Cliff, yo Cliff, ya good?" she asked, snapping her fingers, noticing his eyes widen in her direction.

"Sorry, I just was not expecting you to look like…"

"Like what?" she asked.

"You look like you could assassinate people at the drop of a hat." He joked, trying to deter her attention from his staring to be at her beauty.

"I am the Prophet Warrior,"

His eyes widened, "From the Gnetgnu Text?"

"Yeah."

"How did you survive?" He moved his palm to cup her face.

"They sent me back and sent someone to kill me from within the portal."

"But…"

"I defeated them in the portal."

"No, that can't be." He shook his head, still in shock that he was in the presence of the Prophet Warrior.

"Why not?"

"That's not what I was taught."

"I'm starting to question most things with them."

"There are more unanswered questions than answered," Skyler commented. "How long have you known that world?" Chad asked sincerely.

"I was taken two years ago," Skyler said and stared into his eyes. "Did you suffer the sting of the Mrshti flower?"

"I did not."

"I did…" Hyacinth cringed. "Nothing on this planet feels like that ever did," Hyacinth shook her head.

"I've seen what it did to the Rishta."

"Rishta?" Skyler never heard of that species.

"Wiped out by the Mrshti flower, the last feeling it had was burning, and its death song sounded like nails on a chalkboard."

"The Mrshti sing a song and entrap your soul."

"Hy, people are staring at us." Skyler was worried.

"Let them stare, we'll just tell them we're the latest throuple."

"Excuse me?" Chad laughed, slightly uncomfortable and slightly intrigued. "Put your mask on!" screamed a stranger.

"Put it on now!" said another.

Annoyed, Hyacinth jumped to the top of the Cart Return, "Don't you people have enough to worry about? Worry about your own lives and the stupid scary virus, and leave us alone!"

"Put your mask on!"

Hyacinth spit into the air and laughed, "I'm right here, you wanna challenge? Then challenge, or better yet, mind your OWN FUCKING BUSINESS!"

"She's feisty," Chad looked at Skyler as he put his mask back on. "Just wait," Skyler said, securing her mask in place while rolling her eyes.

"What's the deal?"

"She does not believe the pandemic. She only got back like a month ago, the insanity of no one believing you, recent break up because of said insanity, you know, the whole girl's gone psycho package wrapped up with a bow."

"Your deal?"

"I found her as you did. I'm so glad there's another."

"You have no idea what this has been like."

"I can relate, though."

"10 years, no one…"

"I know," she stared at him and hugged him again.

One man came running toward them. Hyacinth somersaulted off the cart return and ran full speed toward them.

"Oh shit, here we go again." Skyler rubbed her temples, reminding herself to stay calm.

"Again? She's done this before?"

"There's a distinct possibility we will be banned from Trader Joe's for life."

"How often has she incited a riot in the parking lot?"

"Every time she's ever been here…and the Target experience, we'll save that story for another day…"

Hyacinth then leaned down and went through her opponent's legs. She sat up quickly and side-kicked them forward, and their face went into the blacktop of the parking lot. Another came from behind, and she threw them over her shoulder on top of the person she had dispatched.

"Sheep! Fucking sheep!" She screamed.

Another came toward her and smacked her across the face. The strike didn't faze her. She responded with a haymaker to the face of her attacker, breaking his nose.

"If you're going to challenge, be prepared motherfucker!"

She went to bring her fist through their jaw, but before she could continue the fight, Chad bear-hugged her and pulled her away, "NOT HERE!" he warned.

"WHY NOT?" she writhed in his arms, desperately wanting to finish what she started. Or, in her mindset, continue what the world would not let go! His grip was like a feeble crab claw trying to hold a crocodile's jaw in place.

"You are on Earth, and the game has changed." He breathed in deeply, holding her against his body. He came to terms quickly that she was going to be more than he anticipated. He calmly blew in her ear as if he had been trained to do so.

Without consciously understanding, she went limp in his arms as he took her back to her car. Being in his arms made sense, and she allowed her better judgment to stop participating in a riot and be pulled away. "Do you want to come back with us to my apartment?"

"Where do you live?"

"Paramus."

He handed her his phone, and she put the address into his maps. Then, she got into the car with Skyler.

"What just happened?" he asked himself as he looked at his phone. He quickly followed. He couldn't understand how lucky he was to find others with the same impression in their jaws. Above that, he was intrigued by the Prophet Warrior, more than intrigued even.

...

They all arrived at her apartment, "Make yourself at home." Hyacinth said, as she walked through the door, Skyler went over to her designated stool at the kitchen island and busied herself with the centerpiece, "Hy, seriously, if you're not going to prune the plants, I'm going to stop buying them!"

"It's not my fault; there's just not enough sun!"

"Have you two lived together long?"

"Since we met."

"How long ago was that?"

"About a month..."

"That's fast," Chad was intrigued. They argued like they had lived together for years.

"We share a connection, and now you share that too."

"True, but it seems kind of crowded here." He smiled. He felt very comfortable around Skyler, but

Hyacinth put butterflies in his stomach.

"Well, we kind of live here, and we kind of live at my place..."

"Oh, so you're..." he said, confused.

"No, we're not together. We're just, you know, bonded because of what we know that we know that no one else knows, and those we try to tell think we're crazy..."

"I get it." He smiled.

"Caleb, I'm home," Hyacinth called out. There was no response.

"Do you live with someone else?" Chad asked.

"No, Caleb is my imaginary friend, and I am reassuring him I came back safely covered in the virus infecting the air." She made her way down the hallway to knock on the door.

"Oh…" Chad nodded his head, confused.

"She's not serious," Skyler laughed, "You'll learn quickly, she's sarcastic."

"Who's Caleb?" Chad asked Skyler as he sat down next to her.

"A very sensitive subject at the moment."

"Caleb," Hyacinth called out again. "There's someone here I want you to meet! He knows what I know, another person to prove I'm not crazy."

From behind the door, they could hear a muffled, "Is your mask on?"

"No," she sighed, "I'm not wearing the fucking mask in the apartment, and I'm licking your door knob right now!"

"When I die, you will be so mad at yourself for not listening!"

"When you survive, I will scoff at how paranoid you are!"

"I'm not leaving this room."

"Fine, stay hidden in your room, little baby. The big scary virus can't hurt you from your takeout container, but it's obviously on my fucking skin!" She smacked the door.

"Um…she's a bit intense," Chad commented.

"Her ex has pretty much gone insane with paranoia, called off their wedding, called off their relationship completely, ummm, telling her that her experience on the planet was just a delusion she made up to cope with the pandemic…having a therapist agree with him… throwing away all their shared memories…she's actually doing better today than I've seen her in a while."

"Oh…"

"Yeah, and I thought I was the dramatic one, but hey, drama loves an audience."

"What have I walked into?"

"HySky calamity."

"What?"

"That's what I call it; that's the line of paintings in my gallery at the moment inspired by us, and now I have to figure how to draw Chad into the mix." She smiled and pulled out her phone, all the originals she had photographed and posted on her Instagram.

He laughed, "Clearly, you remember the moons…" he stared at her painting. It was inspired by Hyacinth's face, feeling different emotions spaced in the alignment of the seven moons.

"And the stars," she swiped to the next one, showing an abstract of a woman pulled apart, and in the center was one of the formations of the stars that would shine upon the Strythocket hills.

"How were they that color?" Chad felt a connection to the painting. He wanted to see it in person and stare at the intricate details of the planet he once called home.

"How is Earth so different?" Skyler sighed. She missed seeing the orange stars against the dark purple sky.

"Different rules, different moons, different everything."

"Different is the word these past months."

"Earth has lost its balance; you have to admit to that."

"Who did you lose?"

"My uncle, a friend…you?"

"My grandparents, my uncle."

"Has she?"

"No, Hy doesn't have family that she talks about. It's just her and the ex…who lost his shit when the pandemic hit."

"So, a death with a living, lingering component?"

"Indeed."

Hyacinth joined them, "Hungry?"

"Starving." Again, his eyes widened when he looked into hers.

"Then you've come to the right apartment."

She leaned into the fridge and smiled, "Do you like eggrolls?"

"You know I do…" Skyler rolled her eyes and went back to her phone. She had to double her workouts since Hyacinth moved in with her. She made her so many different meals, she lost count of how many were already her new instant favorites.

"Definitely."

"Our allies just expanded. How many more do you think we'll find?" She quickly started chopping the cabbage.

"I saw the symbol, and I knew."

"How did you see it?"

"I was searching for something to meditate to, and the way the song played on the keyboard…"

"OMG, me too!" Skyler yelled.

Hyacinth rolled her eyes as she completed the filling and started sautéing everything, "5 million subscribers for my food channel, and you both found me through my half-ass meditation videos." She laughed as she poured the oil into her fryer.

"You're a chef?"

"I guess," Hyacinth said.

"What's your show?" he took out his phone, "I'll subscribe."

"Greaties of the Eighties," she carefully placed the filling within the wrappers and rolled them up tight.

"How'd you learn how to do that?" Skyler asked.

"Mr. Kim, my downstairs neighbor, owns a Chinese food restaurant. He's a special guest every so often, we call it Kickin' It with Kim." She took the rolls and dropped them in the deep-frying basket.

"That's pretty cool." Chad smiled. "What do you do?" Skyler asked. "I'm retired," Chad said.

"Jeeze, I thought you said you were in your thirties; how old are you?" Hyacinth teased.

"I was a computer programmer…I coded a bunch of apps…when I got back, everyone was so weirded out by me that everyone left, so it was just me and a computer…"

"That seems cool, so what do you do all day?"

"Well, now, not much. They closed all the gyms, so I've been creating one at my house."

"My parents have one on our estate. Feel free to use it." Skyler smiled.

Hyacinth placed four egg rolls on a plate and then put some duck sauce in a small dipping cup and brought it down the hall, "Your virus special is ready to eat you paranoid pussy!" She smacked the door.

"I think bitter barely scratches the surface," Skyler said to Chad. "Awkward…"

"Eh, you get used to it. She'll be different when we're back at my place."

"Where do you live?"

"Franklin Lakes, you?"

"Ho-ho-kus."

"Your own place?"

"Yeah…" he looked down.

"You're one of us if you want a secondary location."

"Full gym?"

"And spa." She smiled. "I'm in."

Hyacinth joined them, drained the next batch of eggrolls on paper towels, then brought them over to the island. "I present to you napa cabbage egg rolls, notice the texture of the cabbage." She grabbed one and pulled it apart.

They each grabbed one and started eating, "These are really, really good."

"5 million subscribers."

"5 million and one." Chad smiled.

SEVEN

Hyacinth made her way to her apartment building again. While she liked living with Skyler, adding Chad stirred confusion within her. The three of them ate dinner together every night, and they either watched Netflix on the couch, cuddled together, or played a game. She was still wrapping her brain around how a 33-year-old computer prodigy with his own house and lifestyle quickly stitched himself into their dynamic. She knew why she was so comfortable around Chad. She couldn't understand why she was so comfortable living with Skyler. She concluded that, for whatever reason, the three of them felt secure with one another because of what they had been through. Every day, at some point, Chad had to touch her jaw and feel the symbol. She did the same. Their connection was intense, and she couldn't get him out of her mind.

She shook her head. She had to return and check on Caleb. He was lost to the world, and while she once wished she could bring him back, she was going through the motions. He left his laundry in a basket outside of his bedroom door, and she took it down and did it for him as she had done before she was abducted. She shot her episodes from her kitchen set and ensured he had food to eat while she was gone with Skyler and Chad. Next to the laundry basket today was a framed picture of the two of them from their first vacation together. She tore it apart with her bare hands, cutting her hand in the process. She entered the spare bedroom and traced the symbol on the wall with the blood. She couldn't wait for September to come and for him to walk in and see it, he painted her as insane, then fine, she'd finish the portrait for him. The dried blood made the bedroom look like a crime scene. She didn't care in the slightest. She went into the bathroom, wrapped gauze around her hand, and then returned to the laundry.

Looking at the picture, she could see how happy they had once been. She looked deeper at her face, her smile was there, but when she looked at Caleb's, it looked more genuine. It was then she started to question if she ever really loved him. Then she realized how deeply she had, and that's why she was so angry. She wanted nothing more than to marry him and share her life with him, and ever since she was back, he was gone, and she hated it. She put his clothes in the washer and rolled her eyes. The summer weather made her sweat in the small room. Then she started to question herself, was she in love with Caleb, or was she in love with the idea of having a family, a husband, and her perfect Sunday morning picture come true?

Her phone rang, she looked at the contact and rolled her eyes, "What is it Cliff?"

"Can you please call me Chad?"

"Maybe I will if you say something inspiring."

"Why are you so hell-bent on going back and returning to the Gnetgnu?"

"Were you in my room again?" she was immediately annoyed.

"I needed to get something."

"Stay out of my room, you creeper!" She teased.

"Stop sketching weird shit on your walls, you psycho." He smiled on the other end, knowing that he left things purposefully in her room when he would sneak in at night so he could find an excuse to go into her room.

"It helps me think."

"You're going back?"

"They didn't realize what they unleashed when they sent me back through the portal," Hyacinth said seriously to Chad.

"What are you talking about?" he asked, concerned.

"They tried to remove my core piece, and now it is lost. They took a part of me!"

"But you can't travel through the portal without it!"

"I was halfway through, and they sent a Gnetgnu guard to take it from my neck."

"What happened?"

"I fought them in the portal, they took it, but I ripped them in half, which means it is somewhere stuck in the portal."

"Is that how we go back?"

"What do you mean *we?*"

"Wherever you go, I go."

"Stay out of my room!"

"You know I can't!"

"This is something I have to do!"

"Maybe you're scared for us both to go back?"

"Maybe," she paused, was she worried because he wanted to go with her, or worried because something might happen to him? She shook her head and refocused her thinking, "But there's more."

"Tell me!"

"I still have my satchel, all my items. I kept it all."

"How did they allow that?"

"I ripped the Gnetgnu in half, and they were defenseless."

"What had you acquired?"

"I kept a trophy from each of my victories and a whole vial of..."

"You didn't!" he was shocked.

"I did..."

"But that was never meant for you. That is why this is happening to you because you violated the sacred law!"

"No, I honored the belief to not believe everything told. They told us the Grshniz would devour our flesh, but when I was among them, no such thing happened."

"I was never in their presence."

"This is why I ensured my satchel was…" She kept it on her person wherever she went. After putting the next set of clothes in the washing machine, she opened it, and snarled. The tiny hairs were petrified and felt like dried pine needles. "A Mustleknapp has been in my satchel."

"Eww"

"Gross…its fur is everywhere." She started picking them out and placing them in the garbage bin.

"How?"

"I don't know, but now I know why it was so heavy in transport."

"Be careful. If a Mustleknapp is anywhere near you, they will…"

"They will what?" She rolled her eyes as another round of bristles cascaded into the garbage.

"Weren't you warned about the Mustleknapp?"

"No, simply that they were one of the oxygen-needing species on the planet. They were merely creatures, nothing more."

"They were once as grand as the Gnetgnu, but due to their treachery, they were banished from the Strythocket and forced to their underground existence beneath the Grehness Gorges."

"I was never told that."

"I was."

"How do you know that is accurate?"

"How do you know what you were told is accurate?"

"I don't! None of us do…"

The Mustleknapp, having heard its species named, slowly emerged from a hole in the laundry room's wall. It sat up on its hind legs, raised its little eyebrows, and slicked its whiskers back, annoyed. It used its front appendages to cross them like arms angrily as it stared down Hyacinth. She turned, and they locked eyes with one another.

It was currently the size of a rat, with a furless tail, but its face did not have the snout of a rat. It was flat and wide, closer to that of an otter. Its ears were triangular like that of a cat. Its grayish-white fur was short and soft like a cotton ball. It could move from all fours to two legs and run as fast from either position. It could easily manipulate its muscles and joints to accommodate whichever it preferred. It had six fingers on its front and back paws. Its eyes resembled a snake and could blink up and down or side to side.

"I gotta go, stay outta my room!" she hung up quickly. She was confused to see the creature in its current form, "You're the Mustleknapp who stowed away in my satchel!"

"You're the Mustleknapp who stowed away in my satchel!" it imitated her voice.

"The Mustleknapp just spoke!"

"The Mustleknapp just spoke!" it swayed its hips as it imitated her again. "You spoke?" she was shocked.

"I spoke." It widened its eyes and smirked its mouth, mocking her ignorance.

"That was not a repeat…" she said breathlessly in disbelief.

"Duh." The Mustleknapp got back on all fours and approached her.

"How do you speak?" she crouched to be on its level.

"With my mouth, dumbass." It shook its head and stood on two legs once again.

"But the Mustleknapp do not have words." She shook her head, confused.

"No, the Mustleknapp speak a different language than the Gnetgnu and, therefore, from their perspective, do not have words, you lamb."

"Lamb?" She asked, confused.

"A witless follower?"

"Sheep."

"Forgive me. My language skills are still developing on this planet."

"You speak like a human."

"I have lungs, a mouth, and a tongue. Why wouldn't I speak like a human?"

"I meant your voice, and you sound like a human."

"You were transported to another planet through a rainbow portal, and me sounding like a human surprises you?" It puckered its mouth once again, mocking her.

"How did you get here?"

"I hid in your satchel, dumbass."

"I know that. I meant, why are you in the laundry room?"

"Well, other than it's warm here, I have access to the whole building from that hole in the wall."

"But you went into my satchel, on purpose?"

"Wow, really, we're stating the obvious?"

"You *wanted* to come to Earth?"

"Yep."

"Why?"

"To escape the planet we were both on, duh."

"Did you follow me?"

"Again, obvious is the choice word here."

"I meant on your planet, you jumped into my satchel on the Strythocket fields."

"I did."

"How did you get there?"

"I heard of the human, who defeated a Quarternewt with a sondya, and found my way out."

"What have you been doing this whole time?"

"You mean other than taking money from your wallet and using your phone to figure out how to speak your language."

"How?"

"Tik Tok, Facebook, YouTube, Snapchat, Roblox, and I downloaded Tinder. You should know there are a lot of desperate people in your area."

"What?" she asked, angered.

"Oh, don't look so shocked. These are hard times, and people still wanna get some."

"No! I'm pissed because you stole from me. You've been taking money from me? For what?"

"Domino's, I don't know what demons created it, but Hawaiian pizza is addictive."

She sat down criss-cross apple sauce and stared, analyzing and assessing the creature. The Mustleknapp slowly leaned closer to her, and she smiled to the side, "You've been staring at me through the vent. You're the reason my cell phone keeps dying!"

"For fuck's sake, really, now you sound just as stupid as Caleb."

"Give me some more credit!" She teased him.

"I will when you earn it…" He tilted his head playfully. "Why learn my language? Other than to insult me?"

"Dish it out, but just can't bring it."

"Take it."

"Whatever."

"Seriously, what's the point?"

"To talk to you."

"About…"

"To tell you the truth…"

"And what is that?"

"Hang on, I want to ensure I say it right…"

"Take your time."

The Mustleknapp stared into her eyes, then took its front paws and placed them on her cheeks, "You are dumb as fuck. The Gnetgnu are highly sus."

"What?"

"You got played." It tapped her cheek twice and then folded its arms.

"What are you talking about?"

"Am I not saying this right?" it shook its head, not understanding if she was confused over what was said or if this was disbelief. Humans were particularly hard for him to understand.

S. LEIGH MEDEIROS

"Are you trying to tell me I am stupid, and they tricked me?"

"Yahtzee!"

"Bingo." She rolled her eyes.

"Whatever, apparently the most intelligent do not post on TikTok."

"Duh."

"Are you ready to hear the sad truth?"

"Why did you want to escape?"

"That's part of the truth. Are you going to interrupt me the whole time?"

"I'm willing to listen."

"Good, get comfortable."

Another person came into the laundry room. Hyacinth grabbed the Mustleknapp and hid him in her satchel quickly.

"Hy, you need to wear your mask!" Mrs. Carter shouted.

"Why?"

"Because you need to stop the spread!"

"Stop the spread, the two weeks has morphed into months, pretty sure a mask doesn't do shit."

"Because people like you don't follow the guidelines!" she shouted.

"Yeah, me not wearing a paper mask will stop a plague from spreading…you all sound insane."

She left the room and started up the stairs to her apartment. The Mustleknapp crawled out of her satchel and whispered in her ear, "Why hide me?"

"Because you resemble a rat on this planet."

"Which one is a rat again?"

"An unwanted creature in apartment buildings."

"I thought it was someone who gets stitches."

She laughed, "You'll find that words have multiple meanings on this planet."

"That is confusing…especially on social media."

"Must be very hard for you, considering this is a new planet and language."

"Not really, humans are simplistic."

"You cannot judge our entire culture from social media."

"Sure I can. Humans do it all the time."

…

She quickly texted Skyler and Chad and told them to come to her apartment ASAP. The three of them gathered in the laundry room. Hyacinth put the dryer on. It was clanky and loud.

"Why did you put that on?" Chad asked.

"So they can't hear us!"

"Who's they?"

"You know, the government?"

"Don't you think they're a little busy right now?" Skyler rolled her eyes. "Besides, now we have to shout at each other. We could easily whisper." She rolled her eyes and turned it off. "Fine."

"Why did you bring us here? We were both at headquarters…"

"Did anyone have trouble getting here?" She started folding Caleb's clothes. "No,"

"Were you followed?"

"No."

"Why are you acting so paranoid all of a sudden?" Chad stated, concerned.

"This isn't like you." Skyler pouted.

"Because I learned a lot today, and I'm still processing everything."

"What happened?"

"We have a lot to talk about."

"Hy, I know you're trying to go back," Chad said sadly. He loved sneaking into her room when she wasn't there and looking at the drawings she'd sketch on the wall. It made him remember the planet he was on so long ago, and he missed feeling empowered with the Gnetgnu by his side. But they were here now, and he couldn't erase the memory, couldn't dwell and be lost in it.

Being in the pool house with the girls finally gave him a sense of belonging, one he had been without since returning to Earth. "What happened to your hand?"

"Nothing." She hid her hand behind her back.

He went over to her and gave her a look, she tilted her head and showed him her hand. He shook his head, concerned, "What was it this time?"

"Glass."

"Did you get it all out?"

"I don't know."

He rolled his eyes. He took off the gauze and looked at the wound. "Skyler, do you have your kit in your purse?"

"Yeah," she rifled through and handed it to Chad. "Since when do you carry this stuff around with you?"

"Since you smashed your hand through the red ball at Target…"

"oh…"

As Chad worked on her hand, he whispered, "Are you going back?"

"Yes, I am." She fully admitted.

"Can't you just relish that you were the Prophet Warrior and let it go? I mean, coming back to reality sucks, but you need to realize that some things are just meant to be. Why are you doing his laundry?" Chad asked, a little jealous.

"Because he can't leave the apartment."

"I agree on so many levels. You need to stop doing his laundry or at least make him fold it. And, you can't go back. Between the pandemic and Caleb going bonkers, it's no wonder you want to, but we need to accept that Earth is our home planet." Skyler was trying to be understanding.

"I miss it too, I miss having my powers," Chad said to Skyler.

Hyacinth was fuming. "You had powers?" she pulled her hand away. He was disturbed as it pulsed blood onto the ground.

"Yeah, didn't you?" he grabbed her hand and gave her an angry look. She tried to squirm away. He leaned down and blew in her ear to quell her escape attempts so he could continue to work on her hand.

"NO!"

"Wait, you didn't have powers?" Skyler was shocked.

"No!"

"So how did you defeat the Quarternewt?" Chad tried to change the subject.

"My sondya," she said sadly. They both started laughing. "What is so funny?"

"What's a sondya?" Chad imitated her voice inflection.

"It's kind of like a sword, but it has…wait a minute, you weren't given a sondya?"

"It sounds so stupid and fake when you say it." They both couldn't stop laughing.

"Stop it! Seriously! It's like a sword, but the blade is doubled and serrated on the outside…ouch!" She gave him an annoyed look.

"Sorry, Beautiful, that should be the last of it," he rewrapped her hand and kissed it.

"Why a double blade?" Skyler asked curiously.

"One for each heart of the Quarternewt."

"Seriously, you couldn't bend the Septtronium with your mind and send it careening to their hearts?" Skyler asked innocently.

"No…"

"You could move the Septtronium?" Chad asked, surprised.

"Of course, couldn't you?"

"No, I could only manipulate the Decttronium."

"Interesting…"

"What the fuck are you two talking about?"

"You didn't bond to one of the elements?"

"No…" she shook her head angrily.

"Wow, you got screwed over." Skyler laughed.

"Ya think?" Hyacinth shrieked.

"So why do you want to go back?" Chad was confused. He gently pulled her hand up and kissed it again, taking every opportunity he could to show her how attached he was to her.

"I don't want to go back for fucking honor." She pulled her hand away and wrinkled her forehead, frustrated.

"Then why?"

"I'm going back to kill every last one of the Gnetgnu."

They stared, shocked; finally, Skyler broke the silence, "Seriously, stop that right now. The Gnetgnu took us in, gave us a purpose."

"They lied through their fucking corner mouths like rotten little shits!" Hyacinth hissed. "How do you know?"

"I have insider information…" She peered over to the hole in the wall.

At that point, the Mustleknapp entered the room, and Skyler screamed. "Gross, quick kill it, kill it!"

"Well, that's a fine how do you do," it said, annoyed.

"It just talked," Chad said, shocked.

"Yeah, It does that," Hyacinth nodded.

"I am not an IT!" The Mustleknapp exclaimed, annoyed. "Then what are you?" Hyacinth asked.

"A Mustleknapp."

"How do you identify?" Skyler asked with the corner of her lip up as though she addressed vermin.

"Using the two genders approach, which I am learning, is no longer the preferred method on this planet. I am, for all intents and purposes, a HE!"

"The Mustleknapp do not speak."

"Rams." He shook his head.

"Sheep." Hyacinth corrected.

"Whatever…did you order my pizza?" He pointed his sixth finger at her. The only reason he would help was if he could have his fix.

"Yes, it's on the way."

"Good." He turned to address the group, but he immediately disliked Chad, "So let me guess each one of you dumbasses defeated the Quarternewt?"

"How is this miscreant talking?" Skyler asked, annoyed.

"Miscreant?" He looked at Hyacinth, offended.

"Sheep," she gestured with her arms to remind him how gullible humans were in his opinion.

"You're the dumbest people alive, and I'm the miscreant?" he gave Skyler a dirty look.

"How are we the dumbest people alive?" Chad folded his arms.

"You mean in addition to believing the lies a living piece of paper told you to be the laws of a foreign planet?"

"Yeah," Chad said, feeling less confident.

"Your planet is in the middle of a viral plague, and you're sitting in an unventilated area with one another after being blatantly told not to do that."

They looked at one another, "He's got a point."

"I can make an elixir. We're fine," Skyler said.

"With what? You think you have the elements needed on this planet?"

"I am the master of the Septtronium."

"Was sweet cheeks."

"Hey!" Skyler snapped at him, offended.

"Septtronium does not exist on Earth. You're naïve, and I believe the phrase is full of it."

"Full of what?"

"Excrement."

"Shit." Hyacinth corrected.

"I did not come back to this shitty apartment building to listen to the lies of the Mustleknapp!" Skyler stood as though she would leave. She did not like the low amenities of Hyacinth's apartment building and wanted her pool house to be where they'd all congregate together permanently. In her opinion, Hyacinth should leave Caleb to rot and stop trying to ensure he was safe, clothed, and fed.

"Why do you assume they are lies?" The Mustleknapp asked, offended.

"Mustleknapp cannot be trusted," Chad said bluntly.

"And you are basing this on…"

"The wise Jom would not lie," Skyler added.

"Oh please, the wise Jom is the biggest liar on that planet."

"Lies!" Chad accused.

"I swear I'll let all you morons stay festering in your plague juices and stupidity if you don't let me speak."

"Alright then, Latheys and Gentlethem, listen to a Mustleknapp and see what we're up against. You are here on Earth because you need to breathe, and then you need to go back to your planet!" Skyler was losing her sanity, thinking the whole story was a lie.

The Mustleknapp took a deep breath and then stood on two legs, it slowly increased its size until it was that of a fox as opposed to a rat. It approached an empty chair and perched, "Now listen closely, my feeble sheep. The Gnetgnu are not who you think they are. They are dominant over the Mustleknapp but fall victim to the Quarternewt every time. That is why they seek the assistance of an Earthly, enslaved person to do what they are incapable of doing. The Gnetgnu are a frail people; they fall victim to plagues regularly, and if you've ever battled one, they tear apart like parchment. The Quarternewt need only take two fingers, and can easily wipe out entire villages.

There was once a treaty between the Mustleknapp and the Gnetgnu, but that was broken by your mighty Jom ages ago, hence why they needed an Earth person. The Mustleknapp is the natural enemy of the Quarternewt. Hurl one of us when curled into a ball, and we will crush them instantly. The Gnetgnu agreed to share the elixirs made from the heart juices of the Quarternewt to fend off plague with the Mustleknapp, specifically to prevent the Frezton Flower from warping our tongues. Your asswipe Jom purposefully infected hundreds and turned their petrified bodies into weapons against the Quarternewt, hoping to exterminate their population. Making them the dominant of the planet."

"Say that one more time," Hyacinth spoke slowly as she finished folding the laundry.

"The Mustleknapp can defeat the Quarternewt, but had no desire to wipe their species from the planet. Why would we? They are of no threat to us. But they were a threat to the Gnetgnu."

"Are you trying to tell me that the blades of the Quarternewt can cut the flesh of a Gnetgnu?" Skyler asked.

"Yes." He smiled and tried hard not to laugh.

"But the hard stone-like body of a rolled up Mustleknapp can crush a Quarternewt?" Chad clarified.

"Yes," the Mustleknapp squeaked out before letting out a loud laugh.

"What is so funny?" Skyler asked.

"Are you fucking kidding me?" Hyacinth was so angry she could spit daggers. The Mustleknapp laughed harder.

"You're fucking kidding me right now?" Hyacinth shook her head in anger.

"What?" Chad was clueless.

"Hy, what's going on?" even Skyler was confused. Her anxiety started to spike.

"Are you trying to tell me that we were abducted to another planet to fight a battle because scissors beats paper!"

"You and a bunch of other sheep." The Mustleknapp laughed so hard he almost fell off the chair.

"Oh, they are dead, DEAD, do you hear me! I am going back to that planet and I am going to rip apart every single Gnetgnu. I will take the almighty Jom and, rip him apart like a playing card."

"Hyacinth, you're talking genocide!"

"What do you think we have been doing this whole time?"

"If we have the timeline correct, then they abduct someone every other year, which means if we don't do something in a year, another Quarternewt will be slaughtered for no reason." Skyler was visibly upset.

"Why do you suddenly care about the Quarternewt?" Chad still did not fully believe the Mustleknapp.

"I killed one because I was told it was for the greater good of the Gnetgnu whom I thought were my new people. I was lied to, I feel used, and I feel cheap! Then I get sent back, and I have just been schooled by a fucking Mustleknapp!" Skyler was angry.

"You're welcome, by the way." The Mustleknapp flicked its whiskers.

Hyacinth got a text on her phone, "Hold on, the pizza is here."

The Mustleknapp happily shrunk its size and ate the pizza while she and the others sat around on a picnic blanket eating pizza and wings.

"You're going to find your way back."

"No, WE, all of us, were lied to. We are all going back together to make this right." She stared into Chad's eyes, knowing that she couldn't stomach the idea of going back without him…and she grew angry with herself for being vulnerable.

"We need to decipher what is real. What if we blindly follow the Mustleknapp?"

"Mustleknapp can't lie," said the Mustleknapp with a mouth full of pizza.

"Says the only Mustleknapp to ever speak to us." Hyacinth pointed out.

"If you want, if you *can* find your way back, which you won't, put a speaker stone on a Mustleknapp. It'll work, and they will tell you we want only calm."

"Calm?" Skyler raised an eyebrow.

"When there is not harm, or the harm is over."

"Peace." Hyacinth rolled her eyes.

"Peace, calm, call it what you want. We only want to do our thing and not be covered by the Gnetgnu and their need for power. It's sickening."

Hyacinth shook her head, "What's sickening is that we were transported to another planet to cheat at rock, paper, scissors."

"Yeah, we were…" Skyler said, finally accepting all the new information.

"Let's kill them all," Hyacinth said determined.

"Oh, we are going to," Chad reassured her, emphasizing the we in his statement.

"And then we will all return home with a piece of Jom to frame."

"You humans do you, I'm staying here."

"Why?"

"There's no Hawaiian pizza on my planet." And the Mustleknapp devoured the whole thing, and then crawled back to the shelter it had made in the wall.

"Wait!"

"What? I'm full of Hawaiian pizza, and want to nap."

"The Gnetgnu told us you had no language, no culture. You were simply vermin."

"Coming from the human who wanted to kill me a half hour ago?"

"Tell us your culture, your traditions."

"The Mustleknapp spend most of their time cleaning our quarters and one another. Depending on your station, you either clean, be cleaned, hunt, or watch out."

"What was your station?"

"Hunt."

"What did you hunt?"

"Food."

"Do you eat Gnetgnu flesh?"

"Would you eat a piece of paper?"

"No, but people smoke paper," Chad said.

Hyacinth rolled her eyes, "Cliff, seriously, keep your commentary for the gag reel."

"Is that why you like pizza?" Skyler asked sweetly.

"There is no pre-made food on our planet, and I enjoy the convenience. There's also the constant fear a Gnetgnu will cover me for fun. That doesn't haunt my dreams here."

"They would cover you for fun."

"Yes, often, the Gnetgnu are not who you think they are. Now if you'll excuse me, I believe your people refer to it as a food-comb."

"Food coma," Hyacinth corrected.

"Whatevs, I'm out." The Mustleknapp went into its shelter.

"We were all lied to," Skyler said sadly.

"Yeah," Chad said. "I can't believe I fell for it."

"I can't believe I fell for the same lie as Cliff," Hyacinth said.

"Why do you tease me all of the time?" He looked at her as if he was hurt.

"Because you are Cliff, and I can." She smiled at him, knowing she did this because she liked him.

"Yeah, Cliff," Skyler laughed and playfully hip-checked him.

"Do you think the Quarternewt have a language?" Chad asked.

"What do you mean?"

"Well, we were taught the Gnetgnu were the dominant species, the only ones with a language and a civilization, the others mere creatures."

"What are you saying?"

"If the Mustleknapp have a language, traditions, a culture, then what if the Quaternewt do as well?"

"We need to hatch a plan to take one from each faction and put a speaker stone on each to get the clear picture."

"What if the Mustleknapp is lying to us?"

"What if the Gnetgnu lied to us?"

"When they sent you back, did you have your satchel?"

"No…"

"Did you have your core piece?"

"No…"

"We were used, expendable. If we died on our mission, then they would just take another."

"How many of us have died?"

"I'm wondering if the great hall had any answers."

"But only two of us had portraits."

"Maybe they thought you died in transit."

"Where did your body double surface? Mine was in the hospital, but I completely traded with my body double," Hyacinth said sadly, remembering her former self fearful before disintegrating into the sand.

"My double was in a coffin at my wake. Imagine their surprise when I sat up…my grandmother fainted," Chad said uncomfortably.

"My double was on my sofa, next to my roommate, who overdosed. The EMT's were with us both when I sat up confused."

"They thought you were dead."

"No…"

"Yes, the hall is not for heroes. It's so they can keep track of who they killed. They're trophies!"

"Those paper fuckers are getting set on fire!"

"Can you humans please keep your voices down? Some of us are trying to nap," The Mustleknapp called from his shelter.

"You know, I have a futon, which might be a bit more comfortable?" Hyacinth offered.

Before they could say anything, the Mustleknapp emerged, shrunk its size down to that of a mouse and crawled up Hyacinth's clothes and onto her shoulder.

"Show me."

"Tell us more?"

"After my nap." He cuddled on her shoulder as the three made their way upstairs.

EIGHT

Hyacinth stood before the camera, "Welcome back to another episode of Greaties of the Eighties! Today, we are going to make Eternal Flame Fondue. I hate to inform everyone that Caleb will no longer be a guest on my show. So, to drown my sadness, I need good food. Don't we all right now? But you may be wondering, why *Eternal Flame*? Well, one, I was in a Bangles mood, and two, I really wanted fondue. Well, more accurately, I wanted to go to Melting Pot, but let's face it, that's not happening anytime soon. To my poor, poor quarantined fans, this sucks, and we are stuck in this perpetual swirl of ridiculousness, but if nothing else, I can get you through, and we can have a sort of Melting Pot kind of dinner. So tonight, we will be making a three-course dinner of fondue. We will start with a gruyere fondue appetizer, then a bone broth main course, and end it with a super simple chocolate fondue with Cointreau. Okay, here we go." She moved the camera and started taking close shots of the ingredients. She recorded herself singing *Eternal Flame* by the Bangles. She recorded her voice-over while sitting on the counter dipping strawberries in the chocolate fondue, editing as she went.

"What just happened?"

She looked up to the vent in the kitchen above the counters. The Mustleknapp came out slowly, and she smiled. He slowly transformed into the size of a house cat, "It's for my YouTube channel. I have a rather large following, and to be honest, since the pandemic, everyone is trying to cook from home. Those two months of repeats offended my sponsors, and I need to make it up to them because they're the big reason I make a living doing this. It seems the masses keep their sanity by seeking solitude on their familiar YouTube channels. But more so, I think everyone has more time than they know what to do with.

They're watching older episodes as if they have never seen my channel before, so this is really good for me, but this is hard to explain to an outsider. Are you hungry? Would you like some?" She didn't fully understand, but she enjoyed being around the Mustleknapp. It was almost as if they were kindred spirits and bonded very quickly.

"How did you make that stuff?"

"What do you mean?"

"Like how did you know to mix the cheese with garlic, and white wine, and all that other crap you threw in there?"

"I'm like a chef; that's kind of my profession, and I'm lucky that my YouTube channel keeps me out of the crazy hours of working in a restaurant."

"Can I try?"

She smiled, "Here," she handed him a fondue fork. "Which one do you want to try?"

"I want the cheese one." His eyes widened.

She heated it for him over her mini double boiler, then spread out the different vegetables and croutons for him to dip. He took a bread cube and placed it in the cheese, blew on it carefully, and placed the whole bite in his mouth. His little tail started to twitch, and his eyes rolled in the back of his head, she smiled grandly, knowing that she made him happy, "What do you think, better than Domino's?"

"Don't ask me to choose,"

"Seriously?"

"The Hawaiian pizza is addictive if you dare try it."

"The only reason I participate in your addiction is to make you happy."

"This tastes way better than anything on my planet."

"I have to say I do not miss the food from your planet."

"How did you survive without starving?"

"I ate the plants and roots of the Snapsha."

"Gross."

"I agree. What did you mostly eat?"

"The petals of the Strythocket were my favorite, but difficult to obtain. Our most often eaten item would be the roots of a Mayna bush."

"What did it taste like?"

"If I took your human garlic and made it taste rotten."

"Gross."

"Yeah."

"Here, try this," she heated the bone broth and then placed a thin slice of scallop in the center, and when she knew it was cooked, she handed it over on a fork for him to eat it.

"That is amazing."

"I figured you'd like it."

"What's what you're eating?"

"Chocolate."

"What's chocolate?"

"It's cocoa, sugar, milk, delicious." She dipped a strawberry in it and handed it to him.

He took a bite, "OMG!"

"I'm glad you like it."

"Do you cook like this all the time?"

"I do theme-based cooking on eighty's songs."

"Why eighty's songs?"

"It was the only thing I didn't think had been done yet."

"What was the song you sang?"

"*Eternal Flame.*"

"What's it about?" He went back and started dipping radish slices into the cheese fondue. "Falling in love."

"That's something confusing on social media."

"What makes you say that?"

"Do you love other humans, food, or objects?"

"Well, that's hard to explain."

"Humans love foxes, cats, and something called a sphinx that looks like a rat."

"Love is a hard concept to explain; there's romantic love, desire love, family love."

"My planet is much easier to navigate than this one. We don't have love, or music like you do here, or videos, or anything like you have here."

"Yeah, well, I put a song to a theme or a food type, keeps people fed and entertained."

"Why that song, now?"

"That song is talking about finding another person to love, and she wants to know if it is a for real love, or if she's in love with him and he's not in love with her."

"Like, what's going on with you now?"

"I guess." She took a small piece of apple and dipped it in the chocolate. "What's an eternal flame?"

"Well, not everyone believes this, but I believe that you're meant to find one person in this life and love them and only them until you die."

"Is Caleb your eternal flame?"

"I used to think that."

"What's really going on between you too?"

"The quarantine has messed with him."

"I thought you broke up?"

"We did."

"Yet you check on him, feed him, do his laundry, treat him like a partner."

"More like a pet." The routine was comforting in light of the current situation.

"So the kitty that I've heard about isn't the real him?"

"You mean pussy." She rolled her eyes.

"That's another word I have questions about."

She laughed, "Caleb has not been himself since I've been back; between my body double being in a coma, then the quarantine, him teaching fully virtual classes, and his grandmother passing away, he's just been through so much. He thinks I have made this all up, and thinks I'm the one who needs help. He called off our wedding and wants me to leave when the lease is up…and I will pick myself up and leave with my head held high, buh-bye Caleb, buh-bye happiness, buh-bye future…"

"Never forget, you are the Prophet Warrior."

"I am."

"You changed your whole body,"

"How do you know?"

"Your engagement picture was framed in your room. You were THICK."

"Thanks?" she laughed.

"I like you better thick than like this."

"I kind of like being shredded."

"You like the warrior moves."

"I do. I can teach you if you want."

"I do not need the Gnetgnu fighting techniques in my brain."

"We're all heading back to Skyler's pool house tonight. Why don't you come?"

"Aren't you afraid of the virus?"

"No."

"Why not?"

"Every expert is different, every statistic is inflated, and to be honest, if I'm going to get it, and that's what kills me, then I can't control that."

"So, you don't believe them when they say the masks are for your protection and everyone else's as well?"

"No."

"What if you gave it to Caleb, and it killed him?"

"It's not like I picked it up with my hand and gave it to him like a present, I could bring home strep throat, bronchitis doesn't make me responsible if he gets sick from it. They are germs. They travel as they see fit, and where they land is not my doing."

"You're very interesting."

"I could say the same about you."

"There's something on your mind?" he tilted his head as he stared at her. "Why were you hiding in the ventilation system for so long?"

"Like I told you, learning how to talk to you."

"Why me?"

"You're my Prophet Warrior," he smiled at her.

She smiled and then tilted her head, "What else is on your mind?"

"Why do you want me to come with you?"

"Don't let this go to your head."

"It's going to my ears?"

She smiled, "I like having you around."

"You do?"

"Yeah, I like you." He crawled up her arm and cuddled on her neck. "Me too."

"Come on, let's go pack a satchel."

He stayed on her shoulder and accompanied her to prepare for the evening. They went into her room, and the Mustleknapp shrunk its size down closer to a field mouse as it stretched out on the futon.

"Why do you do that?"

"Do what?"

"Change your size?"

"You wouldn't change your size if you could?"

"Well, I just find it interesting,"

"Why is that?"

"Well, one, you can do that, and two, you do it whenever you feel like it."

"I do it to fit my current situation. At this size, this little futon feels like a California king-sized bed."

She smiled. They both could hear Caleb crying through the wall. She went to his door and called out,

"Caleb, are you okay?"

"Go away."

"Your laundry is outside the door. There's enough food for three days, and I'll come back to check on you in a few."

"Who were you talking to?"

"What?"

"Who were you talking to just now?"

"I'm talking to you." She rolled her eyes, folded her arms, and slammed her back against the door.

"I could hear you record your show, and then you were talking to someone. Why do you keep putting me at risk?" his sobs grew louder.

"Caleb, it's not what you think. He's been here before."

"HE?"

"Yes,"

"It's not Chad or Skyler. This is someone else. What are you doing with your life?"

She grew angry, "Why do you care?"

"I don't!"

"Yes, you do, or you wouldn't ask."

"Did you replace me?"

"Did you replace me?" she asked back at him.

"Stop it."

"Stop it." She imitated him, annoyed.

"Hy, knock it off! Who are you talking to?"

"My friend, someone who cares more about me in a short time than you have our entire relationship, you fucking pussy!"

"Get out!" He cried, and he smacked the door.

"In my own good time, in my apartment."

"Stop doing this to me! You're going to get me sick!"

"You're already sick, you just don't see it yet." She went back into her room, which was packed. "Come on," she gestured, and the Mustleknapp jumped up like a sugar glider and sat perched on her shoulder.

"Are you okay?" He asked concerned. "No, but I will be…" She smiled at him.

"The people on TikTok fall apart and cry, and vow revenge, and vow lots of things. I've seen a lot of destruction and picture burning for break ups."

"I don't define who I am by how someone else sees me. I know who I am, and I chose to share that with Caleb, but that's over, and never going to happen; I accept that…" she looked down.

"But…"

"Picture burning does sound like a lot of fun."

"I put one in your satchel."

…

Skyler and Hyacinth were on the pull-out couch in the living room of the pool house. The Mustleknapp was lounging on the top, roughly the size of a ferret, watching Netflix. Chad was swimming laps in the pool, and Hyacinth had to keep herself occupied from staring at him for too long. She was horrifically physically drawn to him, and she was annoyed. She loved teasing and flicking him, but she secretly loved touching his muscles and feeling his skin beneath her finger tips. She had to keep herself focused, genocide to the Gnetgnu had to come first, and if the virus ever stopped, Caleb could return to normal. She shook her head, annoyed at herself for even thinking it for a moment.

This proved to her what his grace under pressure looked like in a worst-case scenario, and she would never, ever forgive him. He crumbled when the heat was too hot, just like Rowan, and she hated him for being weak and afraid. She slowly leaned over and watched as Chad kicked off the side of the pool for another lap. She was allowed to find Chad attractive, but that was where it needed to end. She had a clear mission, but a little eye candy couldn't hurt too much.

She sat on her phone while Skyler laid on the couch with her legs over Hyacinth's lap. Skyler giggled at the different images from Instagram, occasionally forcing Hyacinth to watch a video. Before too long, Chad walked into the pool house and saw them. He wanted to grab Hyacinth every time he saw her. He wanted to kiss her, touch her, and listen to her tales. The Mustleknapp looked over to him and let out a low growl.

She looked up at him, "Are you okay?" she asked concerned. The Mustleknapp slowly scurried over and curled up on her chest like a doting pet, and he cuddled with her. "Shhh, I've got you, you're okay," she said sweetly as she ran her fingers through his fur and kissed his head.

Chad rolled his eyes at the Mustleknapp's pathetic attempt to gain her favor. There was a heightened amount of tension growing between the two of them for her attention. Chad already had a low opinion of Mustleknapp, but this one in particular, he wished he possessed the ability to kill it like a Gnetgnu soldier.

Hyacinth received an odd email, and her eyes grew wide. She gasped, "Huh."

Chad, knowing her every movement, picked up quickly, "What happened?"

"I read an email," she said bluntly.

"What did you find?"

"There's a possibility we have found another..."

"What?" they both exclaimed excitedly.

"This email is weird, but I think this guy is legit. Look," She held up her phone, and they read the email asking about the symbol, wanting to know if the Gnetgnu poisoned their minds with the Frezdon Flower.

"Email them back!" Skyler insisted.

"M-I-R-L, do you know where Trader Joe's in Paramus is?" She emailed from her phone. Skyler and Chad were staring at her, "Did he write back?"

"Chill, it's an email, not a text. It may take some time before we hear back from…" The Mustleknapp tried to downplay their excitement as her phone beeped, indicating she had a message in her inbox.

"Can't get there, you can come to me,"

"That's weird, maybe it's like a kid or something." Hyacinth was skeptical. "Do you have a phone number where we could talk?" She emailed him.

He emailed quickly, "If you give me your number, I can call you."

"Not gonna lie, this is highly sus." The Mustleknapp spoke candidly.

"Will you stop it!" Chad quickly lost his patience with the Mustleknapp, "Email him your number!"

"I don't know about this," Hyacinth was a little put-off.

"Email him my number," Chad offered. "Why?"

"This way, you don't have to give him your number if you're uncomfortable." He started to rub her shoulders, the Mustleknapp sneered at Chad.

"I think that's an okay idea," Skyler said. She ran her fingers behind the Mustleknapp's ear, "What's wrong? Are you worried too?"

"Something seems off." He allowed Skyler to pet him, though those were not the arms he wished held him.

"Fine, I will," She emailed quickly, and Chad's phone rang within minutes.

He answered and put it on speaker, "Who is this?"

"I can't get to you. I'm in here for life."

"What are you in prison?" The Mustleknapp asked.

"Feels like it."

"Who are you?" Skyler asked.

"My name is Landon. I've been stuck here for the past four years."

"Stuck where?"

"Bergen Regional, third window on the ground floor,"

"You're in a mental place? How'd you email me?"

"I have computer privileges. We have phones here. I snuck out of my room to use it. Please hurry; they committed me here. Tell them I'm not crazy. Tell them, please."

"Landon, you can't leave your room right now." They could hear a nurse in the background, "Put your mask back on and get in your room."

"Talk to them, I'm not crazy, they know what I know." He spoke to the person approaching him, "Please help me, please, I'm begging you to end this, no one will listen, they treat me…"

The person on the other end interrupted them, "Landon, please, honey, you can't leave your room right now."

"Talk to them!"

"Landon, calm down. I need you to return to your room."

"But I finally found someone who knows! I'm not crazy!"

"Landon, please, calm down, stop,"

"No," he laughed, "I'm not crazy!"

The phone cut off, they all assumed the nurse must have hung it up.

The three looked at one another, "What are we going to do?"

"Poor guy's been locked up," Chad shook his head.

"That was my parent's next move after they forced me back here," Skyler said sadly.

"So, then, how'd you get out of it?"

"I stopped talking about it, and I just wrote in my journal, kept it hidden. No one believed me anyway."

"No one believed me either, they thought I snapped. I had to keep it hidden, I was the only one…" Chad said.

"Caleb doesn't believe me, he's convinced my brain is damaged from the accident, and that I made it up to cope with the pandemic."

"We know the truth,"

"But we're the only ones, we can't tell the doctors at this place what we know."

"I know, but at the same time, we have to help him!"

"But how are we going to get him out?"

"Maybe we can convince him to stop telling them, and then they'll release him."

"We can't even visit him. Everything is still shut down."

"He has a window!"

"Are you suggesting we break him out?" Chad was concerned.

"Seriously, Cliff?" Annoyed, she playfully flicked his forehead and smiled to herself.

"What? You said he has a window. What else would that mean?" Chad defended himself; he always put on a serious face when she did that, but he secretly loved when she did. Since they met, he tried to hide how he felt about her, but it was almost as if it was his destiny to be with her.

"It means we can communicate through the window, write to him, and he can respond, and we won't go inside. What else do we have to lose?"

"What if he is a legit crazy person?" Skyler asked as tears surfaced from her eyes.

"Not everyone who is committed is a crazy person. How insensitive of you. I thought you were all for political correctness."

"Seriously, how do we know he's not genuinely insane and made it up?" She started to rock and shake her head.

"Who the hell would know what a Frezdon Flower is?"

"People can make up some weird stuff. What if his roommate was the actual one on the planet, and this crazy guy just thinks he was there." She was slowly unraveling. Chad quickly entered the kitchen and brought her one of her pills and a glass of water.

"Everything in this life is about risk." The Mustleknapp squeezed her tight. She ran her fingers through his fur.

"But there are some risks that are just too high." Chad once again rubbed Hyacinth's shoulders.

"I didn't know about you or you, but we each took a chance, and now we have each other because of that. I'm willing to risk it again and find out what this person knows," Hyacinth said sadly.

"We can't verify his jaw." Skyler was defensive. She lay across

Hyacinth's lap, and she tried to regulate her breathing. This whole conversation triggered her anxiety.

"If we can convince him to stop believing in front of the doctors, then they'll have to release him, right?" Hyacinth ran her fingers through Skyler's hair and gently rocked her back and forth. The Mustleknapp joined them and used his tail to rub her back.

"And then what?"

"Seriously, Cliff, two for two?"

"What?" He was jealous he wasn't holding Hyacinth. "If he is released, we can verify his jaw."

"It's not going to happen overnight."

"No, but if we can contact his parents, maybe they'll let him out. We don't even know how old this guy is."

"Or if it's a guy." The Mustleknapp commented.

"Or if they're sane," Skyler added. She sniffled and held onto Hyacinth tighter.

"Or if they're genuine." Chad kept the add-ons coming.

"I think this is too risky for me," Skyler said, shaking her head. "I remember being in therapy and saw someone go into a complete manic state, and I am still bothered and freaked out by it. I can't go there."

"Skyler, it's okay," Hyacinth was kind and ran her fingers through her hair, which seemed to be the trick with soothing her, "I can go."

"By yourself?" Chad was concerned. "I am a grown-up."

"You're a baby." Chad made a sad face.

"I'm 25, and if that makes me a baby, then you're a senior citizen, Cliff."

"I'll go with you." Chad offered.

"I'm a big girl."

"She can handle herself," The Mustleknapp was annoyed. He didn't want Chad to have alone time with his Prophet Warrior. He shifted his position across her shoulders, ensuring Chad could not touch her again in his presence.

"I want a second set of eyes on this guy to see if this is real," Chad said. The Mustleknapp blocked his shoulder rub, so instead, he took her hand and placed it against his cheek.

"Fine," she rolled her eyes, "But I'm driving."

...

When they arrived at the facility, the parking lot was closed, "Now, what do we do?"

"I don't know," she kept circling the area.

"How about the corner?"

"And then what? Walk?"

"Yeah, I mean, we can't park in there, and if we did, they'd want to talk to us. Maybe this is best." She parked on the street around the corner. He was staring at her, and she shook her head. "What?"

"Plan?"

"Get to the window, knock, show him the symbol, and see how he reacts."

"You're so brave." He looked into her eyes, longing for her to reciprocate his feelings.

"I'm the Prophet Warrior, I live for this shit." She smiled as she rolled her eyes at him. She hated the dumbfounded look over his face when he looked into her eyes. "Tone it down, hungry eyes; at least attempt subtlety."

"I can't help myself around you."

"Learn." She flicked his forehead and smiled. He reached out quickly, grabbed her hand, and kissed the back of it. She couldn't help herself from enjoying the affection, but she quickly stopped and reminded herself what their current agenda was. "We need to get to the window."

"We need to talk about what this is," he gestured between them.

"You have a crush and need to remind yourself that the bigger picture is more important."

"What's the bigger picture?"

"The bigger picture, getting the answers and me killing Jom, the current picture, figuring out what Landon knows."

"And beyond that?"

"Not right now." She flicked him again, and when he went to grab her hand, she pulled it away too quickly for him to grab, "Focus."

"I am…" He looked into her eyes.

She leaned forward, blew in his ear, and whispered slowly, "Not right now."

The two ducked their way behind trees and the decorative brush of the landscape and made their way to the window. She was about to knock when Chad did it instead. She tilted her head to him, "You'll crack the window." He stated quietly.

She narrowed her eyes, "Maybe now I'll do it just for fun."

"This isn't one of your parking lot riots; we need to be subtle."

"Not exactly your specialty." She laughed, thinking about how obvious it was that he wanted to be with her.

At that moment Landon came into view and banged on the other side. She snapped back into herself and showed him the symbol. He started crying tears of pure joy. He held out his right wrist, the symbol etched into his flesh.

"That's slightly extreme." Hyacinth looked at his wrist. It was perfectly formed as if he branded himself with the symbol.

"Did he carve that himself?"

"I don't know, I don't want to know…he looks like he's about to lose his shit."

"If you were locked into a room with no one, you would look that way too."

"What did they do to him?"

"We have to help him."

She wrote on the paper and held it against the window, "Did you do that?" He nodded his head yes as he traced it. "Okay, I am officially freaked out."

"They tried to make me forget…I had to remember." Landon wrote in his journal. "They told me I made it up, that I was delusional!"

"You're not! We are real!" She wrote as fast as she could.

Landon ran into his room, grabbed another journal and flipped through the pages. He had sketched the Strythocket Hills. Hyacinth's jaw dropped, and Chad felt comforted in the drawing. Landon went through, and he had a perfect depiction of his Hunterna, the Quarternewt nests, and Jom in his ceremonial robes.

Hyacinth wrote in her notebook, "How long were you there?" Landon wrote in his journal, "Two years."

"That's a remarkable amount of time. No wonder he can't adjust," Chad said.

"I was there for a year, and it felt like home. I can't imagine what he feels." She was allowing her past to undermine her strength as her mind focused on the family she left behind in Arizona.

"Hy, are you okay?" Chad wrapped his arms around her. "Stop being nice to me," she said in a low voice.

Landon smacked the glass, interrupting their moment, and slammed his journal to the window, "Get me out!"

"How?"

"Tell them you have custody of me!"

"How old are you?"

"30," he wrote very quickly, "My parents had me declared legally incompetent, and they control all my

decisions."

"How?"

"PLEASE!"

"What's your full name?"

"Landon Charles Grayson Junior."

Hyacinth ran to the facility's front door, as Chad attempted to catch her. Before he could stop her, she rang the bell. A particularly perturbed nurse spoke from the other end, "We are not allowing any visitors at this time."

"Don't give me that *The Wizard is not in* bullshit!"

"Excuse me, ma'am?"

"Ma'am?" Hyacinth's temper flared. "You have no power here!"

"I need you to take a step back and put your mask on."

"You don't understand. You have my brother in there, and I want to take him home!" She rang the bell again, losing herself in the moment.

"We are…" she rang the bell again to interrupt her on purpose, "We are…" she rang the bell again. "So sorry, usually when you ring a bell, the door fucking opens!" She rang it again.

The nurse on the other end must have deactivated it because when Hyacinth went to press it again, it didn't make a noise, "We are currently not offering outpatient care, and the inpatients currently residing here would need their doctor's clearance for a custodial guardian."

"I want my brother!" Hyacinth kicked the door and dented it. She was overly emotional, she transferred her feelings toward Rowan onto Landon, and all she wanted was to bring him home. She thought about his disfigured body in the morgue, and now she could save him. She had to save him.

"I'm going to have to ask you to leave."

"I'm not leaving without Rowan!"

"Who?" Chad was confused.

"Landon!" She snapped her mind back to this moment. She was angry that she let his name leave her lips.

"I will call security if you do not leave."

"Stop power-tripping on your artificial authority, you anonymous cunt!"

"I'm calling security."

Chad pulled her back and approached the intercom, "My apologies, you have to forgive my wife," Chad said. "She is very emotional about her brother. Please kindly, what paperwork is needed to have him in our custody."

"You both need to leave!"

"Please understand, they've lost both their parents to the virus, and she just wants him home." Hyacinth gave him an odd look, his speech was quite convincing. He sounded so realistic, she looked down to discover he was holding her hand, gently stroking the back with his thumb.

"Hold on a moment, sir. I will go speak with our director."

He grabbed her and held her tight against him, "You need to watch your temper, and you need to remember what planet you are on."

"Let go of me," she said seriously.

"Never, Beautiful." He rolled his lips in and bit down as he pushed them forward, "Never."

The director of the facility came out wearing a mask. "Please, ma'am, put your mask on."

"I'm six feet away."

"Please, put your mask on."

"Dear, please," Chad said, placing the mask over her face to a fuming Hyacinth. She smacked his hand away after he secured it in place. "Please be understanding, Dear. This man is taking time out of his day to help us and our current legal situation."

"Sir, please tell me why you are here before I call security?"

"That won't be necessary. Please, just a moment of your time." Her eyes widened listening to Chad speak in such a way, she wondered if he was an actor in another life.

The director explained they would need to provide the death certificates of their parents, the judge's order granting Hyacinth legal decision-making rights as well as custodial guardianship. He gave them the contact information for the legal team. The director was shocked that Landon had a sister, as he never mentioned her or had it on his file.

"My parents didn't want to burden me with being responsible for him, but now I need to take my big brother home with me." She lied and then buried her face into Chad pretending to cry.

"It's okay, Dear," He kissed the top of her head, and he smiled, holding her close to him, getting to kiss her. He turned his attention to the director, "Thank you for agreeing to speak with us. I would shake your hand, but given our current circumstances," Chad paused, "please know we appreciate you taking the time. We will be contacting our lawyer and hopefully, this can be resolved before the week is out." He loved touching her skin, and he was pleased she went along with this.

The director smiled, "Of course, our patients mean the world to us."

They pretended to walk away, and as soon as the director was back behind closed doors, they went over to the window. She wrote on the paper, "Soon..."

"Thank you." He wrote back. "Stop talking about the Gnetgnu."

"Why?"

"They don't understand, but we do. We can get you out, but you need to stop."

"I'll stop."

"Pretend it never happened."

"I can't! It happened!"

"But they don't know what we know."

"How do I pretend?"

"It's easy if you try."

"Okay."

"We WILL be back."

"But this is so hard..."

"My name is Hyacinth, and I told them I am your sister."

Landon nodded, held one finger to the glass, and Hyacinth did the same. It mimicked how they connected to Gretgen, and now they bonded in the same fashion.

They returned to the car. Chad attempted to hide the jealousy, "What does the one finger mean? Are you ET?"

"Who?"

"From the movie?"

"I'm too young for that reference, Grandpa..."

"ET, the Extra Terrestrial?"

"Never heard of it."

"Baby,"

"K, boomer."

"Stop it."

"You're a senior citizen."

"Stop, what's with the one-finger thing?"

"That's how Gretgen trained us, to show we have a genuine connection."

"Why don't you do that to me?"

Hyacinth turned to Chad and held up her finger, and when he went to touch it, she flicked his forehead.

Chad looked confused, "What was that for?"

"You know what that was for."

"I seriously don't."

"Kissing my head, stroking my hair. Seriously, keep your hands to yourself!"

"Or what?"

"What do you mean or what?"

"What will you do to me?" he asked with smoldering eyes.

"I will kick your sternum so hard that you'll have a heart attack."

"You're angry with me."

"Yes, I'm angry with you, duh, Cliff!"

"Why? The lie was convincing, and now we know how to get Landon out."

"You *wanted* to hold my hand."

"Yes, I do." He took her hand and kissed the back of it.

"What is wrong with you?" She tried to hide the smile, but she could tell he had noticed.

"Nothing."

"Keep it in your pants, old man."

"Yes, Dear." He smiled.

"Shows over, take a bow, a cold shower, and get your head in the game. We need to figure out how to get all this stuff together, or even if we can, we might need a different plan."

"Anything for you, Dear." He opened her car door for her.

"Call me that one more time, and it'll be the last thing you ever say."

"Take it easy, honey,"

"Stop it!"

"Is it possible I have found a way to tease you for a change?" He smirked at her reaction to his pet names.

She hip-checked him, and he stumbled slightly, "Enjoy the love tap; the next one will send you across the highway."

"Dish it out, but just can't take it."

She wrinkled her nose at him, "Maybe," she pouted. "I like the way you said that."

"Said what?" She blushed.

"The next one." He smiled and leaned over as she sat down, kissed her cheek and carefully closed her door. She turned her head so he couldn't see she was happy. She shook her head and reminded herself to focus.

Once he got into the car, she hardened her expression, "The next time you…" He interrupted her, "The next time we go anywhere, I am driving," Chad said. "Why?"

"Because you drive like a maniac."

"I like to drive fast. What's wrong with that?"

"Please don't drive so fast."

"Get a grip, Cliff. Let's tell Skyler and the Mustleknapp the good news."

They were driving down the highway, and Chad clutched the seat, "Can you please drive below 90,

please!"

"Senior citizen." She took it down to 85. "Your Highness, can I ask you something?"

"I will point this out once, and only once, and then call you out on it every single time you do it again. You just asked me a question!"

"Do you treat everyone like that?"

"Like what?"

"Like they are below you?"

"You're not below me…"

"Then why do you treat me this way?"

"I don't treat you any differently than I do anyone else. You asked if you could ask me a question, which is a question, so if you're going to ask me a question, ask me what is on your mind and don't ask permission to do so; it makes you sound insecure."

"What I'm going to ask you is a sensitive matter, and I wanted you to be prepared."

"So then ask me, *Can I ask you a sensitive question?*"

"Can I ask you a sensitive question?"

"Get to the point, Cliff." She increased her speed.

"Are you still in love with Caleb?"

"Why do you ask?" she shifted lanes and again increased her speed.

"You're doing it again."

"Doing what?"

"Replying to my question with another question."

"It's a tactic of avoidance."

"Why won't you tell me?"

"Why do you want to know?"

"Because I do…" he carefully brushed her hair back behind her ear.

She turned to him and pretended to be annoyed when he touched her hair, "If you must know, then no,"

"But…" he didn't know how to follow up.

"But what?" Her speed increased. "Calm down!"

"Calm down or slow down, be specific."

"Slow down."

"Fine," she rolled her eyes and slowed to 85 again.

"You keep returning to your old life…you do his laundry, visit, cook for him."

"I do what I do for my reasons," she said through clenched teeth. "I loved Caleb very much, I think…but I do not love Caleb anymore."

"Who do you love?"

"I love an idea."

"What idea?"

"I love the idea of killing Jom."

"That's slightly unsettling."

"I am going back to that planet, and I'm going to tear him apart. That's what I love right now."

"What about when it's done?"

"I'll worry about that when I get there."

"Do I get to be a part of that?"

"Aren't we all connected now?" She tried to be nonchalant.

"We are, but I think…"

"Don't say anything."

There was an awkward silence between the two of them. He desperately wanted to take their connection and make them exclusive to one another, and she was flooded with denial that there was anything between them. He slowly reached out and touched the back of her neck, "Can I ask you a question?"

"What have you learned today?" She laughed to herself.

"Can I ask you a sensitive question?" he smiled, and he made her laugh.

"Another one?"

"Yeah…"

"Go ahead…but I warn you, my patience is dwindling."

"How did you get that scar?"

She was caught off guard, she assumed it was going to have to do with their sexual tension, "Which one?" she wasn't ready to handle either story at this point.

"The faded one, on the bottom."

"I don't want to talk about it." The thought made her forehead crinkle, and her shoulders became tense.

A protective vibe from within him emerged, and he asked innocently, "Please?"

"Why the fuck do you wanna know?" She snapped.

"It's intense, and it must've hurt really bad…this wasn't from that planet, this was from Earth, please…what happened?"

She took a deep breath and wanted to lie, but she couldn't come up with anything that could sound believable, "My mother forgot who I was and slashed me with a steak knife from her food tray."

"What?"

"Yeah, that happened, and as I was bleeding on the ground, my sister had the audacity to ask me how I upset her."

"Why would she do that?"

"My mother or my sister?"

"Either!"

"I have a lot of baggage I'm not unloading right now." She increased her speed with her car and gripped the steering wheel tighter.

It hurt his heart to hear her talk about her horrific past. He wanted to change the subject quickly, "How'd you get the fresher one?"

"In the portal back, the Gnetgnu soldier knocked me off course, and one of the rainbow crystals tore my neck." She was far more comfortable talking about that experience than with her mother. She loosened her grip on the steering wheel and noticed a hidden cop up ahead and slowed the car down. She shook her head, replaying the memory. She hid that whole life from everyone, and she would continue to do so. The emotional scars were far more telling than the physical ones displayed on her skin.

He pulled his shirt up, and on the side of his chest was a scar, "The crystal got me, too."

She smiled and laughed. She ran her finger over the scar. They felt the same, there must be some element in the crystal that they didn't know, and it bonded with the flesh. "Did it change the color of the portal?"

"That was the freakiest part!"

"I know!"

He ran his finger over her neck, he enjoyed touching her. "They're softer than a typical scar."

"That they are," she smiled at him.

"We share something deeper, and you know that."

"Doesn't mean I'm ready to handle it just yet."

"Yet?"

"I have priorities."

"But you and I…"

"I know."

And the two were surprisingly comforted, leaving the conversation unfinished but with closure. She knew she cared about him, and he knew he cared about her. Their mutual painful experience allowed for her to casually admit that she wanted this to go somewhere. There was no need to push the subject at the moment, but they both felt it, and she was frightened by it, and he was desperate for her to see him the way that he saw her. But right now, they rested in the comfortable silence of driving to headquarters.

NINE

Skyler was in the middle of a panic attack, pacing in the kitchen of the pool house with the Mustleknapp pacing beside her on two feet, trying to soothe her. This had been happening for nearly 20 minutes, and he was sick and tired of this nonsense.

"I don't know what else to say!" The Mustleknapp shouted, annoyed, "Um…funny cat videos?"

"No." Tears started to surface.

"Oh, Funny Pics! Do you have that app?"

"Yeah,"

"So take out some funny 2020 pics and laugh."

"Not the best idea right now!" Skyler started hyperventilating. "Quarantine! Hyacinth and Chad are going to see Michael Myers! They're dead, I know it! We're all going to die!"

"Distract yourself with something! You're not going to calm down by freaking out over what ifs."

Skyler started crying harder, "You're a Mustleknapp. You don't have anxiety!"

"I'm starting to develop it with you acting like this!"

"What's taking them so long?" Skyler put her hands to her temples and started shaking her head.

"What do you think happened?"

"They went to the insane asylum! He got out! He got out!" Her words were spaced between each breath.

"They went to a mental health facility. What are you picturing in your head?" He was confused and upset because, she didn't make any sense.

"Hyacinth in a straight jacket…they're taking her away."

"Don't say things like that! They can't get in. They're going to a window." The Mustleknapp placed his paws on her cheeks and tried to center her.

"What if the person is insane and breaks free and tries to kill her?"

"She'll kill them much quicker than they'll kill her. You have to admit that."

"I can't take this much longer!"

"Where are your pills?" He leaped to the other counter, looking for her medicine.

"Xanax is NOT going to help me right now!" she smacked her hand against the island in the kitchen and screamed.

"Well, something better. I'm out of ideas!"

Hyacinth and Chad walked through the door, and Skyler ran to Hyacinth, "Why were you gone so long? What happened? Is he crazy? Is it fake? Did they try and take you too? Tell me! Tell me now!"

"Somebody spiraled while we were gone," Chad commented. "Duh, Cliff." The Mustleknapp rolled his eyes and folded his arms.

"What happened?" Hyacinth asked the Mustleknapp as she held Skyler tight, her body spiraling into hysterics.

"I don't know, I was napping in our bed when she started crying. I came out here, and she was pacing in the kitchen babbling about *Shrek*."

"*Shrek?*" Chad asked, confused.

Skyler shouted, "Michael Myers."

Hyacinth laughed and looked at the Mustleknapp, "Halloween."

"The candy-driven holiday?"

"The movie," Chad said.

"What's the movie about?"

"A deranged mental patient who escapes and kills everything and everyone."

"You humans have the weirdest movies."

"I kept thinking that was going to happen to you." Again, she spoke between gasps as her body continued to hyperventilate from fear.

"Skyler, this place is a hospital, not a prison asylum."

"What'd you find?" The Mustleknapp asked Chad.

Chad poured a glass of water for Skyler and took one of her Xanax out of the cabinet, "Landon was declared insane by his parents. We made up a lie: if they call his parents tonight, they will figure it out quickly. So, we need a plan, and we need one fast."

Skyler quickly took her pill and sat with Hyacinth on the couch, "Is he crazy?"

"Seriously?" Hyacinth asked sarcastically.

"You know what I meant." Skyler took another sip of water. "He has the symbol etched on his wrist."

"That's a bit extreme."

"I draw it on my wall."

"A wall is one thing. Scarring your body is another," Chad said.

"Ever get a tattoo, Cliff?" Hyacinth asked.

"What?"

"That's what a tattoo is, an inked scar. What if he did that so he'd always have it, never lose it, but he had no access to a tattoo artist… he said they tried to make him forget. What if that was the only way he could remember our world?"

"When you look at it like that, it doesn't seem, so…no, sorry, can't lie, still seems creepy to me," Chad said.

"How are we going to get him out?" Skyler asked. "We need to verify his jaw, and if he's legit, that's one thing, but if he's a lunatic, then we need to put him back where he can't hurt himself or others. You can't unleash something like that into the world!"

"Chillax!" Hyacinth said. "Breathe in and out, put your head back and let the Xanax run through your veins."

"This is going to be harder than we thought," Chad said. "Hopefully, they don't call, but I don't know how we're going to get all the information they need to turn him over to us."

"Can we forge the documents and lie our way through this?" Hyacinth asked. She walked over to the freezer and got an ice pack for Skyler.

"I don't know," Chad said as he stared at Hyacinth, gently placing the cold compress on Skyler's forehead. She did have a caring component to her, and he would uncover that love and adoration and find what he had wanted his whole life.

"You shouldn't lie." The Mustleknapp stated as he made his way over to the girls on the couch. He immediately curled onto Hyacinth's lap. Chad stared at him jealously. The Mustleknapp knew what he was doing and purposefully rubbed his face on her tummy, cuddling her while she ran her fingers down his back.

"What we need is a body double."

"Say that again," Hyacinth said.

"We need a body double," Chad repeated.

"How do we get a body double?" Skyler asked, looking over at the Mustleknapp.

"Don't look at me." The Mustleknapp stated, "That's a Gnetgnu thing. I don't know how to breathe life into a replica."

"Wait, but you know how to make a replica?" Hyacinth was confused. "On my planet, not yours, you don't have any of the things I need."

"But this could work."

"What are you thinking?" Skyler asked, completely calm.

"We can't get in, remember?" Chad didn't like the look in her eyes, the Mustleknapp referring to her bed as *theirs*, or how the Mustleknapp got to cuddle all over her the way he wished he could.

"My sweet Cliff, what's the one thing that will always clear a facility, even during a viral pandemic?"

"What?"

"Oh…" Skyler went to answer, and Hyacinth shot her arms up to quell her.

"No, wait, I wanna see how long this takes."

"Stop teasing me," Chad said to her seriously.

"Come on, play along. What's one thing that would make a facility get everybody out as fast as possible, ensuing in chaos as they try to maintain order?"

"I don't know." Chad didn't want to play this game as he was too furious that everyone else got her attention at the moment.

The Mustleknapp sat up, "I know, I know!"

"Give him a chance." She teased the Mustleknapp, rustled his fur, and cuddled him close.

The jealousy coursed through Chad's veins, "A fire."

Hyacinth stopped her cuddle routine and smiled at him, "See, Cliff, I had faith in your cognitive prowess."

"You want to start a fire in a mental health facility and swipe out Landon's body with a lifeless double?"

"Bingo," she said.

"Now that sounds insane."

"Think about it: we grab him quickly and touch his jaw. If he has the symbol, we take him with us; if he doesn't, then he is insane, and we alert the authorities to get him safely back to his cage. We don't need a body double."

"How are we going to start a fire?" Skyler asked. "Molotov Cocktail?" Hyacinth shrugged.

"Do you know how to do that?" Skyler asked, concerned.

Hyacinth smirked, "You've never?"

"That's arson, and no." Skyler was not finding the humor in her nonchalant attitude regarding throwing a Molotov Cocktail into someone's window.

"Arson, expressing yourself…potato, potato."

"I want the background story!" The Mustleknapp said, intrigued.

"Not a chance…not even for you!" she teased him.

Chad didn't want their cute little banter to continue further, "You don't necessarily have to start a fire. You need to have one of the sensors go off. It's how we used to interrupt finals in college." Chad commented.

"Wait, you can do that?" Hyacinth asked, impressed.

"Well, you couldn't do it in your class, but we would do it for one another, you just need to hack the system used to do it all the time."

"I forgot you were a tech wizard."

"I can hack pretty much any system." He smiled at her.

"But what you're forgetting is the actual danger." The Mustleknapp chimed in. He was not about to let Chad have a moment in the sun.

"What do you mean?"

"If a sensor goes off, everyone is so paranoid about leaving their rooms, they'll look out, and when they don't see smoke, they'll stay in lockdown mode."

"So what do you suggest we do?"

"What does their ventilation system look like?" The Mustleknapp smiled.

"You're going to set the building on fire?" Skyler was shocked.

"No, I'm going to set a trashcan on fire. It'll produce smoke, providing validity for when the sensors go off. When they evacuate, everyone grabs Landon and touches his jaw. If he's legit, pull him. They'll mark him as a runaway and put a search out for him. We'll hide him in your apartment. Caleb won't leave his room, and he can lay low. We all can, together." The Mustleknapp lowered his eyes at Chad.

"That's actually not a bad plan…" Chad had to admit. He was very concerned about what his next move would be: to keep a space between her and the Mustleknapp.

Hyacinth ran her finger behind his ears, "You're so smart."

"You're only saying it because it's true." He leaned over and kissed her cheek. She smiled, and the Mustleknapp eyed Chad, who looked like he would burst.

…

Skyler couldn't sleep that night, and she took a shot of tequila, hoping it would ease her to sleep. She left her room and knocked on Hyacinth's door. "Hy, are you awake?"

Hyacinth opened the door with her eyes half closed, "It's 3 a.m., what's wrong? Shouldn't you be in a valium-induced coma by now?"

"I can't sleep…" she looked down sad.

"Oh," it was only with that phrase Hyacinth figured out why she knocked on her door, "Come in."

"You really freaked me out today."

"I know," she pulled the sheets down, "Don't crush the Mustleknapp," he was curled up, sleeping, the size of a fruit bat on her pillow. They lay down in the bed together, and Skyler cuddled her tight.

"Don't do anything like that again."

"Like what?"

"Leave me…"

"Okay." She knew Skyler was being dramatic again and let it go in her tired state of mind.

"If we find a fourth, then I think we should stop the search and start the plan."

"We will."

"We're going to come back, right?"

"Yes, we're going to come back," Hyacinth ran her fingers through Skyler's hair the way Rowan would do to her when she was scared as a child.

"Tell me a bedtime story."

"What?"

"I'm high-strung, need a soothing, melodic voice to bring me to REM sleep."

"Are you serious?"

"Please." She pouted.

Hyacinth rolled her eyes, "Once upon a time, there was a misunderstood virus."

"What are you doing?"

"This has a point; don't interrupt me."

"Fine," Skyler closed her eyes and felt the comfort cover her like a warm blanket as her tense muscles finally relaxed.

"Once upon a time there was a misunderstood virus. It went from country to country, searching for the antibodies to counteract its deadly effects. Every time the virus thought it made a friend, they would stop breathing. The guilt in the virus made it question if it should keep trying to find the antibodies. Then, one day, it infected a beautiful young princess. She fell ill from the virus. The money and power surrounding her body were useless to fight off the virus's attempts at courtship. Then her body stopped fighting, and her inner antibodies realized that the princess's natural immunity was what the virus had been looking for the whole time. The antibodies in her system stared at the virus, and they danced through her trachea and blew out of her mouth into the night sky, together forever dancing in the wind."

Skyler let out a dainty yawn, "That's a pretty story…"

"I'm glad you liked it."

"Should I visit Landon?"

"I think you should."

"Will you take me?"

"Of course."

"I'm driving."

"I figured." She held Skyler close, and they both closed their eyes and peacefully slept. The Mustleknapp awoke an hour later, kissed both girls on the forehead, and then made his way into the ventilation system for his second sweep to ensure his Prophet Warrior was protected as she slept.

…

The next morning, they all set out to visit Landon. They went to the window one at a time to not create too much of a disturbance.

Skyler took a deep breath and sat outside the window. When she was ready, she knocked softly, Landon came to the window, and the two stared at one another. She smiled at him, and drew the symbol on his window with her fingertip. He followed along with her. She drew it again, and he continued to move in sync with her. She stared into his eyes so intensely that she felt her body tense, but not the way it did when she was anxious; this was a romantic nervousness, and as her smile spread across her face, his matched hers.

He grabbed his journal, "Who are you?" She pulled out her sketch journal, "Skyler."

"Your power?" he asked.

"Master of Septtronium."

He smiled, "I'm the master of Marttronium."

"How?" she smiled. She had been told that element was the hardest to bond with, almost impossible for a human to do so.

"That was my element." He wrote and then shrugged cutely.

He didn't look deranged to her, he didn't look unsettling, and she felt an immediate calm in his presence. He was more soothing than her Xanax. She wrote quickly, "How many Quarternewt?"

"12."

Her eyes widened, "Impressive."

"You're really pretty."

She giggled, "Thank you," She placed her hand on the window, and he placed his in the same place.

He sparked an idea in his mind. He ran to his bedside and retrieved an old cigar box. He removed a small vile, and he smiled. He opened it and wrote, "Septtronium."

"How?"

"My shirt was soaked when I was returned."

She closed her eyes and breathed deep. She raised her right arm, and the substance slowly rose in the air. Landon smiled, and when she opened her eyes and saw it hovering above the vial, she smiled.

She beckoned it toward her, and somehow, it was drawn to her so powerfully that it defied physics, went through the window as if the glass was not there and covered her hand like a glove. She stared at her hand, and tears of joy fell from her eyes. She manipulated her fingertips so that she morphed the small amount to resemble a Quarternewt dancing. When she was finished, she wrapped the Septtronium around her neck like a choker and webbed the center to look like a real necklace.

Landon was laughing, and he wished he could hear her voice. He wrote on his paper, "When?"

"Saturday." She wrote back.

He turned around and heard someone at his door, "Go."

She quickly got up and ran to the nearest bush to hide. She was instantly drawn to him. She was angry at herself for ever thinking he was insane; he was adorable, and she wanted to take him home and keep him forever. She couldn't help but feel like Veruca Salt and found her perfect squirrel. She decided that she would visit him every day until they executed their plan on Saturday. She slowly made her way back to the Jeep with a dazed look.

While waiting, Chad turned to Hyacinth and asked, "Can I ask you a question?"

She gave him a distinct look of annoyance, then he smirked as did she, "You did that on purpose."

"Maybe…"

"What do you want to know?"

"The other night, you were talking in your sleep." Her eyes widened, frightened, "And what did I say?"

"Ummm."

"You tell me, and you tell me now!" she looked sick.

"Who's Rowan?" Chad asked. Hyacinth screamed, then put her head between her knees and started to breathe in and out as evenly as she could.

She sat up and tightened her jaw, "Rowan is a type of tree."

"I think Rowan means more…" He remembered her saying it when they first met Landon, and now, a dream.

"You will never know. I do NOT want to talk about this."

"You kept asking *Rowan why?*" he looked at her concerned. "It's a tree and nothing more..."

"Then..."

"Stop it."

"You cried in your sleep, and all I wanted was to..."

"It's none of your business, it is a tree. A rowan is a tree...just a tree." She ran out of the car and went over to a nearby shrub and started kicking it repeatedly.

Chad felt awful he caused this reaction. He wanted to know who this Rowan person was and why he hurt her. His thoughts went to a possible former boyfriend, but seeing her reaction, he feared this was too deep for her to handle. All he wanted was to make her feel better. He got out of the car and went over to her, "I didn't mean to upset you."

"Never say that to me again."

"I won't."

"And if you hear me say that again in my sleep." She looked far into the distance. "What?"

"Smother me." She turned to walk away, and she felt him grab her. "I didn't mean to upset you; I just wanted to know..."

"You're so jealous of everything...leave me alone." She walked past him toward the Jeep. "Hy, please!" He went after her.

"The next time you ask me a sensitive question, be prepared for me to say no and then knee your testicles until they come out your mouth!"

"I struck a nerve, didn't I?"

"No, I'm perfectly fine discussing this with you fucking jerkoff!"

"There it is."

"I'm going to wait for her, and you are not talking to me for the rest of the night." She got in the front seat and slammed the door shut.

He bit his lip and then got in the driver's side, "I didn't mean to..."

"Stop talking."

"Can I sleep in your room tonight?" He asked. She stared at him, "No."

"But how will I know whether to smother you if I'm not there?"

"Fine." She looked down.

He looked away, hurt, and in the rearview mirror, he saw Skyler approach, "She's here."

"What's around your neck?" Hyacinth asked.

"Landon gave me a gift," she held her hand out, and the Septtronium formed into a heart above her palm.

"Is that Septtronium?" Chad asked.

"Obviously, Cliff," Hyacinth said, annoyed, alone with Chad for too long. She was angry he brought up her brother, but part of her understood he wasn't asking her to reveal her tragedy. It was a name he didn't know the context of. For the first time in her life, she wanted to explain her pain to someone, and she hated it. Being with Chad tempted in ways she was unprepared to handle. He always found some excuse to wrap his arms around her or hold her hand. She wanted to fall into his arms and have him hold her as if she were his love. She never slept sounder than when he was beside her, and as much as she complained, she adored when he would crawl into her bed at night and fall asleep.

"I'm curious to see what I can do with this on Earth," she once again placed it around her neck, and this time she spiraled it to look like vines tattooing her delicate skin.

"I have Septtronium…" Hyacinth looked off to the side.

"You what?" Skyler asked excitedly.

"I have a whole jar of it."

"Why didn't you tell me?"

"I forgot…I have all the elements…"

"What?" Chad was shocked.

"They're in my satchel…I have the sand of my body double…"

"Come on, let's go now." She tugged on her arm like an anxious child wanting to go on a new roller coaster.

"Where's your satchel?"

"It's in my apartment… after I met the Mustleknapp, I stopped carrying it around with me. I saw it as a security blanket and it made me feel weak, I detached myself from it…"

"Come on, let's go!"

They piled into the car, and for once, Chad went above the speed limit to get to the apartment.

…

Landon was anxious; he hadn't been outside since the quarantine. He hadn't been anywhere other than this room and the recreation area of the hospital in four years. He didn't know how they knew, but they did. He thought about his time on the planet of the Gnetgnu, studying under Gretgen, recovering from the sting of the Mrshti flower. It hurt him deeply to be abandoned by his new people and to be forced back on Earth. He uncovered what he shouldn't have, and they sent him back half out of his mind, unable to cope with the lies spun around him, guilt over how many he had slaughtered over his time there. He was the only human ever to unravel the lies Jom spun that the Quaternewt were attempting to wipe out the Gnetgnu. Every so often, he would have a flashback to the death around him, and it sent him down a genuine shame spiral.

He could smell the smoke in the hallway and knew the plan was in motion. When the fire alarm went off, he was ready. He gave himself multiple pep talks about how this would work; he would find Skyler, and she would shield them and take him to the others. He'd be free of the cage he'd been trapped in for far too long. They knew what he knew, and he would tell them of his uncovered lies. When they didn't evacuate the building, he went to his door, which was locked. He banged on it, "Let me out!" The fire alarm's blaring sound was disturbing. He could hear multiple screams throughout the floor. The activated alarm should have set off the sprinklers, but no water sprang from the ceiling. He watched as the smoke filled the hallway. He coughed. Whatever was set on fire was laced with some chemical, and it made his eyes tear. "Let me out." He saw one of the security guards walking. He banged on his door, "Fire, let me out!"

He was panicked that the their plan wouldn't work, and that the staff were willing to allow the inhabitants to cough and tear from the smoke. They were more fearful of the spread of the virus than of following established safety protocols. He was angry they would rather keep everyone locked down with the smoke slowly saturating the air than have them evacuate. He shook his head; the world was crazy, not him. He banged on it harder, "Let me out!"

Everything was for naught. The Mustleknapp had set the trash on fire, but they wouldn't let anyone out of their rooms. Landon was scared. He coughed harder from the fumes, then took a deep breath and screamed, "Let me out!"

The nurse came to the door with a reassuring look on her face, "It's okay, Landon, it's a tiny fire. They've already put it out."

"But the smoke, the smoke could damage your lungs. We need to leave."

"We're not evacuating; the fire is already out."

"But the sprinklers didn't come on, we're in danger, we need to leave."

"Landon, calm down. Everything will be fine, and maintenance is on the way."

"No! No! I need to get out of here."

"Landon, calm down. I'll bring you something in a little while."

"No!" hurt and panic were thick in his voice. He was about to break the door down when he felt the air shift in his room, and he froze.

"Shhh," he heard from behind him. He slowly turned around, and found Skyler standing in his room. There was a blue hue where the white of her eyes should be, and the tips of her lips were tinted dark blue as though she had hypothermia. The way the light hit her skin, a blue aura emanated from her body.

"Am I dreaming?"

"Do I look like a dream to you?" She smiled sweetly.

"Is that a trick question?" She was beyond gorgeous, and he could feel his whole body feel comfort in her presence like she was his savior.

She giggled, "Perhaps."

"Your voice is beautiful…I didn't expect you to sound like that."

"Like what?"

"An angel…" His eyes were wide as he analyzed her up close. He finally understood what it meant to look upon your soul mate. When her voice called to him, he knew they would be connected forever.

"First things first," she held her hand out, and he walked over to her, and she touched his jaw. He bit down, and she felt the symbol. She took his hand and, placed it on her jaw and bit down.

"How long were you there?"

"A short time, only two months."

"But you were there."

"I was there, we all were, you're not alone,"

"It's been…"

"Shhh," she placed her hand on his cheek, and he closed his eyes, suppressing tears, "You're with us now…"

"How? I'm stuck here. All I shave are memories."

"Not for much longer." She smiled at him, she leaned over and placed her head on his shoulder and wrapped her arms around him.

"What do you miss?"

"The Strythocket Hills the most, the merging of the moons."

"Every 18 months, the moons merge all into one and then expand and burst into the sky, creating thousands, and over a week, the seven are reformed."

"That sounds beautiful."

He held her tighter; he hadn't had human contact that wasn't someone attempting to restrain him since his time on the planet of the Gnetgnu. She was honest, and this beautiful angel was absolute and holding him. She looked at him adoringly as it was everything he could ever want. It was then his mind wondered, "How did you get in here?"

"Do you want me to leave?" she teased as she pulled herself away from him slightly.

"No, not at all." He quickly pulled her close. If this wasn't real, this was the only image he wanted for the rest of his life.

"You gave me a gift the other day, and by some luck, it sparked Hyacinth's memory of having a whole jar in her satchel."

"What are you saying?"

"I am bonded to my element, and my powers are restored."

"That's amazing."

"She has a small amount of Marttronium if you're willing to try and…"

"I will," he smiled, relieved she was with him, "All this time, being told I was crazy, no one listened. They just kept saying I was delusional!"

"You're not…" She smiled. "What happens now?"

"Well, that's up to you, really."

"What do you mean?"

"Are you ready to leave, Landon?"

"Yes."

"Do you trust me?"

"Yes…"

"Do you need anything in here?"

He grabbed his journals and the small cigar box. "This is it."

"I'm really hoping this works." She laughed. "When Plan A doesn't work, you still have the rest of the alphabet, but I'm hoping Plan B goes well…" She put her hands out and the Septtronium left her skin and formed a bubble around him, "Walk through the window," she whispered.

Landon walked through as quickly as the substance had days ago. Once he was outside, Skyler beckoned the Septtronium, surrounded herself, and joined him outside. The two walked through the woods behind the hospital to where Chad and Hyacinth had the Jeep parked. He marveled at her ability to walk through glass, trees, and bushes.

"How are you doing that?" He asked.

"The Septtronium." She smiled. She quickly withdrew the element, bubbled it around him again, and he walked through a tree. "Thrilling, isn't it?" She greedily took it back.

"You're like a blue angel."

"Maybe I'm your angel?" She smiled at him. "Where are we going?"

"To be with the others, we have a meeting point to get you out of here as quickly as possible before they suspect anything."

They reached the Jeep, and the back door opened. They climbed in quickly; Chad and Hyacinth were sitting in the front.

"Welcome, Landon." Chad smiled.

"Where's the Mustleknapp?" Hyacinth asked with her eyes wide, frightened.

"He's not with you?" Skyler asked.

"No, he was supposed to come back with you!"

"He wasn't outside the window when we left. I figured he returned here..." Hyacinth leapt out of the car, "Don't assume anything!"

"Hy, wait!" Chad called.

"Chad, we need to leave before they realize he's gone," Skyler said sternly.

"We can't leave without Hyacinth!"

"She'll be fine; they're not looking for her."

"I'm not leaving without her."

"Get us to her apartment, and then you can come back for her. We need to move before they put this all together."

"I'm not leaving,"

"NOW!" Skyler pushed the Septtronium forward and took over the steering wheel.

"We said no powers in the car!"

"This is an emergency."

"We can't leave them!"

"We're not! We're coming back for them."

Landon was overwhelmed as the car's engine revved, and they pulled onto the highway, "Okay, okay, I'm steering, I'll drive, let go!" Chad yelled to Skyler.

She retreated the Septtronium and it formed itself back to her skin, the blue returned to her eyes, and for fun, she drew the symbol on her right wrist to match Landon. It was gorgeous with the dark blue color on her skin.

"Only two months, and you can do that?" Landon was stunned.

"This is my element. We took to each other easily." She gracefully curved her hand, and the Septtronium made a puddle in her palm and then weaved down her wrist, criss-crossing and absorbed into her skin.

"I think I'm losing my mind." He put his head between his legs, trying to understand everything around him; he hadn't been in a car in over four years, and the motion was more than he could bear.

"Don't worry, we've got you." She carefully rubbed his back.

Meanwhile, Hyacinth ran to the hospital and jumped to the roof quickly. She found the ventilation system where the Mustleknapp had entered. "Mustleknapp," she called in, she heard nothing. She quickly lowered herself in. The squeeze was tight, but she made it about halfway through the air duct. She was worried he'd been hurt or, worse, captured. "Mustleknapp!" she whispered carefully. She moved as quietly as she could.

She laughed to herself, if you asked her last year where she saw herself in a year, and the last answer in the world would have been in the air duct of a mental facility searching for a Mustleknapp after breaking a person out with a mental health condition. She saw his tail in the distance and was relieved she found him. He was stuck in a very narrow compartment, which was beyond her reach. She did her best and tugged on his tail. She pulled it, and it was NOT the Mustleknapp. It was a dead rat. She gagged and tossed it back in the direction she found it. She successfully suppressed the vomit and then maneuvered her way backwards. She went around another corner, and she thought she saw him. She reached out, grabbed his hand, and pulled him toward her. He wasn't breathing. She started to give him mouth-to-mouth, and then he coughed something into her mouth, and she gagged again. "What the fuck was that?" she spit out whatever it was, disgusted at what it could be.

"What just happened, did you just mouth fuck me?" The Mustleknapp asked, annoyed.

"It's called CPR! You weren't breathing!"

"You crawled into the ventilation system to kiss me?"

"What?"

"You just had your mouth on mine!"

"I know and you coughed something into my mouth, gross." She wiped the back of her hand across her mouth, irritated by what had just happened.

"Uh-oh."

"What? What's uh-oh?"

"What was it?"

"What do you mean?"

"What did it look like?" his eyes widened in panic.

"I spit it out," she reached over, and it looked like a yellow marble. "What the hell is this?"

"I'll take that, thank you," he put it back in his mouth. It looked like he placed it somewhere deep, he didn't swallow it.

"Can we get out of here now?"

"First, we need to talk about you kissing me."

"I didn't kiss you, you weren't breathing, I was resuscitating you."

"Like saving my life?"

"Yeah,"

"By making out with me?"

"Will you stop? Can we get out of the air duct before it…" At that moment she heard the duct shift, "Move, move now."

They made their way onto the roof of the hospital. "You came back for me."

"Yeah, I did."

"Does this mean we're together now?"

"What do you mean?"

"Well, you did kiss me."

She flicked his ear, "I did not kiss you."

"You did something if my core piece came out."

"That's your core piece?"

"Yes."

"It looks like a yellow marble."

"You must've done something out of the ordinary to draw out my core piece."

"I think the smoke hit you wrong, and you passed out."

"You saved my life?"

"Yeah, I did." He leapt into her arms and cuddled close to her. "I'm the Prophet Warrior, and you're on my team. I will never leave you. I will always protect you...and I did NOT kiss you," He perched on her shoulder as she maneuvered her way down the building to get back to the Jeep.

"Your shoulders just tightened." The Mustleknapp commented.

"Because they're gone." She clenched her fists and jaw extremely angry the Jeep was not where it was supposed to be.

"Now what?"

"We walk, or more accurately, I walk, and you relax."

He draped over her neck like a mink stole. "I'm good with that. Why are you so angry?"

"They were supposed to be here. They left us in the lurch."

"That's slightly sus."

"I agree." She fought tears, she hated how easily they seemed to surface and provide meaning to her life, and in these last fifteen minutes, how easily the ones she found important exited her life.

"You've got issues."

"Everyone has issues."

"Them not being here strikes you harder than most."

"While that is true, I don't want to talk about it."

He cuddled close to her, letting out the little purrs to comfort her. She thought about Rowan. She thought about Caleb. Then, the thought of Gretgen entered her mind. He was her trainer, and he abandoned her. They all did, and now Chad had too. She shook her head, angry with herself that she felt anything toward him. Feeling anything, even resentment, meant there was something more…and she didn't like it.

It wasn't long before she heard someone honking their horn at her. She didn't look behind her, she flashed her middle finger in the air and kept walking. The car pulled over with the window down and kept pace with her, "Hy, get in the car," it was Chad.

"No," she kept walking. "Hy, please, let me explain."

"You left two members of our team behind." She kept walking. The Mustleknapp cuddled her close. His Prophet Warrior came back for him, saved his life, and he got a kiss out of the deal. He couldn't help but feel relieved she was mad at Chad. He was still extremely jealous that he got to be a human and he never could.

"I had to get Landon out of sight, seriously we broke out a mental patient from the facility. We had to get him out of sight."

"No one in a million years would believe we broke him out using an element from a different planet that defies space, time and physics."

"Hy, come on. Get in the car, *please*."

"Fuck off!" She looked at him, and just the sight of him struck a chord with her. She lost her composure. "You left me behind, you left the Mustleknapp behind. If I hadn't gone back he would've died in the ventilation system! Not one of you cared!"

"You don't understand…"

"You just left me…" She shook her head. Chad didn't realize at that moment she was talking about more than just him. She started walking faster. "Why would you do that to me? You…you would never, but you did…you left me with nothing!"

"Hyacinth, please. I had to get Landon out of there. I came back for you."

"Too little, too late." She started to walk faster.

Chad pulled the car to the side of the road and ran after her, "I will always come back for you." He grabbed her hand and spun her to face him. "Hy, look at me."

"No," she purposefully looked down.

"I promise you, I will always come back for you." He ran his hand below her chin and gently pulled her face up.

She stared at him, she didn't know if she believed him. "I'm not in a forgiving mood."

"You don't have to forgive me right now, but please, get in the Jeep. There's a lot you need to hear from Landon."

"You left me…"

"I'm here now…"

She turned to walk away, and he grunted, annoyed, and then she felt a strong pull. She looked down, and her waist was surrounded by the turquoise of the Decttronium she had given him. He pulled her back to him. She stared at him. He didn't have nearly as much of the element as Skyler did, but Decttronium was far more powerful, "We said no powers on each other!"

"We also said no powers in the car, but Skyler took control of the Jeep. I didn't bring my Decttronium with me; I was helpless to stop her, but I came back and returned for *you*. I will never abandon *you*! So please, get in the car."

"Fine." She could continue to fight him, but once he bonded with the Decttronium he could keep pulling her back.

She jumped in and buckled up. She didn't look at him and kept her focus out the window. The Mustleknapp cuddled to her chest and again purred to soothe her.

"Landon put a speaker stone on a Quarternewt."

"And?" she asked disinterestedly.

"Jom is corrupt; he confirms the Mustleknapp's story."

The Mustleknapp moved down her body and pointed his finger at Chad, "When I say it, it's sus, but when a human says it, it's legit?"

She rubbed behind his ears, "He's just saying that having two separate sources makes the information more viable."

"It's still insulting."

"I know," she held him close and ran her fingers through his fur. He cuddled close to her and let out a mixture of a coo and a purr, a sound he only made for her.

"Landon knows Gretgen, and he has a small amount of each of the elements if we combine them with your collection, then we can each regain our full strength, which will help."

"Help how?"

"If we can find more traces of the element, then maybe we can activate a portal."

"We still don't know how to activate it or where it exists, it's in constant motion."

"Hy, please, this is a good thing."

"You abandoned me." She felt hurt, "I needed you, and you left me..." she wasn't talking about Chad anymore, and the Mustleknapp tightened his grip on her, feeling the sadness emanate from her soul.

"I didn't abandon you, I... please."

"Pull over,"

"Why?"

"Because I want to get out."

"Why?"

"I don't want to tell you."

He kissed the back of her hand, "I made you a promise, and I will keep it no matter what."

"What if I don't believe you?" she shook her head, staring at him.

"I will never abandon you. How could I?" He looked hurt. She looked away and focused on the passing lights of the highway. "I made you a promise, and I kept it this time, as I always will."

"I don't..."

He pulled the car over and stared into her eyes, "I will always come back for you." She stared right back, "I..."

He gently leaned forward and kissed her forehead, "No matter what happens, no matter where we are, or what we're going through...I will always come back for you."

TEN

Chad and Skyler took Landon out for a drive. He was so relieved to be on the outside, and his information and insight into the Gnetgnu and the Quarternewt were very helpful in finalizing their mission. Hyacinth needed to record another show. She readied the ingredients before starting her intro.

"Welcome back, my YouTubers. Have you all gone Quarancrazy? I definitely have, and I would like to thank my sponsor for their support in making this cocktail possible. You can check out their website by clicking the link below.

So tonight's cocktail, I call the Quarantini, and I can tell you after one of these, you won't be feeling much after. So that is one part Cherry Noir vodka and one part lemonade, balanced with a Black Cherry White Claw. It is delicious and refreshing, and I highly recommend it. Now, back to tonight's episode. As you all know, I've shared with you this whole time that Caleb is no longer a guest star, which means that change is on the horizon, but we're not there just yet. So enjoy our Greaties of the Eighties set for another episode, but know the background will change over time.

"

Tonight, I wanted an episode to capture how I felt, and I confess this song was not originally from the eighties, but the cover was so popular that it warrants recognition. So tonight we are covering *I Think We're Alone Now*, and every food has something hidden and unexpected. For our appetizer this evening, we are making Crab Rangoon, but the secret is that a super mini crab cake is in the center of the creamy filling. Our entrée is beef Wellington. Who would have expected beef inside of a pastry shell?

And for desert, the most amazing chocolate lava cake, with a cherry vodka whipped cream on the side. Why cherry vodka? For one, cherry and chocolate are a wonderful compliment to one another. And the other, honestly, I needed another shot right about now and a shout out to our sponsor."

She went on taping her show and then recorded the song. She sat on the counter, editing when she heard an odd sound from her room. She went to inspect what she heard. The Mustleknapp took a deep breath. He slowly pushed the vial of Marttronium ever so slightly, and it started to tip and slowly made its way to the edge of the counter. Hyacinth screamed, and the Mustleknapp retreated to behind the refrigerator. She leapt forward and caught it before it could shatter on the ground. She breathed in deeply, and then her face morphed into madness. She stared at the fridge, "You did that on purpose! I watched it with my eyes; you're trying to sabotage the mission. Get out here and face me!"

The Mustleknapp shrank to the size of a cockroach, "I…"

"You did that on purpose. Why?"

"I don't want to tell you."

"I'll squish you like a bug!"

"I have no desire to explain myself to you!"

"But yer gonna, or I'm calling the super to let him know a rotten little rat lives in the laundry room."

"I'd rather be a rotten little rat than a stupid little sheep!"

"We are working on a plan to uncover the truth and restore the balance to your planet; you know Landon needs the Marttronium to make this all come together!" she shook her head out of confusion and frustration.

"I know." He confessed.

"Then why would you do this?"

"I don't care about the balance! That's not my planet anymore!"

"So you're just going to abandon your family and people to stay here?"

"My life there was wretched. I like being here."

"You live in a wall, people sneer if they see you, and your only joy is eating Domino's pizza."

"When I come here with you, maybe, but at the pool house is different!"

"You would trade your whole line, all the Mustleknapp in existence, to hide in ventilation systems?"

"I have a lot more here that I will not give up." He looked sad, staring into her eyes. She was the only human ever to love him, "I have you…" he quickly scurried up the fridge to leave through the vent.

"Wait!" She shouted, looking up at him with a desperate look.

The Mustleknapp turned to her with a lost expression, "What?"

"You're avoiding my question. Get over here." He crawled over to her with his head down. "You're always all about honesty, so tell me."

"I don't want to tell you why I did what I did, and I'm also mad I got caught."

"Why do you want to sabotage the mission?"

He crawled onto her shoulder, cuddled to her shirt, and used her collar to wipe a fictitious tear from his eye, knowing his form did not produce such human things, "I know things that you don't."

"Withholding truth is just as dishonest as lying, so tell me."

"I don't want you to go back."

"We've talked about this."

"No, you've talked about this. I listened."

"Tell me."

"I can't."

"Yes, you can." She stroked the fur on his back and allowed him to curl his tail around her finger.

"Hy, you wouldn't understand."

"What wouldn't I understand?"

"You can't go back!"

"Help me understand why you feel that way."

"You're my BAE."

Her eyes widened, "What?"

"You're my BAE, and if you go back, you're not coming back here."

"So why don't you come with me and keep me safe?"

"I am never going back there."

"Why are you really worried I won't come back?"

"You're lucky you made it the first time."

"What makes you say that?"

"If you recall, I saw the assassination attempt,"

"That's right, you were there."

"They trained you too well. You heard something that no other typical human could. I heard it, but before I could poke my eyes out, you were already ready to face them."

"So then, why doubt my ability? I will go there, and then I'll be back."

"Jom never shared with you the whole prophecy, but I know the prophecy,"

"Tell me."

"I can't."

"Yes, you can."

He crawled down her arm and sat on his hind legs on the counter closer to the size of a ferret, "You were told you were the Prophet Warrior."

"Yes, Gretgen trained me."

"The prophecy states that the world will regain balance but only when the Prophet Warrior dies defeating the corrupt."

Her eyes widened. "Oh."

"I'm going to assume Jom never told you that part."

"No…" she wasn't frightened. She grew up her whole life hearing about self-fulfilling prophecies. She would always amount to nothing, and if this was how she got to nothing, then so be it.

"Hy, don't go back. Stay here with me. Let the others go, you're my BAE. We can stay here safe, please!"

"You keep saying I'm your BAE," she smiled, flattered.

"Aren't you?"

"I am."

He smiled, "See, you know it, you feel it!" He leapt into her arms, cooing and rubbing his nose against her cheek.

"Then you know this is who I am, and I must go back."

"You're walking into your death for a planet that doesn't care about you with a war you never started, they abducted you. You shouldn't have even been there!" He crawled around her neck and, as always, hung from her like a fur.

"I have to do this."

"No, you don't!"

"Yes, I do. It's what I'm destined to do."

"Says you!" he slid down her arm and smacked her across her wrist with his tail.

"Ouch!" she pulled her hand away, "What are you doing?"

"I'm trying to make you realize!"

"I realize you're scared."

"You do not frighten me?" He shook his head. "No, you're worried I won't come back."

"Because you won't!"

"I will!"

"I need you to stay with me!"

"I need you to accept that I need to do this. I need you to realize I will be back because I'm nothing if not defiant, and I will come back to Earth. So let's enjoy what we have now. Spend our time together because, in the coming weeks, I will restore your planet's balance, with or without your support. We're doing what's right for everyone."

"You're going for revenge." He pointed out. "Revenge, restoration. Two birds, one stone."

"Why would you hit a bird with a stone?"

"I'll explain it to you later. Come on," he crawled up her arm, and she held him against her heart and snuggled him. "If I'm your BAE, does that make you my Boo?"

"I'll be your Boo, Bae."

She kissed the top of his head, and he smiled. "What do you want to do tonight?"

"Well, I am a creature of habit."

"Go start the Netflix, I'll order the pizza."

He hurried to the living room, fired up the Apple TV, and started cuing up one of their shows. At the same time, she ordered the Hawaiian Domino's pie for him and the other items for everyone else.

...

Hyacinth and the Mustleknapp were on the couch. She rolled her eyes as she ate the wings, her own recipe was ten times better, but then again, she didn't have to cook these herself, and she got to watch the Mustleknapp roll his eyes in ecstasy eating his poison. Her Boo was busy eating his pizza while she was laughing at the television. They were content to be with one another, and the Mustleknapp was very happy sitting on her lap. They both listened to the door creak out of nowhere, and Caleb emerged from his room. He wore a respirator, latex gloves, and safety goggles. When he entered the kitchen, he turned and stared at the two of them on the couch.

"Caleb?" she was confused. He hadn't left his room in so long, he didn't even have a clue Landon had been living there for over a week.

"Hyacinth, what is going on?" he looked at the Domino's boxes and then tilted his head to the Mustleknapp cuddling with his ex-fiancée.

"Tell me that's what he looks like? I've actually got a shot."

"Stop it, he's wearing a mask." She laughed.

"Did that rat just talk?"

"He's not a rat!" she was offended. The Mustleknapp smiled at how quickly she defended him.

"Hy, what the fuck, am I having a fever dream? Did I get the virus, and I'm dying in the hospital?" He uttered while shaking his head, genuinely convinced he was hallucinating.

"Caleb," she rubbed her temples, annoyed at his presence, "Why are you out of your room?"

"Hungry,"

"Oh, I forgot to stick your pizza under the door." She carefully placed the Mustleknapp on the couch and kissed his head. Then she went to the boxes to find the one she ordered him. She knew he hated Domino's, but she saved what she made during her show for him to eat later.

"What is this?"

"Food."

"I don't want to eat this…"

"Then order something else, but you have to be the one to answer the door." He turned and stared at the Mustleknapp, "Is that a rat in my apartment?"

"No, that's my Boo," she said defensively.

"Holla," the Mustleknapp said as he shoved a piece of pineapple in his mouth.

"Am I crazy?" He shook his head back and forth, and a few tears dripped down his cheeks.

She rolled her eyes, "Yes, but for different reasons," she slowly approached him and attempted to place her hand on his cheek. He backed up frightened, "Figured…go back to your room before the big bad virus emanates from your ex-fiancée but is immune to your pizza box."

"We broke up?" He was genuinely confused for the moment, perpetually overwhelmed by the news of the virus, each moment in perpetual fear he would die.

"You called off the wedding, don't you remember?" she had no patience left for him.

He nodded, "You're insensitive."

"You've gone completely off the charts."

"Do you love me anymore?" He approached her gently and held his hand out to her.

Since she had returned, she longed for this moment but felt no joy or satisfaction; she felt nothing staring at his open hand, and she didn't bother to place hers into his. "You're not you anymore. I loved the before quarantine you if he should ever resurface. But let's face it, he won't."

"You only care about yourself." He hugged himself as another tear went down his cheek. She rolled her eyes, "No…that's where you're wrong…"

"You don't know what you're saying."

"When I met you, for the first time in my adult life, I cared about you, and you killed any chance I ever had of caring about others."

Caleb went back into his room and slammed the door. She was preparing herself to fall apart, but she didn't. She felt nothing.

"You were seriously going to marry that?" The Mustleknapp rolled his eyes.

"The paranoia has gotten to him, changed him."

"He always calls you insensitive."

"Your point?"

"It's almost like he's shocked."

"Excuse me?"

"You are insensitive."

"I know that. I don't try to hide it."

"But why was it he could never see it before?"

"Because he loved me…he doesn't love me anymore. The death of his grandmother pushed him over the edge."

"Many people die from plagues, and we had them all the time on that planet. Until it hits you close, you don't get it."

"Who did you lose in the last plague on your planet?"

"45 Mustleknapp total."

"That's a lot."

"I'm a Mustleknapp. In case such a situation arises, we tend to maintain large numbers."

She sat back on the couch, and he crawled onto her lap, propping his head up with one hand and eating his pizza with the other. She rubbed behind his ear, and she smiled at how his tail would twitch at the bottom when she did so.

The door opened, and the rest of the crew walked in. "Did you remember the cheesy bread this time?"

"Dammit, Cliff, yes, I did." She laughed and then saw how serious they were, "What's wrong?"

"I have a question for you," Landon said seriously. "Okay…"

"How did you see your body double wake?"

"The assassination attempt threw off my momentum, they got the timing wrong."

"Did they?" He raised his eyebrows to her.

"What are you implying?" She was confused.

"Did they do that on purpose?"

"How so? They had intended for me to be dead."

"But you saw it?"

"I watched her die."

"The thought has me really freaked out." Landon looked down as Skyler wrapped her arm around him in comfort.

"That would freak me out," Skyler said reassuringly.

"I never met mine," Chad said.

"I never met mine either," Skyler said.

"I'll be honest, it was terrifying." Hyacinth didn't like remembering that moment.

"What happened?" Landon asked. The Mustleknapp cuddled to Hyacinth's heart and made small cooing sounds as he always had done when she was upset.

"I spoke to it…and the puppet acted like me…well, the me

before I was taken…then I watched her disintegrate, and then I gathered the sand, well it looked like sand, and I kept it."

"Where?"

"It's in a jar in my satchel."

"What do you intend to do with it?" Skyler was intrigued. "Safekeeping, I guess. I couldn't just leave it there."

"How did you know she was the double and you weren't?" Landon asked. "What if I'm the double, and I'm not real?"

"The double didn't have a bellybutton."

"How do you know?"

"I asked her to touch her belly button ring because I have one…" she lifted her shirt to show them. It was a bright blue crystal with a dream catcher dangling from the bottom.

"I like your jewelry choice," Skyler said, going over to her and touching it.

"Thank you,"

"So what happened?", Chad asked staring at her sexy stomach with the jewel dangling, enticing him like a moth to a flame.

"I asked her if she had one, and she said no, and then she started panicking that she didn't have a bellybutton at all."

"So what does that mean?" Landon's voice cracked, and Skyler stopped her obsession with the beautiful jewel and went back to soothing him.

"The body double can only copy what the maker sees, that's why she had my scars and why she didn't have a bellybutton, I bet her breasts were shaped but probably had no nipples, and she had the outline of an ass, but no actual butthole."

"Hyacinth!" Skyler chastised. "What? It's probably true."

The Mustleknapp laughed out loud, "Add crude to the list of your character traits."

"Bite me." She rolled her eyes at him. He hurried over and nipped her arm, "Ouch! Don't do that!"

"You told me too!"

"It's an expression, dillweed!"

"Oh…so if someone asks you to pinch them, you shouldn't?"

"Different set of rules."

"Your language is confusing." Now, he rolled his eyes.

"Don't bite me again!" She teased, and she grabbed him and pulled him close. He happily perched on her shoulder.

They all sat around the living room, eating Domino's, watching Netflix. Landon was a happy addition to their crew, and for reasons they couldn't understand, they knew one another deeper than others. They were a bonded unit as if they were on a mission together, had one another's backs no matter what they encountered. But despite his denial, the Mustleknapp couldn't ignore the feelings Chad exuded toward his BAE, and it angered him in ways he had never had to deal with before his Earthly experience.

"Do you think it's been long enough?" Skyler asked. "Has what been long enough?" Chad asked.

"For Landon to move in with us," Skyler smiled.

"What are you talking about?" Landon was confused. For the past week, he assumed they all lived in the apartment.

"This is kind of like our safe house," Hyacinth laughed. "Our headquarters is in an alternate location."

"Really?"

"Yeah, it's almost like you've beaten level one, but the princess is in another castle." Skyler laughed.

"I'd like to see it." Landon couldn't help but smile. Skyler was his princess.

"Then, tomorrow, we'll take you."

"Breakfast?" Chad asked.

"Fast or real?" Skyler qualified.

"What are you talking about?" Landon asked.

Hyacinth laughed, "Oh, yeah, we only eat take out when I'm lazy…and we only order Domino's because of the Mustleknapp."

"What?"

"Hy's a chef…and she's really good…" Skyler laughed.

Hyacinth rolled her eyes, went over to the fridge, and assessed what she could make in the morning. Chad followed her and leaned against the counter. She looked up at him, and he smiled at her and then pouted. "Fine…" she rolled her eyes, "Who wants Eggs Benedict in the morning?"

"Me!" shouted the Mustleknapp from the couch. "Yes!" Skyler exclaimed.

"I haven't had that in I don't know how long…" Landon smiled. "She makes *the* best hollandaise."

Chad slowly approached her, "You know why you're doing this, don't you?"

"Because you all want that?"

"Because you want to make that for me…"

She rolled her eyes, "Don't read too far into this…"

"Will that be the entrée you feature when I'm a guest on your show?"

"IF you were ever a guest on my show, I'd make scratch Cliff bars." She rolled her eyes at him and then flicked his forehead.

While she was distracted in positioning her flick, he grabbed her by the waist and pulled her toward him,

"I'm more to you than a guest."

The intensity of his voice and the way his breath felt on her ear and neck, she stared back at him, "I know…come on, it's getting late."

Landon and Skyler slept on the futon in Hyacinth's former room. Each night, they started on opposite ends, but by the night's end, they were spooning in the center. Chad and Hyacinth slept on the pull-out couch in the living room, with the Mustleknapp strategically placed between them, the size of a large housecat. In the middle of the night, the Mustleknapp shrank size and crawled into the ventilation system to sweep before leaving the next day. She stretched and then turned, and Chad held her close. "Are you awake?" he asked.

"No…" she, quickly cuddled to him and placed one leg around his.

"Can I kiss you?"

"Yes."

He kissed her forehead. "Good night, Beautiful."

She let out a low sigh of happiness, "Good night, darling."

He felt her body relax into a deep sleep. "I'm in love with you."

ELEVEN

Hyacinth set up the kitchen island to house the elements from the Gnetgnu planet for easy storage. She wasn't resentful of their powers, and it seemed as though her strength had increased since the four of them were together. It was almost as if she needed them to propel her to the next level. She was in the middle of doing her meditation when Chad walked into the kitchen for a snack. She was balanced on her right hand, with all other limbs at perfect 90-degree angles. He reached into the utility drawer and took out a rubber band. He aimed carefully and shot it at her behind. She didn't flinch. He did it again. Once again, she didn't move. When he went to do it a third time, she pushed up with her hand and flipped into the air, grabbed the rubber band and then shot it back at him. It smacked his forehead before she landed.

"Ouch!" He pouted.

"Serves you right. I was concentrating, and you were being inappropriate."

"Was I now?" He asked, staring at her with that same dumbfounded expression she could not stand. "Take a cold shower, and take it down a notch creeper."

"I'll do my best, Prophet Warrior." He inched closer to her and stopped as he heard the door open.

She made a pouty face to tease him that his romantic attempts were thwarted by impeccable timing.

"I'm so glad we made this our official headquarters…" Landon commented, returning from the gym on Skyler's parents' estate. He dropped his gym bag on the recliner chair in the pool house living room, oblivious he interrupted Chad and Hyacinth's perpetual drama and sexual tension.

"It's like an all-inclusive," Hyacinth commented.

"How did your show go?" Landon asked, walking over to them.

"Highest number of hits since I've been back."

"That's good, right?" the Mustleknapp asked, leaving their room after a much-needed nap.

"Very."

In her bikini, Skyler came out of her room, "Who's ready for a swim? The pool season is officially open."

Landon's eyes nearly bugged out of their sockets. Her chest looked like something you'd find in adult entertainment, "Are those real?"

"Excuse me?"

"Are those," he pointed to her breasts, "like real?"

She looked down at her chest, "Um, yeah, they're real." She gave Landon an odd look, meaning she was outwardly offended, but inside, she was giggling like a schoolgirl. Since they met, she couldn't get her mind off of him, so she chose this bathing suit to see if he would grab the bait.

He continued to stare, "Can I touch one?"

"What?" she crossed her arms across her chest, forcing her cleavage to expand.

"They look fake." He challenged, hoping he could touch them.

"Too much time in the psych ward, you crazy man."

"Men can do crazy things…"

"Easy Romeo," She smirked. "I'm sorry, I just haven't seen…"

"Well, I assure you they are all me!" she ran her hand down her sternum to tease him.

"I'm sorry, I can't stop staring. They look too perfect."

"What a Cliff thing to say." Skyler continued to move her hand down the center of her chest. "Why am I the butt of everyone's jokes?"

"Calm down, Cliff; that just means you're important to us," Hyacinth spoke with artificial sincerity.

"I think you would have never given me the time of day if I didn't have that symbol in my jaw." His typical derpy behavior morphed into serious.

"Honestly, do you think I give anybody the time of day?" Hyacinth narrowed her eyes at him.

"You know what I mean." He was tired of her constantly treating him as if he were stupid. Holding her that night in her apartment couldn't escape his mind. Now, in the pool house, she would randomly open her door, waiting for him to climb into her bed. Making pouty faces indicating she wanted to kiss him, then constantly belittling his intelligence and flicking his forehead, he grew tired of her perpetual mixed signals. While he felt compelled to pursue her, at the same time, the constant quips and eye rolls were pushing him away. He was so conflicted by her behavior that a small part of him was secretly thinking of backing out of the group to get away from her toying with his emotions, but part of him knew he couldn't walk away from Hyacinth.

"I don't think our paths would've crossed if it wasn't for the Gnetgnu meddling with our sanity, destiny, or anything in between." She sounded bitter.

"So maybe we should see this as positive," Landon continued to stare at Skyler. Neither of them denied how they felt about one another; it was love at first sight.

"The only thing I find positive about the Gnetgnu is how easy they are to kill," Hyacinth said with no concern behind her eyes, leaving an unsettling feeling in the room. "Trust me, I'll kill my fill when we get there."

"Did you have any friends before this, your Highness?" Chad asked.

"Yes," she said, annoyed.

"Name one." He spit back at her.

"Let me guess, Cliff, you were the most popular guy in your circle of friends until they turned on you, thinking you were crazy when you woke up in your coffin. Half them thinking it was a prank the whole time and the other half genuinely ghosted, not sure if they understood what the fuck just happened."

"You're ducking the question." He hated how she was dead on accurate.

"No, I'm averting the question. Expand your vocabulary."

"There they go again, I'm out. See you in the pool." Skyler could feel her anxiety start to trigger at their perpetual drama, and she left the room annoyed but with Landon close behind her.

"What is your problem with me?" Chad stared at her.

"I don't have a problem with you." She shrugged her shoulders and shook her head. "You do. You're constantly underminding me."

"Undermining."

"See, you did it again!"

"You misused a word." She looked shocked, and she had to point that out to him. He set himself up constantly, and she was pointing it out to entertain herself. She found it odd that he was a quote-unquote genius lacking basic common sense.

The Mustleknapp, annoyed with their constant bickering, got between them, standing on his hind legs. "Will the two of you stop this bullshit!"

"Excuse me?" Chad asked, confused.

"The two of you are worse than frenemies. You have a mission together, but your personalities clash, you," he turned his face to Chad, "need to stop setting yourself up with your comments, and you," he turned his face to Hyacinth and tilted it to the side, "need to realize what you are doing." As much as he was jealous, he knew their trust in one another was needed for the mission. It hurt so deeply and profoundly to realize how much his Bae was attracted to Chad.

"She treats me like an idiot!" Chad pointed at her like a child being accused of taking a toy that wasn't theirs.

"You *are* an idiot!" She folded her arms and sat on the recliner, pretending she couldn't hear him.

"I am not! I'm a lot smarter than you think I am!" Now he folded his arms and turned his back to her. The Mustleknapp rolled his eyes, "You both are so basic I can't even right now."

"Why do you act like a dumbass all the time?" Hyacinth stood annoyed at Chad's behavior and put-off by the Mustleknapp's comment.

"Why are you so critical of me?" he turned to her, and he didn't realize how close they were to one

another.

"I'm critical of *everyone*! Why do you think you deserve a fucking exemption?"

"You go out of your way to purposefully dig at me anyway you can, like I did something to you to motivate you to be mean to me, and I've never done anything mean to you!"

"He has a point Hyacinth." The Mustleknapp sang in a higher pitch than his typical.

"I tease you, why are you so sensitive, fucking Soy Boy."

"You just did it again!"

"Hyacinth," The Mustleknapp's tone shifted seriously, like that of a doting father, "Stop acting like a child, and tell him the truth!"

"I don't want to!" she looked panicked.

"You never want to admit how you feel…if you can then maybe, you'll see…" The Mustleknapp looked at her adoringly, he was deeply in love with her, and he wished more than anything he could be human and love her the way he wanted. Part of him feared that would never happen, but the other part knew she needed to be honest with herself. In his logical mind he needed Chad to protect her when he couldn't. He held on loosely to the belief that someday he could be human and then she would fall into his arms as the love he always wanted.

"There's a truth? What are you talking about? A truth to what?" Chad asked.

Hyacinth rolled her eyes and pointed to him as she stared at the Mustleknapp, "See? He's too clueless for anyone to deal with!"

"Tell him the truth, he's on your team, and you can't be a team without trust. What if something happens to you on the planet? I will not be there to stop it! You won't listen to me about staying and letting this go, because you are too stubborn and you can't. But you are never going to let go of how you feel until you let the words out of your mouth. I don't want this to happen, but at the same time if you go back there, I need you as safe as possible to come home to me. So, understand your truth, accept what lies before you, and don't make excuses for what makes you uncomfortable..."

"What TikTok clip did you steal that from?" she asked resentfully.

"While I'm sure it's been said before, it is the truth, you have a mission, and you'll fuck it up if you keep this up. And as much as I care about you all, you and I are Dorothy and Toto, unconditional love, you need to be honest with your Scarecrow. I am confident in the end, I'm still the one in your arms no matter what happens...after all he's kind of a Cliff." He smiled as she laughed.

"What is he talking about?" Chad asked, he didn't pick up on the *Wizard of Oz* references.

"Oh, come on!" She stared once again and pointed at Chad showing restraint.

"Hy, now while I know you're an insensitive Bi-atch with issues of your own, even I have figured out why you treat him this way, and as you tell me all the time, I'm the outsider, well the outsider figured it out. Now I am going to swim in that weird cement thing, you two will stay in here until you are honest with him and honest with yourself...and as always, I am still here for you, no matter what, I am always yours." He got on all fours and scurried out and slammed the door with his hind legs.

Hyacinth clenched her fists and kicked the coffee table. She knocked it over, and had a surprised look on her face from the sound it made. She picked it up and placed it back, Chad smirked and gave a whispered laugh. She sighed loudly and then looked over at him, "Wipe that fucking chode expression off your face for fuck's sake!"

"What did I do to you?" Chad looked sincere.

"What are you talking about?"

"What did I do to you, to make you hate me like this?" He shook his head and looked down at the ground, "I honestly don't know what I did."

"You didn't do anything." She rolled her eyes, "It's nothing that YOU did!"

"It's not you, it's me. That's where we're going right now?" Now, he rolled his eyes at her.

"It's true."

"No, when someone says it's not you, it's me, then it really is you."

"How badly did your ex scar you?" she folded her arms, angry at the accuracy of the Mustleknapp forcing her to face her feelings.

"She was only in it for the money…she never cared about me… but the one before her, she said it wasn't me, it was her, that she just wanted something more, more than what I was willing to give, she posted on her facebook that she ditched the boring computer programmer and couldn't wait for her date with the cop for some real action."

"Ouch."

"Yeah, well, that's that." He looked out the window, and she could tell talking about it brought all the hurt to the surface again.

"Her loss." She stared into his eyes and for a split second she allowed her vulnerable side to peek out.

"You are challenging to understand."

"Not really."

"Yes, you are!"

"How so?"

"You make fun of me all the time, and then when you're about to fall asleep you call me darling, you hold me like you can't sleep without me, but then you get angry with me for holding your hand, and then in the next you're grabbing my arm feeling my biceps…I don't know what you want, or really when I think about it, who you are…"

"I have a lot of baggage." She shrugged.

"Don't we all?" He sideways smiled at her, the way he always did when he looked at her adoringly. Since day one she crept into every thought he had, and now he was hoping she would tell him why she hated him.

"Mine's a bit more of a perpetual, ridiculousness that messes with me and my ability to be nice to other people…I was cold before they took me, and now I fear I grow colder every day."

He rolled his eyes, "I've known that from day one, Beautiful."

There was a long silence between the two of them, Hyacinth walked over to the couch and sat down, Chad stood frozen staring at her. She folded herself in half, then put her hands on her head placing her wrists against her ears, and then he heard tiny sniffles.

"Are you crying?" he was shocked. "No…" she lied.

"You're crying." He got down on his knees before her. "I didn't mean to make you cry." He grabbed one of her hands to his heart; he only wanted love from her. He never wanted sadness. Despite all the hurt she cast in his direction, he wanted to try to comfort her, dry her tears, and make her happy again.

She looked up at him, doing her best to hold the tears in, "I can't do this to myself."

"It's okay to cry when you're sad."

"I don't deserve to be sad."

"You can't stop emotions."

"Yes, you can, it's called suppression."

"It's called lying to yourself."

"I'm not lying to myself. I know me more than you do, and I don't deserve a second chance."

"What are you talking about?"

"I don't deserve anything."

"Happiness is a choice."

"No, misery is a choice."

"Hy, don't do this to yourself," To his shock she wrapped her arms around him and got down on her knees with him on the floor. He held her close unsure of what to do. After a little while he slowly ran his fingers through her hair, her eyes were glistening in his direction, and he felt closer to her than he ever had before, "I'm here to listen, if you're willing to talk."

After a few more minutes, she calmed herself, "I don't mean to be mean to you. I keep pushing you away; you're just easy to tease, and I really like that."

"What does that even mean?"

"You set yourself up all the time for sarcastic comments and pointing out obvious things, and I call you out on it... and I like that."

"You like being a mean person?" He asked in disbelief.

"I don't know if I can share this with you." She shook her head back and forth, she appeared as though she may fall apart.

He gladly touched her cheek, forcing her to stare into his eyes, "What are you trying to tell me?"

"I don't want you to know..."

"Know what?"

"Why I do that..."

"Tell me," He cupped her face, and they stared into one another's eyes.

She sniffled, "I can't..."

"Can't or won't?" he qualified.

"You don't understand what this feels like..." she squeaked.

"Truth is not weakness. You are the Prophet Warrior, but you're still human."

She stared at him and took a long, slow, deep breath, "You remind me of how I felt before Caleb went all virus panicked and broke my heart, that feeling I tried to push away. I see it when I look at you, and it happens when you touch me. When you hold me, you, bring something out of me."

"I do?" his eyes widened.

"I miss that feeling when you see in someone else something more, something beyond the surface, and it's so hard."

"What about Caleb do you see in me?"

"I don't see Caleb in you. I experience the feeling I once had with him, sparked by you."

"Oh…"

"Yeah…it's hard to articulate."

"Try?" he asked desperately as she looked up at him lost, "Please?"

"Butterflies in my stomach, tense shoulders…like the first time you grabbed me in the parking lot, and I felt your jaw."

"Then, why?"

"It's hard for me…"

"You tell me I'm ignorant."

"You're not ignorant."

"Then what is it?"

"Innocent."

"Oh…"

"I miss what it was like to have that innocence around me, and to point it out and see it stay innocent despite everything around us…every time you do that, my heart breaks, not because I miss him, it's not about him, it's about me. Because somehow, I was lucky enough to find it again. I don't deserve to have the chance to be with someone who has the most attractive qualities I want …and I don't want to ever be that vulnerable again…I don't deserve happiness, and I can't allow myself to enjoy it, especially with you…"

"That must be hard."

"The whole time on that planet, whenever I thought I couldn't go on, I thought of my future and how I would get married. I wanted a family, and I wanted to have a baby. I wanted everything. I wanted that kind of life where I made Eggo waffles in the morning, and my kids and my husband devoured them; I never had that growing up, and watching the commercial on television, that was all I wanted…I had the possibility of that future, but he's straight-up psycho now, and I lost that innocence, and then I meet you! I don't know if I could handle losing it again."

"He's caught up in the paranoia, it could go back."

"What a Cliff thing to say."

"You're doing it again."

"Because I'm confessing something to you, but you're not seeing beyond the surface."

"He could come back to you…"

"I don't want *him*!"

"I'm not getting it."

"Don't you realize yet, it's never going to go back, it's changed forever, nothing will go back…it's like when any other tragedy strikes, the rules change, he abandoned me…I don't love him…I don't think I ever did, when I'm honest with myself, I loved the idea of him and nothing more…but I can't help but question if I was wrong to think that I could ever be happy after all that I have done…change…is not an easy concept…"

"Isn't that a good thing?"

"No, it's not."

"What does that mean?"

"When you change for personal growth, that's an important change. When everything changes out of fear or ignorance, you're opening Pandora's box."

"Are you talking about the pandemic?" She sighed, "Oh, Cliff."

"Stop it." He pleaded with her. "There has to be a silver lining to everything we've been through."

"Are *you* talking about the pandemic?"

"The quarantine is helping."

"No, it's not. When you gather the sick to stop a spread, that's a quarantine. When you restrict movement of the healthy, that's tyranny."

"Wow."

"You don't agree?"

"I would say something, but you'll just make fun of me."

"More than likely." She bobbed her head, she wasn't going to hide herself. "I still don't understand."

"Caleb was so innocent when we first met; it was his first time in the states, and everything was so new to him; everything fascinated him, and that innocence drew me to him originally."

"Were you mean and sarcastic with him?"

"All the time, but he never saw me as rude or hurtful. He found me funny."

"I don't think you're funny."

"You think I'm hurtful."

"You're plotting the genocide of an entire culture because they lied to you."

"They lied to all of us; they deserve what's coming to them."

"Hyacinth," he said as he shook his head.

"Your presence is a constant reminder of the loss of that innocence, a reminder I never deserved to be happy because of what I have done. I have severe abandonment issues, and for some reason, karma is making it come around full circle and then I look at you, and I think for a split second I could be happy again, and I have to push it away with my full force, or I will be hurt again..."

"But that's not my fault."

"It's not your fault, but that's why I tease you. I tease you to keep you away from me, and it's comforting, I know that sounds sick, but I get so excited seeing you. I feel something when I look in your eyes, and I have to crush it away, or you'll just hurt me and abandon me like everyone else in my life. I can't stop myself from teasing you. Almost like we're on the playground, and I have to push you in the mud, because if I don't, I will be vulnerable."

"What's wrong with being vulnerable?"

"I don't like that, it hurts too much, so I'll push you as far away as possible."

"You're right. It kind of does sound sick."

"You're such a Cliff, Chad."

"You're doing it again. Why do you want to hurt me?"

"I don't."

"But you keep doing it, and I can't take it. If I have to, I'm going to leave." She sniffled, "I figured."

"Why?"

"Because once again, the thing that brings me happiness is just going to go away again."

"Then..." He couldn't finish his thought as she leaned forward and kissed him softly, gently on the mouth. "What just happened?" he was stunned, it was everything he ever wanted, and he had no idea how to react.

They stared at one another, "Do you get it yet?"

"Kind of..." he had no clue how to understand or process what happened.

"I know we're deeper, but it's hard for me, so I tease you...but don't for one second think it's because I want you to go away..." She leaned forward and kissed him a little longer, grazed her tongue against his and then bit down slightly on his bottom lip.

"What are you doing to me?" Chad asked.

"Telling you the truth," she kissed the tip of his nose and smiled, "Come on, let's go swimming." She stood, pulled her clothes off to reveal her bikini, and walked out the door. He was enamored watching her breasts bounce back and forth as she walked, and the suit Skyler gave her showed the majority of her bottom as if she was wearing a thong as opposed to a bathing suit.

"I'll be there in a minute." Chad sat on the couch, trying to process what just happened. She was mean to him because she liked him. How would he ensure her that he wouldn't abandon her? The night of Landon's liberation flashed to the forefront of his mind. That was why she was so angry with him; she felt as though he left her, not that anything else had happened. She cared about him, and it killed her and made her happy in the same instance. He remembered sleeping beside her and kissing her forehead. Now, she kissed *him*, and he was confused but elated and satisfied in the exact moment, and he wanted to know where he went from here.

The sun was shining, and the wind was warm if it hadn't been for the pandemic, this might have been a beautiful day. She looked over at the Mustleknapp, happily floating on his back. Hyacinth laughed. She thought he resembled an adorable otter in the water. Skyler was on Landon's shoulders as they giggled and splashed. Skyler ran her fingers through his hair, and he playfully tickled her. Hyacinth rolled her eyes, they were like that couple in an ad for anti-depressants. She walked down the built-in steps of the in-ground pool and submerged herself. As she emerged from the water, the Mustleknapp approached her using his tail as a rutter.

"Are you two better?"

"Better?"

"Yeah, did you tell him the truth?"

"Yeah,"

"Where is he?"

"Trying to comprehend. It's going to take him a few minutes."

"You have to stop that."

"I can't stop who I am." She smiled and shook her head.

"That I know."

"But you were right, we're a stronger team when we all know we are cared for and there for each other."

He crawled onto her shoulder and patted her head, "Good human."

She smirked and rolled her eyes. "You're jealous of him."

"I will not dignify that with a response."

"That only means it's true."

"Enough! Now, everyone, stand back, and I will show you the awesome power of the Mustleknapp." He jumped out of the pool and scurried to the diving board. He stood on his hind legs and then increased his size to that of a small wolf, bounced three times, shot into the air like a rocket, and spun until he was a golden, round ball and then crashed into the pool. The water shot straight up and then rained down on them. Delighted with his accomplishment, he got out of the pool, restored to his typical size and bowed.

"Very impressive!" They all cheered in approval.

"The Quarternewts don't stand a chance!"

"Rock always beats scissors." Hyacinth smiled. "Every time!"

Chad came out of the pool house with a dumbfounded look. Hyacinth stared at him. He was a Chad, -with six-pack abs, toned arms, and broad shoulders, with his hair still done perfectly. "What'd I miss?"

"Dammit, Cliff, keep it together." Hyacinth chided him.

"Do it again!" Skyler squealed.

The Mustleknapp sighed, "In a few minutes, need some recovery time."

"How did you learn to do that?" Landon asked.

The Mustleknapp dove into the water and made his way quickly to Hyacinth and crawled onto her shoulder, "Instinct."

"You're born just knowing how to do that?"

"We're not exactly born, but we are created with everything, including our language and prophecies."

"How is that possible?"

"As I said, we are not born in the typical sense."

"How so?"

"A Mustleknapp's reproductive orb is a small clone of its genetic material."

"So it's like laying an egg, like a platypus?"

"It isn't an egg as you have on Earth."

"So, it doesn't need to be fertilized?" Chad asked.

Hyacinth opened her mouth for commentary, and the Mustleknapp smacked her chin with his tail. "No, it is the identical genetic material of the Mustleknapp."

"How do they hatch?"

"Well, they don't hatch; they need to be formed. The instincts of how to hunt, clean, protection, and battle are all in the orb. The prophecies, language, and our history come when the orb is wrapped in another Mustleknapp's tail. The orb's hardened surface softens over time, and when the knowledge has been completely transferred, the softened form transforms into a Mustleknapp."

"So, you don't have baby Mustleknapp?"

"No, just Mustleknapp."

"That's fascinating."

"For you, maybe, carrying one of those orbs on your tail for however long it takes is exhausting."

"It's different?"

"We keep growing as a society, and therefore, more knowledge needs to be transferred. Mustleknapp are wiser, not because they know more, but because they access knowledge faster."

"Are all the Mustleknapp like you?"

"Like me?"

"Sarcastic, funny…"

"We are all different."

"But you're all clones,"

"Forest versus caring."

Hyacinth rolled her eyes, "Nature versus nurture." She ran her fingers down his tail.

"Whatever, Bae, English is a complicated language."

"Is that how all species operate on your planet?"

"No, the Quarternewts have live birth, babies as you call them, but even the smallest Quarternewt can take apart whole cities of Gnetgnu with one swipe."

"Do you know how to speak Quarternewt?"

"No, none of the languages are known to the others. That's why we have speaker stones."

"It's like a Rosetta Stone," Chad said.

"Check you out with a meaningful tidbit to the conversation,"

Hyacinth commented. "What's the Rosetta Stone?" the Mustleknapp inquired.

"This stone held the same phrase in different languages, so early civilizations could communicate with one another even if their native language was different. That's why they named that language computer program after it."

"Oh, Cliff, you never cease to amaze me." Hyacinth smiled, and for once, Chad smiled back at her nickname for him. The Mustleknapp rolled his eyes, sighed and went inside for a much-needed nap.

Chad swam over to her and then pulled her toward him. He whispered to her, "I'm going to sneak into your room tonight."

"For what purpose?"

"I want to hold you."

"Okay." She smiled.

"Do you actually like me?" Chad asked, heavy with his insecurity.

"Maybe…" she smirked to the side and splashed him.

He gladly grabbed her and placed her on his shoulders, and the girls laughed and played chicken fight in the pool. When no one anticipated it, Skyler placed her arm out, summoned the Septtronium and battled Hyacinth with an advantage.

Everyone laughed and giggled as they both went back and forth, and then before anyone could protest. Hyacinth shot straight up in the air, landed directly onto Skyler, crashing down into the water, and the Septtronium retreated from her body. They both looked shocked and quickly surfaced.

They all stopped laughing…they stared at one another, "Did you do that on purpose?" Skyler asked

scared.

"No, I didn't. I was just caught up in our little game. I didn't mean, did I actually do that?"

"Did the Septtronium do that?" Skyler was confused.

"What exactly happened?" Landon was worried.

"I don't know, she landed on me, and I laughed, and then when I hit the water, it just felt like it drained out of me."

"Is it water resistant?"

"No, I had it in me this whole time, and I'm soaking wet."

"Maybe it thought if you couldn't breathe?"

"That doesn't make sense."

Hyacinth rolled her eyes, "When was the last time any of this made sense?"

The distress behind her eyes activated Chad's protective side, and he swam over and held her close. He kissed her head, "It's okay, we'll figure this out."

They each silently left the pool and dried off. They each gave one another a look. For the first time, she felt as though Skyler was angry with her. "I didn't mean it." She looked at her desperately.

"I know that. I'm just freaked out." Skyler started breathing heavily, and like clockwork, Landon grabbed her medicine, Chad poured her a glass of water, and Hyacinth led her through her breathing technique. "I'm okay." She smiled.

Hyacinth hugged her, "I don't know how I did that."

"I don't even know *if* you did that."

"I have to know," Landon said. He held his arm out, and the Marttronium entered him. He went over to Hyacinth, "This is just an experiment, nothing more," he pushed her hard, using the Marttronium to send her backwards.

Hyacinth twisted her body in the air and landed quickly, "I didn't do it on purpose! I don't even know if I did it!" She brought her fist across Landon's torso, and if he hadn't been bonded to the Marttronium, she would have cracked his ribs. With Marttronium lining the area, they bent, broke, and then went back together instantly.

He screamed in pain as they broke and reformed, "You did something. We need to figure it out!" He pushed her again. This time, she twisted sideways to get away from him. She knocked over the recliner as she landed, and it made a loud noise.

Chad instinctively summoned the Decttronium and placed a bubble shield around Hyacinth, "Explain yourself, now!"

Skyler once again summoned the Septtronium as her body took on the color, "Everyone needs to calm the fuck down!"

"You hate that phrase!" Hyacinth commented, confused.

"What are you all doing?" The Mustleknapp was angry, and he groggily came out of their room, "Bae!" He shouted as each of the elements came toward her. He ran toward her, but the elements knocked him off track, and he was cascaded to the side.

"NO!" she screamed as she pushed her arms out. All three of them were tossed backward. Chad thudded against the wall and slid down, Skyler was sent so far back she was on the porch, and Landon landed on the recliner as it flipped back into place. Their elements abruptly returned to the jars. "Boo, are you okay?" She held him in her arms. "Speak to me!"

"You can push the elements away," he said plainly. "I've never seen anything do that before."

"What?" She rubbed his belly, afraid he was hurt.

"You have a power no other human has ever had before." He smiled.

The three looked at her dazed, and finally, Landon spoke, "That's why you never bonded to one. You have the ability to repel the elements from the planet!"

"I don't know how, though…it just happened." She cuddled the Mustleknapp, and he lavishly took in each stroke.

"Your emotion…" Chad smiled. "What?"

"Your emotion can control our elements!"

"Holy Shit, that is so metaphorical right now…" Skyler said as she entered the room, dazed from being thrown away.

"I need a drink," Hyacinth said as she placed the Mustleknapp around her neck. She ran to the cabinet and grabbed the tequila.

"You don't need a drink; you need to figure out how…" Landon tried to stop her.

"Later, right now, tequila!" She took the shot down quickly, and Skyler was at her side, rubbing her back, taking her own shot, trying to figure out what to do next. The two looked at each other and did their infamous double shot, which always resulted in the liquor impairing them that much quicker.

"You can repel the elements!" Chad said as he and Landon joined the girls. "I don't know how!"

The Mustleknapp leaned over and knocked back the bottle of tequila. He smiled, "You don't know...yet."

"Since when do you drink?" Hyacinth asked, confused.

"Since the natural elements of my planet sent me flying into the sky!" He took another one, "That fire liquid is poison."

Skyler picked him up and held him with his head cradled on her shoulder like she was soothing a baby, "You're okay. Just breathe." He cooed for her, not as he did for Hyacinth, but he also wanted to be close with Skyler.

"I am declaring it bed time for myself, I'm overwhelmed." Hyacinth walked over to her room while the others continued to drink and hypothesize about how to train her to move the elements.

When the night was ending, Landon tiptoed into Skyler's room, as Chad did the same to Hyacinth's room.

"What do you want?" she whispered as he crawled into bed with her. "I want to cuddle with you."

"Okay, do NOT crush my Mustleknapp." Chad looked over to see the Mustleknapp asleep on her pillow, this evening, he was the size of a guinea pig.

"Your Highness, can you hear me?"

"Yes," she yawned as she adjusted her head against his chest. She slowly placed her hand under his shirt and placed her palm on his abs.

"There is going to be a day where you fully admit you want me."

"That moment is not now. Tone down the tequila courage." She whispered.

"I can't deny how I feel."

"Neither can I, but I will suppress it until I have my revenge."

"And then?"

"We'll cross that bridge when we get there..."

"Are we there yet?" He asked.

She looked at him, "Chad, not tonight, please."

"What do you think I'm looking for?"

"Well, you know…"

"Hy, all I want is for you to admit you like me."

"I already did that." She yawned and held him tighter. "So…"

"So what?"

"Do you want me?"

"Ugh."

"I know you want me…"

"I do. I *want* you to be quiet."

He looked down, defeated, "Hy…"

"I want you to be quiet, and I'm going to snuggle my face onto your chest…and you're going to wrap your arms around me, and I'm going to touch your skin…" She sniffled, "I'm going to allow my body to cuddle onto you and enjoy every moment of it. You're going to touch my skin and stare at me while I breathe in and out. Then we're both going to fall asleep feeling comforted and wanted, and then I'll wake up in the morning and tease you again." She kissed his chest over his shirt, then she looked over at him, "Do you object?"

"No…but…"

"But what?"

"Can I kiss you goodnight?"

"Yes," she said quietly.

He leaned over her and kissed her gently. He moaned ever so slightly, and she smiled and then kissed him again. "I like doing that."

"Me too," she admitted, then she cuddled closely to his chest, and he wrapped his arms around her tightly.

When he realized she was asleep, he whispered, "I will make you happy."

The Mustleknapp stirred after another hour. He did not succumb to the tequila the way humans do. For him, it gave him a buzzing sensation that lasted about a minute, and then he was back to sober. He shook his head and realized Chad was with his Bae. His face snarled into a dirty look; he did not like how he looked at her. She was *his* Bae, and he only needed to have him adore her long enough to keep her safe on the Gnetgnu planet. When they got back, he'd cleanse the circle of Chad. He crawled over, kissed Hyacinth on the forehead, and sneered at Chad. The Prophet Warrior deserved so much more than someone unworthy like Chad, and the Mustleknapp was honest with himself. He hated him.

TWELVE

"If things were normal, we'd all go out to dinner, or if I had my way, we'd be on vacation somewhere tropical." Skyler pouted.

"That sounds like you." Landon smiled as he handed her the piece of tape.

"Well, since life is upside down, I guess headquarters will have to do." She smiled as she hung the
Happy Birthday sign along the hood of the stove top.

"Well, the more important thing is that we're all together." Landon couldn't help but smile at her adoringly as if she were the only female on Earth. Then he gently took her hand and pulled her close to him. He kissed her softly, "If I have to be stuck in a government-forced shutdown with anyone, I'm glad it's with you."

"When they lift travel restrictions, we are going somewhere. I don't know where just yet, but we're going there for at least a month!"

"Anything for you." He smiled.

Her eyes dilated, staring into his eyes. She couldn't get over how infatuated she was with Landon, "How do I know we're both not just high on angel dust and this is an illusion?"

"You never know that, for certain, even if there wasn't a pandemic."

"Am I dreaming?" She ran her fingers through his hair and stared into his eyes.

"Should I pinch you to find out?" he teased.

"Where would you pinch me?" She gave him a sexy look with her eyes.

He grabbed her behind and pulled her toward him, "Wherever you tell me." She giggled, "I'm obsessed with a crazy man."

"I'm infatuated with a dramatic artist."

"We've only known each other for how long?"

"Not long."

"I will follow you anywhere, I will do anything. You and I are why romance still exists even in these crazy times."

"I want you so much." She squeezed him tight, and he picked her up and spun her around the room as she wrapped her legs around him.

"I am the luckiest man in the world."

"Because we are meant to be…" she kissed him repeatedly.

"Do we have enough time?"

"They'll be here in 45 minutes."

"Then we have enough time." He happily carried her into her bedroom.

The two of them couldn't get enough of one another, and they were hoping Chad and Hyacinth could find between themselves what they had with each other.

…

Hyacinth wrapped everything up in the apartment. She went to Caleb's door and knocked, "There's enough food to last the next two days. Your clothes are in the basket."

"Get out."

"Caleb, when you realize…"

"Hyacinth, the lease is up in September, and I will be renewing in September, and I will be renewing it without your name on the lease."

"I know, so kick me out when September comes…" she sang, changing the song lyric to fit her current situation.

"I know that is still a ways away, but if you could stop coming here sooner."

"This is my apartment, and as long as I am paying half the rent, I'm going to use the kitchen for my show. It allows for consistency for the viewers. Even you, in your paranoia, must realize how comforting it is to see something has not changed."

"The sooner I no longer have to hear your voice, the sooner I will heal."

"Caleb…"

"Get out!"

"Sleep tight, don't let the virus bite," she said with an evil twinge to her voice. She grabbed her satchel and went into the kitchen. She went into the fridge and purposefully blew on all the food, then licked the handle and laughed.

"Childish much?" The Mustleknapp asked from his perch atop her counters.

"Even you have to admit this is over the top."

"Over the top of what?"

She rolled her eyes and smiled, "Come on," she opened her satchel, and he jumped down. "Where are we going?"

"Home…"

"Are we going to move in with Skyler permanently?"

"Yes, eventually, slowly moving myself out of here, piece by piece."

"Her place is way nicer than this place."

"I know."

"So then…"

"Stop now, or I will not make the Strezma syrup you requested."

"Still, are we leaving here one day, never to return?"

"Do you need to move anything out of your maze?"

"What if I want to stay here?"

"You are more than welcome to, but when the lease is up, I won't have access to this building. You're not a technical tenant, so I can't get in to visit you."

"What if you and Caleb made up?" He asked, secretly hoping she would deny this up and down and confess it was because she loved him more.

"We're not going to." She shook her head and rolled her eyes, "Even if he returns to his sanity, thank you, NO, thank you."

"Then why do you keep coming here to check on him?" He narrowed his eyes, suspecting her ulterior motive.

"To make sure he eats, make sure he's okay," she said without thinking. She ignored the glares from the tenants staring at her for being unmasked in the hallway.

The Mustleknapp rolled his eyes, analyzing her demeanor, "I don't buy it."

"Then don't," she didn't bother to put her mask on as she walked through the hallway. She twirled it around her finger to mock anyone who rolled their eyes. Wouldn't it appear odder that she was speaking to her satchel than wearing a mask? No one even questioned that she was talking to someone. They were all so fixated on her exposed nose and mouth and didn't bat an eye to the deep voice that answered from her satchel.

"Seriously!"

"We were together for a very long time. We have been through so much before all of this nonsense, and he's not in his right mind, you can't just walk away from someone like that. You should be there for them, even if they're not there," she said as though she read from a script, without genuine concern or care.

"Still don't buy it."

She clomped down the stairs whistling, ignoring the looks from the other tenants of her audacity of not wearing her mask, "Well, that's the answer I'm giving you. If you don't like it, oh well…"

"But it's not the truth."

"Maybe part of it is…maybe part of it's not. How would you ever know for real and for true?"

"Can you please just be honest with yourself?"

"What is it with you and honesty?"

"Mustleknapp do not lie."

"Why?" Her eyebrow went up at the concept.

"We simply do not lie. If you lie, you do not deserve to be a Mustleknapp,"

"What happens if a Mutleknapp lies?"

"They are killed immediately unless they escape and kill themselves from the guilt."

"But you can give someone a piece of a puzzle without the whole picture."

"That is not lying."

"Still deceitful."

"But not a lie."

"I'll remember that."

"I'm sure you will use it against me at some point."

"More than likely."

"You want revenge too hard."

"No, you justify leaving chunks of information from the bigger picture out because you say that it is still honesty when it means you're still just as full of it as lying about it."

"Bae…"

"Shut it!" She stood outside her apartment building waiting for Skyler to pick her up when Chad pulled his Jeep over and rolled down the window, "Get in, Beautiful."

"Why?" she was annoyed. As of late he kept trying to spend more time with her than was typical, she found it harder and harder to fight her feelings for him, her vulnerable side exposed more and more. Seeing him pull up in his car with his perfect smile, calling her beautiful and looking at her as though she was all that mattered in the world made her feel like they were slowly entering a romantic relationship, and she hated and adored it simultaneously. He rubbed her back the previous night they were together until she fell asleep. She hated admitting that she slept sounder with Chad in her bed.

"We have an errand to run before we go home, Beautiful."

She rolled her eyes at him, then tightened her jaw, "Why did they send you?"

"Can you get in the Jeep, please?" The sincerity behind his eyes was growing stronger, another obstacle for her to fight. Her mind kept replaying kissing him, sleeping beside him. These feelings were stronger within him, but he knew they were within her, too.

"Fine."

"Why are you so upset?" He gently ran the back of his hand over her cheek, perturbed at the look on her face. She just stared at him as though she could cry at any moment.

The Mustleknapp crawled out of her satchel and sat in the back seat stretching, "I made her have another realization about herself, and she's upset."

Chad gave the Mustleknapp a dirty look from the rearview mirror, "Why did you do that?" He gently took her hand and kissed the back of it.

"What?" the Mustleknapp asked innocently.

"Do not rub your fur in the backseat, it turns to needles once it leaves your body."

"The same thing happens to your five o'clock shadow, and no one complains about you!"

"I don't leave my stubble in the back seat!"

"Just in the bathroom sink." The Mustleknapp rolled his eyes. "Yeah, in MY bathroom that no one else uses."

"Except me."

"No one invited you."

"Well, I can use whatever I want, when I want, because they all have vents."

"And that's just fine, but if you want stubble-free sinks, go play in Landon's sink."

"Listen, you sack of…"

"Can both of you shut up for five seconds?" Hyacinth shrieked. She ran her fingers through her hair and stared out the window.

"What did you do?" Chad asked angrily at the Mustleknapp. "I asked her a question, and she lied."

"I didn't lie! I just didn't tell the truth!"

"That's the same thing!"

"No, it's not, remember? You said not showing your full hand was just fine in your quest for honesty."

"I always show my hand?" The Mustleknapp held up his paw and wiggled his fingers.

"It's poker slang. Watch something more than TikTok!"

"Don't be mad at me because you're having a BM!"

"A what?" Chad was confused.

"BF, bitch fit!" She rolled her eyes.

"Whatever."

"What did you ask her?" Chad was angered; he had a whole night planned, and the last thing he wanted was that stupid Mustleknapp ruining it.

"Why does she still go to the apartment even though she is no longer wanted there?"

"I pay half the rent; it is still mine, and I am allowed to be there!" She slammed her hands against the seat, and it shook the Jeep. She sat on her hands, worried that she had rocked the car in such a way.

"There's something else."

"It's MINE! Why do I have to sacrifice what's mine because he's a fucking clueless fuckwad?" She couldn't help herself and smacked her hand against the windshield. Chad was startled by the noise.

"Calm the fuck down." The Mustleknapp rolled his eyes. "Go fuck yourself!"

"Masterbate? I cannot."

"That's not what she meant!" Chad held in the laughter.

"She's hiding from herself again, and she needs to face herself before facing a foe on another planet with all the advantage if he discovers her vulnerability."

"The Mustleknapp does have a valid point."

"Shove it, Cliff!" she pulled her knees up to her chest and

wrapped her arms around them tight. She breathed in and out the way Skyler did when she lost her composure.

"You struck a nerve." Chad gave the Mustleknapp another angry look.

"Be honest with yourself!" The Mustleknapp chastised from the backseat as he rubbed his fur in the upholstery like a back scratcher. "The only one you're terrified of is yourself!"

"Shut it!"

"I will not! You are your own worst enemy in every way definable."

"Fine!" She shouted, "You really wanna know why I go back there all the time?"

"YES!" They both exclaimed.

"You're not going to like it! You don't want to know, and you're both stupid and nosey!"

"Be honest!"

"Fine! Because when Caleb realizes that his madness has ended the best thing that ever happened to him, and he begs for forgiveness, I will turn to him and laugh as I watch his heart break in front of me. And then I will delight in watching the regret scar his soul, and I will walk out of the apartment, never to return, leaving him alone to grieve in a shroud of his misery and stupidity. I want nothing more than to be there when reality re-enters his world, and when he finally realizes he was the one that ruined everything, I will smile at his misery and bathe in the joy of his insanity…"

There was silence.

"Wow…" Chad finally broke the tension, "That's intense."

"Bae, I'm starting to worry about your emphatic revenge desire."

"You need to understand something very crucial about me and who I am."

"What is that?" Chad asked.

"If you dare to throw me in the Chateau d'If, be prepared for me to go full-blown Monte Cristo on your ass!"

"What does that mean?"

"Dammit, Cliff, read a book!"

"What are you talking about?" He asked, genuinely confused.

"She means, if you betray her, she will take more than her share in revenge." Even the Mustleknapp watched the IMBD trailer to understand what she always referenced.

"Oh." Chad parked the car.

"I never got my revenge..." She stared out the window and thought about Rowan. He was the ultimate betrayal, and she channelled Caleb's descent into madness as her surrogate moment for getting back at him for leaving her. Rowan left this world and never returned. She would never have her moment to scream and yell at him for abandoning her, for taking away her only sense of security in the world, the only person she ever wanted to be close with. She saw Caleb's loss of self as a similarity, only now there would come a day when she would get the satisfaction of watching true heartache, the way Rowan never saw her die on the day she held his hand in the morgue.

"What are you thinking about?" Chad asked. "Leave me alone." She looked out the window. "Hy," Chad tried.

"Don't..." the Mustleknapp said, "I pushed her too far."

"Yeah, I know!" Chad gave him another dirty look from the rearview mirror, he was reluctant to leave the car or even blink at this point, staring at her.

The thoughts of her brother exhausted her, and she felt slightly dizzy sitting in the Jeep. When she realized where they were, she asked, "Why are we at Trader Joe's?" her voice was forced and tired.

"Because Skyler has made a request for dinner tonight, and it's something that we all want, and so we're getting the ingredients, and you are not going to start a riot. We are going shopping and nothing more."

She got out of the car. Part of her hoped he picked her up because of something more, but then she shook her head. She didn't deserve special treatment, she didn't deserve to celebrate, and she grew angry at herself for thinking he had something planned for her, as if by some power he knew that today was her birthday. Everyone forgot again, just as her family did, and she reminded herself that she shouldn't expect anything special, this was just another day, nothing different.

If she wanted a celebration she should have told them about today. In her realization, she reminded herself that death to the Gnetgnu was the primary objective, and being distracted by how infatuated she was with Chad was a nuisance. She couldn't comprehend why she wished he spontaneously knew today was her birthday, and he wanted to make her feel special. She stomped her foot on the blacktop, making a dent. She once again told herself to remain focused. Revenge was her goal, nothing more.

"We'll be right back. Do you want the window open?" Chad asked the Mustleknapp.

"Just a crack, I'm going to catch up with my inner slumberjack."

"Shouldn't be too long." Chad went to leave.

"Oh Chad," he called with his eyes closed, "Remember, she's my Bae, hands off."

"No matter what, you're still not human."

"No, but she loves me more than she'll ever love you."

"Again, I can give her things that you can't."

"She's kissed me more than she's kissed you." The Mustleknapp boasted. Chad shook his head in anger, wanting nothing more than to kiss her every chance. The Mustleknapp cared about her profoundly, the same way Chad did, and they would both fight to be her top priority even though the Mustleknapp spent more time cuddled against her than Chad ever had. He finally joined her, and she looked at him, annoyed for waiting. As soon as he could, he grabbed her hand. She looked confused, "Oh, come on, please?" he picked her hand up and kissed the back.

"Fine." She complied. She enjoyed the smile that came over his face when she walked into the market holding his hand. Without realizing it, she, too, was smiling. As soon as he grabbed a cart, she dropped his hand and playfully stood on its edge so he would push her, "Is there a method to your madness, darling?"

He handed her the list, "I think that's everything."

"I have a majority of these things in my apartment." She rolled her eyes.

"So now we'll have them at headquarters. You can cook, and you should share your talent."

"Why did you pick me up?" She asked out of nowhere.

"So you could make sure this was to your liking."

"Why not just send me a list? Or have Skyler's house manager take care of this?" She asked as she turned to the next shelf to retrieve the items.

"Because I was going to do this to surprise you, but I knew you'd make fun of me if I messed it up again."

"You walked into that last one!"

"I did not!"

"I asked you to pick up truffle oil, and you brought home a trifle and olive oil."

He laughed that she referred to headquarters as home. Part of him wanted them to have a house, have a life together. He was more than just in love; he was captivated, "I'm not a chef."

"But you have seen a cooking show before. Truffle oil was the trend of a decade, along with sriracha and anything aioli."

"What is aioli?"

"A pretentious way of saying mayonnaise."

He pulled her close and placed his hands on the small of her back, "How'd you learn to cook?"

"Trial and error." She looked to the side and remembered cooking in the kitchen with Rowan.

He could tell he sparked a memory, "You didn't go to culinary school?" He ran his hand down her cheek.

"Nope." She stepped away from their embrace, covering her feelings as best she could.

"Then, how?"

"I have a natural affinity for flavor I guess."

"But how did you learn how to balance everything?"

"Trial and error." She repeated herself as she grabbed the capers from the shelf. Then she stood on the edge of the cart, and Chad pushed her down the next aisle.

"You never went to school?"

"Nope," she looked along the aisle, "Hault!" He stopped the cart, and she got down and grabbed a bag of flour, sugar, baking soda, and baking powder. She got back on the cart edge and smiled, "Mush, Cliff!"

He rolled his eyes, and did his signature move of crushing on Hyacinth pulling both of his lips inward and ran them through his teeth before he smiled to the right, "Can I ask you something?"

She shook her head, "You just did my dullard."

"Did you go to your prom?"

"No."

"Why not?"

"Didn't have the opportunity."

"Nobody asked you?" Chad asked, shocked; she was so beautiful, even in her most sarcastic moments, her lips begged to be kissed. In his mind, a more perfect creature than Hyacinth had never existed.

"I dropped out when I was 16." She looked off to the side as if she was talking in an interrogation.

"What?"

"I dropped out when I was 16," she slowly said and articulated each word.

"My shock was not because I didn't understand you, your Highness, it was because I am surprised. You speak too eloquently for someone with a lack of education."

"I didn't drop out because I was failing. I dropped out for other reasons." She looked down as they reached the produce section.

"Then why?"

"I don't wanna talk about it."

"Why won't you open up to me?" He touched her shoulders and then ran his fingers through her hair.

"What are you babbling about? I talk to you all the time." She pushed him away.

"You talk at me often, you tease me even more, and you hide your real self from me every chance you get." It frustrated him how she teased him all of the time, dominating him in her way, hiding how she felt about him. Why couldn't she just put down her guard and tell him how she felt about him? Every night, he held her close. He could feel she loved him.

"I do not," she picked up a Roman cauliflower and placed it in the bag.

"What the hell is that thing?" He looked disgusted as if she had put something unnatural into the cart.

"This is how I make the soup you like so much." She held it up to him, and he grabbed it and his mouth was wide open in shock. "What?" she asked concerned. He laughed, "Look at the center."

"What?" she asked. "Just look!"

She looked down then moved it around, "It looks like the Strythocket hills."

"I know, right?" Cliff was smiling from ear-to-ear beneath his mask. "Here on Earth this whole time." Hyacinth froze, "What did you say?"

"What?"

"That phrase you just said? Repeat it."

"I know, right?"

"Dammit, Cliff," she said, frustrated.

"Here on Earth this whole time." He couldn't wrap his mind around what she was grasping for, but he wanted desperately to journey with her. He'd follow her anywhere.

"I know how we find the portal," She stared in front of her, seeing something that no one else could.

"What?"

She ran her finger over the center, "We have to find where on

Earth this formation is. Once we do, we can use the three elements and travel through the rainbow portal."

"You're serious."

"Think about it, all aligned, the elements, the scenery, the alchemy, the location is all that's missing, and we'll be there." She smiled. He leaned down and kissed her over her mask. "What was that for?"

"You're a genius." He smiled behind his mask, and she could see the little wrinkles on the corners of his eyes. "I can't wait to tell the others."

"Do you really think this plan will work?" she asked excitedly.

"It's going to work."

"How do you know?"

"Because you designed it, Prophet Warrior."

She smiled at him, wrapped her arms around him, and kissed him over his mask. Someone from the distance screamed, "6 feet apart!"

Hyacinth pursed her lips and then shouted, "We live together, cocksucker!"

Chad quickly slung her onto his back, piggyback style, and pushed their cart to the check-out, "You don't have to curse out every paranoid person you come across."

"Have to…no…*want* to…absolutely yes." She enjoyed holding onto him; he was like a muscular teddy bear that she perpetually wanted to cuddle but kept denying herself the pleasure. She cradled her face on the back of his neck and breathed in the smell of his cologne. She didn't realize she let out a small moan of happiness.

"Stop it! You missed how scary this was when it all started." He'd lean over the rung up items, she'd grab something and hand it to him. Every time he tried to reach for something she did it faster. He couldn't help but smile at her playing with him in this fashion.

"If you recall, I was in the middle of being brainwashed and murdering a Quarternewt while you were all brainwashed that a plague was something you could escape." The cashier gave her a weird look, and in turn, she rolled her eyes, "Come on, be realistic, a virus

that knows the distance of six feet and can't live on Amazon boxes…
doesn't that seem odd to you?"

"Don't mind her. She hit her head a few years ago, and the injury
is still impacting her."

"Stop making excuses for me!"

"Stop giving me a reason to!" When their task was complete, he
twisted her off his back and into his arms, then placed her inside the
cart, "Stay or else!" He flexed the turquoise color from within his eyes
as a warning.

She hadn't realized he bonded to the Decttronium before picking
her up. Skyler seemed to be the only one who couldn't conceal its
presence. Then she shook her head. Skyler had far more than either
Landon or Chad of their element. Perhaps a small amount could be
concealed, but the amount she had made it blatantly obvious. It
didn't matter, she folded her arms as he unloaded the recyclable bags
on top of her. He took out his wallet, paid for their order, and then
pushed her out of the store.

"Why don't you let me speak my mind?" She removed her mask
as soon as they were out of the store.

"Spouting your opinion in public is a Russian roulette for the
mentally unstable." He kept his on until they made it to his car.

Her eyes widened, "Can you say that again?"

"Excuse me?" they started placing the groceries in the trunk of his
Jeep. She smiled, "Please."

"Spouting your opinion in public is a Russian roulette for the
mentally unstable."

"Ooh, talk protectively to me, baby," she said seductively.

He blushed, "Hy, one of these days, you're going to set off
someone that you shouldn't, and they're going to hurt you."

"Nothing can hurt me, I am the Prophet Warrior."

"On the planet that only we know about, for reasons we don't
understand and are trying to get back to for revenge purposes," He
wrapped his arms around her, "So you can't act like you have the

same power here, find one idiot that wants to snap and throw acid on you because of your personal opinion, and it's going to happen."

"And once I've beaten them to the ground, they'll never do it to anyone ever again."

"But you will be horrifically deformed." He stared into her eyes, slowly cradled her cheek, and then slowly kissed her.

She laughed, "You'll still chase me."

He rolled his eyes and sighed, "Probably. Can you just admit to yourself why you do this?"

"People are stupid."

"No, there's more."

"You sound like the friggin Mustleknapp." She pushed his hand away.

"They cannot be trusted."

"Says you…" she looked down, angry he was trying to be serious.

"They cannot. They withhold the truth like you are doing right now."

"Then what's the truth, genius?"

"You're so mad at yourself for believing Jom that you're refusing to believe any of this has the slightest iota of being real."

"You're not even close."

"I'm a little close," he pulled her toward him.

"No, you're saying that because you want me to be deeper than I am."

"You are as deep as the Mariana Trench, deeper even."

"I'm as surface as it comes. Everyone is stupid and blindly following what they are told."

"Just like you did."

She looked down, "Stop it."

"Beautiful, when will you realize how close we are?"

"We're not close."

"Should I use another metaphor?"

"That was a simile, Cliff."

"You're doing it again."

"I know…" she looked into his eyes.

He leaned down and kissed her slowly, "There it is." When he was done, he looked down and bit his lip.

She narrowed her eyes at him, "You're hiding something from me."

"What are you talking about?" he had a guilty look.

"When you don't want me to know something, you always do that!"

"Do what?" he looked down and bit his lip again.

"You ARE hiding something from me!" She seemed panicked and pushed him away.

"Hy, stop it!" He was overly concerned.

"There's something…I can feel it. I can see it in your eyes!" She felt vulnerable and went into a defensive mode as if what he was hiding was meant to hurt her, another betrayal she would need to endure.

"So what if there was?" He tried to sound nonchalant. "You know I hate when you keep information from me!"

"This isn't information."

"You knew the Quarternewt more than any of us, and yet you held back that you could move their nests with your mind because they are made from Dectrronium."

"I didn't think it was important at the time."

"It was, always has been, and now you're doing it again." She looked at him horrified.

"Hy, this is not…"

She interrupted him, "What more do you know you're keeping from me?" She started to slowly back up from him, she was slowly losing her sanity, the hurt and betrayal that he was keeping something from her was cutting through her. She couldn't help but flashback to seeing her brother in the morgue, another betrayal was more than she could mentally process at the moment.

"We've talked about this. Remember, trust one another, we have to totally trust one another or this will never work." He stared at her, desperate. He loved her so much, and he was trying to keep her from spiraling away from him yet again…she kissed him. That had to mean something.

The Mustleknapp stirred from his nap in the back seat. He quickly jumped up and made his way to the edge of the trunk. "What's going on?"

"He's hiding something!"

"Hyacinth, stop this!" Chad said seriously.

She kept backing up, and someone in the parking lot honked their horn as she was in close range to be hit. She sprang up in the air and landed on the Jeep's roof.

"Bae, knock it off!" The Mustleknapp called to her casually.

"No, he's hiding something. What is it now? Are you going to sabotage the mission? Are you creating a potion to keep us from going?"

"Hy, stop being paranoid… I'm not hiding anything related to the mission!" Chad pleaded, and he slowly inched toward her and grabbed her waist as she made her way back to the ground.

The Mustleknapp started to lose his mind with laughter in the trunk and couldn't help but hold his sides from hurting so much, "This is so amazing, cheese and crackers. I've never laughed this hard before."

Hyacinth was angry and walked over to him perched on the trunk and stared at him, "*You* know

something."

"Bae, I know everything," he patted her right cheek with his paw twice. "Tell me!"

"No."

"Why not?"

"Because you need to learn how to trust, Cliff."

"My name is Chad."

"Shut up, Cliff," the Mustleknapp snickered. "Even the Mustleknapp makes fun of me."

"He's hiding something!" She looked terrified. "He is." The Mustleknapp stated.

"How do you know?"

"Because I hide it too, and I want you to trust me and him."

"Since when are you a Cliff supporter?"

"Again, standing right here!" He held his arms out to indicate he was within three feet of them, clearly hearing their conversation.

"I am not a supporter of Cliff; I have been and always will be all about you. You once again have the opportunity to be honest with yourself."

"You and honesty." She rolled her eyes.

"I am asking you to search within yourself and trust."

She turned and looked at Chad, "I'm driving, give me your keys."

"No, this is *my* Jeep."

"And you want me to trust you,"

"Of course I do, Beautiful." He stared into her eyes with the love and devotion that made her melt and feel defensive in the same instance.

"Then you need to trust me."

He rolled his eyes and sighed loudly, "You MUST do the speed limit." She wrinkled her nose, "I MUST drive this Jeep."

They got into the Jeep, and she watched in the rearview mirror as the Mustleknapp buckled himself in,

"What are you doing?"

"Bae, I love you, but super cereal, you drive waaaay too fast."

"I do not!"

"Who taught you how to drive?" Chad asked, concerned. "I did."

"Do you even have your license?"

"Yes, I do." She backed the Jeep out of the parking lot and onto Route 17, and she was up to 90 miles per hour by the time she reached the exit for Skyler's house. When she parked in the driveway, she turned to a stunned and pale Cliff. She eyed the Mustleknapp in the back seat, who was smiling.

"Bae, we gotta get you a Bugatti Chiron."

"That would be amazing." She smiled at him, then looked at Cliff, "Blink your eyes so I know you're alive."

He blinked twice, "That was…"

"Exhilarating?"

"Terrorizing."

"The correct word would be terrifying."

"I can use whatever word I want; I may never recover from that experience."

"I think you liked it," she licked her lips at him while he pulled his in and bit down with his teeth. The Mustleknapp crawled over and wrapped his tail around Cliff's neck, "Don't get any ideas!"

"No ideas," Chad said, hiding that he was planning on kissing her at any moment.

"Never any ideas." Hyacinth went back to her teasing mode and flicked his forehead, "Get out of your head, we've got shit to do."

They exited the car and carried in the groceries while the Mustleknapp crawled up her back and sat across her neck like a mink stole. She walked into the pool house and out jumped Landon and Skyler from behind the kitchen island, "Happy Birthday!"

She looked shocked and smiled; she never had a surprise party before. It was slightly unsettling; she could feel the genuine anxiety that Skyler always described to her build within her stomach. She turned to Chad and whispered, "This is what you were hiding?"

He smiled, proud he could keep the secret from her and give her this moment, "Trust…we need to work on your trust level." He didn't realize she was feeling overwhelmed, but he could pick up on her uneasiness, hugged her quickly, and whispered in her ear, "Just breathe."

"It's your birthday!" Skyler squealed, enjoying the moment, "You got the ingredients for your birthday episode. I've got all the equipment, and it's your first episode with three guest stars."

"Lick the bowl, Landon." He held his arms out like part of a barber shop quartet.

"Screw it up, Skyler." She did the same.

"And Chad." He quickly jumped next to them. She smiled wide, "I can't believe you did this!"

"We even matched the 80s song to the flavor theme!"

"What did you pick?"

"*Walking on Sunshine!*"

"Why'd you pick that?"

"Because every dish has lemon in it! And lemon is yellow like sunshine!"

"That's so amazing."

"So start it up!"

. . .

When everything was finished and all her friends were eating, she recorded herself singing. Chad quietly came into her recording room; the one Skyler had installed in what once was the library of the pool house.

"What are you doing?" She asked. "Maybe I want to listen?"

"You want me to sing this song to you, don't you?" She smiled mischievously.

"Whenever I see you, I'm walking on sunshine," he smiled, then bit his lips and rolled them over his

teeth.

"Fine," she rolled her eyes, "But you cannot make a noise…or make a face…or touch me!"

"I'm going to sit in this chair and not move at all, I just wanted a live concert from the best singer I have ever heard."

"Your flattery is tainted."

"How so?"

"You are biased because of how you feel about me."

"Even if I hated you, your voice could win every reality show in any country."

She smirked, "Thank you." She started the playback and recording, "I present to you, my followers, *Walking on Sunshine* by Katrina and the Waves…I dedicate this song to my special guest stars," The music started, and she rocked her body in time with the music and started to sing, *"I used to think maybe you loved, now baby, I'm sure."*

Chad stared at her and couldn't help but smile, and he labeled himself as her sunshine, and he would go to whatever lengths it took to ensure that would always be the case.

…

When the recording was finished, and Hyacinth edited everything to her liking, the others were already enjoying shots in the living room. She popped in her USB and replayed the song. All four of them and the Mustleknapp danced around the living room, each taking shots of limoncello as they did so.

"When did you realize you could sing?" a happily buzzed Skyler asked her as the two collapsed on the couch together when the music stopped.

With her frontal lobe compromised, she spoke the truth, "One day, my brother turned to me and started singing *Time after Time,* and I started singing it with him, and he was shocked. I didn't know if what I did was good. I just did it, and I've done it ever since." Hyacinth took another shot.

Chad plopped beside her and put his arm around her so she was leaning on his shoulder, "You have a brother?"

Hyacinth froze for a second, "Kind of."

"What?"

"I have a brother, he's just not around anymore."

"Where is he?" Landon asked innocently.

"He died."

"Oh…"

"How'd he die?"

She exhaled under the pressure of talking about the incident, "Car crash…"

"Drunk driver?"

She laughed uncomfortably, "No…he crashed on purpose…

suici…" she couldn't finish the word, "It was a long time ago… doesn't matter anyway."

"Hy, I didn't mean to…"

"You didn't know…" she took another shot, "Who wants another lemon bar?"

"Me!" The Mustleknapp insisted as he jumped on the island in the kitchen for her to cut him another

one.

The three looked at one another. Chad shook his head, "I didn't know," he whispered.

"Go get the present. That'll help ease this weirdness." Skyler told Landon. He quickly walked to her room to retrieve the present they had gotten her. "She never told me this."

"Me either."

"Holy Fuck!"

"I know…"

The Mustleknapp gobbled down the lemon square, "Why do you put powdered sugar over the top?"

"To balance sour and sweet."

"You need to balance sour and sweet in more ways than one." He raised his whiskers at her.

"Whatever Jiminy!"

"What's a Jiminy?"

"A cricket."

"I am not a flat bat for sport!"

"No, but sometimes you pretend you are my conscience."

"What reference is this?"

"Pinnocchio."

"Is that on Tik Tok?"

"Use the Kindle." She rubbed behind his ears.

The three came in, "Come on, we have a special present for you."

"Why did you do this?" she looked at Skyler, then Landon, and then focused on Chad.

"It's your birthday, and we're in a ridiculous quarantine, and we are planning the destruction of the

Gnetgnu, while bringing peace to the Quarternewt..." Landon was babbling.

Skyler slowly reached her hand over his mouth, "How about it's your birthday, and we got you a gift."

"Who told you it was my birthday?"

"It was on your channel from last year. Caleb gave you a birthday present, and you used the immersion blender in the episode," the Mustleknapp said.

"You told them?" She looked confused.

"Yeah." He smiled back. Chad was fuming on the inside.

"Thank you," she looked into his eyes, "Thank you to all of you," she said to the group, blushing. She opened the box and pulled out a replica of herself, "You had a custom action figure of me made?"

They all smiled, "It looks too much like you."

"It eerily does…OMG, this is amazing as fuck!" she squealed. She manipulated the movement of the figure and couldn't stop laughing at how close it resembled her. "Thank you." They all hugged her.

The Mustleknapp quickly scurried to her satchel and took out an odd-looking metal orb. "I made you this," he held up for her.

"Boo, you didn't have to do that!"

"I wanted to."

"What is it?"

"A puzzle orb."

"What's a puzzle orb?"

"The tradition of the Mustleknapp, the significance remains a mystery to our people." Landon picked it up, "This is much heavier than I thought."

"The whole thing is forged from Fluctotious on my planet, but I settled for steel on this one."

"Where did you find steel?"

"Scrap yard."

"How did you weld it?"

"The heat from my tail."

"I think it's beautiful." Skyler stared at the design. It was so intricate, almost as if M.C. Esher's Relativity concept was recreated in orb form.

"So, how do I open it?" Hyacinth found it just as fascinating and couldn't wait to open it. "You need to figure that out. Think of it as a tangible riddle."

She placed her hand over the first layer, and then it trickled downward. The separate layer sprang up, revealing two possible paths to continue tracing, "Whoah!"

"Told you." The Mustleknapp smiled.

"Thank you," she kissed him on his head. She went over to Skyler and kissed her cheek.

"What was that for Buzzy Buzzerson?"

"You bought me a doll…I know they freak you out."

"It's not a doll, it's an action figure." She clarified, giggling.

"Dolls freak you out?" Chad asked, confused.

"Specifically, sleeping porcelain baby dolls," Skyler tried to laugh it off.

"Those things are creepy as fuck, they look like dead babies." Landon snarled in disgust. "Exactly!" Skyler's eyes widened.

"No matter, I still appreciate that you did this, out of your comfort zone for me."

"I'd do anything for you." She wrapped her arms around Hyacinth.

The Mustleknapp looked slightly jealous, and Chad seized the chance, "Group hug." The four embraced and the Mustleknapp twitched his tail in anger.

"Who wants to go for a late-night swim?" Skyler asked. "I'm down…" Landon said.

"Count me in," the Mustleknapp quickly exited the door. They could all here him jump in belly flop style.

"We'll catch up," Chad said as he carefully grabbed Hyacinth's hand.

While Skyler and Landon got changed, Hyacinth and Chad started cleaning up the kitchen. She took the lemon bars and cut a tiny bite-sized piece, and as Chad turned around, she put it in his mouth and smiled. She got powdered sugar on his lip, wiped it with her thumb, and then placed the sugar on her tongue, "Thanks for helping to clean up."

"Sure thing." He was stunned, her eyes were so beautiful that he felt sheer arousal from watching her lick the sugar off her thumb. She went over to the bottle of limoncello and had another shot, "Hy, slow down."

"It's my birthday."

"You weren't going to tell us," he said slightly seriously.

"No, I wasn't." She answered honestly, candidly, the way she was, as always.

"Why?" he sounded almost hurt.

She was confused by his feelings about her not directly telling him it was her birthday, "It's not important to me..."

"It is to your friends, the Mustleknapp, and me."

"Why is my birthday important to you?" She rolled her eyes.

Skyler and Landon walked out and heard the attitude in her voice, and watched her fold her arms at him, "Again?"

"Get out now, go, go, go..." The two ran past to get away from yet another Hyacinth and Chad drama scene.

"Do I matter to you?" Chad asked. "Cliff..."

"And can you, for once, call me Chad?"

"Why?"

"Because that's my name..."

"Chad," she said, annoyed. "I'm working on the teasing thing, but you know you set yourself up, and I just seize the opportunity."

"You know how I feel about you, and you constantly push me away."

"You don't know me!" She went running into her room, and he blocked her, "Don't think I won't send you flying across this room. You know I can."

"I know you can kill me in less than 30 seconds, but you won't."

"You really wanna test that theory when I'm pissed at you?"

"Why are you pissed at me?"

"Because you're pushing the issue again."

"What issue?"

"You're trying to take you and me to the next level."

"Because we are the next level, and you just keep pushing it away."

"I'm not pushing anything away…I'm just…"

"Hy, why didn't you tell me about your brother? Why didn't you tell me you dropped out of school?"

"Why does that matter?"

"Because it kind of uncovers why you're such a closed-off bitch!"

"Shut the fuck up!"

"I will always tell you the truth and how I feel!"

"Fine, that doesn't mean I have to give a shit about it!"

"You know you love me!"

"Don't force those words out of my mouth!"

"I don't, the way you feel does!"

She pushed him with both hands. He flew into the air and landed on the sofa with a loud thud. He flew into the air and landed on the couch with a loud thud. He sighed and winced in pain. "Chad!" she ran over to him quickly and realized she knocked the wind out of him, "I…I…"

"Get away from me," he said between clenched teeth.

"I didn't…I was…No, I didn't mean for this to happen!" she went to reach for him, and he pushed her hand away.

"I don't care anymore…" He stood slowly, wincing in pain. "Chad, no…please…I…" she held back tears.

"I am not your punching bag…" He turned away from her and slammed the door to the pool house.

She could hear him start up his Jeep, she felt awful for once. She pushed him away, again, and she knew it was because he knew how she really felt about him. She sat on the couch and pulled her knees up to her chest. She heard the door open and lifted her face slightly. A wet Landon in a towel came into the pool house. He took a bowl of strawberries out of the fridge and then grabbed the Limoncello. "While the three of us are having a great time celebrating your birthday, you look miserable."

"Then I'm glad you're all happy." She squeaked out, feeling awful about Chad and how she reacted to her realization that she loved him. She didn't want to love him…she didn't want to love, she didn't want anything ever again, and it was only after he turned away from her how hurt she felt without him. She longed for his touch; she wanted to laugh when he bit his lips. She wanted to try to touch his arms. She wanted to pretend to be mad when he took her hand. All she wanted was to hold him close to her and revel in how he loved her, unlike anyone she had ever met.

Landon tilted his head, "What did you do?"

"I pushed him away again."

"Figuratively or physically?"

"Both…"

"Hy, you need to remember how powerful you are. You forget that you're strong, like freaky strong."

"I know, but…"

"You need to channel the strength from your physical body to your emotional self."

"What if I can't?" She stared at him with tears in her eyes.

"Then maybe that's the bigger issue, the bigger problem, the one you actually want to push away."

"Did you learn that in therapy?" She hated it when another person spoke reality to her.

"Yeah, I did; everyone should have a therapist. They help, have you ever seen one?"

"Just the one Caleb made me talk to after everything,"

"Does Caleb know about your brother?"

She thought, "No, he only knows about my mother and Chrysanthemum, I never told him I had a brother…"

"And what does that tell you?"

"More than I want to admit."

"Because you need to heal from that pain before you're ready to share it with another."

"The man I was going to marry knew nothing about me beneath the surface."

"Because you hid it, kept it there, and he was so surface, he didn't dig to find it."

"What does that make me?"

"Guarded?"

"I guess…"

"I think you weren't meant for Caleb."

"How do you figure?"

"You've told more about yourself to me, Sky, Chad, and even the Mustleknapp, ten times what you've told Caleb…I think you saw something and wanted to play pretend, but we bring you to reality."

"We never saw reality until we all came back."

"That I know."

"Are you happy now?"

"Very." He smiled sweetly, "I can't thank you enough for forging us into a unit. We all belong together."

"How is that possible?"

"You don't need to understand how something works to know that it does…"

"Thanks Landon."

"Take a minute, come on and swim, it's a beautiful night, and it's your birthday."

"I'll be there soon."

She took out her phone, she wanted to call Chrysanthemum, she wanted to call Caleb, but neither of them wanted her. She could try and call her mother, but she doubted she knew who she was anymore, let alone when or where she was. It was then she realized why she really wanted to call them, she wanted an aversion from her desire to call Chad and beg him to come back to her, tell him the truth.

She wanted to feel comforted, but she was alone. Abruptly her mind stopped in its tracks…she wasn't alone, she had Skyler, Landon, the Mustleknapp, and if she would stop fighting herself she could be with Chad. She finally texted him, "If I asked you to come back, would you?"

He didn't answer her, she knew it was delivered, but the little bubbles that implied someone was responding didn't appear. She went into her room, she didn't want to put on her bikini and swim, she didn't want to do anything. She cried alone on her bed, tears running down her face. She buried her face in her pillow, and wished she could melt into a small puddle and sink within the Earth and be forgotten by everyone and everything, forever gone, spread so thin beneath the Earth that no one would notice her gone.

She heard the front door open and assumed they were done with their moonlight swim, and she listened to a gentle knock on her door. She slowly got up from her bed and wiped her eyes, which were-bloodshot from crying. She opened her door expecting Skyler, and there was Chad. "You came back?" she sounded shocked, relieved, and terrified at the moment.

"I made you a promise: I will always come back for you," he said, then he leaned down and kissed her

forehead.

"I am horrible to you."

"I know." He let out an awkward laugh.

"I lost my temper, I do *not* want to hurt you."

"Physically or emotionally?"

"Either." She slowly touched up and down his arms, fighting her emotions. "All I want, is to make you happy."

"I'm too messed up to deserve to be happy."

"I don't believe that." He took his one hand and placed it on her cheek, she cradled toward him as he ran his thumb back and forth on her cheek.

"I do,"

"Then we need to work on fixing that because you do deserve to be happy," he ran his fingers through her hair.

"No, I really don't…I'm far too selfish."

"Who told you that?"

"Reality."

"I disagree, you're stubborn, and you're judgmental, very sarcastic, and you don't know how to always empathize with others…"

"This pep talk is not helping." She turned away from him.

"Why can't you admit that you want me?" He gently placed his hands on her shoulders.

"Stop it." She placed her hands upon his, hoping they would never let her go.

"I know why."

"Why, then?" She snapped, she spun around facing him, pushing his hands away, then tugged on her own hair, "College educated, super smarter than me, retired at the age of 30 computer genius! Why?" Her voice grew louder with each utterance.

"Because you love me." He smiled slightly, because he knew it, it was confirmed in this moment seeing her reaction.

The fear choked her worse than a Quarternewt, "Stop it!"

"I know it, everyone else knows it, that's why the Mustleknapp is so jealous of me, because he can never have you in the capacity that I can."

"Stop…" she shook her head trying to deny what was in front of her.

"I care about you, and I want to know everything, and be your everything, and it scares you, because the last time you thought you could love, he went crazy and abandoned you when you needed him the most."

"How do you know all this?" she looked up at him hurt, for her she wasn't thinking about Caleb.

He cradled her face, "Because somewhere in all of this madness, I found in you what I've needed my whole life," he leaned down to kiss her forehead and she shot her face up and kissed him on the mouth.

His eyes widened in shock. "What are you doing?"

"What a Cliff thing to say."

"What?"

"You're talking to me about how you feel about me, and why won't I just admit that I love you, and yet you're shocked I kissed you?"

"I wasn't expecting…" He stumbled in how to react.

She leaned up and kissed him again, and he fully reciprocated, and ran his fingers through her hair with one hand and touched the small of her back with the other.

"Hy…"

"Shhh…" she kissed him again, and then wrapped her arms around his shoulders. "Hy, stop."

"Why?" she kept kissing him as did he, too weak to stop, needing her touch, excited that she was finally going to admit that she wanted him.

"Not like this," he protested while she kissed him again and now she ran her fingers through his hair as he moaned.

"Don't you want me?" She kissed him harder and gently bit his bottom lip.

"I do...you have no idea…" He absorbed her insecurities at every turn to continue to be close to her, how every moment with her brought meaning into his world, she was his reason for breathing every morning, for researching every possibility to get back to the Gnetgnu to fulfill her desire for revenge.

"Then why?" she looked confused, if he wanted her and she wanted to reciprocate, why didn't he seize this opportunity when she was vulnerable? She was finally willing to admit everything to him.

"You're emotionally charged up, you've been drinking, and I want so much more than just a birthday hook-up." His expression was serious, very un-Cliff of him.

"What do you want?" She shook her head confused.

"I want you." He took her hands and kissed them both, "So much more than just the physical you...I want to know the origin story of the Prophet Warrior. I want to tell you about me, and then we need to be serious about where we want this to go...because I know what I want, but I wish I knew what you

want..."

"I don't get it, I'm practically throwing myself at you, and you're rejecting me?"

"No, not at all."

"I don't understand."

"I want more than just sex."

"What's your endgame?" She asked suspiciously.

"After we get back, there's only one future I want."

"And what is that?" she sniffled, she looked down, she lost any hope that he wanted her. "Me and you together...forever." He cupped her face and she looked at him with disbelief. "But I'm..." she shook her head.

"Hy, you have some serious baggage you need to handle, and I will be there with you, I will stand beside you through quarantine and back, to another planet so you can have your revenge. But when the dust settles on all of that, I can't see myself going back to my old life, because the only life I see, is with you and me together."

"But I'm so fucked up!"

"You have a past, we all do, and yours is filled with pain, and I will not leave you because of what you tell me!" He leaned down and kissed her mouth, and she ran her fingers over his face while she kissed back.

She couldn't contain her emotion and started to cry again. He held her close to his chest, and she held him tight, "You'd rather listen to my emotional baggage than have sex with me?"

"I don't want a hook up from you, I want a mutual relationship with you, where you love me, because I love you." She stared at him and then placed her hand on his cheek, he smiled staring at her, "Open your heart, let it all out, I'm not going anywhere."

"My big brother killed himself when I was seventeen, he was my world, the only one who understood me, the only one who cared if I was around. *He* abandoned me when I needed him the most." She sniffled, "My mother had a stroke when I was sixteen that's why I had to drop out of school, what pushed Rowan over the edge. Rowan is so much more than a tree…he was my big brother, my protector, and he killed himself while I was left to rot…still want this nonsense?" She went to pull away, and he held her closer.

"I want you, always…"

"I don't understand why!"

"You don't need to understand why I need you, but I do, and I appreciate you for sharing that with me."

He slowly ran his fingers up and down her back while she held him close to her.

"I abandoned my family…I don't deserve to be happy."

"What family did you abandon? Like a kid or something?"

"No, my mother and sister, I was never right after my father left us, I wasn't emotionally connected to either of them. I can't remember if I was like that before he left or after, Rowan was my protector, my everything, he was the only family I ever loved, the only one who understood me, and I would fall asleep in his arms, and then he'd carry me into my bed…I'd awake every morning angry he put me back in my place, and I'd run to his room and jump on him and he'd tickle me till I couldn't breathe…then he'd make my breakfast, and take me to school…and when our mother fell apart…when everything went to shit… he fucking left me!"

"That actually explains a lot," he said sarcastically.

"And now I'm done talking." She turned to walk away.

"Dish it out but just can't take it?" He held her close, and then kissed her mouth. "I guess so."

"How old were you, when your father left?"

"I don't remember, I think I was 5."

"And your mother had a stroke?"

"And after my brother killed himself, she tried to kill herself, and she messed herself up pretty bad. Taking care of her was our job. But when Rowan killed himself, her care became Chrys's job, and I had to work every day all day. I was losing my sanity. Every day was more misery for all of us. When I was 18, I ran away from them. It was the only way I could see myself having my own life, the way Rowan always told me I should…it was wrong to do that to them…"

"That doesn't mean you don't deserve to be happy."

"I don't deserve anything…"

"I disagree."

"Why are you looking at me like that?"

"You know how I feel…how do you feel?"

"Confused."

"How do I confuse you? I'm nothing but forward with you, and how I feel about you…"

"*You* don't confuse me, *I* confuse me." She clarified.

"Because you feel guilt?"

"It's a weird kind of guilt."

"Help me understand."

"Like I shouldn't be happy, because I left them in misery."

"You are the controller of your own life."

"That's what I always tried to believe, but every time I think I'm happy something catastrophic happens!"

"Like what?"

"Appendicitis! Infected wisdom tooth! Being abducted! A fucking pandemic!… You… Fuck you!… You look at me like I could finally be happy!" She pushed him away and shook her head as she spouted off each answer.

"Because I am going to make you happy!" He followed her closely.

"Stop saying that?" she shook her head back and forth, "Because I don't get the happy ending!"

"Of course you do, because we both deserve a chance at happiness!" He grabbed her and held her close.

"You torture me."

"How?"

"I see you, and I feel…"

"You deserve this!"

"But I abandoned her!"

"Your sister?"

"I betrayed her the same way Rowan betrayed me."

"No, you lived, there's a big difference."

"It's hard to describe our dynamic together…"

"Try?"

"We were never close, I never looked at her like she was my sister, she always said I was the downfall…I never understood what that meant as a child."

"But now?"

"Part of me wonders, if she blamed me for him leaving…I called her when I got back from the planet."

"And?"

"She hates me…and she's allowed to. I question her loyalty to our mother constantly."

"Why is that?"

"She always said to my mother that children weren't Pokemon cards and she didn't have to catch them all…I never understood that."

"Siblings are complicated…"

"Do you have brothers or sisters?" She looked up at him and tilted her head to the side.

"I have a brother,"

"Is his name Kyle?" she asked with a devilish smirk on her face. "No!" he rolled his eyes at her, "His name is Brad."

She started to laugh, "Chad and Brad?"

"Stop it!" he laughed too.

"It's just so you, Cliff."

"Is it?"

"Yeah," she pulled him close to her and kissed him again. "Why is it so easy to feel this way about you?"

"Because we're meant to be, but you want to punish yourself."

"You're sure you don't want to take this to the next level?"

"We'll get there…" he kissed her and couldn't help but smile.

"Come on, let's go swimming." She pulled off her shirt and her bra in one motion, she took his hand and placed it on the center of her chest, "Help me?"

"You're such a tease…"

"I'm not a tease, I'm all for seeing this through, you're the tease, telling me how much you want me and then saying we need to wait."

He ran his hand down her bare back and then kissed her neck, "Don't misunderstand me, I want the physical you like you would not believe, but before I enjoy that part," he kissed her neck again, and ran his hand over her bottom, "I want the emotional you, because I have never wanted to be closer to another person more than with you. I want to understand what makes you act the way you do. You are the other half of my being, and I will wait until we are ready, to physically combine our beings."

"Why don't you speak like this all the time?"

"Maybe I do, but you don't hear me?"

"Chad," she whispered, and he reached down and kissed her. She ran her fingers up his shirt to touch his bare skin.

"You have no idea how hard this is."

"I have an idea," she grazed between his legs.

"That's not what I meant." He smiled. Then he walked over to the top drawer of her dresser and took out her bikini, he slowly placed it on her and tied it in place. He took down her pants and got down on his knees, and kissed below her bellybutton as he pulled up her bikini bottom. He stood and then gently smacked her bottom and she laughed.

He went into his room and changed. When he returned, he quickly grabbed her and threw her over his shoulder so they could join their friends in the pool. He threw her in, quickly and then jumped in. She saw her Boo and swam over and gave him a look, "And…"

"Has the drama llama made its way back into the bitter barn?" The Mustleknapp asked his Bae. "Yes."

"Good, keep it that way!" He smacked his tail in the water and splashed her.

"You are so dead." She swam after him and dunked him under. When he submerged he went after her and pulled her under the water.

Once they reached the bottom of the pool she was confused, she wasn't scared, she stared into his eyes, and he smiled. Then he touched their noses together, and they closed their eyes, and he projected into her mind the Strythocket Hills, the seven moons, and the orange stars against the indigo sky. There was a shell around the two of them, keeping them as intimate as possible. He projected into her mind the first moment he saw her, she was training with Gretgen, then he showed her saying the prayer on the Strythocket Hills after she defeated the Quarternewt and him crawling into her satchel. She smiled wide and stared at him, then he grabbed her hands and brought her to the surface, she slowly opened her eyes to a confused and somewhat panicked Skyler.

"Are you okay?" Skyler swam over to them.

"Yeah." She was fine; she was still smiling from the image he had shown her. The three stared at her confused, "What's going on?"

"You were down there for five minutes!"

"What?"

"Five friggin minutes!" Skyler shrieked. "Five seconds." Hyacinth clarified.

The Mustleknapp emerged from the water, went over to the side of the pool and stretched out,

Chad swam over to him, "What the fuck was that?"

"Oh, did I not mention that ability to you?" The Mustleknapp smiled sideways knowing full well what he had just done.

"That's not fair!"

"Nothing is fair in love and war."

"Stop it!"

"She's my Bae, and I gave her a gift." He started to shake the water from his fur in Chad's face. "What did you do you double crossing ass muncher?"

"And why should I tell you?"

"Because I have to keep her alive on the planet you're too much of a pussy to go back to!"

"She can now do something, no other human can do…"

"What did you do?"

"Cliff, never forget, she will always be mine!" He smiled, stood up on his hind legs and strutted his way inside.

They all stared at her, "What happened?" Skyler asked upset.

"It was amazing…it was beautiful…it was as if serenity was surrounding my whole body." Her face had never come alive with such pure happiness since any of them knew her.

"Better than sex?" Skyler asked in disbelief.

"Yeah…like ten times better than the best orgasm you've ever felt!" Hyacinth shook her head in disbelief, "In what felt like a second I have moments upon moments of beauty and silence, and just pure…joy…and it lasted far more than a second, and it never stopped!"

"That's impossible!" Landon shook his head, questioning if she wasn't just oxygen-deprived.

"I didn't know the rodent could do that," Chad said under his breath.

"Hold on!" She swam down to the bottom of the pool, and she didn't need to breathe. She closed her eyes and felt the gentle rhythm of the water, from the others wading eight feet above her. She sat on the bottom and imagined he was with her, she leaned forward and envisioned his nose leaning up against hers. From within the house, he could feel her, and he projected into her mind again. Instantly she saw clearly how to unfold her plan for revenge against the Gnetgnu. Then she saw her return with Chad, she saw Skyler and Landon's wedding day, her and the Mustleknapp gazing at the clouds eating malted milk balls, she saw everything…she grew overwhelmed with everything she saw and the feelings within her body, she eventually made her way to the surface. "How long?"

"3 minutes," Skyler said concerned.

"It was an ongoing proverbial orgasm that lasted and lasted,"

"What happened?"

"I don't need to breathe below water." Hyacinth smiled like she never had before. The sensation was unique. She couldn't describe the happiness she felt.

"What?"

"I can just go down there, and stay there…it's weird, but I can…and it feels…I can see…" She smiled wider. The gift he granted her brought her happiness that no other sensation could offer. "I saw our mission, what we need to do, I know where the speaker stones are stored." She collapsed onto Skyler who was giggling uncontrollably.

"Tell me!" Landon urged and he pulled the two of them to the shallow end to sit on the steps.

Chad immediately grew angry, he knew the Mustleknapp did this on purpose. He left the pool and went to find the Mustleknapp, but he had sequestered himself into Hyacinth's room and locked the door. "This isn't over!" He yelled at the door.

"Once you get back it will be!" The Mustleknapp threatened.

"You know something you demented little weasel!"

"I am not a weasel I'm a Mustleknapp!"

"It means you're deceitful, you literal pain!"

"I believe Hyacinth says something about masturbating when she wants someone to disappear."

"Go fuck yourself!"

"That's it!"

Chad smacked his arm on the door, "Get out here, you know more than you're telling!"

"I know everything Chad." The Mustleknapp curled into a ball on her bed. He knew something that he would never tell them, that he would never tell Chad especially, and he grew weak and emotional thinking about Hyacinth returning to his planet. "Leave me alone!"

Chad put his arm out and the Decttronium entered his body, he was about to break the door down when he heard her.

"Chad?" Hyacinth walked in with her wet hair down her face, the towel wrapped around her, he was immediately distracted, then encompassed his emotional desire into the sound of her voice, "What's going on?"

"He did that on purpose!" He pointed to the door. "What are you talking about?" She was confused. "He wants you."

"What are you talking about?"

"Hyacinth, look at me." He searched beyond her gaze, convinced he'd be able to see if the Mustleknapp had brainwashed her somehow.

"I am…you look like you're about to lose your mind, your eyes are blazing turquoise! Were you going to use the Decttronium on my Mustleknapp? Have you lost your mind?"

"He did that on purpose!" His anger increased when she referred to that miscreant as hers.

"What are you talking about?"

"He gave you something I could never give you, to have you want him more!"

"You're overreacting…"

The nonchalant attitude behind her voice infuriated him beyond what he could stomach, "There is going to come a moment where you need to make a choice, and I can't explain it, but there will, and I don't know what you're going to choose…" Against his better judgment, he released the Decttronium back into its jar and out of his system.

She ran over to him, and placed her hand on his cheek, "Look at me, what just happened?"

He saw a genuine care behind her eyes, his whole being was invigorated. "I can't stop myself, I'm jealous."

"Over my Mustleknapp?"

"Stop doing that!"

"What?"

"Calling him yours!"

"You're that level of jealous?" She raised her eyebrow at the thought.

"I can't take," he grabbed her by the waist and held her close to him, "I can't compete with the way you feel about him."

She shook her head, "Oh Cliff, really we're going there?"

"No, don't dismiss this so easily! You love him."

"Your point?" She answered without answering, it was hard for her to utter those words.

"You admit it?"

"Admit what?"

"You love the Mustleknapp?"

"Again, your point?"

"But you won't say?"

"Say what? You're acting weird."

"Why can't you love me the way you love him?" He stared at her for longer, they all knew how she felt about the Mustleknapp, that wasn't hidden on any means, and yet here she stood and all she had to do was utter the words, and yet she challenged it. Part of him thought she was more perturbed by the word itself as opposed to the concept.

She pushed up on her toes and whispered in his ear, "He's not human."

"Oh..." He took that to mean she could love the Mustleknapp without fear of ever being hurt, because they would never be together in the traditional sense. He leaned down and kissed her mouth, she feared loving him because she was vulnerable, he would prove his dedication to her, and she would love him more than she ever could a Mustleknapp, "There will come a time where you have to choose..."

"I choose to end this conversation."

"Why?"

"Didn't you not want to open up a can of worms because I'm vulnerable, I've been drinking, and it's my birthday?" She mocked him.

"Yes, but..."

"So right now, I choose to eat the rest of the leftovers, because we're all hungry." She kissed him again and then kissed down his neck and whispered in his ear, "You're the one who pumped the brakes, not me."

"Because I want to be closer to you…"

"Your jealous side is kind of sexy." She bit her bottom lip and then ran her hand down his bare chest. Skyler and Landon came crashing in, "Stop being so serious!"

"Seriously, Chad you look like you're going to burst."

"Because I'm fighting with the Mustleknapp, and he's being a douche!"

"Calm down," Hyacinth's voice was soothing, a tone she rarely used. She ran her arms around his shoulders and hugged him.

"I hate that phrase," Skyler rolled her eyes. "We know, we know," they all echoed.

"One of these days you're gonna say it again!" Landon joked.

"Not gonna happen."

"You never know," he started tickling her.

"Come on, we're all hungry, forget the Mustleknapp for right now, do you want more piccata?" Hyacinth tried her best, unsure how to quell his tension. He grabbed her by her waist and squeezed her gently, he wanted to kiss her over and over again. He smiled, then slung her on his back to carry her to the kitchen. She shared herself with him tonight, he was going to hold her all night long, and she was going to be his girlfriend and so much more. That jealous, deceitful little Mustleknapp would never get to keep her the way he could, kiss her, touch her, and be her emotional partner to start and then become her physical partner. He was going to get all of Hyacinth, the only girl of his dreams.

They all pulled the leftovers from their dinner and happily picked at the different items. Hyacinth went to grab a change of clothes from her room.

"Why is my door locked?"

"Like I said, the Mustleknapp is being a douche." Chad rolled his eyes annoyed.

She rested her ear on the door, "Boo…you okay?" she was soothing in her speech, she always provided him with every inch of her patience, unlike the rest of the world.

"I'm fine." She heard from within.

"Do you want me to come in?" She tried the door knob again, and was very upset he locked her out.

"I'll be out in a minute or more."

"Boo, you're scaring me…"

"Bae, it's all good…just need a minute, k?"

"You know why I don't like this door locked."

"Please Bae, just a minute, I'll be out soon."

"Do you want another lemon bar?"

"No, I want more soup."

"I'll heat it up for you." She heated up a portion of soup and the Mustleknapp emerged from her room, the size of a Rottweiler, which was not like him. Skyler's eyes widened and she gave Landon a look. He shrugged then looked over at Chad confused.

"Like I said, douche."

"Enough you two! Boo, you want crème fraîche on top?" she asked unmoved by his change in size.

"Please," he smiled.

She kissed the top of his head and handed him his bowl. Chad's lips tightened and he stared at the Mustleknapp as though he was going to access the Decttronium and squeeze him to death.

"Oh, this is some shit ass freaky furry drama." Landon shook his head.

"Babe, chillax dude, n-y-l!" Skyler tickled him as she shoved another bite of lemon bar in her mouth. She took the tequila off the shelf and she and Hyacinth did two shots back-to-back the way they always did.

"This is the best birthday ever, and I have you all to thank for it," Hyacinth said sappily as the tequila hit her hard.

"I love your tequila talk," Skyler laughed, and she took a third shot. "Easy!" Hyacinth took it from her and had another.

"Okay, both of you are nuts." Landon laughed and took the bottle, now he had a shot. "Coming from you, should we be insulted or complimented?" Hyacinth giggled.

Landon laughed at himself, "Complimented!"

Chad rolled his eyes, "You're all drunk." He took a shot of tequila. "I have an idea," Skyler said.

"What?" Landon smirked.

"Let's watch a movie and we'll all be together tonight…"

"Wait, what?" Hyacinth asked while laughing.

"NO! Not like that…" now she couldn't stop laughing, "I meant, let's pull out the couch, put on a movie and fall asleep together."

"I can do that." Landon laughed, the pressure of performing while this level of buzzed would be off his mind.

"All for it," Chad said staring at the Mustleknapp. "So am I," the Mustleknapp said defiantly.

While the credits rolled from the movie, they were all exhausted from drinking and swimming. Skyler was in Landon's arms, and the two passed out happily embraced with one another. Hyacinth finally understood that they were a couple. It wasn't hidden anymore, and their mutual attraction grew into something far more substantial.

Hyacinth used Chad's bicep for a pillow, and he was enamored with the feel of her body touching his, so he could feel her breathe. The only thing that annoyed him was the fact that the Mustleknapp shrank down to the size of a hamster, and curled into a ball on Hyacinth's chest, once again flaunting how close they were to one another. Chad could not deny his jealousy, but at the same time he was comforted at how he could offer her so many things the Mustleknapp never could. When the Mustleknapp got up to do his evening sweep, Chad pulled her closer and ran his fingers up and down her arm.

"Hy, can you hear me?" she didn't respond, "I love you."

She cuddled to him and then made a cute sound, "Chad, what are you doing to me?"

"What do you mean?"

"You make me want you," she wrapped her leg around him and held him close.

"I love you." He breathed in relief that he could say it to her so easily. He had known for a while, and saying it gave him a certain level of comfort.

"And so it goes." She whispered.

"What?"

"That's the song I sing to myself about you."

"What are you talking about?" he was confused, she was definitely buzzed, he couldn't tell if she passed that stage and into drunk.

She smiled, and she sang/spoke, "When we get back…*So I would choose to be with you, that's if the choice were mine to make, but you can make decisions too…and you can have this heart to break.*" She collapsed on his chest.

He smiled wide, he wanted nothing more than to kiss her, but she was clearly out, and he was content in being by her side. "1 choose to be with you…I will always come back for you." He held her tight, she was too important, too everything, and he needed her.

THIRTEEN

Hyacinth walked into the pool house with two bags of groceries, she went over to the kitchen as the Mustleknapp emerged from the bedroom the size of a house cat.

"Did you get it?"

"Of course I did. I always take care of you, Boo!" she reached into the bag and tossed him the malted milk balls he requested.

"That I know, doesn't mean Trader Joe's always supplies my fix."

She giggled, "And how's the crack today?"

He took one out and devoured it, "These are so friggin good."

"If you find me an 80's song about sugar or milk, I'll feature them in an episode, and I'll make malted milk ball shakes, fudge, cookies, and then use them in a mole sauce on steak."

"I'm on it," he scurried over to her, grabbed her phone out of her back pocket, smacked her backside with his tail, and went into their room to research the song.

She kept putting groceries away when Landon and Chad came back in after spending two hours at the gym. Chad smiled seeing her in the kitchen, he went up behind her and started kissing the back of her neck. "What are you doing?" she asked playfully.

"Nothing." He smiled as he kissed down her neck. "Stop…" she giggled, she didn't want him to stop.

"Never," he ran his hand down her side and then pulled her hips back toward him. She giggled again, and then let out a sigh of satisfaction, "Take a shower."

"I will…" he kissed her again, "Can we spend more time together tonight?" He asked hopefully.

"Where you ask me personal questions and I answer or where you finally throw me down and fuck me?"

"The former."

"Tonight." She rolled her eyes.

"I can't wait." He kissed her neck a few more times, ran his fingers through her hair then went to his room to change and shower from working out.

Skyler came into the room wearing a very low cut halter top and Landon's eyes looked like a cartoon character, "Hey, Babe." She smiled at him and winked as she walked into the kitchen.

"Skyler, what are you wearing?" he could barely keep the saliva in his mouth.

"My new outfit, what do you think?" She turned around and the shorts she wore were cut high enough half of her behind was exposed.

"I think after I shower, I may have a heart attack." He walked over and kissed her cheek, "I missed you, Baby Girl." He kissed her again.

"I'll take that as you approve…"

"Provided we're the only ones…"

"It's quarantine, where the fuck am I going?" She kissed him hard, and he grabbed her backside and even though his eyes were closed, he still rolled them in the back of his eyes at the touch of her.

"You are amazing…"

"And guess who gets to have me at the beginning and end of every day," She teased him as she twitched her nose.

"I'm the luckiest man alive," he kissed her again, then left to shower.

Skyler couldn't wipe the smile off her face, then she looked over at Hyacinth and asked, "Are you sure we need to go back?"

"What do you mean?"

"Aren't you happy?"

"No…" she lied quickly. "I'm happy…"

"I can see that." Hyacinth busied herself putting away the groceries, she shook her head thinking about how over the top Skyler and Landon were, but then again Skyler was eccentric, she never hid that about herself. She wondered if she and Chad looked as lovey dovey as they did. She quickly pushed the thought aside, for the first time in what felt like an eternity she was looking forward to feeling the way she felt around Chad, and the way he kissed her made her melt on the inside.

"Seriously, what if we just let it go?" Skyler could see Hyacinth's mind wandering, and she was hopeful it walked far enough to agree with her.

"Then another human will be abducted, another defenseless Quarternewt slaughtered, we have to do this, stop them from hurting anymore of us."

"Why don't I believe you?"

"Mostly because I'm lying about my true motivation."

"There it is." Skyler rolled her eyes.

"Those ideals are still true, wouldn't you prevent another person from going through the insanity of thinking you're crazy when you're not?"

"Not if it meant losing Landon!"

Hyacinth laughed, "You're in love with Landon…this is more than just getting some!"

"Yes! Okay! Yes, I am in love with him…I don't want to lose that."

"You won't…"

"How can you know?"

"I saw it…"

"What?"

"Never mind, we are coming back, all four of us, and then the two of you can ride off in the sunset and be blissfully happy knowing the planet is restored to balance and no unsuspecting human will be targeted again."

"Tell me right now why you really want to go back."

Hyacinth tensed her shoulders and jutted out her jaw. "You don't want to know."

"Either you tell me, or I wrap you in a bubble of Septtronium and entrap it in the floor boards until you talk…" Skyler was serious.

"Stooping so low to use powers in the house and threaten me simultaneously?"

"It's not a threat. It's a warning, tell me!"

"I'm going to kill Jom with my bare hands for lying to all of us. That's what I want, what I'm in love with, and what I'm doing this for, for *me*."

"That is extremely selfish of you!"

"Have I ever hidden that from you?"

"No, but you're willing to jeopardize our lives so you can get what you want."

"I never sugar-coated any of this. Besides, you'll all be protected. You'll have your elements."

"That doesn't mean that we don't risk something happening to one of us!"

"Jom is going to die by my hands, and I am going to laugh manically, and that is that!"

"But look at what Jom has given us!"

"What has Jom given us other than lies and betrayal?"

"Each other!"

"His optimism has worn off on you!"

"Like your cynicism hasn't?"

"Look, I am very grateful that we are all together, but how many more lives will they destroy?"

"We can be like a rehab, we can find them and…"

"Stop it! If you want to back out of the mission because you're having second thoughts, then that's fine, but I am going back…with or without you…with or without any of you." She slammed the fridge shut and ran out the front door.

"Hy!" Skyler went to the door, but would never be fast enough to catch her. She debated summoning the Septronnium and going after her. She shook her head, she knew it would end with Hyacinth shutting down and them getting nowhere in this debate. She knew that even if Hy was being selfish, it was irrelevant; the bottom line was they needed to stop the abductions, they were the only ones who could.

The Mustleknapp scurried out of their room, roughly the size of a ferret, and jumped onto the island, "I found a song!" he called out. He shook his head back and forth, "Where's Hy?"

"I upset her…"

"Did she run?"

"Yep…"

"What did you do?" The Mustleknapp asked seriously.

"Suggested we don't go back." She held her arm out, and he climbed up and wrapped his tiny arms around her.

"While I would love that, you know she can't let it go."

"But why risk it?"

"Even though she's doing this for her revenge, she makes a point, you could stop abductions."

Skyler bowed her head, "She always says she's selfish, but I'm selfish, too. I'm happy with Landon. I want to stay here and swim, have her cook, and all of us just be…"

"And we will…after you all come back."

Skyler cuddled him closely and scratched behind his ears, "Coming from the only one not having to go back."

"Oh, please, you know as well as I do, you are going to fill your body and your satchel with as much Septtronium as you can muster."

"Fuck yeah I am." She finally smiled.

Chad walked in, with his perfect hair, his perfect everything, but the light behind his eyes dropped when he didn't see Hyacinth in the kitchen. "What's going on?"

"Nothing, go back to your room and stay out of my sight for a day!" the Mustleknapp sneered, his body grew stiff beneath Skyler's grip.

"Fuck you, you knock off Furby!" Chad shook his head, "Where is she?"

"I upset her." Skyler confessed, "I asked if perhaps we didn't go back and just stayed here."

"You know she can't have that."

"I know, but…I thought for a second that maybe…"

"I'll find her," Chad said as he walked out the door, but not before holding his arm out so the Decttronium could bond with his body.

"She needs her space, leave her…" The Mustleknapp went to go after him, and Chad used the Decttronium to push him backward. The Mustleknapp flew through the air and landed on her bed.

Skyler put her hands out, and the Septtronium bonded with her body. "Don't you dare!" she moved the element backward and shut the door to the bedroom, "Don't hurt him because you're jealous!"

"You know he's hoping I don't make it back." The turquoise behind his eyes grew more profound as his anger grew.

"That's not true." She quickly put her bubble around herself. Both their emotions were heightened, giving their powers a surge of supremacy.

"It's true; ask him, he won't lie to you, he'll duck the question," Chad spit the words at her.

She turned her head with an attitude, "You know she loves me too. Are you going to throw me across the room?"

"You're not deceitful like he is."

"He's not deceitful if it wasn't for him…"

He interrupted, matching her attitude, "If it wasn't for him, she'd never know where the speaker stones are, or how to summon the portal!"

"You don't want to go back either?" Her expression softened as she stared through his eyes into his soul.

"Other than bonding with the Dectrronium to full capacity, no I don't."

"Then why?"

"You know why…" Chad stormed out.

She removed her bubble, took out her Xanax, and swallowed it dry. She opened the fridge to find Hyacinth's freshly squeezed orange mango juice that she loved. She poured herself a glass and shook her head. "Why can't we just be happy?" she wanted Hyacinth to fall in love with Chad and the four of them to enjoy these moments together. It was summer, and they all could eat, sleep, swim, and stop focusing on the pandemic or the planet that robbed them of their minds for far too long.

After his shower, Landon walked out into the living room and noticed her eyes were once again deep blue. "What's going on? Baby Girl, are you okay?" He was upset to see her this way.

"I don't want to go back."

"Why not?"

"Because what if I lost you?"

"We're all coming back."

"We don't know that."

"I'll make you a promise."

"You can't promise that you won't die!"

"No, but I can promise you that everything happens for a reason, and everything works out in the end."

She ran over to him and grabbed him tight. "Without you, I'll never be alright."

"Shhh…I've got you, Baby Girl." He held her and ran his fingers through her hair, "Come on, let's do something to cheer you up. Tell me what you want, and I'll give it to you…"

She smirked and bit her lip, "I want to go to the golf course in the back and play Septtronium versus Marttronium."

Landon smiled and put his arms out as the element forged with his skin, and his eyes turned from dark brown to light blue. "This is going to be fun."

"You have no idea." She formed a bubble around herself and started to run. Landon chased after her and the two made their way to play with their elements.

The Mustleknapp shook his head from landing so abruptly on the bed, he could hear the argument in the next room but ignored it. He was nervous, and he kept debating how he would sever the bond between Chad and Hyacinth once they returned. He needed him to love her to keep her as safe as possible on their journey; he knew that Chad would give his life to keep her safe. In the same thought, he feared how Hyacinth had grown attached to Chad.

She was *his* one and only. She was *his* eternal flame. He would never play second fiddle to Chad and his stupid, perfect hair. Then again, if being with Chad made her happy, that was all that mattered. Then he smirked. They had no way of getting through the portal, and they still couldn't find it. He relaxed on her pillow, taking in her scent, and he napped until she would come home again, make him delicious food to eat, and dive to the bottom of the pool with him and play the only way they could because no other human had the gift he had given her.

. . .

Chad found her sitting on the edge of Bald Mountain. She looked so beautiful, staring at the horizon's formation surrounding the most elevated place in all of Bergen County, with no fear of falling over the edge.

"Hi, beautiful," he said he didn't want to sneak up on her and scare her. He laughed to himself at the thought; he doubted anything could truly scare Hyacinth with the exception of commitment.

"I don't want to talk about it," she said without looking at him.

"You never do. That's not new, but there is something new that I can't help but smile about."

"What?" she looked at him lost.

He sat beside her, leaned over, and kissed her on the mouth. "I think that might be my favorite thing to do."

"I don't understand why."

"You don't need to know why. That's for me to know." He put his arm around her, and without consciously realizing it, she cuddled her head to his shoulder, breathed out slowly, and sighed in satisfaction, as though she had found her happy place.

They were content in silence for almost fifteen minutes before she whispered, "Will you feel sadness when I kill Jom?"

"You're doing it again." He laughed.

"And what is that?"

"Talking like a narrator or something."

She looked down, "Are you going to be mad at me when I kill him?"

"No, I won't."

"What will you feel then?" She took his hand and started to trace the lines of his palm.

"Honestly?"

"Always."

"Relieved."

"Why, because I'm stopping the corruption of an entire civilization? Putting an end to human suffering from abductions?"

"No…"

"Then why?"

"Because you will have finally ended Fernand Mondego, and I get to take you home and love you for the rest of my life."

"Cliff, you read a book for me." She smiled.

"I always have, and always will, do anything for you."

"Prove it!" She teased him.

"I already have,"

"What are you talking about?" she was confused.

"Do you remember what you told me about the location of the portal?"

"Yes."

"I wrote an algorithm and started searching geographical points, and I found a 99.9% match to the formation."

"When were you going to tell me?" She exclaimed impatiently. "I only found out after I showered, but you were already gone." She wrapped her arms around him, "I'm going to kill Jom."

"I know."

"And you love me anyway?" she clarified in such a way that she still could not believe it.

"Yes, I do."

"I'm not sure if I should be flattered or confused."

"Flattered." He kissed her again.

She stared at him, "Where is the place you found?"

"It's in Rockleigh."

"We need to show everyone."

"We will, but I need something first."

"What?" she looked at him confused. "I need to tell you something."

"You just did," she shook her head at him.

He leaned over and kissed her, "I'm in love with you, Hyacinth."

"That's a dangerous predicament to be in."

"Am I your Mercedes?"

She smiled wider, "Answer me honestly. Did you read the book, or did you watch the movie?"

He pulled up his phone and opened his Kindle app to show her. He downloaded the book and finished it. "I'm currently reading *The Wizard of Oz*...am I your Scarecrow?"

She rested her head on his shoulder. "No..."

"I'm not?" He sounded hurt.

"She says goodbye to him...I have no intention of saying goodbye to you."

He put his arm around her, "If nothing else, after all those years of suffering, I get to be here with you." She didn't want to dwell in his pathetic love story, "Come on, let's show them the location, figure out the timeline. We need to go back, stop Jom, rescue the planet."

"That's not your motivation…"

"No, but it is a realization."

"You are the leader of your own destiny, Beautiful."

"Why are you really doing this?" she looked into his eyes with a higher level of intensity than was her typical look.

"To give you what you want…because I'm in love with you, and if this will make you happy, then I will do it."

She reached into her pocket and pulled out a Cruzer Fit USB, "This is for you."

"What is it?"

"I recorded you a song, but I'm not ready for you to hear it yet."

He thought about her birthday, her drunken rambling. She didn't know he already knew, "Hy."

"When we get back, I want you to listen to it."

"But only when we get back?" he raised an eyebrow.

"I'm in love with the idea of killing Jom, and I am not in a place where I can focus on anything but that until it's over."

"You have to have your revenge, Monte Cristo."

"I do."

He leaned over and kissed her again, "So let's tell everyone what I found, so I can give you what you want…but…"

"What?" she knew where this was going.

"There's something I need first," he looked at her and smiled to the side. "What?"

"I need to kiss you…" He leaned over and kissed her. She wrapped her arms around him, kissed him harder, and slowly drew him closer to her. Her hips started to graze up on him. "I'm still not there yet," Chad said honestly.

She straddled him, "Do you want to make out with me or what?"

"I do…"

"Maybe *I* want your kiss right now."

"I will always give you what you want." And he gladly kissed her.

…

The Mustleknapp was asleep on her pillow. She smiled when she saw him and leaned over and kissed his forehead. He stirred gently.

"Hey, sleepy head."

"Where were you?"

"We showed them the location for the portal…Landon's working on the timeline right now."

"Where's Chad?"

"Working out."

"Skyler?"

"What's with the 20 questions, Boo?" she changed her clothes and brushed her hair. "Please don't go," he said seriously.

"I'm not going anywhere, my clothes were all sweaty, and my hair is frizzy as fuck."

"That's not what I meant!"

"What then?"

"Don't go back to my planet."

"I have to go." She dismissed him quickly. "No, you really don't, you really, really don't!"

"Stop." She turned away from him.

"When was the last time you checked on Caleb?"

"It's been a while."

"You're distracted…"

"Weren't you the one chastising me for going there in the first place? "

"Hy…"

"No response because you know I'm right."

"You've changed."

"I have not."

"You have, you've lost your focus."

"What makes you think that?"

"Because you're infatuated with Chad!" He slammed his fists down in anger. He would never accept them as a couple. It couldn't happen. He would get rid of Chad if he had to once they returned.

"I am not infatuated!" She brushed her hair faster and fixed it while looking at herself in the mirror.

"You love him."

"Why does everyone assume that?" She didn't stop her task. "I have eyes dumbass, you love him."

"I love the idea of killing Jom!" she slammed the brush down, and it made a clunking noise as it cracked the marble of her dresser; she clutched it tighter, surprised it was still intact, "That's what I love. That's what I have fought for, and once I have had it, I will finally know true satisfaction, and I will be able to move on with my life!"

"I disagree."

"Excuse me?"

"I think you'll kill Jom and feel nothing."

"What?"

"You will kill him, feel nothing, and your blood lust will grow until you kill more."

"Now who's sounding ridiculous?"

"You are not going to find the answers for what really bothers you by killing anything on that planet."

"Bullshit."

"Your father didn't leave because of *you*…Rowan didn't kill himself because of *you*," he said with a straight face.

"Excuse me?" Her eyes widened in anger as he knew these things.

"You heard me."

"How did you…"

"You and I are bonded. I gave you an incredible gift, and as such, I gave myself one in return."

"For someone who boasts honesty all the time, you never told me that."

"As you taught me, I just didn't show my whole palm." She rolled her eyes, "Hand," she corrected.

"Whatever, I don't lie."

"You withhold the truth, which is lying by omission and just as deceitful, you rotten little rat."

"You are walking to your own death, you selfish, suicidal little girl."

"Get out!"

"You think that getting revenge on Jom will fill the void Rowan created,"

"Shut it!"

"Your father left and you filled the emptiness with Rowan, and you made him more in your mind than anything else!"

"Shut it!" she threw her hairbrush across the room and it became lodged in the drywall.

"You wanted your revenge through Caleb, and when you realized you would never get it, you shifted your focus. You're using Jom's lie as your excuse for the ultimate revenge."

"So you're a fucking psychologist now? Did they teach you that on TikTok?"

"Restoring the planet will never restore your family!"

"I don't want them!"

"What do you want?"

"I want you to shut the fuck up!" She ran out of her room and paced in the living room. Skyler was in her studio painting her frustration, Chad was working out, and Landon was in the field using the Marttronium to find when the portal would be in the correct location, she was alone with the Mustleknapp. For the first time, she wanted to throw him across the room. She started to pace faster in the room.

He came out slowly, "Calm down…"

"Now I know why Skyler hates that phrase."

"Why?"

"Because it means nothing…"

"Am I still your chimney?" He perched on the top of the couch moving his head back and forth watching her.

"My what?"

"Conscious."

"My Jiminy and you're acting as my conscience."

"Your problems are deep-rooted,"

"You watched my pain like a documentary and didn't bother to tell me, and I'm beyond pissed at you right now."

"It was the reaction when I gave you the breathing power…would you trade it back if I didn't know?"

"I can't answer that right now."

"You don't have to go back!"

"I WANT to go back!" She stopped and stared him down, "And not because of anything that scarred my psyche because I am going to kill Jom. I'm not going to lose my sanity because of it, and I will come back here and live my life!"

"And what does that life look like?"

"I won't give you the satisfaction of knowing my future; you know my past, and that's enough."

"You don't see yourself coming back."

"Yes, I do!"

"You saw Landon and Skyler; you saw me and you, but that was a memory, not a projection. You saw everyone return, except you."

"You can't see yourself, a projection's not a fucking mirror."

"That's why you're okay with going back because if you don't survive, you won't feel remorse."

"What do you know of remorse?"

"I have remorse for abandoning my planet, my species, but I know that this is the right path for me."

"And this is the right path for me!"

"No, it's a path you want for you."

"Stop it!"

"Just stay!"

"No, I know how to get there, and I am going."

She went to leave. She didn't know where she would go, but she wanted to be away from him, he yelled over to her, "There is something I have to give you before you go."

"Then give it to me so I can leave here."

"I will, but I need a ride."

"Where?"

"Your apartment."

"Fine, if that'll get you away from me!"

"It will, I don't know if I can stand being here these next few days."

"What?"

"I…"

"Shut the fuck up, get in the back seat of the car. If you so much as make a sound I will turn around and you can go wherever you like, and I will never care again."

They drove in silence. There were several moments where he thought he wanted to say something, but seeing her face, he knew she meant what she said. Her threat would be real. Typically, she'd grab him and place him in her arms or her satchel. This time, she left the door open and waited for him to emerge. She grabbed him by the back of his neck and carried him as if he indeed was a rat. He felt foolish and was angered at her handling him in such a way. Then he took a deep breath and reminded himself that he had upset her, and she truly was hurt at his realization.

Once they entered the apartment, she dropped him at her side without looking at him. She looked around the apartment as if she hadn't been there in years. Everything seemed to look the same. The Mustleknapp immediately went to the top of her cabinets and into the ventilation system. She saw the laundry basket outside Caleb's door, fuller than it had been.

"Worthless little baby," she muttered. She walked over and placed it on her hip; she didn't bother to knock on the door or say a word to Caleb. She routinely made her way down to the laundry room. She went back upstairs and dusted the apartment. Then she cleaned the kitchen; it hadn't been used since she left, the only thing she noticed was the abundance of takeout boxes. She walked them downstairs to the dumpster. She didn't put a mask on, and as Mr.

Kim walked in he rolled his eyes at her.

"Hy, where you been?"

"Oh, um, Caleb and I broke up."

"What?"

"Yeah, um, I'm just here to clean out some things, and yeah."

"I so sorry honey, um…put on your mask."

"No, I'm good, thanks; if you're worried, then you should stay away from me, apparently I'm poison," she could hear him talking to her, but she didn't process the words or think about it too deeply, she went upstairs.

She walked into the kitchen and traced the symbol she etched into the kitchen cabinets, "Why did you take me? What was it about me? Why did you do this to me?" She punched the cabinet, and it broke easily. She shook her head and kicked the piece on the ground. It bounced off the fridge, and she had to jump up to avoid it smacking into her shin. "There are billions, why us? Why did you do this to us?" She shook her head and purposefully arched her back to stop a tear from falling.

"Why did you keep Landon for so long? Skyler for so short? Of all the pretty boys in the world why did you pick Chad? Why…"

"I have to be honest with you," The Mustleknapp came down from the top of the cabinets.

"What?" the adoration that once lit up her smile in his presence dissipated quickly.

"I have something that belongs to you, and I don't think it does what you were told it does, but I want you to have it, just in case it does something."

"What is it?" she didn't look at him, part of her didn't care. He held out her core piece, "I grabbed it in the portal."

"You've had this the whole time?" She was angry with him, she felt betrayed yet again.

He nodded his head yes as she took it, "I hold it close and it makes me think of you, and how I want more than anything to be human, so I can be with you. I want you to kiss me the way you kiss Chad. You're my eternal flame, Bae."

Tears dripped from her eyes and her anger melted, she stared at him and couldn't help but immediately forgive him, "Then you hold onto it for me, and when I get back, give it to me then."

"This is not the thing that will travel the portal, that was a lie they told you."

"I know, but if you've had this the whole time, and it brings you comfort, then you hold onto it, and

when I come back…"

"You're not coming back!" he slammed his paws down in frustration, "Don't you see that?"

"I don't believe that!"

"Well I do, and I need space away from you, because you can't see how I feel, and how scary this is for me." He placed her core piece in her hand, "My core piece keeps me safe, and keeps me alive."

"Your core piece came out when I resuscitated you."

"That is the first time that has ever happened, which is how I know we're meant to be together."

"How?"

"You already know, you're my match, my core piece wanted to be within us both simultaneously."

"No, I blew into your mouth and it popped out."

"But when I'm close to you, I feel it move."

"You never told me that."

"I just did."

"I *will* bring this back to you."

"But not the way I want…" He thought about holding her core piece.

"What?"

"If I were human, would you kiss me?"

She leaned down and kissed the top of his head, "You don't have to be human for me to kiss you."

"No, I meant really kiss me…like you did that night."

"I didn't kiss you! I gave you mouth to mouth resuscitation." She took her core piece and tied it around her neck.

He increased his size until he was the size of Chad. He concentrated harder than before and flattened his paws so they were closer to hands. He morphed his body as best he could, he looked half human and half Mustleknapp. He stared at her desperately, and wished she was his wife, "What about now?"

"How did you do that?" she was overwhelmed.

He leaned over and kissed her mouth, "I will find a way to be human for you."

"Mustleknapp, you can't…"

"You're my eternal flame, and we were meant to be together."

"Mustleknapp…" she looked down.

He sang to her in a gentle tone that was balanced and melodic, she was captivated, "*I believe it's meant to be darling, I watch you when you are sleeping, you belong with me, do you feel the same, am I only dreaming or is this burning an eternal flame.*"

"I didn't know you could sing like that…" she whispered.

"If I was human, who would you choose?" He slowly brushed her hair back.

"What?"

"If I was human…who would you choose, me or Chad?"

"You're not human; maybe that's why it is so easy for me to love you so much."

He kissed her again, then wrapped his tail around her, there was a heat that surged through her body and she let out a slight gasp and when she opened her eyes, she stared at him. He whispered, "I know your life, now you know mine." He had transferred everything to her, she knew everything about the Mustleknapp, their prophecies, their instincts, he gave it all to her. She saw her death, as he viewed it, and it frightened her. She backed away from him.

"Why would you show me that?" She saw a horrific golden light, and her whole being torn to pieces as she screamed in agony falling to the floor of the great hall, tears involuntarily fell from her eyes, her whole body torn asunder.

"Because maybe now you'll stay!"

"It's not real…it's not!" She shook her head, the future was never solid, perhaps this stood a chance to change.

"Bae, look at me." He held his paw-like hand out to her, but she didn't take it. She was coughing and choking from her own hysterics, she shook her head repeating the word *no.* He had to go over and grab her and breathe with her to calm her down. He kissed the back of her neck, over and over again. Each time he did, he sighed, sounding human, and then she made a soft gentle noise of enjoyment, and with each additional kiss they grew slightly louder. "I love you," He held her closer, "I am going to be human someday…but only for you, and when you die, I will die."

"I refuse to die like that!"

"That's what's been…"

She interrupted him, "I am different! I am not a prophecy; I am so far beyond your tales…"

"How?"

"I don't know, I just know."

"You can't change…"

"You were next in line to lead the Mustleknapp."

"You had a clone to take your place, I have one to take mine, I have no desire to lead that planet."

She breathed as though she would pass out, he held her tighter, "I'm not going to stop until I have killed Jom! Your predictions are not absolute, they are mere calculations, but even the most powerful statistic can be wrong! Don't leave me now! Change the image and come with me!" She held him as tight as her arms would allow, and he delighted in her touch.

"I was meant to be here, on this planet, with you…I am going to be human, and we will be together, because we love each other…"

"You can't know that!"

"I know everything, Bae." He quickly spun her around so they were face to face, he tapped her cheek twice, kissed her once more, then quickly shrunk down to the size of a mouse and scurried to the spare bedroom, and locked the door behind him.

She gripped her core piece and felt particularly macabre, "I am coming back!"

Caleb abruptly emerged from his room, as always with all of his gear on, "What are you doing here?"

"Cleaning the apartment, doing your laundry, and waiting for the moment you snap out of this."

"Hy, what's going on?"

"Go back to your room you worthless sheep."

"You need to leave!" He shook his head back and forth in disbelief that she showed up again, it had been long enough he figured she was gone permanently.

"I am…and there is a chance, only a chance, not an absolute, that I'm not coming back." She wasn't speaking to Caleb at this moment. She was honestly speaking to the Mustleknapp curled up on her pillow in the spare bedroom, "But that's a risk I'm willing to take. And while my motivation is selfish, the aftermath is for a greater purpose. So even if I'm selfish, who cares? I'm going to save the sanity of another and the life of a creature I don't understand in the same instance. And yes I am risking my life, I'm risking our future, but I have to do this, or I will never stop questioning why I didn't take this chance. I can't live like that, and you know it! I love you, please know, I *love* you. I don't know how to love others, but I love you, forever and for always.

And I'm sorry for the hurt you're going to go through waiting for me to come back, with your false belief constantly questioning if I come back, but I don't believe it. But you are every thought I have, and when I lose the will to go on, I'm going to think of coming home to you, and that will drive me forward. The thought of a night without you curled up on my pillow hurts more than you can ever understand. You were right, unconditional, that's you and me, because I'm so fucked up that I can't allow myself to be happy…but you always make me happy just by being you. You don't even have to try; I just see you, and I know. But I'm going back; maybe it is to sabotage myself. That's just who I am, I guess. But I will be back to hold you and be with you. I promise you that I will give you my core piece when this is over; it is yours, it always has been, and I realize now that it always will be. I will do whatever I can to give it back to you. When I get back I will make you lemon bars, buy you malted milk balls, and order you Domino's for the rest of our life together, but not until I do this first.

This is hard on you, and this is hard on me, but I will come back to you because I love you, because I'm stubborn, and because you may be the only being on any planet that knows me better than me. I love you…I love you more than I ever knew I could, and I hate that you're away from me, but if this is what you need, I will give it to you. My heart is breaking that you don't want to snuggle

with me tonight, but again, if you need this, I will give it to you…"

"You know I don't understand your metaphors." Caleb was upset.

"Oh please, go fuck yourself," Hyacinth kicked him and rolled her eyes, he fell backward, having his knees swept out from under him, and she left the apartment satisfied with the sound of his grunting from the pain of falling.

The Mustleknapp pulled himself into a tight ball on her pillow, "You have to come back to me…I can't live without you Bae, all I can see is your death." He wished he knew how to cry, because he wanted to in this moment. He cuddled closer to the pillow, taking in her scent. "Come back to me."

FOURTEEN

Hyacinth balanced on her right hand, keeping everything at 90 degrees. She thought about the Mustleknapp and a single tear leaked from her eye. She focused herself and then switched her hands. She tightened her core and before she could switch positions again, a powerful force wrapped itself around her waist and propelled her toward Chad.

"You need to stop that!"

"I can't help it!" He smiled at her, "You seem more miserable than normal this morning, only do 500 push-ups as opposed to a thousand?"

"Ha ha, very funny."

"Is it?" He tilted his head, knowing full well she already did a thousand push-ups today.

"Can you quell your jealousy for one moment, you know I miss him!"

"He didn't leave you, he's just trying to understand why we are going back." He lifted her slightly with the Decttronium so she was at eye level.

"And not being here in the same moment."

"Honestly doesn't bother me."

"Not shocking." She rolled her eyes, then he placed his hand on her cheek and gently kissed her. She thought about the Mustleknapp kissing her, and felt conflicted. Raising an eyebrow at herself, she made out with a Mustleknapp… now here she was kissing the most handsome human she ever met, felt guilt and stopped kissing Chad then asked seriously, "Why are you going back?"

"I'm getting sick of that question." He gently retreated the Decttronium and placed her on her feet again.

"Is there something more than just supporting me?"

"Don't spiral out of control, please, come on, today is our dress rehearsal, and you need to bring your A
game."

"I don't know who to trust anymore…"

"Trust us," he intertwined their fingers and pulled them toward his chest, he stared into her eyes, "We are a team, and we are going to go back, we're putting a speaker stone on a Quarternewt and then we are going to help them restore balance."

"What if you have to kill again?"

"If I have to kill again, then I will."

"For what purpose?"

"What are you talking about?"

"When we were there we were all convinced it was for protection…what happens when you kill for vengeance…or when you kill for fun…"

"Hy, please, you need to chill." He squeezed her shoulders trying to massage her.

"I'm not ready to chill or relax," She flung her arms up breaking his connection to her, "What are you going to do when you see me rip apart the Gnetgnu for the sheer fun of it!"

"You wouldn't do that!"

"I wouldn't?"

"No, you wouldn't do that!"

"You don't know me!" she turned on her heel to leave the room.

"I know you!"

She was angry and narrowed her eyes as she turned around to face him, "No, you don't! You never have, you see me and you want a relationship, you're in denial of what lengths I will go to in order to bring them all down…for the fun of it…I don't care if I save someone in the process, I want to feel the paper tear between my fingers! That's all I care about!" She walked away from him and he followed closely behind her.

"I don't buy it!"

"Well, then that's just too bad for you!"

"Please…" He held her close and blew in her ear, she melted onto him. "Please Beautiful…please, stop doing this to yourself."

"What if I can't?"

"Then I'll hold you till you can." He kissed the side of her face and down her neck.

"What is wrong with me?"

"Nothing…nothing at all, I will hold you, support you, no matter what I am here."

"Until you're not!" She cried harder.

"No, Beautiful, that's not me…that's over…please…shhh." He ran his fingers through her hair, held her close and kissed the top of her head.

Skyler walked in, "Seriously, the Soap Opera Drama better get the fuck out of this space!"

"Shut it!"

"No, I will not, the two of you just need to fuck and get it over with, that's why you're still mad at each other, because the tension is too high."

"Shut it!"

"We have a dress rehearsal in like a half hour, you have plenty of time, just go get it done so we can all fucking concentrate." Skyler left and slammed her door.

"I am not fucking you!" Hyacnith sneered at Chad, she pushed him away.

"That was not my suggestion." He laughed innocently.

"Then what? WHAT is going to fix this?" She kicked the island sending the it into the air, she was still shocked at her strength, but made sure it was back in its place.

"I know what I want."

"And what is that?" she looked over at him annoyed.

"I'm going to come over to you just like this," and he walked over with his hands innocently up in the air,

"Then I'm going to grab your waist like this," he did so, "Then I'm going to hug you." He did.

"Then what?"

"That's it, just hug you, because I need you."

She breathed in his scent and then ran her fingers through his hair. She breathed out slowly, turned on by touching him. "Chad…"

"I know…I will wait until we get back…because we have to focus on killing Jom, and then, all my focus will be on you." He kissed her forehead.

She knew why she was really mad at herself and not him, she confessed to him, "The Mustleknapp told me something, and it is confusing me."

"What is that?" He adored when she would open up to him. "You're going to be jealous, and think without logic."

"I am cool, calm, and collected, especially with him gone."

"You're happy that I miss him?"

"No, I'm happy I don't have to watch him cuddle onto your chest like he owns you."

"He said he was going to turn into a human." She assessed his reaction and could feel the intensity within his shoulders.

"That's impossible."

"He morphed to your size and then flattened his paws like finger tips and he sang to me. Then he kissed me, on my mouth."

"He did WHAT?" He couldn't hide the anger, "I swear I'm going slam his scrawny ass into a wall when we get back. He had no right!"

"He's jealous of you because he wants to kiss me the way you do."

"He never will." He leaned down and passionately kissed her making her swoon, she never kissed anyone the way she did him. "When we kiss, it's more than a kiss." He kissed her again and again and she grabbed his shirt, and moaned in enjoyment. He whispered to her, "You know you feel it."

"He asked me if I would choose him over you." Chad's eyes grew wide, "What did you say?"

"I said it was never going to happen because he would never be human."

"If he could…who would you choose?" He asked jealously.

She pushed him away and looked away, "I already made my choice, and you'll know the answer when we get back."

She walked into her room and slammed the door, she needed to prepare herself for dress rehearsal. Chad's smile spread across his face, he knew she would choose him. All he had to do to win the heart of the woman he loved was travel out of the galaxy, slaughter an entire race of aliens shaped like paper, talk to a newt-like dragon about balancing peace on that planet, and then somehow return to Earth alive…simple really.

…

They made their way to the field. This was where they would be catching the portal. Skyler's eyes were deep with the dark blue of the Septtronium, Chad's turquoise with the Decttronium, and Landon with the light blue of the Marttronium. They all took their places, and with Hyacinth in the center they could see the portal's movement, but tomorrow night it would be over this space. The three of them were playing with their powers, while Hyacinth went back to the Jeep and cried alone in the back seat.

She thought about Rowan, what she always wanted to say to him, "You left me when I needed you more than ever. You took the easy way out, like a coward, but that didn't match you at all. You were so much stronger. Was it the drugs that weakened you or your sanity? Did you have the same illness she did? You told me I was the Wild Card…what did that really mean? Was I an accident? Because she had me, did that break her? Did that break him? Why were you the only one that loved me?

Chrysanthemum never did, she always turned her nose up at me, was that because I was the baby? Or because she was old enough to hear them argue over me? What was it about me? No one ever told me…I have no answers, you were the only one who had them, and they died with you. You told me to live my life, and I did. She can hate me all she wants, I don't care, I'm living my life and some alien dipshit screwed it up. Now I am going back to kill him. It doesn't have anything to do with you, other than I'm the Wild Card. You taught me to never question what if. I see my opportunity to seize what I want and I'm taking it.

I have never given much thought into what would happen after I die…just that I was going to live before I got there…unlike you…I don't know if I can ever forgive you. I feel like I will never forgive you. Getting my revenge on Jom will never bring me the closure I need from your betrayal."

She pulled her knees to her chest and did her best to calm her nerves as the tears streamed down her face.

When she sensed they were close she pretended she was laughing at something on her phone. They all knew her well enough to know she was faking, but none of them wanted to cross that line with her.

Landon went to say something, and Skyler covered his mouth with her hand and shook her head, he nodded to show he understood. He licked her hand and she gave him a playful look and then wiped it on his shirt and wrinkled her nose at him. He smiled widely and then leaned over for a quick kiss on the cheek.

"Did you want to go see the Mustleknapp before we leave tomorrow?" Skyler asked concerned, she didn't want to push Hyacinth away when they were so close to the launch of this mission. "No, we had our moment, and he needs his space, besides, the mission is all that matters."

"Really?" Chad asked. Skyler gave him a look and then pinched him with the Septtronium. "Yes, it always has been."

"There's nothing else?" He couldn't hide the hurt within his tone. Skyler went to pinch him again and he deflected her attempt with a Decttronium bubble.

"Not going there! We have the chance to prevent abduction."

"It will be worth it, imagine if we can save the sanity of another person?" Landon chimed in. "He's right, so we need to relax tonight," Skyler encouraged.

They drove the whole car ride in silence with no eye contact toward one another. Once they arrived back at the pool house, Landon broke the dead silence, "What's for dinner?"

"Leftovers, there's stromboli and quiche in the fridge." Hyacinth smiled. She looked over and Chad gave her an odd look. "Do we need to talk?" she asked pretending to sound cheery.

"Yes…"

She rolled her eyes, "I'm so sick of this." She whispered to herself. "So am I," Chad answered her annoyed.

Landon started taking out the leftovers, "I never remembered relationships being so complicated."

"Not everyone fits together as easily as we do Babe." She walked over and helped him.

"True, but even before my abduction…" he looked off the side remembering, that time was always a gray area for him.

"I know what you mean, if I liked someone I saw them, if I didn't…I didn't…"

"If someone didn't want me, I didn't go out of my way to keep going after them, why doesn't he…"

"Because he knows what I know."

"And what's that?"

"She wants it, she doesn't want to admit that she wants it."

He grabbed her close to him, "Do you think we would have ever met if it wasn't for this?"

"No, but I'm glad we did."

"I wouldn't trade it for anything."

"Neither would I…" she kissed him.

"Can I ask you something, hypothetical without you freaking out?"

"We talked about this, and yeah we can try but it's gonna take…"

"No, not that." He giggled.

"Oh…" She blushed.

"What if after we get back…we, well…" he didn't know how to approach her about this subject. "What?"

"I am still an anonymous individual to put it bluntly; I don't know if anyone is looking for me, or if they assumed I'm a missing person. I have no job, no money, no nothing."

"I don't care."

"I know *you* don't care but there's something *I* want to give you but I have no means of paying for it."

"What do you want to give me? I can buy it for you…"

"See that's the problem." He looked deeply into her eyes, so in love with the angel that saved him, the princess that stole his heart. What he found in her in this short time went well beyond every romantic stereotype he had ever seen, read, or dreamed of in his entire life.

"Does it bother you that I have money?" Skyler looked back at him with the same level of intensity. Usually, once a guy saw her lifestyle, they stayed for free-loading, but not Landon. Landon gave her every ounce of attention and affection that she desired, and she never had to feel pressured or different. He was truly in love with her and who she was.

"No, not at all…"

"Is it a hit to your manhood that I buy what you want to give me?" She was confused.

"No, Baby Girl, it's just that…"

"Just tell me…" she said nervously.

He immediately picked up on how her anxiety starting to trigger, he gently placed his hands around her rib cage and mimicked the deep breathing she would do to calm herself, "I want to surprise you."

She smiled, and felt relief, "So I'll give you my Amex."

"What?"

"You wanna buy me something?"

"Yes."

"But you don't want me to know what it is?"

"Yes."

"Then I'll… I'll add you to my Amex," she said easily.

"What?"

"I'll put your name on my account and whatever you want you just charge to the Amex."

"Seriously?" He was shocked she suggested such a thing.

"Yeah, seriously."

"How do you know I'm not gonna do something stupid?"

"You're not, you're my Babe…and I trust you." She kissed him slowly and made a yummy sound and smirked when she was done.

"I love you, Skyler."

Her eyes grew wide, "That's the first time you ever said that to me!" Tears dripped from her eyes. "It's true."

"I love you too!" They started kissing in the kitchen and he lifted her onto the counter as they made out after their professions of love for one another.

"My room now!" Skyler demanded.

"Anything for you, Baby Girl!" They kept kissing as they made their way to her room.

With Skyler and Landon occupied in their own romance, Hyacinth was at the end of her rope with Chad. She closed her door, sighed and turned to him. "What's going on?"

"I need space away from you right now." Chad turned away from her.

"Why?" It hurt her heart to hear it, didn't he just profess to her this morning that he was never going to leave her? Defensive she quickly squared her shoulders, this whole talk about being with him had to wait, or did it?

"Because you keep telling me the mission is all that matters, but that's not what matters to me!"

"What are you babbling about?"

"Hyacinth, you know how I feel about you."

"Please, you and the Mustleknapp both need to stop this ridiculous love game, I don't want to play."

"I want you."

"I can sense that from how you look at me."

"Hy, I want to marry you, I want to be your everything."

"Chad, that's…"

"I want to be the husband and father you make Eggo waffles for…"

"Chad…"

"I can't accept that that's never going to happen because you're going to go back to the Gnetgnu and die for your revenge."

She picked up easily, quickly on the panic within his soul and rolled her eyes, "I am not going to die by their hands. I am far too strong."

"I can't sit here, and not mourn that you are going to die on that planet."

"Not you too!" Her heart was bleeding, he was no different than any other man in her life, she gave up all hope at that point.

"It's a possibility!"

"I could get hit by a bus tomorrow, that's a possibility!" she sneered disgusted at him, always saying that he was different. He was going to abandon her, just like all of them before him, just like the Mustleknapp.

"The Prophet Warrior does not have ancient texts suggesting she dies by a bus when she restores planet's balance!"

"Stop it!"

"I can't."

"Why?"

"Because I'm fucking in love with you, I have known it since the moment we met!" His sanity was unhinged thinking about her death.

"Stop it!"

"I knew as soon as my hand touched your face that we were meant to be together."

"Does being the master of Decttronium come with psychic vision now too?" She asked sarcastically.

"You're walking into your own demise, and you don't care what that would do to me!"

"Because I know something you don't!"

"What's that?"

"I'm not going to die there!" She stamped her foot and her bed rose in the air, as always, her eyes widened, and he couldn't help but enjoy her innocence in that moment.

He shook his head and tightened his jaw, "That's really why you're so comfortable with telling me how you feel only after we get back."

"What does that even mean?"

"You are so afraid to be loved that you're completely okay with the idea of never coming back to Earth so you never have to be vulnerable to me. You'd rather die than utter *I love you*."

"Stop it!" She smacked her hand against the wall, cracking the drywall. "Shit," she said quickly. "I will not, you want to run and hide, be my guest, but I will not run from how I feel!"

"How do you feel? Please tell me again you fucking hopeless romantic! You can't go a day anymore without saying it, does it feel real to you yet? Because there is only one thing I want right now!"

"You want to kill Jom."

"I am *going* to kill Jom."

"And then what?"

"We return to Earth." She shrugged.

"Then I'm going to marry you," he said certainly.

"Stop..." she shook her head, confused by this interaction entirely.

"No, I'm going to marry you, we're going to have a family together, and we are going to grow old together."

"Stop!"

"Never, I love you more than I ever knew was possible, and I am not going to stop because you are afraid of what you feel."

"I have no fear."

"Yes, you do, that's why you keep shoving me away, because you can't handle that you want me, and that's why I can't be here with everyone tonight."

"Why?"

"Because I need to distance myself from you, because it will compromise the mission."

"How?"

"Because you are the only one I'm going to be focused on! You say the mission is all that matters but it doesn't to me! I can't focus in your presence, I will only care about you and your safety…"

"You can't do that!"

"I can't help it!" He grabbed her face and kissed her, then turned his back and walked away.

She whispered to herself, "First my father, then Rowan, then Caleb, then the Mustleknapp, and now you too…ironic how everyone who loves me can't be with me at the same time…I guess now I can confirm it, you were wrong yet again, it's not you, it's me." She crawled onto her bed and brought her knees to her chest and hugged herself as tightly as she could. A tear ran down her cheek, "Don't cry, I've got you," she whispered to herself.

. . .

Skyler, Landon and Hyacinth were sitting in the living room playing Cards Against Humanity. They were hysterically laughing. Skyler took another shot of limoncello.

"Slow down," Landon teased as he tickled her. "We have a hell of a day tomorrow."

"That's why I need the extra shot!" She laughed.

"Are you ready for tomorrow?" Hyacinth asked them. "I am, but I'm a little scared at the same time."

"This plan will work, we need the truth."

"I know we do."

"Where's the Mustleknapp? I figured he'd want to see all of us one last time, just in case," Landon commented innocently.

"He's still angry with me at the moment, he's somewhere in the ventilation system in my apartment building I believe, he does his best in mazes."

"Why is he so mad?"

"He doesn't want me to go back, he's convinced I'm going to die."

"But everything we have uncovered, all that we know, we're all coming back." Landon smiled.

"I know that, you know that, we all know that, but there are two males battling for my attention, and they can't handle that my only focus is to kill Jom and not falling over them spouting sonnets and other love shit."

"Who do you love more?" Skyler asked with a sneaky smile on her face.

"Not you too!"

"Indulge me…"

"Please…" she rolled her eyes.

"If you had to choose, the Mustleknapp or Chad, who would you pick?"

"That's not a fair question…only one is human."

"If we made the Mustleknapp human…who would you choose?"

She smiled and took another shot of limoncello, "I know the answer."

"Which is?" Skyler was ready to burst playing into the triangle drama. "It's easy, the one I adore the most."

"Who is?"

"Me." She laughed.

"So, what happens when we arrive on the planet?"

"When we arrive, we are all one, so we are equal to one another, we risk all of us for each of us," Hyacinth said.

"This conversation went intense rather quickly," Landon said uncomfortably. "I have an idea!" Skyler shouted.

"What?" They both turned to a smiling Skyler.

"Landon, you get the limoncello, I'll grab the mini quiche from the fridge and we should swim in the moonlight to calm our nerves."

"I like that idea."

"I just need a few minutes," Hyacinth said sadly. "What's wrong?"

"I'm just…"

"Take all the time you need, we'll be splashing away."

"Thanks."

Hyacinth pried her hairbrush from the wall and brushed her hair as she thought about Chad. He left her just like everyone else, he constantly spouted he was different, but turns out he was just the same as all the others before him. She was disappointed in herself as she wished he was close to her. She hated this feeling. He said he needed to clear his head before their mission, he really just didn't want to accept that he wasn't her top priority. She was mad at herself for ever revealing she liked him. She laughed to herself, he wasn't her type. Then she thought deeper, did she have a type? What did it matter anymore?

She was going back to seek her revenge, and if she didn't make it back, to Hell with it. Killing Jom was all she wanted, and she was going to get exactly what she wanted. She had an internal debate with herself, did she want to kill Jom or did she want to make Eggo waffles for a loving husband and finally feel like she was part of a real family? It was then she realized she was part of a family, just because it didn't match the commercial didn't mean that it wasn't real. She sniffled back a tear, her eyes were red and puffy. There was a knock on her door.

"Seriously, I said give me…" she opened the door and it wasn't Skyler. "Hi," it was Chad.

"Hi,"

"Were you crying?" He asked concerned. "No." she lied.

"Yes, you were," his heart broke in half. Once again, he made her cry without even trying.

"What're you doing here? I thought you needed space from me."

"Tomorrow is the day,"

"Yeah, I know."

"Do you remember what I told you?"

"You tell me lots of things, Cliff."

"About when we get back."

"Yes," she looked at him seriously.

"I've been absorbed this whole time about whether or not you make it back."

"Slightly obsessively." She shrugged him off.

"What if I don't make it back?" He carefully eyed her reaction.

She never considered that an option, she never questioned his arrival back to Earth, "With that mentality you won't," she laughed the thought off defensively.

"Hyacinth," he looked at her seriously, with a smolder in his eyes. "What are you thinking about right now?" she asked.

He leaned down and kissed her. "I want a taste of what I'm fighting to come home to." She kissed him harder and wrapped her arms around his shoulders, he kissed her lips, then down her neck, and then grabbed her with both hands and lifted her onto him. She squeezed him with her thighs, "Easy warrior," he warned her.

She smiled, "I didn't mean it, Chad…"

"I love it when you say that."

"Say what?"

"My real name."

"Chad." She blew in his ear, "Is this going to happen now?"

"Do you want it to?"

"Yes." She looked beyond his eyes and into his soul.

"I'll always give you what you want." He lowered her onto the bed and kissed down her chest and slowly ran his hand up her shirt and gently touched her breast above her bra. She quietly gasped. "Are you okay?" He asked concerned.

"It's been so long."

"Too long." He quickly undid her bra and then pulled up her shirt. With her topless he started sucking on her nipple while caressing the other breast. She kept moaning quietly, and then she ran her fingers down his back and pulled his shirt up. He sat up and took it off, "Do you want this to happen?"

"You know I do," she said. "Do you want me?"

"Yes," She smiled.

He went back to kissing her mouth as she held him close allowing their bare chests to touch.

"Hyacinth…"

"Yes…"

"I'm going to take this to the next level…"

"What are you going to do?" She smirked.

He slowly kissed his way down her chest, then down to her stomach, once he reached below her belly button he pulled her pants and panties down in one motion. He lowered himself down and she rolled her eyes in the back of her head and moaned louder in delight. She had no idea Chad was that skilled with his tongue. It was only in this moment she finally realized how long his fingers truly were, and she ran her fingers through his hair as he continued. Before she could moan another moan she cried out as she twitched into orgasm. When she was through he gently licked, happily enjoying this moment, and then he looked up at her, "That's your noise?"

"What?"

"You sound…" he couldn't stop smiling. "What?" she was slightly nervous.

"You sound amazing." He wiped his mouth with the back of his hand and then started kissing her neck.

She smiled and then reached her hand down and grabbed him.

"Holy Shit."

He laughed, "What?"

"That's all you."

"Yeah, I know." Now he rolled his eyes at her.

She grabbed him and started to stimulate him, now he was the one moaning. She slowly shifted their positions so she was on top of him, she unzipped his pants and took him fully out. Then she started to place him in her mouth. He was moaning. He happily enjoyed each moment, he carefully touched her breasts while she had him down her throat. He kept breathing heavily. He was about to burst and he pulled her off of him.

"What's wrong?"

"I want the whole experience," he said seriously at her. "Are you sure?"

"Yes."

He placed her tenderly on her back and then parted her legs gently, he stared in her eyes, "Are you okay with this?"

"I want this to happen."

"Okay," he slowly placed himself inside of her. She moaned as he went deeper, she gasped, having never felt anything like this before. "You okay?"

"Yes, it's just..." He felt amazing.

"Shhhh." He kissed her neck over and over again, as he slowly entered her deeper and deeper. "Chad..." she moaned again.

"I love you," he whispered, "You don't have to say it back, but I want to tell you..." She looked him directly in his eyes and smiled, "I love you," she whispered back. "Do you mean that?"

"Yes, I always have; you deserve to know that."

He kissed her hard and held her close, "Are you okay?"

"I'm okay."

He gained in speed, and she couldn't help but cry out as he kept going in and out of her, she couldn't contain her excitement, and for the second time she cried out in delight as her body succumbed to a second orgasm. He smiled as she finished, "I will fight to come back to that sound." He grabbed her hands and intertwined their fingers and brought them up over her head.

"I will fight, to ensure you are there to make that happen."

They kissed one another repeatedly, and then she felt him come within her as he now cried out in satisfaction. He collapsed next to her, and for the first time, she held her arms around both his shoulders. She cuddled her head onto his chest and held him close, he kissed the top of her head, "That was better than I ever thought..."

"That was…that was…" she held him tighter, he was everything she fantasized and more.

"I will fight for us."

"I will fight for us."

"Do I get the honor, to call you mine now?" He stared into her eyes, with full sincerity.

"Do I get to call you mine?"

"I always have been."

"When we make it back, I am forever yours."

"Hy…" he wanted to tell her so many things.

"Shhh," she kissed him, "I love you, Chad." She smiled at him.

He felt as though he could cry, "I love you, more than anything."

"So hold me," she lowered her body over him, he held her tight, and couldn't wipe the smile off his face. He never thought she would say it back, and she finally did, and he felt closer to her than he ever had before. They both closed their eyes and drifted into a peaceful sleep.

Skyler and Landon were cuddling in the pool, "Do you think they made up?" Landon asked innocently. "I'm gonna go with yes."

"Are you ready to go inside?" He asked as he kissed her neck. "Not just yet." She turned around and starting kissing him. "Are you sure?"

"They're busy, it's just us." She whispered into his ear as she undid her bottom bikini string.

FIFTEEN

The four of them were all silent in the Jeep. They drove to the sight in the field, each denying that there was a distinct possibility they would not return. Another part of them was hyped with the idea of bringing the planet of the Gnetgnu to balance. Chad only wanted Hyacinth to feel the satisfaction of slaughtering Jom and then return to this world so that he could love her as his partner, his wife, his everything. Landon wanted to ensure that no other human would be abducted, and face the same debilitating psychosis he had endured once returned to Earth. Skyler was surface level wanting to save the Quarternewt. Still, she sincerely wanted to stay with the four of them in the pool house, funded by her parents, enjoying each other's company and be content in that lifestyle for the rest of her days. A more significant part of her wanted to gather as much Septtronium as she could so she and Landon could play fight on the golf course with one another.

"When we get there, if we're separated, the first point of order is to get to the third Strythocket tree on the Epson edge of the hill, are we clear?" Hyacinth asked.

"Crystal," Skyler said.

"What?"

"That means yes, Cliff." Hyacinth rolled her eyes.

"I know what she meant, it's just confusing considering we are going to travel through a portal of crystals, choose a different expression."

"What happens if we die on our way?" Landon asked.

"No matter where we are on the planet, it should not take more than seven moons to get there. On the reverse of the moon's cycle, if we are not all together, then one of us has died, and we will move on to the next checkpoint," Hyacinth said coldly.

"Could you at least pretend to be concerned?" Skyler asked.

"None of us have died in the portal. I doubt we will this time," Hyacinth said matter-of-factly. "What if this doesn't work?"

"This is going to work."

"Once we are reunited, we need to retrieve a speaker stone."

"The speaker stones are stored within the bottom of the third Strythocket tree on the horizon, it should not be difficult."

"Then to the Quarternewt."

"We can do this."

"We will do this, now."

The four left the Jeep, and none of them gave one another eye contact. They walked to the field and stood in their spots. Once Hyacinth was in the center they could see the portal. It was traveling in the opposite direction as it had the previous day, then came within 3 feet of them.

Hyacinth could hear Skyler start to breathe erratically, Chad and Landon made no noise, "We may be unsure of the outcome, but we are going to do this! We are going to make right what was wrong! We are going to do something no other humans have ever done!" it was then the portal came within a foot of them, then disappeared.

They all turned to Landon with narrowed eyes, he looked panicked and shrugged, "Okay so there is a distinct possibility that my math was slightly off."

"Okay...so we will do this tomorrow," Hyacinth said. She threw her arms up in frustration, broke the configuration, and stomped her way back up the hill.

"I can't believe I was off by…"

"You're human, doing something inhuman, it was a miscalculation…" Skyler wrapped her arms around him trying to comfort him.

"It's okay, we can figure it out tonight," Chad said, slightly relieved. The four returned to the Jeep feeling defeated.

"Is anybody hungry?" Chad asked to fill the silence.

"I could go for something," Landon said sheepishly.

"You wanna drive to Hackensack? Get some White Manna?"

"Yes, yes I do," Hyacinth said confidently.

Skyler pulled her phone out, "I'll order. You drive." Hyacinth looked out the window and started laughing. "What's so funny?" Chad finally had to ask.

"This whole messed up situation." They all started to laugh. Hyacinth laughed and then shook her head,

"I'm trying to find the right word to describe this feeling."

"What do you feel?"

"Our adrenaline was so pumped up for this moment, and I was giving that monumental movie speech

and then to see it flit away so easily…"

Skyler started to laugh uncontrollably in the backseat. "You went all William Wallace on our asses…"

The girls continued to laugh, and then Skyler shrilled in laughter, which meant she had something on her mind that was making her laugh, "What?" Hyacinth had to know.

"I know how to label this…" she kept laughing. "What?" Hyacinth smirked.

"Pre-mature ejaculation…"

"YES!" Hyacinth agreed, and now the two girls were even more hysterical.

"Hey, that only happened like one time!" Landon said.

The two girls laughed harder as Chad rolled his eyes, "TMI dude, TMI."

...

Hyacinth felt her body careen forward. She landed on something soft and familiar, she rolled her body to brace the momentum. She looked up and she was on the Sprythocket plane…only half a day's walk to the Strythocket hills. She smiled, she was finally back. She grabbed her core piece, it was still the same, completely unchanged. She started her journey in solitude, her first thought was whether Chad had made it through successfully, then she shook her head and reminded herself that she had to separate her personal feelings for him. This was about death to Jom, that came first. She would die in sacrifice if she knew Jom would die as a result. She didn't care…Jom lied to her, and she was going to ensure he paid for his betrayal. She could not allow her personal feelings to jeopardize the mission, they needed to be equals.

She enjoyed the beauty of the orange stars; but she wished she could stay longer in their presence, chart them, and make her own constellations. She felt a sense of comfort in the stars, and then she started to wonder if they were stars. She labeled them as such, but honestly, they could be planets, moons, or something different. All she knew was they scattered about the sky like strategically placed glitter on an indigo canvas. She heard no sounds, not the Mrshti flowers moaning nor the Frezdon flower gleating.

She walked, silently unable to understand anything around her without her speaker stone. She reflected to when she was first abducted, she could hear. There were sounds, but it was primarily low chatter. Perhaps the Gnetgnu's speech differed. Then again, her speaker stone was the first point of order when she arrived. She remembered them jamming it into her jaw, the pain…she didn't hear anything in the portal. There was no white noise, and she couldn't hear anything until she placed the speaker stone back into her jaw. Part of her wondered if it would hurt.

She stared at the pools she passed on her way, they were identical until her finger slowly sent the spirals outward, the first puddle she came across was stagnant, she had come in contact with these before, and just assumed they were dried, nothing more. Now she pulled for the Decttronium to be removed from the puddle, and it left and traveled to the next, which rippled with turquoise. Then she pulled out the Septtronium and it traveled across her visual field to a puddle several feet away. The puddle was originally Marttronium, and now the light blue color shined brighter.

She could see the hills on the horizon, and she started to run. She was delighted that she was faster than she had ever been. She took that to mean Landon, Skyler, and Chad were there as well. She reached the third tree and saw no one. She looked around and went into a knot in the tree. The amount of the stones were abundant. She grabbed a handful and placed them in her satchel. She took one and placed it in her jaw, the moans, gleating, and songs of the plant life of the planet filled her brain. Then she heard the most gorgeous sound she knew on any planet.

"Missed you, Beautiful."

She turned and Chad was standing with his arms out, she ran into him and he held her tight, "You made it! Where is everyone?"

"Look up…"

She did and Skyler and Landon were nestled in the branches. "Hurry up!"

"What?"

"It's the night of the seventh moon merging, which means they are all going to come together and then explode into thousands of moons, it's the most beautiful sight you have ever seen."

"No, we have to get to…"

"Shhhh." Chad placed his hand on her cheek, "We're all here, your revenge is going to happen, but for one night, we all get to witness something truly unique, something no humans have ever shared with one another; please, please Beautiful share this moment with me?"

"But we have to…"

"Please…"

"You're delaying this, they'll be distracted."

"I'm already distracted." He leaned down and kissed her forehead, then blew in her ear.

"Fine…" she conceded.

Chad flung her over his shoulder and climbed up the tree. Chad held Hyacinth in his arms, nestled in a branch, while Landon held Skyler in another. They looked up to the sky and watched as the seventh moon absorbed the others. They turned to a shade brighter than gold and then rotated so quickly it was as if the moon was perfectly round and still. When the explosion occurred, it was as if seeing something more beautiful than the aurora borealis. Hyacinth gasped at the sight, and Chad kissed her neck as they enjoyed this moment.

"When the light emerges, we will journey to the Quarternewt," Chad said. "But we could gain miles if we…"

"Your Highness, we just traveled from one planet to another and saw the explosion of moons to form thousands to be reforged. Enjoy this moment for what it is, something you and I have experienced together that no one else ever will. And when we return to Earth, this will be something we share, that is all ours, and now we are going to snuggle in this tree and rest because our journey to the Quarternewt nest will require full strengths."

"Well, when you put it like that." She smiled and rested her head against his chest. The four rested and slept in the safety of the Strythocket Tree. They would not fall victim to a Mrshti Flower or a Frezdon Flower. Given how this was the night of the seven-moon explosion, the smell of the moon chips would hide their presence on the planet entirely.

…

As the daylight crept on the planet Chad squeezed her to him, "Last night was so amazing."

"I've never seen something like that before."

"Aren't you glad we took a moment and enjoyed it?"

"Yes and no…"

"How so?"

"Yes, it was beautiful and we enjoyed it, but we lost half a day's journey in merriment when the death of Jom is all that matters. We need to get to the realm of the Quarternewt."

"We will…"

"We won't if we don't treat this with utmost seriousness."

"You're doing it again!"

"What?"

"Talking like that!"

"Like what?"

"You're talking, I don't know, like a video game…"

She rolled her eyes, "I will not be deterred from my revenge because you want to stare at a moon."

"I know," he shook his head, "Because you won't love me until this is done."

"I didn't say that…"

"What are you saying?"

"I will not be derailed from my desire."

He kissed her forehead, "I have a shred of hope that your dedication to this feeling of revenge is even an iota of the dedication you will have for our relationship."

"Cliff, not now!"

The four started the journey, "This was so much faster with my Honturna." Landon commented.

"I know. I wish mine survived the journey."

"What do you mean?"

"My Honturna died from the heat of the Quarternewt nest," Hyacinth said. Landon started laughing, "Seriously?"

"Don't mock me! It was really sad for me!"

"Honturna are immortal," Landon said.

"What?"

"It didn't die. It just melted and wanted to change shape."

"What?"

"Yeah, um, your Hunterna was probably assigned to you by Jom, and it melted when it was told to, and then it reformed and left you high and dry."

"Please tell me you're making this up to fuck with me right now…" Landon shook his head, "Nope."

"How do you know?"

"Their blood is pure Marttronium."

"Does that mean you resurrect?" Hyacinth asked in a low tone. Landon put one finger up to his mouth to tell her to keep that fact quiet.

"Seriously?"

"Like I said, Hunterna are immortal."

"Oh, I am going tear that playing card motherfucker apart so hard, and then I'm legit flossing my teeth with his threads!"

"Easy, Hy." Chad tried to place his hand on her shoulder.

"No!" she shrugged him off her, "I was lied to, we were all lied to, and I cannot believe you are not feeling the same anger. You were locked up in a mental institution! You were forced to leave college and move in with your parents! And you were alone, every friend left, and your brother gave up! How are you not dying, aching to tear them apart?"

"We are, but not as heightened as you…"

"Well then, maybe I'm just…" She froze in her steps, "No one move."

"What? Did you…" Landon also froze.

"What's going on?" Skyler walked beside Landon and saw the Mrshti flower on the ground. "Oh, it's so pretty." She went toward it, listening to its sound, "Wow." The sweet, soft music sent a wave of calm through Skyler's brain that hit harder than oxycodone and Xanax combined. The sound was more adorable, and more precious than any lullaby, and the smell that permeated her nostrils was a mixture of cotton candy and gardenia.

"Baby Girl, NO!" Landon wrapped her in a blanket of Marttronium and pulled her toward him, "Don't listen, don't listen."

"It's so pretty, I want to touch it." She used the Septtronium to slowly make her way forward.

"Don't!" Landon doubled his efforts.

"I want to touch it," her face turned to the side. She had fallen victim to its song.

"Chad," Hyacinth called, "Pull out her speaker stone now!"

"What?"

"NOW!"

Chad used the Decttronium and removed her speaker stone. Skyler collapsed into Landon's arms. "What just happened?"

"The Mrshti flower has the most potent venum, poison, whatever you want to call it,"

"Never felt it myself, but I saw what it could do." Chad confessed.

"Consider yourself fortunate. When it touches you, it's worse than a bullet ant bite."

"The pain alone made me crumble for days," Hyacinth said.

"What?"

"It is the worst pain I have ever known, and if she touched it, you risk your sanity because the pain makes you long for death, almost as if you were set on fire," Landon said.

They continued moving forward. Hyacinth grabbed a jar, captured the Mrshti flower, and sealed it shut.

"Why would you do that?"

"Never know if I need one…" She smiled. "You're not taking that home with us."

"I had one originally, but I lost it in transit."

"Maybe that's a good thing; that flower alone wiped out an entire species."

"So have humans, and we're expected to live amongst them," she smiled devilishly as she placed the jar
in her satchel.

"If it stings you, I will tell you I told you so."

"If it stings me, then I deserve it for mishandling it."

"What am I going to do with you?"

"Walk faster so we can get this over with."

"I don't think…"

She rolled her eyes, then turned to ask Landon, "How is she?"

"She'll be fine."

"We should settle down for the night," Chad said.

"What?" Hyacinth was annoyed.

"We can't make the realm within a day's walk, we need to sleep and be ready for a fight tomorrow."

"But if we travel through the night…"

"Hy, calm yourself; we need to be at full strength; we can't burn out before we get there, and Landon has been carrying Skyler this whole time. There are Hushcru trees two miles from here, we can sleep in the branches and continue tomorrow."

"You are delaying this too long!" She started to run from them.

Chad used the Decttronium, and without him realizing it, more from the surrounding puddles bonded to him, and he extended the element twentyfold than he had before.

He encased her in a vine of the element and pulled her back to him, "We are not as strong as you here, your Highness. We rely on elements, and if you want all of us to do this, that we are all equal, then you need to slow down." He gently blew in her ear, and she instantly calmed.

"I just want him to die." She collapsed onto Chad.

"I know." He kissed the top of her head and smoothed her hair.

Landon cradled Skyler in a bubble of Marttronium and pushed her on. Chad still had Hyacinth laced with the Decttronium, weary if he should release her, so he carried her on his back as he did on Earth. He wanted her as close to him as possible. He knew if she desired, she could cast out the element and run, but her feelings for him were stronger than ever, and he could feel her palm search for his heartbeat as they journeyed forward. Once they were settled on tree tops Hyacinth turned to Chad, "I'm going to kill him."

"I know." He tried to look in her eyes, but she refused make eye contact with him.

"I'm going to like it." Her bloodlust grew within her, it was stronger than it had been on Earth, almost as if an animal instinct had over taken her better judgment.

"I know." He tried to hold her still and she continued to fight and shake, "Please, Hy, please look at me."

She stared at the turquoise in his eyes, and was momentarily hushed, "And yet somehow, seeing this rise within me, you still want this?"

"More than anything…"

"Then I'm worried for you." She grabbed him and stared in his eyes, "I've grown inhuman here."

"I can see that."

"Then why?"

He slowly held her until her ear was against his chest, "Can you hear that?"

"Yes…"

"I'm still human, and we're connected, I'll be human for us both until you get what you want." A single tear ran down her cheek, "I want him to die."

"And he will."

"Now!"

"Soon." He continued to cradle her as she continually cried.

In the other tree Skyler fluttered her eyes open, and she stared at Landon unable to hear anything. He carefully placed her speaker stone back in. "I'm sorry Baby Girl, but you were hypnotized by the Mrshti flower."

"It was so pretty, I wanted to touch it," she said groggily.

"I know, they are very beautiful, but the burn from their touch is more painful than you could ever imagine."

"You were stung?"

"I was…"

"And…"

"I wished for death…at one point I could no longer form coherent thought, the pain never stops, you never habituate to it, you are constantly burning, and there is no light at the end of the tunnel, and depending on how long you touched the flower, is how long the pain will last."

"Tell me more…" she cuddled close to him as he touched up and down her arm. "I touched it for less than a second, and the pain continued for well over a day."

"That must be awful."

"It was…I begged Gretgen to end the pain, but he waited, and was patient as I screamed and seizured from the pain."

"I'm so sorry you went through that."

"Well it taught me a valuable lesson."

"What was that?"

"When I heard their song after that, I paired it with the pain…so I never fell victim to it again."

"Thank you for keeping me safe." She nuzzled herself closer to him.

"Always will, Baby Girl." He kissed the top of her head and then gently ran his fingers through her hair.

"Can I ask you something about what we talked about before we left?"

"What?"

"You wanted to buy me something…" she gently rubbed her hand down his thigh.

"Yes…"

"What do you want to buy me?" When she reached his kneecap she swirled her finger around and then made her way back up.

"I want to surprise you."

"Okay, then I won't ask what I was going to ask…" She stopped touching him.

The curiosity got the better of him, "What were you going to ask?"

"If it was jewelry…" She looked up at him and smirked.

"Maybe…" He smiled back at her.

She squeezed him tighter, "I love you." Her mind flooded with the adorable charms on a brand-new Pandora bracelet, filled with all things Landon.

"I love you too!" He held her among the branches and they snuggled staring as the thousands of mini moons started to forge together. Their evening was going smoothly as opposed to Chad and Hyacinth, her impatience was getting the better of her.

Chad held Hyacinth, "I love you so much, please relax."

"I can't…" Instead of crying, her whole body grew harder as if she would turn to stone. "Look at me!"

"No!" she turned away.

"Stop it!" He held her tighter, he could feel her tense up as if she would leap from the tree, he tethered her to him with the Decttronium so they were bubbled together.

"What are you doing?"

"Ensuring you don't fall from the bough."

"You want to suppress me, but I will never be that way!"

"Are you talking about the mission, or are you talking about our relationship?"

"We don't have a relationship." She pushed the element away from her, and it receded into Chad at an alarming rate. He couldn't hide the teal color from entering his skin and hair. "Yes, we do…" he said calmly, as if his element kept him solid for her.

"What are you talking about?"

"We love each other, you've told me…I know you do, but you don't want to say it now, so you can concentrate on killing Jom, but…"

"On this planet, at this moment, if I don't kill that paper fucker I will never return to Earth and make Eggo waffles like the commercial. If I can end this here, then everything you ever wanted will be yours."

"Why are you trying to sell it to me?" He shook his head at her.

"What do you mean?"

"I'm going to have that with you, because this is going to happen. I just don't need to have it instantly. I can sit back, wait and do it right."

"How?"

"Because your past is really what's motivating this revenge, and I don't have that back story."

"Don't talk about me like you know me!"

"I do." He held her tighter, "I always have," he carefully blew in her ear to calm her, and for whatever the reason she melted onto him and kissed him repeatedly. He seized the moment and wrapped the two of them in a cocoon of Decttronnium. She allowed herself to cuddle onto his chest as she had done on Earth and she finally sighed in relief. They all felt settled in the trees together waiting for the morning to complete their journey.

SIXTEEN

The heat from the Quarternewt nest was abundant as the sweat dripped from each of their brows. The smell was a mixture of gym socks and melted rubber. Between the heat and pungent stench, they each wrinkled their noses as they approached. They could see what appeared to be steam slowly seep out from the base of the nest and surrounded their ankles.

"What is that?" Skyler asked having never seen this part of the planet.

"Apparently the ground was overcooked in the microwave," Landon said sweetly. "It's just residue…it won't hurt you."

"Unless you graze your ankle on a Mrshti Flower because you can't see the ground," Hyacinth said bitterly.

"Remind me to wear boots the next time we're here," Skyler said, disgusted by the steam.

"The whole point of this is so there won't BE a next time," Hyacinth said as she carefully stepped, fearful of what lurked beneath the myst.

"So, what exactly is the plan?" Landon asked again.

"Place the speaker stone on its jaw so we can speak to it, like we planned, get their back story, explain what happened, tell them our intentions, an open dialogue conveying how remorseful we are, and how we're here to restore the balance, end the abductions; a.k.a. get Earth out of the plucking zone." Hyacinth switched her tone to severe and determined.

"Okay, but what if that's not where it is meant to go?" Landon shook his head.

"What do you mean?" she stopped moving and stared at him.

"The Gnetgnu placed them in our jaws…but they kept them on the sides of their mouths." Landon feared what would happen attempting to shove the stone in the jaw of a Quarternewt.

"You're bringing this up now?" Hyacinth asked flabbergasted.

"Well, I mean…"

"You couldn't share this realization *before* we traveled between worlds to get here?"

"Calm down your Highness." Chad tried to grab her to blow in her ear to calm her down, but she wiggled away too quickly.

"NO! You are the one who has slaughtered the most, did they ever beg for life or make a sound?"

"I heard noise, but then again, they didn't have a speaker stone, and it was so long ago…I don't know."

"You're being a little loud," Skyler cautioned as she quickly placed her bubble of Septtronium around her for protection.

They all heard what sounded like a synthesizer going out of key. They all turned as an older Quarternewt rose from its nest.

"Plan?"

"Just keep trying to put speaker stones near its mouth and jaw."

They quickly climbed to the top of the nest and jumped inside. The creature sat up and stared and appeared dazed. The four threw the stones at the beast, who grew visibly annoyed. It summoned the Decttronium from its nest to push them away when Chad lifted the nest and the creature backward. Hyacinth ran toward it, shoved a speaker stone into every appendage she could muster. It swatted at her like a mosquito. She placed the stone within what she thought was its ear but was more like a decorative horn when it smacked her hard, she fell to the bottom of the nest.

Before she could stand, it kicked her hard and she went careening into the air. Chad quickly placed his arm in the air and sent the Decttronium to retrieve her. Then, Skyler climbed from behind, then dropped another speaker stone in its ear, and promptly scurried away in her bubble until she was safely beside Landon.

"What the hell, man?" The Quarternewt yelled. "I'm trying to sleep, and you humans come barging in here throwing pebbles at me. What the hell?"

"You know we are humans?"

"You're those things we've been warned about to stay away from, you're like worse than the Mrshti flowers…" The Quarternewt rolled its eyes and then used its talons to flick each of them out of its nest.

"Wait! Please, we just want to talk!" Skyler said as she clutched to the outside of the nest and then swung herself back inside.

"What? No way, not falling for it."

Hyacinth came crashing down, immersed in Decttronium, into the middle of the nest. "Fuck's sake Chad, couldn't make it a clear fucking landing!"

The Quarternewt screamed as if a demon was in its presence, "You fucking monster!" it went to flick her too, but it was propelled backward by Chad.

"Did the speaker stone attach?" She asked.

"What a Cliff thing to say," Chad smirked at Hyacinth. She rolled her eyes.

"I think it worked. I mean, it's talking," Landon said.

"Then ask it a question!" Skyler squealed.

"I'm not an IT! What is wrong with you humans?"

"Sorry, I didn't want to assume your gender…" Skyler was always the politically correct one. "What the hell is a gender?"

"Well, it's a way of discriminating between…"

"Shut it!" Hyacinth interrupted, "Where is your speaker stone attached?"

"Stay away from me! Baby Killer!" The Quaternewt lifted its tail threateningly.

"What?"

"You're the Baby Killer! You murdered a baby Quarternewt! We all know who you are! Betrayer of your own kind! What the fuck, dude? Why the fuck are you in my nest? You're a disgrace!"

Hyacinth looked shocked. "What?"

"You're a disgrace! How could you do that to your own kind?" It yelled louder.

"I'm not a Quarternewt, I'm a human…" she put one eyebrow up while the others looked at one another

confused.

"You are bound to the Quarternewt!" it pointed to her core piece.

"What?" She was confused.

"You were meant to be with the Quarternewt, you are our Prophet Warrior!" Again, it pointed to her core piece, "A gift you don't deserve!" It then pointed to the jewel between its eyes that all Quarternewts had, each a different shape and color.

"What are you talking about?" She asked, shocked throwing her arms up in the air in frustration.

"You were supposed to defeat Jom for our people! Instead, you slaughter your own kind! You killed a baby that fell from its nest, you are a disgrace!"

Hyacinth became unhinged, "I was *abducted* by Jom, who told me that you were demons to destroy their civilization! I killed the babe meant to destroy their entire race! I was preventing the genocide of a species."

"You murdered an innocent baby because you believed what you were taught! You never questioned their teaching!"

"Because…because…" She didn't know what to say.

"You didn't want to know, you ridiculous little follower! Fuck off, Baby Killer!" Again, its tail was up, ready to swipe them as far away as possible.

"Everyone, please calm down!" Skyler said from inside her bubble.

"You hate that phrase!"

"Well, everyone is pumped up when we really need to start a reasonable dialogue."

The Quarternewt jumped to its hind legs and then crashed forward on its front legs, sending Landon, Chad, and Skyler into the air. Hyacinth clutched to the nest fragments below her, fearful of what would be their next move. The others used their elements and reached out to the nest. The Septtronium and Marttronium fizzled upon touching the nest, and as such, they each reached out a second strand and bound to Chad, who could easily bond to the nest.

"I didn't know!" Hyacinth was defensive, "I had a hole drilled into my jaw, and the first faces I saw told me I was meant to rise above the anguish and bring *their* people to balance. I never knew what it meant!"

"At least you killed the baby's giver!"

"What do you mean?"

"It never occurred to you why it was so easy to take down an alpha? You're a friggin chode."

"Excuse me?"

"The only reason it succumbed so easily was because you killed their baby not more than six months beforehand! And you didn't even bury it! You didn't give that slaughtered innocent a chance to resurrect!"

"Wait, you can do that?" Chad was confused.

"You are some Decttronium Lord and have free travel among the Quarternewt, but seriously, dude, think about the company you keep. Your companions had best leave my nest before I take my wrath out on all you douche bags! I was fucking napping, and you bed bugs came creeping in to destroy my bliss. Fuck you, fuck all of you!"

Before the four could protest, the Quarternewt raised them into the air and propelled them backwards, but Chad held tight with the Decttronium. Skyler clung to Chad and pleaded with the Quarternewt, "We only want to speak with you. We were deceived and want the truth! Where is your leader? Where is the one in charge, please? We journeyed here not for your lives but for your teachings!"

"This shit's legit?" The Quarternewt stared at Chad.

"Legit…we have more speaker stones," He held his hand up, showing them to the Quarternewt, "We only want to talk and understand why we were lied to."

"You stay here, do not move. You've already infested my nest. I will not let you infect anyone else's, you stupid little bugs." The Quarternewt quickly flew away as they stared. Within moments, it returned with two additional Quarternewt. The Quarternewt took the speaker stones and placed them into their ears.

"What the hell, man? I was totally napping, and you interrupt me for what?"

"Are those like real humans?"

"Is *that* the Baby Killer?"

"Yeah, and she's…"

"Why the hell would you bring me here to see the Baby Killer? Fuck her!"

"Are you out of your damn mind? Don't interrupt my napping!"

"Please, I'm asking you both to please stay and talk with us!" Hyacinth spoke, "I was deceived by Jom, we all were, we came back here to bring your people peace!"

"You were the ones who ruined it to begin with!"

"We didn't know!"

"Well, now you know, how does it feel, Baby Killer?" The other two Quarternewts uttered while encircling Hyacinth. Then they both turned to Landon and let out an annoyed grunt. "And get that piece of shit away from us, don't you know better?"

"I didn't know!" she shook her head. Chad immediately went to her side and said, "I don't know anything!"

Chad blew in her ear gently.

"Ah, the Decttronium Lord is her spirit guide, figures…pathetic."

"What are you talking about?" Landon asked.

"Marttronium has no business in our nests, save it for the Mustleknapps; you're just as gross…fuck off, dude!" the other said disgusted.

"I came back to this planet to kill Jom." Hyacinth looked at each of them, "I killed your kind for reasons I was brainwashed to believe, but I will not be so naïve again…I will destroy every Gnetgnu on this planet, one by one. For fun, for vengeance, for my own reasons that you don't need to know!"

"Damn, she's a feisty one."

"She *is* the Prophet Warrior."

"Doesn't explain the bitchy human shell." The Quarternewt rolled its eyes.

"No way is she for real right now." The other protested, "Our Prophet Warrior wouldn't kill a baby and then return to kill its creator."

"That's her, check the piece!" The three quarreled with each other, and pushed each other in the chest with each utterance.

"No way, seriously dude, she could've killed the Prophet Warrior and took the piece."

"Ugh, if she did it woulda turned soft dipshit."

"Seriously, dude, she's the one in the pictures, or I've gone Mustleknapp."

"Shut your fucking tongue!"

"Totally, check it…"

"What the hell is happening?" Hyacinth looked at her friends.

"I think the Quarternewt are debating whether to forgive you or not." Skyler looked confused.

"Jim needs to see this." The Quarternewt pointed its talon to Hyacinth.

"True, Jim needs to make the call."

"Jim'll know what to do!"

"Who the fuck is Jim?" Hyacinth was annoyed at being left out of the conversation. Finally, the three turned to her, "Our leader!"

"Your leader's name is Jim?" Hyacinth asked in a monotone voice.

"Don't judge fucking human, you blindly believed someone named Jom, so shove it and suck it fuckwad!"

"Is it slightly unnerving how speaker stones take on our language so flawlessly?" Chad asked.

"Seriously Cliff!" Hyacinth shrieked. "What, it's true."

"Listen to the Decttronium Lord! He is wiser than all you bugs, especially you Baby Killer!"

Before any of them could say a word, a black tar enrobed the four of them, and there was no escape.

. . .

Hyacinth was encased in a cage of Bronttronium, an element that none of them knew existed, the black tar that had enrobed them and brought them to a place in the middle of the nests that none had ever ventured before. She was so flustered by the Quaternewt's reaction to their presence that she couldn't channel her emotion to see if she could repel it, the way she had the other elements.

She was in a panic, and tried to center her thoughts, but couldn't. The others were bound together with their elements entwined with one another, the Quarternewt knew how to mix them in such a way that not one of them possessed the power to escape. It broke her heart to see them each wallowing in pain from being pulled too tightly. She knew Skyler was falling apart, Landon couldn't break free to comfort her, and Chad's only thought was to get to Hyacinth, but he was futile.

A Quarternewt came over to the cage, it was an alpha, and stared at each one. It leaned over and licked Chad's cheek and then shook its head in disapproval. It turned to Hyacinth in the cage, then moved the Bronttronium with its mind and approached her aggressively with its tail up and its talons drawn, she didn't retreat to the back of the cage like a frightened animal. She stood proud in her stature, she was not afraid to die, and she was not afraid to be hurt, she jutted out her bottom jaw and then mouthed the words, "Fuck you."

The Quarternewt had a speaker stone but without her actual words, there was no translation. The Quarternewt, based on

Hyacinth's posture and jaw, assumed she was hostile and stabbed her through her shoulder with their front talon and held her high in the air. All the Quarternewt chanted in gratitude for the torture. Those without speaker stones sounded like synthesizers going up and down the scales. It echoed behind the twenty or more who took the speaker stones. The higher the Quarternewt raised her body, the deeper the wound, and by the time she was high enough for the whole clan to view, Hyacinth couldn't help but scream as the blood dripped down and seemed to splatter with each of her heartbeats.

"Hyacinth!" Skyler screamed as she started to hyperventilate.

"Look away, Baby Girl." Landon tried to comfort her, entrapped within the elements he once controlled, all congealed together made him futile.

Chad's heart broke in half, "Stop! Please stop!"

A random Quarternewt turned their head to the side, "Doesn't feel good, does it?"

"What are you talking about?"

"Watching one of your own die, for no reason…"

"We were deceived."

"Maybe you were, maybe you weren't…did you not take a moment to think what it might feel like to lose someone you loved? Whether they were good or not, that was a being that meant something to someone." The Quarternewt left quickly.

Hyacinth did her best to swallow the pain in her shoulder, she grew light headed from the blood loss. She would not crumble from this, she channeled her inner strength, she thought of killing Jom, she remembered her training with Gretgen. She contorted her body and then flipped in such a way the talon was removed from her flesh and she landed atop the beast.

She kicked it in the eye, and then dove toward her friends. She pulled their elements toward her to detangle the mess and then pushed them back until they were freed. There was shock and stares from the Quarternewt observing the Prophet Warrior work. She placed herself in the center as the three formed a triangle, their eyes each saturated with the color of their element. For fun, channeling the same feeling she felt when she moved their elements, she melted the cage from afar, and the Bronttronium was pulled around the triangle, protecting the four of them.

"Are you okay?"

"Seriously Cliff?" her voice was drained.

"Please…"

She knew he was dying on the inside knowing there was nothing he could do to stop this from happening to her, "There is a stream of blood from my shoulder and I just jumped 50 feet from the air…I'm gonna need a minute."

"A minute if you're lucky," Landon said, fearful of breaking their formation.

"How do we fix this?" Skyler asked lost. "Does anyone have a white flag?"

"Coward." Hyacinth rolled her eyes at Chad. "What if they hurt you more?"

"I can take anything, stop treating me like a fragile human, I am more, I have always been more…"

"You sound sick." Skyler started to choke up.

"You have your elements, that's your power…I have me…I am my power."

"Then use it!" Landon yelled.

"We have wronged you," Hyacinth spoke. "We have journeyed to right the wrong!" From the crowd she heard repeatedly, "Baby Killer!"

"Disgrace!"

"What the hell man?"

"You took down your own people!"

"You are not MY Prophet Warrior!"

"Fuck off!"

"Why did you bother to come back?"

"Kill her!"

A small Quarternewt, possibly an adolescent, came out from the crowd with a speaker stone affixed to its ear. "Why did you kill?"

"Because I was taught to do so, and that by doing so I was saving my people," Hyacinth said. She looked the creature dead in the eyes without hesitation.

"They weren't your people."

"I didn't know that."

"Why didn't you question it?" It tilted its head ever so slightly, but didn't raise its tail.

"I believed, because I was scared, and believing in something when you're scared can be comforting."

"It was still stupid." It shook its shoulders and rolled its eyes.

"And I can see that now, but I didn't in the moment." She matched its movements.

"Leave the formation, and approach me proper."

"You want me to leave them behind and come out, unprotected to speak with you?"

"Seriously? I said proper, shouldn't that be enough simple human?" Hyacinth approached the juvenile; Chad instinctively placed a Decttronium bubble around her. "You are loved by the Decttronium Lord."

"What's a Decttronium Lord?"

"A master of the element, who can bend, shape, and kill at the will of the Decttronium."

"Then, yes I am." She bobbed her head back and forth.

"He loves you…but you are frightened."

"Seriously? We are in the middle of a battle between Earth being severed from this planet and trying to restore a balance within here, I'm bleeding to death from a shoulder wound, and you want to focus on the pathetic love story? This is a tale of revenge for fuck's sake."

"Not the way he sees you…"

"Oh can we please just focus on me killing the corrupt Jom?"

"What?"

"Everyone is so wrapped up in this shit!" She gestured to her and Chad, "Yes, we fucked, it was awesome, he's in love with me. We are not some reality series for everyone to gawk upon, we were both abducted onto this planet and to be honest all the fuck we want is to right what we fucked up and then go the fuck home!"

"Why did you return? You are the first ever to do so…"

"I am going to kill Jom." She threw her arms up in the air frustrated, and the pain from the doing so, made her cradle her shoulder. Her hand was covered in blood, and she knew if this went on, she'd never get her revenge, she really would die on this planet.

"Why?" Its eyes grew wide, trying to be empathetic to the most significant threat to their people.

"Because he lied to us, we are only four strong, but how many over the years have been brought, brainwashed, and then killed your kind? It's not right, and this is where it will end." She strained to keep herself upright, her body was weak, and slowly losing its ability to stand straight.

The juvenile tilted its head to the side, "There is another on your planet you intend to seek once this is complete?"

"Have I given an indication of such?"

"You have a Mustleknapp hair, surrounding your core piece."

She looked down, he must have done that before she left, "And if I did?"

"Mustleknapp cannot be trusted!"

"Says you! You are berating me for believing one species over another, and now you are telling me another species is worse…Guess the fuck what! I don't care! I don't give a flying fuck! I want to kill Jom, he lied to me, he lied to all of us, and I want to rip his paper like being into nothingness and then play with the dead threads!"

"You're intense!"

"You've entrapped us, and ripped by fucking shoulder apart, I wronged your people! I didn't mean to, I was LIED to! So now I'm going to go fuck up all his shit, is that good enough for your mob? I'm going to go fuck him up and kill a lot of stupid paper fuckers!"

"You're different from your others."

"They have elements, I have me." She turned to see them standing in their formation, protected for now at least. She didn't know what would happen next, but she doubted this was going to end the way she predicted.

"You are potent." It snarled.

"I'll take that as a compliment," she said with a dead-pan face.

"Prophet Warriors are destined to die." It cautioned.

"We are all destined to die, the question is merely, when."

"Why do you wear your core piece around your neck?" It asked confused. It was only then they both realized the mob was listening intensely to their conversation, as if they were engrossed in some kind of intense pod cast.

"Where do you wear yours?"

"The core piece knows where the core piece belongs," it pointed to the space between its eyes, their core piece was purple and in the shape of a triangle.

"I was given this by Gretgen," and at that point she fell to her knees, the blood continued to drain from her shoulder, "I was told this was how I would earn my way to enter the portal and return to my home on Earth."

"That's not true." It scoffed.

"I know that now." She matched its inflection.

The juvenile slowly reached out its talon and beckoned the Dect-tronium away, as it was restored to Chad, he dropped to his knees. The juvenile touched the shoulder injury. Hyacinth breathed in deep and swallowed the pain, it stared at the liquid that was on its talon, "What is that?"

"Blood."

The Quarternewt leaned forward and smelled the wound, "Your blood smells weird."

"Your blood feels weird."

"Because they are one, and you never saw it until it was too late."

"Not 100% sure of the right reaction to that statement..." She did her best to keep herself together.

"Are you always this sarcastic?"

"You don't even know what that means!"

"I know my planet's interpretation, and the speaker stone has labeled it as such in your language."

"Define it for me then." She rolled her eyes defiantly. If this was how she was going to die, she wasn't going to be placated by anyone or anything.

"Using irony to prove your point."

"Ding ding ding we have a winner."

"I'm not sure if that is endearing or annoying…"

"It's one or the other, and many are confused by it." Hyacinth looked down, realizing how no matter what planet she was on, she was always misunderstood.

"This is your blood?"

"Yes."

"This is my blood?" The adolescent pierced its skin and held it out to her.

"So does that mean we're connected somehow?"

"Sort of, only if you combine them." The juvenile mixed the two on its palm and then touched it to Hyacinth's shoulder who screamed at the sensation as though she was being stabbed through the heart… she fell completely backwards, as if she finally died.

"Hyacinth!" Chad screamed, he went to walk toward her, and Skyler and Landon held him back. "Look!" They exclaimed.

They watched mesmerized as the combination of the bloods healed her shoulder, the juvenile carefully took Hyacinth in its arms and walked her to the center of the quadrant they were in. From above a large shadow cast upon them all. Jim was coming to assess the situation.

They brought her before Jim. And he looked down at her, she braced herself for the worse, and as she closed her eyes tight, she whispered, "I'm sorry." Jim pulled her toward him and embraced her closely, he licked her shoulder repeatedly.

After what seemed like twenty minutes he raised her up over his head, "This one is different!" Jim called out to the crowd watching the disappointment in his people who were anticipating a slaughter. "The

Prophet Warrior! OUR Prophet Warrior! The one to end the imbalance, she is here, she is the one!"

At that point Hyacinth felt her core piece attempt to burrow into her skin, she winced in pain. "What's happening?" She looked frightened.

Her core piece stayed on the surface but no longer required the necklace, it was simply adhered in place on the base of her throat. Despite her attempts to remain as sharp as possible in the given conditions, she collapsed unconscious into Jim's arms. He handed her to another Quarternewt who flew out of sight.

Chad screamed, "Hyacinth!" the nests all around him rose several feet in the air. "Silence him!" Jim called.

A Quarternewt bashed Chad over the head with their tail. Landon looked over panicked at Skyler, "This is not good."

"It's going to be okay." Skyler was convincing herself more so than Landon.

"We are prisoners, Chad is unconscious, they just stole Hyacinth."

"We are here for peace!" She said as she breathed slowly in and out of her mouth.

"They don't see it that way."

"We have to show them."

"How? What do you want to show them?"

"I don't know."

A Quarternewt sniffed the two of them, they both turned away with their heads down and their eyes shut. The outlook was grim, and they both clutched to one another in fear for their lives. They grabbed Chad and held him tight, and then through some power they never knew existed, Landon projected an image of when he was abducted, and the Quarternewt all gathered around. It was like watching a group of people watching a drive-through movie, as they all finally saw the deceit of the Gnetgnu, and even without speaker stones, could finally understand.

...

Hyacinth slowly regained consciousness. She was in a Quarternewt nest but was highly puzzled about how she got there. She sat up and looked around her. She now recognized the winding vines to be the Barttronnium. The Quarternewt had somehow mastered blending this element with Decttronium, which revealed how Chad was able to move the nests so flawlessly. Where was she?

At that moment Jim stood before her, "How long were you with Jom?"

"A year."

"And he taught you that we were demons?" he started circling her on all fours.

"Yes." She didn't bother to trace his movements, she could feel his movement within the nest and kept her gaze to the sky. "And you believed him?"

"I did."

"Why?"

"I was abducted to a planet I didn't know, I was told I had a purpose, a reason for the anguish, I never suspected I was being lied to…"

"Naïve." Jim rolled his eyes.

"I know that now." She looked down feeling sorry for herself, she was naïve and now that she was here, she was cautious she was being lied to all over again.

"You only just awoke."

"I have…" She wanted to ask so many questions to verify this was the truth and not another lie.

"What was your first thought?" Jim stopped moving.

"Excuse me?"

Jim lowered its neck to be directly in front of her face, "Tell me, what was the first thought in your mind?"

She stared into his eyes, "Where am I…"

"Your first thought went to you?" he sneered. "I guess." She shrugged.

"Not wondering where the Decttronium Lord exists?"

"No, my first thought was where am I."

"What of your team?"

"I can't be of use to them, if I am lost," she said philosophically.

"So where are they now?"

"Who?" she didn't know where any of them were, she didn't have any sense or presence within her that they were near.

"The Lords of the Elements?"

"You make them sound like a punk band." She scoffed.

"I do not understand…"

"Sorry, Earth slang."

"Explain slang." He sat comfortably on the floor of the nest, and Hyacinth sat beside him. "Words that exist, or newly made words with a meaning defined by culture and not a book."

"Example?"

"Highly sus."

"I do not understand that phrase." He put out his talon and she placed her hand on it.

"Means suspicious…"

"Distrust?"

"Yeah."

"Why do you make up new ways to say the same thing?"

"I don't know…" She looked around her.

"You're trying to find your way out…"

"Yes."

"Why?" it was peaceful in the nest, and she could rest.

"I do not know your intentions, other than you could've killed me but you didn't."

"I would never kill my own Prophet Warrior," Jim said casually, "Why not stay here in the nest?"

"I need to know where I am."

"My nest." He smiled.

"But where is your nest? Before I can save my friends or seek my revenge, I need to know where I am and what I'm up against."

"Self-centered?" he questioned.

"I can't save them or help the planet if I don't know where I am…"

"The more important question is why are you here?"

"I came back to fix what I messed up, and I am hated by your people, and the only thing I want is to kill Jom."

"Our people."

"Your people, our people, I only want to kill Jom."

"Jom has lost his way." He spoke sadly.

"How do you know?"

"I created him to be understanding, and now he's corrupted."

"Created?" she was confused.

"Yes."

"You made him?"

"Yes." He widened his eyes, "That is the definition of created, is it not?"

"How?"

"I used threads from the Chrchum tree, stitched them together, and then used the sacred powder beneath the Mrshti flower's origin space, to create Jom."

"Wait, so you made all the Gnetgnu?"

"Of course, with a different formula, Jom is the only Jom."

"Why?"

"To quell the Mustleknapp."

"I don't understand."

"When this planet was forged iotons ago, the Quarternewt reigned, out of nowhere one day three Mustleknapp appeared, and crushed several of our nests. They wanted to be the dominant species. We were defenseless against them, the only advantage we had was the ability to resurrect if our pieces were still within the nest."

"But Mustleknapp only want peace?" That was what she was taught after having his tail wrap around her. She felt it, she knew it, they wanted all the fighting to stop.

"The Mustleknapp cannot be trusted. They withhold the whole truth revealing only what they want you to see."

"What does that mean for their end goal?"

"They want only peace, but peace does not mean what you think it does as it does on your planet."

"What does that mean?"

"Peace on their terms, meaning they are dominant, everyone else is dead, and they have the whole planet to themselves."

"I don't believe it!" she shook her head back and forth, her heart broke thinking of the Mustleknapp in this way. Her Mustleknapp wasn't like that, or was he? He often withheld the whole picture, but it always revealed itself over time, he knew it would unfold in the correct fashion.

"So easy to believe Jom, and yet you doubt Jim?" He cradled her face with his talon, looking at her adoringly.

"I know the Mustleknapp." She smiled thinking about when he wrapped his tail around her.

The thought projected into Jim's mind, "Ewww, you mated with a Mustleknapp?"

"No!" she said defensively.

"It wrapped its tail around you!"

"Yeah, so?"

"That's mating according to their kind!"

"What?" Another detail he failed to mention.

"He mated with you."

"No, he sang to me, and then kissed me, and because I said we were never going to be together because he's not human…"

"Stop lying to yourself."

"Holy Fuck, no more of this conversation, he showed me my imminent death and their prophecy is hypothesized, that doesn't make it real! He showed me what he knew!"

"You know what they allow you to know, the whole picture belongs only to pure Mustleknapp." She kept shaking her head, "No, he wouldn't lie to me!"

"Jom lied, and you believed him, and now you think I am a liar?

But I'm sure there are times when you can see the deceit of the Mustleknapp."

"I don't know who to trust!" She looked up at him with her eyes wide, feeling comforted in the nest with Jim, still wanting revenge on Jom, and slightly grossed out about the Mustleknapp.

"Trust your training."

"What?"

"You were taught to see beyond the obvious, see beyond the battle, you were trained by Gretgen."

"Yeah, as the Gnetgnu Prophet Warrior."

"Who do you think made Gretgen?" She paused, "You trained the trainer."

He smiled, "Trust your training. What do you see now?"

She closed her eyes and then touched her core piece that was now merged to her flesh, "I see one of us not getting back, only three will make it back…"

"Choose."

"What?"

"Choose, which one of you will not make it?"

"I cannot make that choice!" She was horrified.

"You are the leader…"

"No, I'm just the assertive one."

"Assertive?"

"Stand up for what I believe in and not back down even if others see me as wrong."

"Are you assertive or are you a…" He appeared deep in thought, "The Earth word meaning bitch?"

"Fine line Jim." She laughed.

"Choose, of the four of you, who does not survive?"

"Who would you choose?" She tried to turn it back on him. If he was the mastermind behind her training, then he already knew the answer.

"It's not about me, it's about who you would choose."

"I can't make that choice!" She shook her head.

"You must…if you wish to kill Jom."

"That's not fair!"

"What about any of this has ever been fair?"

"I want to kill him, but not if all four of us have to separate."

"Unfortunately, that is what is needed, if you want to kill Jom, which I am not okay with by the way."

"If you are not okay with it, why would you allow me to do it?"

"I will allow you to confront him, slaughter the corrupted that follow the blinded order to kill without logic."

"What if I kill him?"

"What if you don't?" he pondered to her.

"You think I will grow tired and not have the strength?"

"You have more strength than you know how to handle."

"Then why?"

"If you want to slaughter Gnetgnu, have your final revenge, then one of you will perish…choose…and choose wisely."

Hyacinth curled into a ball and squeezed her legs tight, she slammed her fists down on the nest and watched for a brief moment the Barttronium and Decttronium separate then forge back together quickly. She looked over every scenario, and she finally made her choice, "Chad."

Jim was perplexed. "How did that decision come to be?"

"If I am forced to choose, I took each person and looked at the aftermath of their death. If Skyler dies, then Landon would be lost, if Landon dies Skyler would be lost, if I die Chad would be lost, but if Chad dies…" she held in the emotion as her throat grew thick. "I know how to handle when love leaves you, I'm not saying that I would be fine, but I know how to carry on…so if anyone should die, I would spare Chad the anguish of living without me…"

"Conceited much?" Jim didn't like her answer. "What? You asked me to choose!"

"I did, but you're so selfish it's kind of odd for a Prophet Warrior."

"How am I selfish?"

"A true leader is ready to die for their cause, their team, you were willing to sacrifice the one who loves you the most."

"I was ready to spare him a world without me, if I die Landon and Skyler still have each other, but that would leave Chad with nothing, that's not fair to him!"

"Because you love him?" He smiled at her and winked.

"Seriously, is every planet obsessed with whether or not I love Chad?"

"What do you mean?"

"Never mind, I played your stupid game," She stood and stretched, "Now, if you don't mind, there is a Gnetgnu leader that I need to tear apart."

"You no longer care what happens to your team?"

"They have bonded with the elements of your planet; they need only throw a hand in the air, and their enemy will perish,"

"So before when you asked *Where am I*, it wasn't so you could find your friends."

"I have had time to process and think since then."

"So, you are willing to allow Chad to die, so you can kill Jom."

"You made me play your stupid game! I don't want any one of us to die, we are here to fix what we broke, nothing more."

"You can't take back the lives you all stole."

"No, we can't, but we can prevent the Gnetgnu from taking another human from Earth to do the same, and that is what I intend to do."

"For honor, for your people?"

"For the sheer pleasure of ripping that asshole in half…"

"You need to be careful Prophet Warrior, your insanity is growing the longer you are here."

"I want to rip Jom apart, and until that moment comes, I don't know the meaning of the word sanity."

"Your team will be released, but I release you first, and see if you are true to your word."

"I am going to the Strythocket and I am going to rip them apart."

"Then you will need this." He took her forearms and gently traced from her elbow to her wrist. The sensation was burning, but she swallowed her suffering. When he was finished she looked and she had small scars strategically placed on her arms.

"What is this?"

Jim smiled, "You are of the Quarternewt, we were meant to find you first, but we didn't…Jom corrupted our Prophet Warrior, and now our Prophet Warrior has returned, and to be honest, do what I cannot do, bring myself to hurt my creations. You are the only humans who ever traveled here, and I have given you a gift."

She stared at the scars, she touched one, and it felt as though she was running a fever. "What do they do?"

"Think about ripping a Gnetgnu apart."

She did and tiny Quarternewt razors emerged from the scars. "Holy Shit."

"What?"

"I mean, I'm surprised, pleasantly surprised…scissor beats paper." She smiled.

"You are the Prophet Warrior of the Quarternewt texts, you were meant to restore the balance."

"Which means *I* will die."

"So, you will not get your choice."

"But if Jom is dead, and I can restore the balance, then it will be worth it…"

"What of Chad?"

"I love him, and he deserves someone better than me…" she spoke honestly.

"Why see yourself so unworthy?" He lightly brushed her hair with his talons.

"I am unworthy to be your prophet, and you have given me another chance, rescued me from the mob. I need to restore the balance of your planet. Jom is corrupt, but if you made him…" she stared off into the distance.

"What are you thinking?"

"It can't be…"

"What?"

"I don't know yet, but I will speak to him and find out, I will not kill without clarifying why he has done this. I will get the answers I have festered over all this time, and I will get you the answers into how he came to be corrupt."

Jim lifted her out of the nest and placed her on the ground, "Go…"

She started running at full force. From within another nest, Chad, Skyler and Landon watched from within another cage as she abandoned them.

"What is she doing?" Skyler asked hurt.

"She's going to get her revenge," Chad said heartbrokenly. "The only thing she's ever really wanted."

"Or she's going to restore the balance, and save us all," Landon said hopefully, "You can't assume anything in this world."

"Did she ever love me?" Chad looked at Skyler.

"Oh please." The Quarternewt guarding them scoffed, "Why do you take everything so personally?"

"Because I love her," Chad stared out on the horizon wishing her face would appear, and release them from their cage.

"That's the worst decision you'll ever make." The Quarternewt rolled its eyes.

"Why would you say that?" Chad slammed his hand on the bar of the cage.

"Because there are only two outcomes for the Decttronium Lord if he falls in love with the Prophet Warrior…"

"And they are?"

"Either he saves her, or he kills her."

SEVENTEEN

Hyacinth arrived to a whole row of Gnetgnu who were challenging her arrival to Strythocket. She rolled her eyes as they came toward her. They swayed their appendages in the air at an attempt to frighten her.

"Oh, come on!" She screamed. She charged into the fray and flexed her new Quarternewt blades on pack upon pack of Gnetgnu soldiers. She was enjoying the moment, and she couldn't help but smirk to herself as she ripped dozens in half with a single back hand. After she slaughtered the first wave the second approached. She recognized several from her time in the Great Hall. She cared not, and anyone that attempted to attack her after being torn in half by her razers was then torn apart with her bare hands. She still had no care or regret for her slaughter. She never thought of Chad, Skyler or Landon.

She only absorbed herself in the death around her. She continued tearing the Gnetgnu to shreds. It wasn't until she was about to tear the next wave apart, when she came face to face with Gretgen. She stared into his eyes, and it was only in that moment she fully reflected on what she was doing.

He bowed, folded himself in half prepared to die at her hand, and instead of tearing him apart she quickly grabbed and rolled him up tight and stuck him in her satchel. She was a ruthless killer, but she could not deny what they had, he needed a speaker stone and she would explain what happened, and he would understand, he was the only Gnetgnu with feelings, because of her teachings. She knew he didn't understand her, she was hoping the sincerity in her voice would quell him, "I am taking you with me, I will not allow anyone to harm you, we are connected. You cannot deny this, that is why your eyes long to see me."

She continued to kill all those around her when she sensed something approaching. She looked to the horizon and saw Chad along with 50 Quarternewt coming to assist in the slaughter. She closed her eyes and thought of Chad, as he ran, she pushed Decttronium toward him, and he absorbed it as he ran faster. She closed her eyes and concentrated her mind to him and uttered, *I love you.* She waited and within moments she felt the ground vibrate and she swore she heard in the distance, "I will always come back to you."

She refocused herself, she didn't need to concentrate on slaughter, Chad was here to take care of the small battle, she need only fight what was in front of her to get to the Great Hall. Chad loved her so deeply, he understood that she went to this length for the right reasons, and he supported her decision. She killed every Gnetgnu that came toward her, they stood no chance with her Quarternewt blades.

She pushed open the doors of the Great Hall as she had before, she felt euphoria knowing she was close to getting what she wanted. She saw the portraits of Chad and Skyler, and she couldn't help herself but climb atop the pillars and pull them down. She rolled them up and placed them in her satchel. They survived, they didn't need to be belittled as trophies.

Jom was readying an elixir at the altar of exception. He worked diligently, knowing that Hyacinth and her army of Quarternewts along with the element Lords were drawing near. He had been waiting for this moment for too long, and he was prepared; knowing more than she realized.

Hyacinth ran faster and faster; she made peace knowing she was the Prophet Warrior, and only with her death would the worlds be balanced and order restored from the power-hungry Gnetgnu corrupt since creation. She hoped Skyler, Chad, and Landon would be able to take the rest of them down. Chad knew within his soul that she loved him, and that was all that he needed, if she died at least, he knew the truth. She understood now, she was the Prophet Warrior but for the Quarternewt, that's why she was never afforded powers. She had to use her newly gifted sharp razors on her arms to take down Jom. Being bound to the Quarternewt for this short time, she felt more alive than she had the whole year of training. Was her sanity slipping, or was she finally seeing clearly? At this point, she couldn't tell anymore.

She kicked open the doors and stared at Jom from across the room. "What did you do it for?"

He answered her in his native language.

"Put in your speaker stone and truly face me." He did so, "You cannot understand."

"I am the Prophet Warrior, the one meant to take down the corruption of the planet, and I will take you down with my final breath. But before I do that, I need to know why you wanted to throw the world off balance."

"Your human mind cannot understand the damage and history of the Quarternewt."

"The Gnetgnu have done more damage to the Quarternewt than the Mustleknapp."

"And when you attempt to wipe out the Gnetgnu, the Mustleknapp will rise above as the dominant species, forever leaving the Quarternewt in peril."

"Your goal is the same, wipe out the Quarternewt and you dominate the Mustleknapp, they are too peaceful to take you down. You broke the treaty."

"Indeed, I did." He continued his task and at no point looked at her.

"Why Jom? Why did you have Gretgen train me to be the Prophet Warrior?"

"Because you are the Prophet Warrior."

"Of the Quarternewt, not of the Gnetgnu!"

"True."

"Then you know I am going to end you," She flexed her arms. "I will tear through you with a single backhand with my Quaternewt gifted arms, and then rip what's left of you with my bare hands."

Jom smiled widely, "Not before I crush you Quarternewt." He tilted his head. "Paper does not beat scissors."

"Yet again, you fail to see beyond what is given to you…"

"What does that mean?"

"Just because I don't show my whole hand…"

"What?"

Hyacinth didn't understand; she stared at him, then the outer body of Jom morphed into a human-sized Mustleknapp. His maniacal laughter was unsettling.

"Who are you?"

"I am Jam, the leader of the Mustleknapp, and after I crush you, all the Gnetgnu will be gone, and we will dominate the planet!"

"But Mustleknapp cannot lie."

"They cannot lie, but that does not mean I have to reveal the whole truth."

He started to swirl his body into the round hard stone he would propel into her and crush her body. A tear went down her eye, all of this was for naught. She bent down on one knee, this was all her fault. If she had never come here, she wouldn't have doomed the Quarternewt or wiped out the Gnetgnu. She sniffled her tear back, she was about to die, the image the Mustleknapp had shown her was true. She didn't allow her hysterics to take over, he saw her death and tried to warn her and she ignored him. She swallowed deep, accepted what lie before her, she would go out with dignity. She bowed her head as she could hear the squealing sound of the approaching attack. "I didn't see, until it was too late…I love you." A single tear went down her face and as the sound became deafening, she covered her ears to drown it out, which lifted and opened her satchel. Gretgen flew from her satchel screaming a term she didn't know. "NO!" she called, holding her arms out to him, only inches from clutching the edge of his bottom appendages.

He stretched out the edges of his body covering Jam and sealed his sides shut. Hyacinth looked up shocked, "Gretgen, NO!" Gretgen stayed strong as the squealing from inside grew louder, there was a deafening sound like something popped and the Jam exploded within the seams. There was a wave of Gretgen's paper around the room like confetti. Hyacinth grabbed the pieces as the tears flew from her eyes. She got down on her knees clutching the parchment, "You were always the Prophet Warrior," she sobbed. "You sacrificed yourself for your people."

At that moment Skyler arrived with Jim. "What the hell happened?" she ran over to Hyacinth and grabbed her tight.

"Jom was not Jom." She took her by both arms and stared in her eyes.

"What?"

"Jom was Jam."

"Who the fuck is Jam?" Skyler asked confused. "Leader of the Mustleknapp."

"Jim, Jom, Jam?"

"I'm letting that one go," Hyacinth said blankly. "Then where is Jom?"

They looked around the hall. Jim was startled, "It is impossible for a Mustleknapp to have beaten a Gnetgnu, he must be alive."

"But where?" Skyler shrugged.

Chad came running in, his eyes located Hyacinth; the blood and bruising on her face disturbed him,

"What happened?" He ran to be at her side, he wanted to kiss her, but knew she wanted the mission to take priority over their relationship.

"Paper cuts." She laughed. He quickly took a cloth from his pocket and started wiping off her face.

Jim leaned over to Skyler and whispered, "How long has," he pointed to Chad and Hyacinth. "Ugh, the drama since the beginning, but the mutuality recently."

"It's kind of cute."

"He's in love," Skyler said sweetly, "Since day 1."

"Of course he is, he is the Decttronium Lord." The manner in which he said it indicated to Skyler that Chad never had a choice in the matter, that he was destined to be with Hyacinth.

"I guess he saved her."

"So far…"

Skyler was about to press Jim to clarify that last statement when Chad came rushing over with Hyacinth,

"What happened?"

"Jom was Jam!" Skyler squealed.

"Who's Jam?" He asked, entirely in the dark.

"Jam was the leader of the Mustleknapp!" Hyacinth was still angry about that, how she walked directly into a trap. He would still be alive if she hadn't demonstrated compassion for Gretgen.

"But Mustleknapp beat Quarternewt." He ran his fingers over her skin worried something had harmed her further than the Gnetgnu battle.

"Gretgen," she said sadly. "Gretgen was the Prophet Warrior the whole time, and just didn't know it." She took a piece of his torn flesh and handed it to Chad, she gave another to Skyler, and another to Jim. It was then she realized this foursome was missing a critical player, "Where's Landon?"

Chad looked down, "I don't know how to say this…"

"Where's Landon?" Skyler looked panicked.

"He didn't make it."

"What?" Skyler screamed. "Define, didn't make it!"

"He melted in the nest, he fell through the cracks, and I tried to make a net of Decttronium, but he fell straight through."

"Do you have the body?" Jim asked quickly.

"He is with the Quarternewt."

Skyler started crying, "Why? Why did this have to happen?" She bubbled the Septtronium around her as she screamed and fell into a panic attack.

"Skyler stop!" Hyacinth called to her, but it didn't work. Skyler was falling apart within her bubble, which seemed to grow at an alarming rate. Hyacinth gently pulled the Septtronium from her body and she crumbled to the ground.

"NO!" she cried weakly.

"He is not dead." Hyacinth fell to her side to cradle her. "But he…"

"No, his Marttronium melted, he will be restored."

"That's not possible." She looked at her as if she was the biggest liar she had ever heard.

"It *is* possible."

"I don't believe you…"

"He is the Marttronium Lord on this planet, and he merely needs time, he is not gone, he is not dead!"

"Why?"

"It's the same as my Hunterna remember, the Quarternewt's nest heat had him melt, that's all, he can come back, we just need to follow the alchemy."

"I'll do whatever it takes, we need to go now."

"I do remind you, Element Lord, that there is unfinished business we must tend to here before we go back," Jim stated thoughtfully.

"What's more important than Landon?" Skyler squealed. "It's not a matter of import, it's a matter of opportunity."

"What does that mean?" Chad asked, confused.

"Oh, Cliff, you never cease to amaze me." Hyacinth rolled her eyes and flicked his forehead, "Because this was meant to be, we stopped the Mustleknapp from destroying all Quarternewt, but I fear for the Gnetgnu. Did we kill them all? Did any survive?"

"Where is Jom?"

"Jim, you made him. Can you sense him?"

Jim shut his eyes and clutched the gem affixed between them. "There is the presence of Jom and there is a small thumping of Jam in the Mustleknapp gorge."

They all looked around the hall trying to figure out where Jom could be trapped.

"Do you think Jam sent Jom to Earth?" Hyacinth asked the group.

"Impossible, how?"

"How was a Mustleknapp disguised as a Gnetgnu?" Hyacinth said dryly. She turned her gaze to Skyler, who was desperately searching, all she wanted was to be with Landon and bring him back to her.

"Point taken."

"Jim, walk around the room, does your sense of Jom heighten?"

Jim closed his eyes and tripped on the altar. He grunted, annoyed. "The presence is stronger if I move in this direction." He continued to move about the room.

Hyacinth started to laugh, Chad gave her a confused look, "What is so funny?"

"We traveled through space and time to play hot or cold with a Quarternewt."

The two started to giggle. Then Skyler lost her mind, "Landon! Stop laughing! Landon is dead!"

"We will restore him. We are on a planet with that technology, we will not leave without him. I told you, we all leave together," Hyacinth said assertively.

"I don't believe you!"

"Doubt me now?" Hyacinth was angry, "I have told you no lies, withheld no truths, he will be restored, you need to remember who you are, where you are!"

"Hy! Stop!" Chad said.

"What?" she shook her head.

"Again, you've entered video game narration. Knock it off!" He flicked her on the forehead, and she smirked.

"Element Lords, come here." They walked to Jim, who stared at the tomes of ancients. "The feeling is strongest here."

The three looked at the objects, the sphere for the Mustleknapp, the Rectangle of the Gnetgnu, and the Blade of the Quarternewt. Hyacinth picked up the sphere, "My birthday present."

"What?"

"My Mustleknapp gave me a puzzle that he made for my birthday."

"Your Mustleknapp?" Jim had a weird inflection in his voice.

"Well, he's all our Mustleknapp."

"He is NOT mine." Chad put his arms up.

"He's part of our family," Skyler said, "And so is Landon! So can you get to the point so we can get back there sooner than later!" She gave an annoyed look to Hyacinth.

Hyacinth started to trace the patterns the way the Mustleknapp had shown her, "He called it a puzzle orb."

"It's a sphere," Jim corrected.

"Sphere, orb, really we're going there?" The sarcasm was heavy in her voice.

"Can you open it?"

"I can try," she continued the patterns, and as she did a small labyrinth emerged. She ran her finger through the maze and when she reached the center the orb popped open, and a folded piece of parchment fell to the ground. "Jom?"

The parchment started to flutter and flap as it unfolded, and the fundamental Gnetgnu leader emerged, Jim quickly placed a speaker stone on his most precious creation. The eyes on his parchment moved about irratically, "What happened?"

"Jom!" said Jim.

"Jim?" Jom was shocked. "Where is Jam?"

"Jam was corrupt, and placed you in the sphere of the Mustleknapp, he took over the world, he banished the Mustleknapp to cover his tracks, and he abducted humans from Earth to slowly wipe out the Quarternewt."

"That's a lot of information. How long was I in there?"

"I don't know, I'm just glad you're free." Jim looked as though he was close to tears.

"Who are these humans?" Jom looked confused. While he knew what humans were, he had never seen one before.

"I am the Prophet Warrior of the Quarternewt."

"I am the Septtronium Lord."

"I'm Chad,"

Hyacinth shook her head back and forth and sighed. "Your power, Cliff."

"Oh, I am the Decttronium Lord…and sometimes she calls me Cliff."

"Stop talking."

"There is another of us who has fallen in battle. Can his flesh be restored?" Skyler asked desperately. "What is he made from?"

"He's human, but he is the Marttronium Lord." Jim quickly spoke, slowly inching his way closer to Jom. "Where has he fallen?" Jom inquired.

"The Quarternewt nest."

"He is with my people. He is the Marttronium Lord, I do not fear," Jim stated.

"Jim, I have missed your voice."

"And I, yours, Jom."

The two kissed and embraced passionately. Hyacinth's eyes widened, "What the…"

"Don't speak, don't say anything, because I don't want to know," Chad stated.

"What is happening?" Skyler whispered.

They continued kissing, Hyacinth was confused, "Dude, what the fuck is happening?"

"Again, I don't wanna know…"

"Will this new Jam be as corrupt as before?" Jom stared lovingly into Jim's eyes.

"Only time shall tell…"

"From what line does it descend?"

"I warn you, the head of the line has disappeared…but it is the Jentra line."

"The Jentra have always been a loyal, honest, and steadfast ally of the Gnetgnu and Quarternewt."

"Wait, did you say Jentra?" Hyacinth's eyes widened.

"Yes, have you heard of it before?"

"Once." She smiled and thought about the Mustleknapp waiting for her back home. His actions, while he saw them as treason, were for a greater purpose. His thoughtful birthday gift granted her the knowledge to save Jom, and now his line would join the Jam, Jim, and Jom leaders to balance the worlds.

That's why he always spoke in riddles, he unraveled what they never could and ensured that the planet would be saved. He wasn't a deceitful little rat, on the contrary, he was a hero.

"Then the Jam, Jim, Jom is restored." Jom once again kissed Jim.

Hyacinth couldn't help but laugh out loud. Chad nudged her, "Now, who's being a Cliff?"

"I couldn't help it! It looks like a demented gecko licking peanut butter off a playing card."

"And thank you for that image."

"Seriously, sorry to interrupt, but can you restore our friend?" Skyler's heart was broken thinking of returning to Earth without Landon.

"He is not a friend; he is the other half of your human soul," Jim stated. "Yes," Skyler said sadly.

"I know the feeling differently." Jim smiled and stared at Jom.

"Bring his body, Jim. Would you be able to spare a vial?" Jom asked lovingly.

"For his sacrifice, I too shall make one." Jim pierced his heart and filled a vial with the indigo substance, and handed it to Jom.

"Wait, you can just do that on cue?" Hyacinth asked in disbelief.

"Yes, but only for small doses."

"So, we waved mass genocide on your people because the corrupt Jam couldn't get your blood donations fast enough? Or was that just part of the cover story?" Hyacinth was annoyed. "Compassion." Skyler reminded.

"What is blood?" Jim asked.

"It is that which courses through the veins of a human to keep their body alive," Chad said.

Skyler and Hyacinth stared at him, "Damn, Chad."

"Bring me the body, and it shall be restored for your journey to the human planet."

Skyler outstretched her arms as the Septtronium created a shell around her body to make the journey to the Quarternewt nests faster. Chad grabbed Hyacinth and secured her to his back, "What are you doing?" she asked.

"Making damn sure I don't lose you now," He summoned the Decttronium, which surrounded them. "I'm going back to Earth with you, alive, and I'm going to kiss you every day."

"I love you," she closed her eyes, relieved they were going home.

"I love you forever, for always, with all of my heart."

When they arrived at the nests, Landon's lifeless body sent Skyler into an emotional and panicked state. She screamed so loud all the Quarternewt backed up, covering their ears. Those with speaker stones took them out until she finished. She wept over his body, her whole being shaking from the anguish.

Her tears dripped onto him as she clutched his body, then gently kissed his frozen lips.

"Wait, are they like…" Chad was so clueless.

"Yeah, since like day one? Are you that dense, Cliff?"

"I didn't realize they were,"

"Cliff, you never cease to amaze me."

Jom leaned over Landon's body, and he mixed the tears from Skyler with the blood from the Quarternewt and then pushed his paper appendage down Landon's throat, maneuvered through his body and directly inserted the combination into his heart. He backed up and asked, "Remind me again, who was he?"

"Landon," Chad answered.

"Cliff, take a break for a second," Hyacinth shook her head, "He was the Lord of the Marttronium."

"The Marttronium Lord?" He asked, confused.

"Lord of Marttronium, Marttronium Lord, same-same."

"Then he is precious indeed."

"The rarest of all Lords."

The Jom took to the closest puddle holding the substance and placed a handful down Landon's nose.

Within 10 seconds, Landon sat up and started coughing.

"LANDON!" Skyler wrapped her arms around him.

"What happened?" He held her confused. The last moment he remembered was them in the Quarternewt cage, watching Hyacinth running away.

"You died! You fucking died!" The tears continued to run down her cheeks. He couldn't tell if they were of fear or joy.

"I what?" He didn't understand.

"You died, but you're back. Don't ever leave me!" She squeezed him as tight as she could. "What happened?" Landon held her close and looked at Chad for answers.

"The heat from the nest, you fell through, your power compromised, it was awful. I tried to save you, but the net broke, and you were gone," Chad said, saddened.

Landon held Skyler closer to him and kissed the top of her head, "It's okay, I'm okay, I'm here, it's okay, calm down, Baby Girl, I'm here."

"I hate that phrase!" She sniffled.

Chad again gave Hyacinth a confused look. "How long has this been going on?"

"Like I said, pretty much since the beginning."

"Oh…"

"You are such a Cliff."

"Stop calling me that."

"I can't," she wrapped her arms around him and squeezed him tight. "Easy, Prophet Warrior."

"I was not their Prophet Warrior. It was Gretgen the whole time, I'm part Quaternewt." She flexed her arm at him to reveal the blades.

"You're still my warrior, and you have to stop squeezing me. I will break."

"I'm not going to break you," she smiled, "I'm going to make you whole."

"Element Lords, we can never thank you enough for restoring order to our planet," Jom said.

"We can ensure the balance and keep our clans at peace. We are stronger together, we always have been," Jim eagerly took Jom's appendage and then once again pulled him in for another kiss.

"Dude, what the…" Landon was confused.

"Don't go there," Skyler interrupted.

"Now, can we go home?" Hyacinth said.

"Where is home?" Jim asked.

"Earth."

"Humans, you can stay here. You are welcome here," They both smiled.

"True, but we are not Gnetgnu, Mustleknapp or Quarternewt. This is your balance, not ours," Chad said proudly.

"I grant you free access through the portal of the Quarternewt," Jim said and handed Hyacinth a jar of

purple powder.

"I grant you free access through Gnetgnu portal," Jom said and handed her a jar of white

powder.

"I am sure when the Jam comes of wisdom, he too will offer you access,"

"Go in peace, rejoin your Earth, and enjoy its riches."

"Thank you."

Hyacinth saturated her index finger with the powder, smirked, and flicked Skyler's forehead. They all smiled as her body disappeared, pulled back into the portal. "Are you ready?" she teased Landon.

"Send me home," Landon smiled. She did the same.

"I think this may be one of your happiest moments flicking me." Chad smiled.

"Just wait till we go home." She smiled playfully to the side.

"What do I have to expect?"

"I love you…that's all that matters anymore." She smiled and flicked his forehead with the powder.

Before she could leave them, she turned to Jom and Jim, hugged each one, and took care to be overly ginger with Jom, "In case either of you are ever on Earth, you dial these numbers into something called a phone, and it will summon me." She handed the cloth to Jom.

"You are the Prophet Warrior of the Quarternewt."

"I was the warrior, and now I want to go home." She sprinkled the powder on herself and felt her body pull backwards through the rainbow portal.

EIGHTEEN

Chad could feel the air knocked out of him, ten times worse than when Hyacinth pushed him onto the couch. He started to breathe regularly. He forced his eyes open, and Landon was standing over him. Landon smiled and called out to someone, "He's awake!"

Skyler appeared in view next, and she smiled, "Welcome back!" Her voice sounded like her, but everything seemed to be muffled and in slow motion.

"He's still coming through," Landon commented.

"It's okay, he will." Skyler smiled, and she and Landon picked him up and brought him somewhere. He couldn't see. He could barely hear. All he knew was he was back on Earth. His brain cut out, and he fell asleep immediately in the back seat of the Jeep.

It was nighttime when he awoke with his faculties about him. He sat up, and in the field, he saw Skyler and Landon lying on a blanket, gazing at the stars. He winced and then stood.

"Hi," he said plainly as he approached them.

"You're awake!" Skyler ran over and hugged him.

"That took way too long." Landon also came over to embrace him. "Where's Hyacinth?"

"We don't know." They both looked down, upset.

"What do you mean you don't know?" His heart broke in half.

"She hasn't appeared, and we can't sense her, and we were worried about both of you, but then you appeared...so we're just going to keep waiting for her."

"Why isn't she here?" He dropped to his knees and felt his heart shatter at the thought of her being lost. "She'll be here; we know she will."

"How do you know?"

"Because we won, we finished what we needed to do. Why wouldn't she come through?"

"She sent us back, but what if something went wrong when she sent herself back?"

"You can't think that way."

"Without her... I can't think."

. . .

Skyler walked into Hyacinth's apartment. Caleb left his laundry to be done outside his door. The basket was overflowing. She rolled her eyes and went into Hyacinth's room with the false hope that she was inside, but she wasn't.

Caleb exited his room without his mask, wielding a baseball bat. "Who are you?"

"Wow, no mask this time. Has your paranoia subsided?" She didn't bother to look at him.

"Who are you?" He raised the bat higher.

"Don't recognize my voice?" She walked over, and Caleb backed up. She reached out and took the bat away from him. Caleb stood with a dumbfounded expression. He was scared and overwhelmed, and since she took away his only defense, he didn't know what to do. She rolled her eyes and looked just like Hyacinth as she did so, "It's Skyler."

"Oh, um...it's nice to meet you in person." He held his hand out to shake it.

"Where's your precious mask?" she held her hand back to emphasize *don't touch me.*

"Um…I don't think I need one anymore."

"And why is that?"

"I had the virus, I got over the virus, and now I'm here, waiting for her to come home."

"You are such a fucking asshole, and seeing you in person, I'm glad she's not here to see how pathetic you look." She started twirling the bat around, debating if she would keep it or not. She enjoyed how heavy it was. Metallic bats were hard to come by. When she thought about it deeper, most things were hard to come by these days.

"Where's Hyacinth? She's not answering her phone. I need to find her!"

"You're not the only one." She spoke with her jaw clenched.

"I need to tell her…"

"You're too late!" she interrupted, "There's nothing you could say to her to bring her back to you now!"

"What?"

"Do you have any idea how much of a nightmare you were?"

"Look, you don't know me." He was defensive, "You don't know what we had, what I will do for her to

show her my remorse,"

"Please, you can't fix it, and that's what's making you angry, that you can't blame her!"

"Stop pretending you know me!"

"Nope, I don't know you at all. All I know is that you threw her past in her face before you broke her heart and then expected your laundry done, your food cooked, while you placed every gift, every memory, every sentimental shared item outside your door to remind her every day that she came here that you were right and she was wrong; you made her feel worthless and then finally she realized that she had more power and control than you ever had." She inched toward him.

"What do you mean?" He cowered backwards.

"You only feel crushed by someone if you allow yourself to be vulnerable to them. She realized that she didn't have to be vulnerable to you anymore, and I'm proud she realized that. She is so much better than you…you're a fucking pussy falling apart; acting like her being a typical person meant she was attacking you and your health."

"I may have…"

"Overreacted?"

"Not exactly, but…"

"Shut the fuck up."

"What are you doing here exactly?"

"I will remind you that this is still her place until September, and she gave me her key. So, I will come here whenever I feel like it until September, but I'm sure as shit not doing your laundry or cooking you any food, so learn how to be self-sufficient, you asshole. Has summer vacation quelled your ridiculousness?"

"Listen, I…"

"I don't want to fucking hear it!"

"You sound like her…"

"Good…because she has more clarity than anyone else on this planet, and you don't deserve her. I came here for two reasons: one, I already confirmed you're alive and still a vapid tool bag, and the other…" She looked around the apartment for him.

"What is it?"

"Where is our pet?"

"Your pet?"

"He's our…umm…"

"Up here."

She looked up and saw his furry little face, and she smiled. He was the size of a ferret, gliding down from the top cabinet and into her arms. She cradled him tightly and he purred, "Come on," she tried to look hopeful.

"Is that a rat?" Caleb looked confused.

"He's not a rat! Fuck's sake, he's our friend, and he only came here to check on you, and you don't deserve any of us!"

"Did she?" the Mustleknapp whispered, concerned that Skyler was the one to retrieve him and not Hyacinth herself.

"Not here, not in front of him."

"Did it just talk?"

"He's not an it, you insensitive simpleton!"

"He looks like a tool shed I preferred the mask," The Mustleknapp said to Skyler.

"Toolbag."

"Whatever."

"What's going on?" Caleb shook his head.

"Nothing that concerns you," she held the Mustleknapp closer to her, and he made the cooing sound he would make for Hyacinth to comfort her.

Caleb stared at the two of them. "Skyler, wait, please, you need to…"

"I don't need to do anything…" she laughed, "You pushed her away because of your fear. You ruined the best thing that ever happened to you, and you'll never have it back again. Buh-bye Caleb, enjoy your life without Hyacinth."

Skyler turned with the Mustleknapp in her arms, clutching the baseball bat with every intent of smacking him with it if he dared try to stop her. She walked with her head high without looking back to see the true heartbreak on his face, "He's totally crying right now." The Mustleknapp held in laughter.

"That's what she wanted, and I can't wait to tell her about it."

"Where is she?" he sensed something was wrong.

"No one knows…"

"Wait, what?"

"She didn't come back through the portal," Skyler said sadly.

"Where is she?"

"I was hoping you would know."

"I don't."

"Then we lost Hyacinth." She held in tears.

He shook his head back and forth, "No! No!"

"We restored the balance, and your original line will take over as Jam…within time…Jim and Jom gave Hyacinth portal powder for both lines to send us back. And told us we were always welcome. She sprinkled me first, and I arrived back to Earth, where we started. Then four hours later Landon arrived…then eight hours later Chad arrived…and now it's been 36, and she still hasn't…"

The Mustleknapp held her close, "We will figure this out."

…

Chad took his laptop and sat in the field waiting for her. He hadn't left the field since his arrival. He placed his earbuds in, took the flash drive she had given him and played what she had recorded for him.

She was blushing and looking down…he smiled. She recorded this a few days before they were planning to go back, "I'm not really good at the whole, showing love thing…and you're really good at it, and I know that can be frustrating, but I went through some thoughts about us, and I think this song really captures how I feel and I wanted to share it with you, but not have to share it with you at the same time, which is why I'm recording it. We're like Schrödinger's relationship. So, this song has been on my mind for a while now, and it always makes me think of you, this is for you, Chad…" and she sang *And So It Goes* by Billy Joel.

The tears streamed down his face as Skyler pulled up in her Smart Car with Landon and the Mustleknapp.

"Any change?" Skyler asked desperately. "None."

"Where is she?" The Mustleknapp pointed his 6th finger in Chad's face almost as if he blamed him for her not coming back.

"I don't know."

"But she was alive when you left?" Now, he turned to Landon.

"She sprinkled us with the white powder from the Gnetgnu. Jom was Jam," Landon said.

"Skyler told me."

"She sprinkled Skyler first, then Landon, then myself, and then…"

They looked to where the portal would come through, and they all stood dumbfounded as the rainbow portal shifted to a reddish-brown color. Its shape morphed to look closer to a twisted tube before breaking into several pieces, then blinked in and out as if the signal was compromised. Before it disappeared the final time, something came from the sky. It was propelled to the Earth with great force, and they all ran the 3-mile distance to get to it. There was a large crater in the ground, and steam coming from its content. But it was not Hyacinth. It was simply her core piece, coated in blood and flesh.

"Where are you?" Chad asked, desperate, staring at the sky.

The Mustleknapp clutched the piece to his heart. "She promised me she would bring this back to me...she kept her promise...but this is not what I meant..."

"Then why isn't she here?" Skyler stamped her foot.

"This can't be happening." Landon shook his head.

"I told you all, the Prophet Warrior doesn't get to live."

"But she was alive! We were all coming back!"

"This can't be real!"

"But it is..." Skyler said sadly.

"NO! This is NOT how this ends!" Landon screamed, upset.

"Is this the end...or the beginning of something tragic?" Chad looked as though he didn't see anything in front of him, that his world had come crashing to an end.

"What the fuck does that mean?"

"We have to figure out how to live without her..." Skyler bit her lip, Landon quickly handed her one of her pills and a mini water bottle.

"There is NO life without her..."

"For once, I agree with Chad..." The Mustleknapp looked down sadly.

"Where is the portal?"

"We can't see it anymore!"

"But we have all three elements! In excess, we have them!"

"But the portal has changed. Everything has changed."

Chad started to cry. The Mustleknapp crawled over to him, and they mourned together, feeling the anguish of the loss of the love of their life.

"What are we going to do?" Skyler looked into Landon's eyes, lost.

"Honestly…I don't know…" then the two of them cried, trying desperately to understand why she was able to send her bludgeoned core piece back, but the portal was gone, and she was lost to the world.

"I made her a promise…and I will keep it…" Chad sobbed, holding the Mustleknapp to his shoulder. "Sometimes keeping a promise looks different than the one you envisioned…"

"Fuck!"

"Calm down!"

ABOUT THE AUTHOR

S. Leigh Medeiros resides in the United States with her family. She spends most of her time battling her cat for access to the laptop. She finds most of her ideas for writing in her kitchen.